Time of Parting

Time of Parting

A Novel By

ANTON DONCHEV

translated from the Bulgarian by Marguerite Alexieva

William Morrow & Company, Inc.

NEW YORK 1968

Contents

Note to the Reader

The story is narrated by two separate people who witnessed the events described, and later chronicled them from two different points of view. Each chapter of the book is an excerpt from one of the two chronicles. The first chronicler is a French nobleman, usually referred to as the 'Venetian', who was captured by the Turks at the siege of Candia and accepted Islam. During his captivity, he learnt Bulgarian, and, at the time of the story, he is acting as interpreter to Karaibrahim, the commander of the Turkish detachment which has been sent to convert the Bulgarians in the Elindenya Valley to Islam. The second chronicler is a Bulgarian priest named Aligorko, who happened to be in Elindenya when the Turks arrived. Although both the 'Venetian' and Aligorko write in the first person, any possible confusion as to authorship is avoided by the device of prefacing each excerpt from Aligorko's chronicle with a verse from a Bulgarian folk-song. The action takes place in 1668.

Characters in the Book

MANOL, a shepherd, on whom his fellow villagers in the Rhodope mountains look as a leader, because of his courage and fine character.

MOMCHIL AND MIRCHO, his sons.

KARAIBRAHIM, a Janissary, sent to the Elindenya Valley of the Rhodope to convert its inhabitants to Islam.

POP (Father) ALIGORKO, a monk, on whose chronicle the narrative is partly based. The chapters narrated by him begin with an excerpt from a folk-song.

THE VENETIAN, a French nobleman, related to the King of France, taken prisoner by the Turks at the siege of Candia in the Cretan War, and forcibly converted to Islam, who has been taught Bulgarian by a fellow-captive and interprets for Karaibrahim. He is the narrator in those chapters which do not begin with a folk-song.

SYULEIMAN AGA, the Turkish owner and ruler of the Valley.

GYULFIÉ, his fat wife.

OLD GALOUSHKO BELIA (The White One), a miller.

GORAN, SHERKO, AND STRAHIN, Galoushko's sons. Strahin was handed over to the Turks many years ago in payment of the *Devshourmé*, or blood-tax, by means of which the corps of Janissaries was recruited.

ELITSA, Galoushko's beautiful daughter.

SEVDA, a shepherd's widow.

VRAZHOU KEHAYA, another of the shepherds.

ISMAIL BEY, chief of the Yurouks, a nomad Turkish tribe of shepherds, a wise and upright old man.

GRANNY SREBRA, an old woman of nearly a hundred, who leads the survivors of the massacres in Chepino to Elindenya and founds the new village of Momchilovo.

SHEIKH SHABAN SHEBIL AND MOLLA SOULFIKAR SOFTA, Mohammedan divines, sent with Karaibrahim to convert the population to Islam by force.

HASSAN HODJA VELKOV, a Bulgarian Mohammedan, who has become a hodja.

DELYO, Syuleiman Aga's *bilyuk-bashi*, or sergeant.

Notables of the three villages of Elindenya Valley.

PART ONE

Sunset is like Dawn

First Excerpt

When Karaibrahim had reached the crest of the hill, he stopped his horse. At his feet lay the valley.

To the right of us was a precipice of red rusty-looking rocks, a sheer drop, with spruces growing at its base. Even the tallest trees reached less than a third of the way up the stone wall. When I bent down from my horse, I looked down on the wings of two eagles circling above the forest.

Opposite us, many miles away, there rose another mountain slope, as steep as the walls of the precipice, blue-black with the pine forests growing over it. Only there, a strip of snow divided the black forests from the grey sky, and the foothills were lost in mists. The forests lay in folds along the slopes and came towards us, growing lighter, until they melted into the nearest spruces, which had green branches, quite pale at the new tips. I looked upon them and could not believe that if I approached that black abyss opposite, I would see the same green trees.

Behind Karaibrahim and me, the mules of the two hodjas stopped —Sheikh Shaban Shebil, the one-armed, and Molla Soulfikar Softa, the stout one.

'Is it here?' the stout one asked in a whisper.

Karaibrahim did not turn to answer him. Then I tore my eyes away from the mountain before me and saw his face. We had arrived.

Far down, at the bottom of the valley, flowed a river, which rose slowly to the peaks the farther away from us it went, and there the two steep slopes of the mountain drew nearer to each other. Three villages could be seen along the river, each one higher and farther away than the other. They were like piles of rocks, for the houses were built of stone and roofed with stone tiles. The beams of the barns had turned grey and had acquired the same colour as the stones. Around the first village, there were pastures dotted with yellow flowers. The soil of the few ploughed fields was light, with darker patches which lay over them like the shadow of clouds. The walls of a castle gleamed white on a hill near the first village.

Everything around us was green and black with forests. They went right up to the tops of the mountains, giving them a finely serrated outline.

The forests looked asleep. The trees were so still they seemed to be made of stone. The tops of the huge spruces to the left of us stood out against the grey sky, as delicate as the icy flowers which a hoar frost leaves on a window. They were very delicate and very fine, so that even a child's breath would have stirred them, but there was no breath. There was only a white transparent little cloud, a frozen breath, which hung motionless above the valley. A narrow band of mist stretching over the slopes before us, but that did not move either.

From the long file of horsemen behind us came the sound of voices and the thud of horses' hooves, but they did not break the surrounding stillness, just as a handful of pebbles would not stir the depths of a vast green lake.

Karaibrahim was still staring at the valley.

The sun appeared for a moment on the snowy ridge opposite and illumined his face. Then I saw that the mountain was alive, and its tremor pierced me like a sudden chill.

A rock rose at Karaibrahim's back. Water was flowing down it, but its flow was imperceptible. The fine transparent stream of water cast a glass robe over the rock, invisibly covering the furrows of the black stone. When the sun shone forth, the rock began to shimmer in a myriad of tiny sparks, as though the whole mountain were shaking. The transparent robe shimmered and shook with a blinding thread of gold in each fold, and each spark no longer flowed downwards, but seemed to echo like a cord in the same place. Karaibrahim's face remained immovable and concentrated amid the radiance of the shimmering mountain.

The sun went out. To the west, towards it, a wall suddenly seemed to crash down, and we saw ten, twenty ridges of mountains pierced by invisible rays, transparent, light interlocked with each other, behind, above one another, now darker, now lighter, until at last one could not see where the mountains ended and the sky began.

We were in the heart of Rhodopa. We had journeyed two days to this spot, and there was at least another two days' journey to the tops of those ghostly mountains which hovered before us.

The whole detachment of horse—Karaibrahim, I, the two hodjas, the twenty Spahis and the hundred men-at-arms—dismounted and knelt down upon the broken red stones of the old Roman road, to praise Allah in evening prayer. And the one-armed hodja had just raised his voice when the tones of a bell echoed over the mountains. There was a monastery somewhere there, and, like us, the monks were speeding the day and the sun.

The tones of the bell were borne over the mountain, pure and transparent like the distant peaks, falling in folds like them, now darker, now lighter. The tones met their echoes, and the echoes returned to a new tone, while the spruces rose like the spires of a cathedral, and their tops were outlined against the sky like slender, black crosses.

A sob rose in my breast, and I bent my head lower still, while my lips repeated the words of the Mohammedan prayer. Neither mockery, nor despair, nor resignation had succeeded in uprooting the old faith.

The ringing of the bell and the hodja's intoning died away and ceased almost simultaneously.

Karaibrahim rose to his feet and whistled softly to his horse. The Arab stallion knelt down, Karaibrahim threw a leg over the saddle and the horse rose without an effort, tossing back his noble beautiful head, with its soft lips, wide red nostrils, and shining eyes.

The detachment began to descend into the valley. The sun had hidden itself, but day had not yet left the valley.

'We must ask someone,' the fat hodja spoke again.

Our guide had run away the day before.

On the left, from the side of the steep slope, came the tinkle of a small bell. Two small red cows were grazing on the yellow meadow above the rocks, and beside them knelt a little cowherd, looking down on us.

'Tell him to come down,' Karaibrahim turned to me, speaking Turkish.

'Come down!' I called.

The little cowherd drew out a long pipe from somewhere and began to blow on it.

'Come down!' I cried once more.

The little cowherd thumbed his nose at us.

The hodja swore, Karaibrahim thrust a hand into his red saddle-bags and drew out a pistol.

The little cowherd rose to his feet, whistled to his cows and dashed away up the yellow meadow. The small red cows gambolled after him like goats, their bells tinkling; the little cowherd was laughing.

Karaibrahim flexed his left arm and raised it across his chest; on to its wrist he dropped his right hand holding the pistol. The little cowherd was running and the broad muzzle of the pistol, ornamented with silver flowers, covered him. A yellowish-green bag, the colour of the meadow, flapped from his shoulder.

He ran for a long time, still covered by the muzzle, until he vanished amid the straight, strong fir trees. Karaibrahim lowered his pistol. From the forest came the little cowherd's laughter, more ringing than the bells of his cows. The echo returned it, as if the mountain were laughing.

'Why didn't you shoot, Aga?'[1] the fat hodja asked.

Karaibrahim did not answer; his eyes were fixed on the stones beneath the horse's hooves.

The fat hodja winked at the one-armed hodja. The latter returned the wink, and, as he had only one eye, for a moment his face grew blind and terrible.

The abyss on the right disappeared, the road entered a forest, then came out into the open. Sloping meadows stretched on either side, and, since the road was cut into the earth, the grass came up to the horses' heads.

Huge stone crosses had been thrust into the meadow on the right, some of them taller than a man. They were of ancient stone, which had kept only the form of a cross, eaten away, broken, most of them lying on the grass. They were not stone-coloured, but looked as if they had been painted, because they were all overgrown with lichens—orange, violet, pale-green, like the flowers in the meadow, which had once been a cemetery. The lichens had grown one upon another in broad patches of colour; they had grown and died, and new lichens had grown above the dead ones. One cross, near the road, had just been broken, so that one could see the stone— white standstone, light, untouched, without a single stain. Under the lichens, the stones remained young, virginal and pure.

Lower down, below the stone crosses, stood wooden crosses and monuments, thrust into the ground. Two men were standing there. When we approached them, we saw that one of them was holding a human skull in his hands.

This was my first encounter with Manol.

The two men stood above us, and the grave, which was probably in front of them, was hidden from our sight by the grass.

One was tall, but so broad-shouldered that his height passed unnoticed. His black hair fell over his shoulders, bound by a strap across his forehead, and a short black beard framed his face. A dark red, knee-length cloak, tied across his chest, covered him. The white sleeves of his shirt, embroidered in red at the wrists, showed beneath it. Around his waist he wore a broad leather cartridge belt, into which only a knife was thrust, and beneath the belt there

[1] For notes see p. 98.

was a red waistband. White leggings, held in place by black straps, bound his brown, black-braided trousers at the knee.

The other was a priest or a monk, with long fair hair, and a long black cassock—the hair so pale that it was almost white, while the cassock had grown grey, and green at the shoulders, from the sun and the rain.

Both were bareheaded.

Four or five huge sheep-dogs, as shaggy as bears, with iron collars around their necks, jumped out at the edge of the meadow above the road, their teeth bared.

When we drew near to the shepherd and the priest, Karaibrahim stopped his horse. From above the two stared down on us in silence, and the black-bearded man still held the white skull in his hands, at his breast.

The dogs growled deeply, threateningly. The black-bearded man raised his hand, and the dogs lay down above the road, their heads stretched out on the grass and their eyes seemed to be turned to the sky.

Karaibrahim nodded to me. I did not say a word, but signed to the men to come down on to the road.

The black-bearded man bent slowly down, his hands were lost in the grass. When he straightened up again, he was holding a black fur cap. He set out across the cemetery as if he were going away from us, and the priest followed after him. Then they came down on to the road—the black-bearded man jumped down from the meadow with surprising lightness, but the priest leant on his hand in getting down. As they set foot on the road, the black-bearded man jammed his fur cap on and turned his steps towards us. He wore sandals, but the priest was barefooted.

They stopped in front of the horses.

Karaibrahim and Manol stared at each other. Now Karaibrahim was looking down from above, while Manol was looking up. I knew that Karaibrahim was angry, although nothing showed on his face. The shepherd should not have put on his fur cap before the Turkish Aga, for a hat is a symbol of freedom and dignity, while it is seemly that the *rayah*[2] should stand submissively before him, with covered head.

'Ask him if he speaks Turkish,' said Karaibrahim.

The man shook his head—he had understood Karaibrahim's words, but either did not know, or did not wish to speak Turkish.

'Ask him the names of those villages,' I heard Karaibrahim's voice say.

The man was silent, and I repeated the question in Bulgarian.

'Prossoina.'

'And the second one?'

'Zagrad.'

'And the third?'

'Podviss.'

Karaibrahim and Manol were looking each other straight in
the eye. After the first glance Manol did not look at me again. I
felt angry and miserable, because I realized that he had taken
my measure, and wanted nothing more to do with me, as though
I did not exist. After that, whenever we met, he never looked at me
—as though I were not there.

'And that white house?'

'Syuleiman Aga's *Konak*[3],' answered Manol.

'What is the name of this pass?'

'Miloto Gospodi.'[4]

I looked at the eyes of both of them. Karaibrahim had half-
closed piercing eyes, one a little narrower than the other, as if
he were perpetually taking aim. Manol's gaze was like a hand—
one felt it upon oneself, searching as if he wanted to find something. He always looked for something in people's faces. And
like a hand, his gaze could caress, or strike a sore spot. It could
gather one in, or cast one aside.

I felt Karaibrahim's anger rising. He had met a strong man,
a steady man—one could see that the shepherd was like a big
tree and deep water—it needed a storm to shake him, a rock to
come crashing down to raise a wave. But there was something in
his look, which made me think that if you aimed well, even the
slightest breath would make the leaves quiver, and ruffle the mirror-
like surface of the deep.

Since I had fallen into captivity, and since those terrible hours
on the ship, I had got used to standing aside and watching: to
see what would happen. I did not meddle. I let nothing reach my
heart. But now I felt a certain agitation, when I realized that these
two men would clash.

Karaibrahim was looking at Manol. He thrust a hand into his
waistband, drew out a coin—I did not see this, I felt it—and threw
it down at Manol's feet. The silver rang softly as it struck the stones.
Karaibrahim was thanking Manol for his words. He was insulting
him.

The shepherd did not bend down to pick the coin up.

Karaibrahim spurred his horse forwards. The shepherd did not
move. The horse was almost on top of him. I heard the dogs growling.

'Come.'

The priest spoke—he had been silent so far.

The shepherd stepped aside and Karaibrahim passed on.

Only now did I look at the priest. Two blue eyes, enormous in the light, shone in his face. He looked quite young and full of *joie-de-vivre*.

I passed him on my horse, and he closed his eyes, perhaps in relief. The light in his face went out and, just as once the sun has hidden itself behind the mountains, one has a clearer view of the forests, hidden until then by a veil of light, thus did I see his face. The sunken sockets, the wrinkles around the eyes, the cracked, burnt-looking skin, the pale lips of a sufferer. The priest was no longer a young man, and he was weary.

Whether the two had waited on the road for the entire file of riders to pass them, each of whom could raise his *yataghan*[5] and cut them down, or whether they had gone up to the cemetery, I discovered only when the path turned far ahead and I looked back. One hundred and twenty riders one behind the other, at five feet distance, and each horse three feet long, that is a lot, that is one thousand feet, a quarter of an hour's journey in the mountains, an endlessly long time. A chain one thousand feet long with one hundred and twenty links, each armed with a *yataghan* and pistols.

They were still standing on the road.

Turning back, I heard Karaibrahim quietly saying something to the one-armed hodja. I caught the words : 'Afterwards break the crosses . . . .'

Then I realized why Karaibrahim had set out with his detachment of horse across the wild mountains—he was coming to turn that valley at our feet to the True Faith.

Second Excerpt

> Last night, shepherdess, there passed
> As many as three files of slaves.
> The first file, shepherdess,
> All lasses with plighted troth.
> The second file, shepherdess,
> All newly-wedded brides.
> The third file, shepherdess,
> All brave young lads.

In the year 1668 of Our Lord Jesus Christ, two years after the Grand Vizier Ahmed Küprüli had laid siege to Candia, in the month of grass, which is the fifth month after the beginning of the

year, the holy Christian forest called Rhodopa suffered a terrible
fate. And in the preceding years there had been omens, which we,
in our blindness, were unable to divine.

A black shadow had darkened the moon, and we all thought
that the setting of the crescent was at hand.

Hail had fallen, each stone as big as the fist of a grown man,
so that it killed the birds of heaven as they flew, and the wild
beasts as they hid in the forest.

Tremors had shaken the earth, and brought down towns and
villages; they had destroyed Mosul, too, and high waves had
wrecked the ships in the harbours.

When the Hungarian city of Offen was burnt down, and even
the canon on its walls had melted, and the slaves in their cells
had killed each other, sixteen pairs of Christian slaves were found
burnt to death, chained two by two, having met their death in
the flames in each other's arms.

The year before had been barren, so that the shepherds ate only
meat, while the other folk had nothing but roots and herbs. The
Grand Vizier put bad money into circulation, and folk no longer
had faith in the silver, so that there was confusion in trade and
the crafts. The Turks were collecting taxes for ten years ahead,
because the Franks, the Germans and the Spaniards had intervened
on the side of the Venetians, and the end of the Cretan War was
not in sight. Venetians landed on Bulgarian soil, one day's journey
away from the Sultan's capital, while Venetian ships fired their
canon at the Turkish Sultan himself, when he went hunting at the
foot of the Rhodopes. I saw shepherds who had embraced Venetian
sailors, with iron helmets on their heads and crosses on their breasts.
The Albanians, who drove flocks from Macedonia to Constantinople
along the shores of the Aegean, said that banners would soon be
unfurled in their mountains.

In that troubled spring I set out from the monastery on Mount
Athos with a bagful of holy books, copied by hand, to go to
Rhodopa with the shepherds, who were returning after spending
the winter grazing their flocks on the pastures along the shores of
the Aegean Sea. The lambs had grown strong and were gambolling
around their mothers; the wool had been shorn and sold. And the
flocks of sheep set out for the north, towards their homes in the
mountains, together with the birds which were returning to their
nests.

In the village of Podviss there lived a man by the name of
Manol. After every man's name, the name of his father is spoken,
for many men have the same name, and a man with but one name
is alone, but the name of his father binds him to other folk, so

that it is known whence his blood has flowed and what his roots are. But Manol knew neither his father's nor his mother's name. He was the first of his family, the first of a great family, although it had no great roots, and when his grandson said that he was Manol, the son of Momchil, the son of Manol, that was a great name.

There passed three files of wretched slaves. The first file—maidens whose troth was plighted, the second file—men in the prime of youth, the third file—newly married brides. Manol's mother—no one knows her name—bore Manol at her breast, and no one knows what she called him. And when her milk ceased flowing and her strength left her, she untied her gaily patterned apron and tied it like a cradle between two pine trees. And in the cradle she placed her nursling—that the breeze might rock him when it blew, and the rain bathe him when it fell, and a doe suckle him when it came that way.

No doe passed by, but Karamanol, the *haidout*,[6] passed by. For the last nine years, since the Turks had carried off his wife and slain his sons, Karamanol had made himself master of two passes—both Rozhen and Eshek Koulak—and he did not let so much as a bird cross them. Any bird that did fly across the passes never returned. No one knew where he spent the night and where he spent the winter, for he always went alone with a rifle and two pistols. In the ninth year, his bile overflowed, and he began to kill whomsoever he met. He would even unearth the bodies of his enemies from their graves and break their bones with a cornel stick or marble stones.

He was pursued by three beys and two sultans.[7] Then the *Yurouks*,[8] too, rose against him, and he realized that his end was near. When Daoud Aga, the father of Syuleiman, asked him from a high place across a deep river why he beat dead bodies, Karamanol answered him that he had but a short while to live, so he did everything out of spite, to provoke the Lord and the Devil.

This Karamanol took the nursling from the cradle and carried it with him across the forests, and at his heels went the five chieftains with their men, for they had sworn that their beards would know no razor until they had caught him. Karamanol would go down to the villages, seeking a nursing mother, and would give her the orphan to suckle, then take to the mountains again. The beys cut off the breasts of the mothers who gave milk to Karamanol's foster-son; they would dash their babies down on the stone thresholds; they placed an armed guard with a rifle beside each mother; but the women feared Karamanol even more, or perhaps it was their maternal pity that was the stronger. Thus Karamanol descended into one hundred villages, and one hundred mothers

suckled his foster-son. When little Manol began to stand on his
legs, Daoud Aga shot Karamanol with a silver bullet, but he was
unable to fire a second time, because Karamanol shot him in the
heart. The wounded *haidout* dragged himself to the mill of Old
Galoushko Belia (the White One) and gave him the child. For
three days, the mortally wounded Karamanol cut and whittled the
muzzle of his rifle, which had held two passes for nine years, and
made a *kaval*[9] of it. And when he had blown on it and the *kaval*
had begun to play, he dragged himself back to the forest—to die
somewhere in the wilderness there like a wild beast, that his
enemies might not make a mock of his head. To his foster-son he
left only the iron *kaval*.

Old Galoushko called the child Manol, after his foster-father,
and when he grew up folk began to call him Manol of the Hundred
Brothers, although they might have done better to have called him
Manol of the thousand brothers, for one hundred mothers had
suckled him, and together with him his foster-brothers were growing
up all over Rhodopa.

What a wonderful sun shone over that Aegean Plain, what grass
grew under the hooves of the white lambs, how the Rhodopes
towered in the distance when on St George's Day the flocks rose
like grey and black clouds, and set out for the mountains. Everything that had life had come out into the plain and the mountains
—to work, to rejoice, to bear fruit, as long as the blue sky shone
above and as long as a man walked God's beautiful earth, and
did not lie in it. What stout shepherd's feet trod the beaten tracks,
what sinews stretched the braided trousers, what forelocks the
breeze played with, and what red cheeks were blown out as the
men played their bagpipes and *kavals*. Where are they now? It is
a good thing that man does not know what awaits him. The bags
were full of raisins, figs and oranges, and various gifts for sweethearts, sisters and mothers, who were watching the snows on the
peaks of the Rhodopes, and waiting.

There were fifteen thousand sheep in the three villages, Prossoina,
Zagrad and Podviss along the River Elindenya, below the Monastery
of St Elijah. How many can the fine men have been who walked
beside them—two hundred, three hundred? Half the sheep were
Syuleiman Aga's, the others belonged to the peasants. But how many
sheep there were in the *Yurouks'* flocks, which followed them—
black flocks, white flocks, mixed flocks—no one knew.

Beside the pack-mules and horses there went a riderless saddled
horse. Its owner had been slain, as early as the autumn, when
Albanians and our men fought at a bridge, so they were bringing

his horse back, to arouse the sorrow of his wife, who would lean her forehead on the cold saddle. Yet he had married only last spring. But it was said, softly, that when she heard the terrible news, his bride had not tied a black kerchief down well over her brows but had pulled back a white kerchief to show her fair hair, and had begun to leave her gate unbarred at night. His sheep had been sold and with them his dogs, but five of them had returned, and as they had no flock, they fought the other dogs, of which there were three times as many as the shepherds. That is why these dogs went with Manol the Hundred Brothers, at whom even mad dogs never barked. Even the worst dog would grow quiet at his look, and lie down at his feet, so that the shepherds said to him, 'It's a good thing you were not born a thief, Manol.'

And when the plain began to rise gently, and the snowy breath of the mountains struck our nostrils, the shepherds prepared to put the flocks in order, to pass through the first mountain villages. The owners brought out the big goats, which led the flocks and bore the *chans*,[10] and gathered them on a meadow. The finest of them had to be chosen to walk first and wear the biggest bell. Some of them were wonderful to look upon, larger than donkeys, yet two of them were a span higher than the others and their horns were a span longer. One of these goats was Manol's, the other belonged to Vrazhou *Kehaya*.[11] And as the shepherds were wondering which to choose, someone suggested that they cut down a straight tree and weigh them, and another said that two should mount them, and see which would go the farthest. And quite near there was a steep place, a thousand feet long. Vrazhou asked that each of them should mount his own goat, which was unfair, because Vrazhou was not much of a man at all, so light that he would leave no tracks even if he walked over snow, and half the weight of big Manol. But Manol did not refuse, and seated on their goats they set off up the hill. A little before reaching the top, Manol's goat fell, and Vrazhou's reached the top. So he was given the biggest bell to wear, walking at the head of the flock.

But Manol did not touch the fallen goat, he merely signed to his son Momchil, who was pale with fury, to slaughter the beast.

'But, Father . . .' cried Momchil.

Manol looked at him and Momchil drew out his knife. Manol had such a gaze—he could see a black ant on a black stone.

The following day, the flocks set out across Rhodopa. At their head walked the big goat with the biggest *chan*, after him came fifty-two goats, each with a silver *chan*. Four full chimes of *chans* echoed over the mountains, so that a ringing and a song were wafted over them, sweeter than the song of Mount Athos, when

the bells of the monasteries ring out. The rams with the *chans*
were numberless, but they took smaller steps, so the *chans* swung
more quickly and their song was not as festive as that of the goats.
One hundred bagpipes skirled behind the goats. Each shepherd
blew on either a *kaval*, or a pipe made of a willow branch, or a
whistle of Aegean reeds. The youngest shepherd boys whistled
with grasses or pear leaves. Dogs barked, pistols were fired, and
lambs bleated.

I walked among this river of living creatures, of men and beasts,
and my heart was like a mirror. The Lord's joy and blessing fell
upon me like a ray of light on a mirror, and I sent that ray wherever
I turned my eyes and blessed the men and the animals, and the
sparrows at the side of the road, and the grasses and the clouds.
One should not send God's blessing where one wills, the Lord
knows better upon whom it should shine. And my mirror proved
to be misted and broken.

That evening Manol came to me and told me that we should
hurry ahead, for there was something we had to do, and I was to
help him.

I thought he was angry about his goat, and wanted to be farther
away from the men and the merry-making.

The following day, before sunrise, Manol came, leading two
saddled horses. And with him came the dead shepherd's five dogs,
for Manol dared not leave them with the flocks.

Then the bells of the flocks were left behind us, and were barely
audible behind the folds of the mountains. And Manol said to
me :

'Three years ago, when I reached Plachliv Kamuk,[12] I learnt
that my wife had died the day before.'

In these parts, it is the custom, when a man dies, to bury him
wherever they wish, and some bury their dead even in their yards;
but when three years are over, they dig up the bones, wash them,
and after putting them in a wooden chest, they leave it in the ossuary at the church. And I saw that Manol was carrying in his horse's
saddlebags not gifts but a chest for the bones, and a goatskin full
of milk. And I had wondered at the milk before, for until the
lambs are weaned it is sinful to drink ewe's milk.

We journeyed all day long over the shortest paths, and the dogs
ran with us, and before sunset we reached the top of the pass
Miloto Gospodi, where there was a very old cemetery. Manol's
wife was buried there.

And when we had dismounted, we set out amid the crosses. Here,
unknown Christian folk had wished to leave a memory of them-

selves, but time had got the better of them, and had effaced the words and the names. Only the crosses were left.

Here, along the heights, there had been snow until quite recently, and the meadow was all wet, and the grass still short and wiry. And when a man's foot trod on it, the earth in ferment rose and filled our footprints with water. After that, the grass straightened up, and in a minute there were no longer any footprints. And it whispered and rustled, so that the graves were full of sound, as if young wine were fermenting, as if beneath the earth something secret and hidden from the men above it were taking place.

Manol knelt down at his wife's grave, which had sunk during the winter, and began to dig it up with his broad knife. He scooped up the soil in his hands and placed it beside him. And various tiny insects moved in the handfuls of soil, and the earth still whispered something. With folded hands, I murmured a prayer.

Then the skeleton appeared, but first of all the bones from the waist to the knees were bared, and the brownish-yellow bowl of a woman's womb, open as if crushed by the weight of the soil. And it was the colour of the earth, of a bowl of unbaked clay, still wet. In that womb Manol's sons had ripened, those bones had separated that the fruit might emerge from them, so that new fruit might fill them.

Little by little, caressing the bones, Manol bared them one by one, and finally he took out the yellow skull. And kneeling on the edge of the grave, he paused, holding in his palms the skull of his wife, and looking upon it with bent head. Thus, years ago, he had held in his hands his wife's head, her warm cheeks and her heavy plaits of hair. Yet one could not tell whether the skull was that of an old or young person, a man or a woman, handsome or ugly— it was just a skull.

Many heads will be spoken of in these chronicles, before 'amen' is written at the end, and then they were still on folk's shoulders, smiling and looking about them.

Then Manol said quietly :

'There is nothing written on her forehead. Yet she used to say that it was written on everyone's forehead what would happen to him.'

And taking out a white towel, he began to wash each bone in milk, and wiped each one separately and put it in the chest. And just then the bells of the Monastery of St Elijah, hidden in the forest, rang out.

The sound had barely died away, when the dogs, which lay beside the stone crosses, jumped up and began to growl, and the sound of horses' hooves was heard.

And, at the bend in the road, Karaibrahim appeared, the man
who ruined the Valley of Elindenya. After him rode his bloodthirsty men.

And Karaibrahim and Manol stood facing each other, the one on
horseback, the other standing on the earth.

Yet Karaibrahim was handsome, like a fallen angel, and garbed
as a Saracen. A red silk mantle, all embroidered in gold and silver,
fell to his knees. A yellow shield was on his left arm, and a green
spear at his right knee. A *yataghan* hung at his waistband, and the
silver handles of two pistols, as sharp as the beaks of birds of prey,
peeped out of their holsters on either side of the saddle. His rifle
was at his back in a red leather case. On his head he wore a turban
of white cotton, with a cap of purplish red material interwoven with
gold, and black feathers waved from his turban. There were handfuls of precious stones scattered over him and his horse, and the
horse cost twice as much as the precious stones.

And he did not speak to us, but said everything to a horseman
at his right knee—a stranger, neither a Turk, nor a Bulgarian,
with a gentle face and a soft beard, with a vague smile on his fine
lips.

Karaibrahim and Manol only spoke two or three words to each
other, and Karaibrahim's wrath grew steadily. And when he spurred
his horse towards Manol, one of the two would have died, if I had
not told Manol to draw aside. And perhaps I made a mistake when
I stood in the way of fate, for Manol would probably have killed
the haughty Karaibrahim, and then the fate of Elindenya would
have been different. But then those great deeds, of which folk
will talk as long as Bulgarian speech is heard in Rhodopa, would
not have been done.

One by one, the Turks passed us, and each of them Manol
looked in the eye. Not a Turk raised a hand against us, and what
was more wonderful, the dogs did not even growl.

When the last horseman had passed, I asked Manol why he had
looked so fixedly at each man. And he answered :

'I sought to see a face like those of my sons, and in my sons
I seek the faces of my father and my mother. For every man whom
I meet may be my brother.'

Thirty years ago, the black storm of the *devshourmé*, the blood
tax, had swept over the Rhodopa, and thousands of the Rhodope
boys had gone to fight under the Prophet's sacred flag.

'These are Spahis,' I said to him, 'and the little Bulgarians who
were carried off became Janissaries. Janissaries only march on foot,
but these were horsemen.'

'I know,' he answered.

And he said not one word more about the Turks, but he could not but be anxious, for they were going towards his villages.

When we returned to the grave, Manol made me write the years of her life on his wife's skull. But I wrote with a piece of charcoal only the year of her death, and placed a cross on it, for, when one thinks of it, only the year of death and only death are of significance, and only through their death do folk show what they are worth.

Manol placed the skull upon the other bones, picked a bunch of fresh flowers, and placed it upon the bones, too, and where he had taken up the chest, we set out for Old Galoushko Belia's water-mill.

Third Excerpt

> At Neda's the sun was shining.
> It was not the bright sun,
> It was Neda herself—
> With black eyes like a doe's,
> With long lashes like basil,
> With white teeth like pearls,
> With a slender figure like a *samodiva's*[13]

And when we reached Old Galoushko's water-mill, which is at the spring above the village of Podviss, Manol dismounted and led his horse by the bridle. And when we came out on to the meadow in front of the mill, we saw Elitsa, standing on the marble stone to the right of the door, combing her hair with a comb made of bone. For when it was unbraided, Elitsa's hair swept the ground, so she had to comb it standing on high. And when she braided it, her hair reached the middle of her calves, and the braids were as thick as her hand. The colour of her hair was like a chestnut that has just been hatched from its green egg.

Then Manol stopped and gazed at Elitsa. I saw on his face an expression which I was unable to make out. His teeth were clenched and his lips slightly parted. His eyes I did not see.

Elitsa jumped down from the stone and ran to him, and her hair dragged after her on the grass. Manol had grown up at Old Galoushko's, who had not been an old man at that time, but a young one of twenty-five. When Manol's son Momchil was three years old, Elitsa was born, so that Elitsa and Momchil had grown up together, and Elitsa was like a daughter to Manol.

Then Elitsa looked at Manol's face and stopped.

Since the autumn, when I had seen her last, she had matured by a year, and now, as Manol looked at her, she matured by yet another year. She dropped her eyelids, so that I did not see her eyes, but her lips pouted and her breasts swelled her white shift.

I looked at Elitsa, and turned my eyes to Manol. I saw him with new eyes—he was still young, barely a few years over forty, his beard was black, without a single white hair, his back was straight and his shoulders thrown back.

They were silent for a long time, one step away from each other, and instead of Elitsa speaking first, Manol was the first to speak :

'Good day, Elitsa.'

It was evening, although it was lighter than up there on the pass, because a wind had arisen, and the sky had cleared, and the nut tree was whispering something to itself.

'Welcome, Manol,' Elitsa replied.

And, for the first time, she did not say *'Baté*[14] Manol' to him. She stood before him not knowing what to do. On previous occasions she had thrown her arms around his neck, and had looked into his bag to see what gift he had brought her.

I often saw how women did not know what to do when they stood in front of Manol, wringing their hands and biting their lips —that is how the frightened does quiver and run hither and thither before the cage of a bear in captivity, although they know that it will do them no harm.

But Manol still stood there motionless and looked at the girl —until Elitsa turned, gathered her hair up over her arm and ran back into the water-mill.

Manol rubbed his brow and strode slowly after her. At the door, from the darkness of the mill, Sevda, the young widow of the murdered shepherd whose dogs were returning with Manol, came out and stood before him. When they saw her, the dogs dashed at her and thrust their heads into her apron, yet she did not drop her hands over them, but stood at the door, her palms crossed at the back of her white neck. It was true : there was no black kerchief on her head, and her fair hair shone gold, uncovered. Yet she was as beautiful as Mary Magdalen, or as Dalilah, who took the strength of Samson.

When he saw her at the door, Manol slowed his steps, then moved aside and turned his back on her, staring at the spring. This was no ordinary spring, but a little lake, about twenty paces wide. In the middle of it a jet of water shot up from the heart of the earth, as high as a man, and as broad as a round table. And the water cast up fell like a waterfall, like Elitsa's hair, only it was silver.

And when it fell in the lake it roared and gurgled by day and by night.

'I have brought your dogs,' said Manol, but he still stood there with his back turned.

'Manol *Kehaya*,' the woman said quietly, and amid the roar of the spring her voice insinuated itself and span out as soft as a spider's web. 'Manol *Kehaya*, why don't you take me? You are a widower and I am a widow, we would suit each other well.'

But he did not answer her and did not even look at her.

'Are you afraid?' she asked him.

This time Manol looked at her over his shoulder, but again he said nothing to her. And he seemed to forget her words, deep in his own thoughts.

'I care neither for priest nor wedding ceremony,' Sevda spoke again, low and softly, and one could hear that there was no impudence or mockery in her voice. 'Take me into your house that I may lean my head on a man's shoulder. I am tired of putting my head on a cold pillow, and one as hard as stone.'

'Who waits at the threshold when the sun goes down? Who sings at night, when the moon shows itself?' Manol said to her.

'Those are lads, Manol, mere lads and they cannot stay quiet. It's a man's shoulder I need, and not only a hand stretched out to me.'

And Manol said:

'Are you not ashamed before the priest?'

'He is no man and does not understand me. Yet you have been a widower like me these three years now.'

Manol replied:

'Not like you.'

'Yet I saw your eyes, didn't I, when you were looking at Elitsa?'

'Be silent!'

He said this quietly to her, but she trembled all over, grew pale and sank back into the darkness of the mill.

'Father Aligorko,' Manol said to me a little later, 'call Old Galoushko.'

He seemed to be afraid of entering the water-mill, where the two women had hidden.

I did not see Elitsa and Sevda. Old Galoushko was hammering a mill-stone. I touched his shoulder, for he had grown slightly deaf, more from the roaring of the water and the rattle of the mill than from old age, for he was not very old, although he had gone grey. And even before his hair had turned white, he had been called the White One because of the flour and the purity of his soul. He was hammering and singing a long-drawn-out song to himself, and the water murmured beneath our feet.

He turned and smiled at me, but he alone had such a smile— gay, sad, wise and gentle.

'Welcome, Father Priest,' he said to me. 'There is no grain, none at all. Famine awaits us.'

Yet his smile and his words soothed my heart, which weighed heavily in me after the meeting with Karaibrahim.

'Turks have gone down into Prossoina,' I told him.

When I saw that he began to pant and his eyes began to glow, because thirty years ago they had taken a son of his for the *devshourmé*, I added what I had said to Manol:

'They are not Janissaries but Spahis. An Albanian is at their head. They are many.'

'My sons are already big, they cannot be changed, and the agas will not take them. I have no grandsons,' the old man said, but his smile was crooked.

I said to him.

'Manol is waiting for you.'

'Manol, did you say?' he said. 'I did not hear them setting out from the villages to meet the sheep at Plachliv Kamuk.'

I asked him:

'Isn't Mircho here?'

And he answered me:

'He is grazing the cows.'

He was already at the door when he answered me, for he loved Manol as his own son, having reared him from his first year.

Outside Elitsa and Manol were standing opposite each other. She had braided her hair and placed a white kerchief on her head.

'Why do you comb your hair in the meadow, to be frightened by people?' Manol asked her.

'The stone has been here ever since I remember,' Elitsa answered.

Then Manol bent down, put his arms around the marble stone, which was about as high as his waist, gathered his strength, raised it, and, walking a few steps heavily, dropped it on the ground at a hidden place, beside the walnut tree. The tree shook, and yellowed leaves fell from it.

And when I turned, I saw Sevda beside me, she had come out noiselessly after Elitsa from the other door. She was breathing heavily and looked very frightened.

Fourth Excerpt

The road dropped steeply down and the hooves of the horses rattled on the round cobblestones. An old and mighty forest still rose on both sides, but each time that we came out onto a meadow we saw before us to the right the stone tiled roofs of the first village, and each time they had come nearer. And the big white house, the *Konak* of the local Aga, still drew the last light of the day and shone in front of us on the opposite slope of the mountain.

We did not see when the horsemen emerged from it. We saw them when they were crossing the humped stone bridge over the river—about thirty or forty men, who were hurrying to meet us. From high up we could see them spurring their horses.

We met outside the village where the road crossed a broad meadow. As soon as they came out from the forest opposite, the leader of the men from the village stopped his horse. His horsemen came out to the right and left of him and ranged themselves like a curved bow, bent towards us. And we rode up to them in a straight file like an arrow.

We approached them at a walk and before stopping I managed to look them over well. At their head was an elderly man on a huge horse, like those which had been bred in the West for centuries. They used to be the battle horses of the heavily clad knights but now they drew huge wains and ploughed with double ploughs. It was strange that such a horse should have found its way into the heart of Rhodopa. The men were armed, but it was apparent that they had mounted their horses in a hurry—some were riding without saddles, some were hatless and straw stuck out of their hair, while the hands of others were muddy. We had come upon them while they were at work, but they held their arms with accustomed and experienced hands, these servant soldiers, and stared at us from under their eyebrows without fear. Around the Aga there were five or six men, armed with pistols, daggers and *yataghans*, on well-groomed horses—these were probably the bodyguard. Karaibrahim stopped his horse in front of the Aga, and without speaking a word for a minute or even more, examined the men in front of him.

As I did my best at all costs to avoid every unpleasantness and complication, I realized at once that here, too, a conflict was coming to a head. We had come from above, from the gateway of prosperity, as Constantinople was called, and we looked down from above, while these men were in their own homes, and it seemed that neither our appearance nor our number could frighten them and make them look up to us from below.

'Who are you?' Karaibrahim asked.

'And who are you?' the man on the big chestnut asked.

His voice was quite calm, so was his smooth face with a white beard, trimmed to the length of a finger. Everything about him was neat—his turban, his beard, the features of his face, his purple garment and his white fingers. He bestrode his horse slightly bent, without swaggering, his muscles relaxed, looking at us with open eyes, without curiosity, a strong confident man, who had mastered himself. Every hair of his beard obeyed him. He did not challenge, neither did he yield.

'I am the Spahi Karaibrahim, the emissary of the Vizier Nehmed Pasha, may Allah bless his name. These are my men.'

Karaibrahim was as tense as a tree bent down. All the time he gazed around as if he were preparing to jump. If the man opposite him was like a sated beast of the cat tribe, Karaibrahim was a falcon. If the man opposite was as smooth as a river stone, Karaibrahim was as sharp as a flint.

'I am Syuleiman Aga.'

'I bring you greetings and instructions from the Vizier.'

Karaibrahim merely turned his head, and his clerk stood beside him, and handed him several scrolls.

'Here is Mehmed Pasha's letter for you.'

Syuleiman Aga nodded and one of his men drove his horse forward. The clerk kissed the seal and handed the scroll to Syuleiman Aga's man.

'Here is a letter from the *Beiler-beg*[15] of Roumelia to the *Kaimakam*[16] of the Prossoina region,' said the clerk.

'I am he,' said Syuleiman Aga.

'Here is a letter from the *Cadi*[17] of Philibé to the Cadi of this place.'

'I am he,' said Syuleiman Aga.

'Here is a letter from the Sheikh Vani to the Hodja of Prossoina.'

'Are you, perchance, a hodja, too?' Karaibrahim asked.

'I am not,' said Syuleiman Aga, 'we have a hodja.'

For the first time a glint of mockery shone in his eyes like a white spark.

'Why do you welcome us as brigands?' asked Karaibrahim. 'Your men have not yet taken their hands from their pistols.'

I saw now that Syuleiman Aga bore no weapons; he did not even have a waistband into which he could thrust a knife. But on his

right side on a white horse sat the chief of his men, a man without a hair on his face, a beardless one, and both his hands lay on the butts of his pistols. The beardless one held his head slightly raised and stared about with wide open eyes. He had a peculiar look—open, curious and shameless. His heart could be seen through his eyes, and there was nothing in it, it was empty. One of his eyes was fixed on Karaibrahim, the other one—on me.

'Why did you not send a man to inform me, so that I could welcome you as is fitting?' Syuleiman Aga asked.

'When you open the letters you will understand,' Karaibrahim replied. 'And now lead us on, for it will soon be dark.'

Syuleiman Aga was gazing at him thoughtfully. It seemed to me that I could easily read his thoughts. He was the master of this valley, and he probably did not have much sense of the existence of others above him. No one meddled with him, no one gave him orders. And now an insolent Spahi had come, bringing a hundred horsemen with him, and was inviting himself to stay with the Aga.

'Welcome,' said Syuleiman Aga. 'No one remembers our ever having turned anyone away from our villages.'

He was still the host, and we—his visitors.

He drew the reins of his horse, the horseshoe of horsemen broke up before us, and Karaibrahim rode forward. I hesitated whether to follow him, for there was no need of an interpreter here, they were speaking Turkish, but I felt that he was calling me beside him. When we had almost drawn up abreast of the Aga, the latter turned his horse and set out ahead of us, leading us. Behind me rode the beardless bodyguard with the bare face and the shameless look.

When we came out on the broad meadow, Karaibrahim rode forwards and took his place beside the Aga. The huge stallion, feeling that another stallion wanted to pass ahead of him, began to growl like a bear. He was altogether like a bear, with short legs, a huge head and a shaggy mane and tail. He couldn't neigh, he growled. But Karaibrahim's stallion neighed clearly and piercingly.

'Aga,' I said, unable to restrain myself and passing to his other side. 'Where did you get that horse?'

He slowly turned his head towards me.

'You are not a Turk.'

'I am a Frank,' I said.

He pointed somewhere towards the summits that rose before us.

'There are ruins there, folk call them the Tourla. Two or three hundred years ago, there was a Frankish stronghold there. The Franks bred such horses. My forebears took some from them, and set aside the colts and fillies which looked like them. These horses are no good for the mountains, but they bred them.'

For three hundred years this man's forebears had bred horses who were no good for the mountains. It was no accident that the Aga was so well-dressed and smooth—for three hundred years the river had smoothed the stone. Without meaning to, I almost said that I knew my family tree from the time of Charlemagne.

When the Aga rode on ahead again, Karaibrahim said quietly to me :

'Thirty-nine men welcomed me. Three and nine are twelve. That's a good omen.'

I understood him at once. He was looking for an omen in the number of those who welcomed him. I was a soldier, a hunter and a gamester, too, I fought duels—a man cannot guard himself from prophecies, and good or bad signs, from malisons, cards and amulets. But in Karaibrahim it was like a disease. He believed that everything was preordained, yet he constantly sought for the signs which fate—according to him—as constantly showed him. He counted the bullets in his bag, the trees along the road, his soldiers, the persons who welcomed him. He watched to see with which foot he got up and with which foot his horse set out. But I felt that his feeling for all that was preordained was nevertheless stronger than these petty questions asked of fate.

'Thirty-nine is divisible by thirteen,' I said.

I saw his face go black and was amazed that he should take my words so seriously. We were already entering the village.

It was not quite dark yet. The sun had gone down behind the summits some time ago, but the sky was still light.

That was why I was able to see the marvel of the stone bridge of Prossoina.

On the parapet of the bridge, women and girls had placed their freshly washed rugs to dry—they were preparing to welcome the shepherds. What rugs they were, what colours, what a wealth ! I shall never forget them. On both sides of the bridge there was rug next to rug. The sunrise and the sunset flamed there, a flower-covered meadow lay between blue-green brooks, snowy drifts reflected the violet forests of evening.

The village was made of stone—grey-brown, the colour of a deer in winter; the stones were grey, so were the tiles on the roofs and the beams of the barns. And a rainbow lay over the humped bridge on the river.

Even Karaibrahim stopped his horse.

Then from the other side of the bridge, women and children began to rush forwards and to seize their rugs. They tossed them over their shoulders, and their feet stumbled beneath the wet wool and water dripped in their tracks. They took down the forests, the meadows and the snow-drifts, they extinguished the dawns, the sunsets and the fires. Only the wet white stone was left, curved in two arcs, like the two walls of a fort. An hour later the damp of the rugs would have dried.

The mountain was hiding its wealth from us and showing us its cold stone breasts. Those rugs had not been spread out to welcome us, uninvited guests.

Karaibrahim looked on, both eyes half-closed. People seemed to be fleeing from his look.

Behind us, the Spahis stirred; one heard exclamations of wonder, admiration and delight. They were delighted at the sight of the women's strong waists, the bare calves, the eyes and the bosoms. Just as a pack of wolves will stop after a long run, and lick their chops at the sheepfolds found at last, so the Spahis swallowed at the sight of the rich village. There were cheese pastries here, chickens, and gaily coloured rugs, on which you could throw down the housewife, while the men were bleating with their sheep along the Aegean coast. It might so turn out that these same women and girls might appear in the slave market in Adrianople.

Syuleiman Aga pointed to his *Konak*.

'There is room for all of you there.'

Karaibrahim merely nodded and spurred his horse.

I counted thirty-six windows in the *Konak*, only in the wall which faced us. It was broken up like the wall of a fortress, and after every six windows a big room with three windows jutted out. The windows were all on the second floor, the first one was built of stone and had narrow loopholes. But the stone was barely to be seen, because it was overgrown with green crane's-bill, which had turned red here and there. In these regions, when they build, they put crane's-bill roots between the stones. The upper floor was whitewashed, the roof was made of slates, three tall doors opened beneath the windows, and at the right corner there was a stone tower. Beyond the *Konak* tower, on the lower land, a church was to be seen—a church topped by a cross, and there were crosses on the tombstones around it. A wall began right next to the church. A man was standing on the wall, staring at us. There must have been fifty feet between us, and we could see that his hair was fair.

Karaibrahim, who was riding next to Syuleiman Aga, asked him :

'What is that man standing on the wall?'

'He's a Russian, a groom.'

'What is he, a believer or an unbeliever?'

'An unbeliever. I bought him from the captain of a galley.'

'Then he's a slave, is he?'

'He's a slave.'

'Aga, sell him to me.'

Syuleiman Aga did not appear surprised at this strange request. 'I paid six thousand *akchés*[18] for him,' he said, indifferently. 'If you still want him, he's yours.'

Karaibrahim drew a pistol from the right holster of his saddle, and without stopping his horse shot at the man on the wall. The groom threw his hands up to his head, swayed, clapped his palms together and fell backwards. He vanished from the wall.

Syuleiman Aga did not even turn his head.

Karaibrahim said to me :

'He fell backwards.'

There is a superstition that you must look to see how the first man killed in a battle falls, so as to understand who will win it. If the first victim among your troops falls backwards, you will retreat, if he falls forwards, you will be victorious. It follows that if the first of your enemies whom you kill falls backwards, the victory is yours.

'Aga, that holds good for battle only,' I said to him, quietly.

'It is a battle,' he said, and his voice rang out over the rattle of the horses' hooves, for we were just entering the dark tunnel into the courtyard. Our road took us under the buildings, and brought us out into the inner courtyard.

What do I remember of that first evening? I was tired, I looked and listened as through a mist.

I remember how I expected to emerge from the gloom of the tunnel at the entrance, and how we entered another green gloom, as if we were under water. The entire inner courtyard was covered by the branches of a huge tree, a plane tree, or as they called it here a *chinar*. Syuleiman Aga's father had spared the tree and erected his buildings around it. There were two more inner courtyards. Later I measured the walls of the yard, they were more than twenty-five feet long on each side. The tree covered an eighth of an acre of land. It had six branches, its bark was quite smooth, yellowish-green, so that the whole tree looked as if it had been peeled. Its bole must have been about ten feet around.

That tree is not there any more. All its six branches were broken when the *voivodas* hanged over one hundred Turks on them at the same time. Its bole was burnt when we set fire to the *Konak*.

Our men of Karaibrahim's detachment were scattered around the rooms of the middle inner yard. When Syuleiman Aga himself took the men to the rooms, Karaibrahim said not a word. For himself, however, he asked for a room that did not look out on the unbelievers' church.

But when he saw where they put our horses, he asked to have his stabled separately.

He was quite right. It would have been a crime to have such a horse kicked and maimed.

The Turks know how to breed horses the like of which we French cannot even dream of, although we boast of our horses. When we capture Turkish horses, we spoil them in six months. When Turks capture our horses, they train them well in six months.

When the Spahis saw that they were all quartered in the *Konak*, they began to murmur—they had hoped that they would roam the village. And when they learnt that the food for men and horses was to be paid for, and that it would be food taken from the peasants at that, they were furious. If they had not feared Karaibrahim, who knows what they would have done.

Every four houses were to look after one horse. A boy was provided to serve as a groom to every ten horses. Twelve *aspras*[19] were to be paid for every kilo of oats, eight *aspras* for a hundred-weight of straw, one *aspra* for one *oka*[20] of bread, three *aspras* for one *oka* of meat, and five *aspras* for a load of wood.

And at that time a Spahi received twelve *aspras* a day. Instead of growing rich, they would have to open their purses. But what if they had to pay for their servants, too? Besides the twenty Spahis and their servants—most of them Turks—there were Wallachians and Moldavians, Tartars, Kurds, Circassians and Arabs—one hundred and twenty men all told. One hundred and twenty *aspras* would have to be paid for the bread alone.

The angry Spahis went to Karaibrahim. He looked at them with one eye half-closed, as he calculated something. Perhaps he was pleased that Syuleiman Aga had angered his men.

Then the beardless one came with his mocking, shameless look and informed them that the Aga was paying for everything, because the Spahis were guests.

The Spahis thanked him modestly—they were after all courtiers —and Karaibrahim closed his eyes still further.

We had arrived. For the first time since I had been taken prisoner at Candia, we had stopped somewhere. We had been making for this valley and so far we had been travelling towards it.

I left the *Konak*, and went and stood a few feet from the gate. I looked around.

There was a starry sky above me, and around me—mountains. The mountains stood there like a wall—one could not see which summit was closer, and which farther back, as if in the darkness the more distant ones had come up, taking their place beside the closer ones, so that they stood there like a black, even wall. Above the wall, the sky shone and shimmered in a kind of radiance as if fires were burning behind the mountains.

Above my head the sky was darker, with bright, calm stars. A cloud moved across it but it was so transparent that it did not hide the stars, but merely dimmed their radiance. I could hear a river flowing somewhere below the *Konak*.

The mountains breathed a threat, but the sky and the river promised calm. I was calm, I drew deep breaths of the cold air and looked at the stars.

I was alive. I was the captive Abdullah, and the captive Abdullah was alive.

It seemed strange and impossible to me that I had once been a French nobleman with a pompous title. It seemed strange to me that now, somewhere over there to the south, behind these mountains, lay Crete, and on it was Candia. I remembered the deserted streets covered with pieces of fallen plaster, cannon balls and bodies, the walls riddled with holes, and the earthworks slippery with blood-stained mud. There could not be such a thing. There was only a circle of mountains, a piece of sky above them, and in the middle—the slave Abdullah.

I remembered Julian of Cappodistria, who had let the Turks enter his castle, and then had blown up both them and himself. I remembered how I had admired his bravery. Yes, but he was dead, and I, Abdullah, was alive.

Abdullah had neither past nor future. Abdullah had no aims. He had only one aim—to survive. To live. He had no path, but he had discovered that human paths led nowhere. The important thing was that he was walking. He had a step.

Deprived of kin, friends, wealth and prejudices, Abdullah had discovered that he possessed the most important thing—life. Silks and feathers, armour and mistresses, festivities and the chase had hidden this most important thing from his predecessor the French nobleman, Abdullah was left naked, and felt that he was alive.

What was everything else worth? I was Abdullah and had the moment.

Abdullah had this moment, the stars and the mountains. The centuries before him, the day before, the morrow and the centuries after him—they belonged to someone else. He had today, the evening, this moment. What were the stars, the mountains and the air worth if Abdullah did not have the moment? The whole world sank in darkness. Abdullah lit it up, holding his moment in his hand, like a candle. Everything could be given for that moment.

Life breathed in my face like a wind, it flew over me like a cloud, it flowed at my feet like a river. Can you catch the wind, a cloud and a river in your hand? Can you hold them? So that they won't slip away from you? To live meant to have and not to have. And not to want to have.

Abdullah had understood—if you could not hold anything, you must not reach out for it.

Abdullah did not reach out—he enjoyed the only thing he had —the moment—and did his best to enjoy it, without wishing to retain it. For after it came another moment.

Only one step remained between me and happiness—to vanquish the thought that the moments would have an end, that one moment would be the last and, after that, I—Abdullah—would go. But the wind would blow, the clouds would fly, the river would flow. And I would not be there.

In the daytime I managed to vanquish that thought, but at night it vanquished me. It was evening now, and I could not determine which was the stronger—the joy of having the moment, or the fear that one might not have anything.

That is why I did not want to go back to the *Konak*, and stood at the gate gazing at the stars.

I said to myself :

'Rejoice ! You are alive !'

I knew that this calm around me would vanish, that this quiet valley would ring to screams and groans, and would grow red in the light of fires. That was the following moment. I was gathering my strength, so that I would be able to keep calm even then, to stand aside and not to reach out. Nevertheless, I didn't entirely believe in Abdullah—I had known him only a very short time.

Could I help anyone? No one can help anyone. A moment cannot be lent.

Karaibrahim startled me. He always moved noiselessly. Looking at the mountains without raising his eyes to the sky, he told me :

'They have given you a separate room next to that of Syuleiman Aga's *bilyuk-bashi*,[21] Delyo. Listen well to what is said.'

I would have to eavesdrop. I studied Abdullah attentively— it did not hurt him much. One could pay anything for a moment.

My room was spacious; it had three windows and was entirely panelled with wood. Two of the walls were nothing but cupboards. I opened them—they were empty. The wood still smelt of resin, and perhaps the fragrance came from the window beneath which the forest began.

That very first evening I had something to tell Karaibrahim. Footsteps stopped at the neighbouring door, I heard an unfamiliar voice—rough, direct and full of mockery. I thought it must be Delyo's, and afterwards I learnt that I had not been mistaken.

'Whatever you do, you'll make a mistake. If you please the *tsar*,[22] you'll displease the shepherds. If you please the shepherds, you'll anger the *tsar*. So do whatever you think, but remember— the end of your rule has come.'

'Silence, dog,' Syuleiman Aga's voice replied. 'I still feed you— do not bark at me.'

I lay down, but I did not manage to fall asleep. I was alive, but everything around me was alive, too.

The house was alive. Its walls, its roof, its door, its windows, and its floors were all alive. Something creaked, cracked and rustled with invisible steps, and settled itself for sleep. Not only what I saw was alive, but the heart of the wood and of the stone lived, too.

Through the window came the other, the big life. It, too, brought life to the house, a new, second life, with the swaying of the flower in the pot on the windowsill, with the breath of air in the room, and the creaking of the old gate.

Outside the wind was alive, the forest was alive and the river was alive. And each of them sang its song.

After that first night, for hundreds of nights on end, I listened to the song of the wind, the song of the forest and the song of the water. Quiet, barely audible songs, songs sung from a full throat, the songs of the storm and the torrent. From the song sung when man rejoices that he has a roof over his head, when the mountain is singing outside, to the song which tells him that his roof is a mere deceit, that the mountain can do what it wills with his roof and with him.

That night I listened to the wind talking to a loose board under my window. The two voices could clearly be heard—the shrill high whistle of the wind, as if a snake grass were whistling, and the deep, full dull buzz of the quivering board, which was pleading.

I fell asleep. When I awoke the next morning, I heard that the board was no longer quivering, but was knocking with a hollow regular sound. The wind had torn it out.

Fifth Excerpt

Karaibrahim and Syuleiman Aga had their first talk in the *kyoshk*[23] that looked out on to the inner yard with the fountain. Besides the two of them, I was there with the three hodjas—Sheikh Shaban

Shebil, Molla Soulfikar Softa and the Imam Hassan, the son of
Velko.

I thought that everything was preordained and only wanted to
see how Syuleiman Aga would maintain his dignity : to see how the
man who, until yesterday had been master of the valley, would
submit to Karaibrahim without humiliating himself. What else
could he do? I did not think about the people whose fate was
being decided. Actually it had already been decided. But I was
alive.

Karaibrahim had removed his turban and was bareheaded. He
was bald and had shaved the remaining hairs of his head so that his
skull shone. He suffered no hair to grow anywhere on his body—
except his moustache and a horn of hair in the middle of his forehead. I have seen other bald men, too, on whose foreheads tufts
of sparsely growing hair are left, but Karaibrahim's tuft really did
look like a horn. His hair probably used to stick up at one time,
because the hairs of the tuft were hard and straight, and perhaps
Karaibrahim put something on them to make them stand up
straight and shiny.

Karaibrahim was lean and his skin was smooth and shiny, like
a barber's strop. He was so lean that no moisture appeared to have
been left in him—neither sweat, nor spittle—to say nothing of
tears. As I looked at him, I remembered that the Spartans considered
it shameful to sweat or spit, because the constant exertion of the
body should evaporate and dry up all these superfluous liquids.
When, later, I saw Karaibrahim's blood, I was surprised.

Syuleiman Aga clapped his hands and demanded coffee for us
all, but Karaibrahim refused and said abruptly :

'Old Mohamed Küprüli has forbidden coffee.'

It was obvious that he wanted to pick a quarrel, that he had
come to accuse and attack.

Syuleiman Aga answered calmly :

'Old Mohamed Küprüli, may his memory be holy, forbade coffee,
but his son, the present Grand Vizier Ahmed Küprüli, may his name
be glorified, has again allowed Believers to drink it.'

Karaibrahim said as sharply as before :

'The Grand Vizier is at Candia and has the unbelievers by the
throat. Every one of the Faithful, wherever he may be, must think
how to help him.'

And he stared fixedly at Syuleiman Aga, while the Aga, for his
part, calmly examined him as he sipped his coffee.

I did not see what hold the Aga could find to overthrow
Karaibrahim. At that moment the latter appeared to me as one
hammered out of polished stone. Not a sinew quivered or beat on

his face or his skull. Can you get a hold on a polished stone? It was only when I looked at the tuft of hair on his forehead that I thought there must be some hidden weakness which one might seize upon.

'I think of Ahmed Küprüli every day,' said Syuleiman Aga. 'Later I shall show you the sword he gave me at Belgrade, when the Janissaries cut the ropes of his tent, because they no longer wanted to fight. I cut down the one nearest to me.'

And he looked at Karaibrahim.

Karaibrahim said to him :

'And you lived? Where were the comrades of the dead man?'

Syuleiman Aga turned the cup he had drained on to its saucer, shook it and said :

'Around him.'

Both were looking each other straight in the eye. I vaguely sensed something. Syuleiman Aga appeared to know that Karaibrahim was a Janissary, and wanted to annoy him.

Karaibrahim returned to Candia.

'When the Grand Vizier gathered us around him, before sending us here, he said to us, "Remember that Rhodopa is the shore of the Mediterranean Sea and no one can dominate the sea if he is not in possession of its shores. When you set out to return, you must see nothing but minarets, and not a single cross." And to the Aga of the Janissaries, the Padishah's most gallant swordsman there, he said : "Today the battle at Candia is being decided along the shores of the sea. I need you here, but you are needed there a thousand times more. Go to Constantinople and crucify Rhodopa. Mehmed Pasha is to set out from north to south, and Abdi from east to west. Where you meet, you must build a big mosque".'

Since the Grand Vizier had given the order, since the Aga of the Janissaries himself had come to convert the Bulgarian lands to Islam, instead of staying at Candia, what was Syuleiman Aga still waiting for that he made no *temaneh*[24] and did not say 'All honour to him'?

'When the Padishah, always the victor, may his years be multiplied, was out hunting in Despot, and that is not very far from here,' said Syuleiman Aga, 'the Aga of the Janissaries was with him. We have known each other since the Persian campaign. He made me a present of a pair of silver pistols.'

From the little valley, threads as fine as cobwebs stretched towards the wide world—towards Küprüli, towards the Aga of the Janissaries, even towards the Sultan himself. Syuleiman Aga added :

'And the Padishah, always the victor, gave me a gold bow, because I hit a bear and a stag with fine horns at a hundred paces.'

Karaibrahim was silent.

Syuleiman Aga raised his overturned cup and gazed at the strange marks left by the coffee grounds.

He was dressed all in silk, with a purple garment embroidered in silver and gold, and he had rings on his fingers. But it seemed to me that, beneath the garments, I was beginning to see his body like that of a wrestler anointed with oil. You tried to grasp him, and he slipped out of your grasp.

It was becoming interesting. At that time the shepherds were arriving with their flocks and playing on their bagpipes and *kavals*. But their womenfolk were trembling behind barred gates.

Then Sheikh Shaban Shebil shouted roughly. His turban was yellowed, he had a yellow eye, a yellow beard and yellow teeth. He probably suffered from some kind of jaundice. All his skin was as yellow as old parchment on which loathsome secrets are written. Looking at him, with his one eye and one arm, I thought that he was surely also deaf in one ear. And his eye was dull, like dirty water, like swill, and one did not know what monsters were bred down below in the darkness of the waters. Several times, without wanting to, I had touched his only hand and had shivered. It was as if I had touched a snake—so wiry, hard and tense was his hand. The strength of both hands had gathered in it, so that his muscles stood out and quivered. And the strength of his look was concentrated in his only eye.

That man numbed me; whenever he smiled at me, I felt nauseated. At such times I found myself again in the rolling hold of the galley, amid the darkness and my excrements. And whoever passed could do as he liked with me.

The Sheikh was shouting:

'The Padishah, holy be his name, set about putting the unbelievers in their place as soon as he inherited the throne from his father. I remember, it was the year 1035 of the Hegira when the representative of the Prophet on earth saw from his palace that the emissaries of the Princes of Wallachia and Moldavia wore red stockings and yellow slippers. And he ordered them to be beaten severely, and let them go their ways barefoot. After that the Padishah himself walked in disguise about Constantinople—may Allah permit us to spend our days there—taking two disguised executioners with him. And wherever he saw an unbeliever in coloured garments, he thrust him at the executioners, who cut off his head on the spot. And when they encountered an Armenian wedding, the Victorious One saw that the bridegroom had yellow stockings on. Before the bride's very eyes, he was beheaded. And instead of sleeping in her arms, he slept in his grave. For a pair of yellow stockings! The

Padishah himself ordered heads to be cut off! And what did my amazed eyes see in your valley? The first thing I saw was a shepherd in a red cloak. The women go about as if they were dressed for a wedding, in red aprons, with white kerchiefs and strings of gold coins around their necks. It is said—an unbeliever is to wear an iron chain at the most, and any garment that shows is to be black, or blue only. And their waistbands are to be made of horse-hair. Why have I seen women on horseback? Since the Janissaries have vowed to go on foot, unbelievers may not mount a horse. If they are ill—they may mount a donkey, and even so, the saddle is not like a Turkish one, but must be a pack-saddle, for carrying wood.'

'Hodja,' Syuleiman Aga said to him. He was carefully looking at the spots in his coffee cup, and appeared moved by the mysterious signs. 'Hodja, one hundred paces before my *Konak* and one hundred paces behind it no unbeliever may remain on his horse. He gets down and removes his fur cap. Otherwise he loses his head. Not long ago I had a head cut off for such a thing, and now I pay the widow, because the deceased left six little children who are starving.'

' But otherwise you admit that they ride?'

'There are no carts or boats here. Everything travels on the backs of horses or donkeys. People cannot always go on foot.'

'So you admit it, very well. Even if you don't, it is so. I saw you holding some of your men by the hand, and realized that they were unbelievers. Yet it is said that the Believer shall not give his hand to an unbeliever.'

'Hodja,' Syuleiman Aga interrupted him, 'did you eat bread this morning?'

'I did,' the hodja answered tartly, but surprised.

'Did you drink milk?'

'I did.'

'And you had a bite of meat, too, didn't you?'

'That is so.'

'Unbelievers sowed the wheat, an unbeliever's wife milked the sheep, and an unbeliever slaughtered the lamb. And unbelievers guard my house, too. How can the hand that feeds me defile me? If what enters my body and passes through my heart is given by an unbeliever, can the touch of his hand defile me?'

The one-eyed hodja was silent in confusion. He snorted, wiped his neck, and his eye shone in a sinister way, while he gathered his strength to wrestle with the Aga again.

Karaibrahim was silent.

Molla Soulfikar Softa spoke up. He was a fat man, and looked as if he had been all stuck together from balls. Someone had played at threading balls together and making a man. One ball was his head. Two little black balls—his eyes, a little red ball—his nose. A big ball stuck straight onto his head without a neck, was his paunch, which had swallowed his breast and shoulders. Two balls next to each other formed his arms, one up to the elbow, the other—from the elbow down. The fingers looked like a rosary of balls, one for each joint. He was a sycophant, a hypocrite and a bloodthirsty man.

'Let us leave the unbelievers and remember the Believers. Have you seen a veiled woman in the *Konak*? I have not, and I was unable to distinguish a Believer from an unbeliever among them. They all have uncovered faces, and every man can soil them with his glance. And they say that the entire mountains are full of *Yurouks*—Turks, and Believers, yet their women go unveiled. What are you about, Hassan Hodja, I ask you? And why are there no signs on the gates of the houses to show where the unbelievers live? Leaving aside that there are houses two storeys high. Suppose a Moslem beggar were to enter and call down the blessing of Allah on an unbeliever's house? That is a great sin, Hodja.'

'There are no beggars here. No one begs. And there are public rooms[25] in all three villages.'

Who said this I don't remember. It was all one—Hassan Hodja or Syuleiman Aga.

Hassan Hodja sat with his legs crossed and stared the two other Hodjas straight in the eye. He looked like a brother of Syuleiman's, neat, with well-trimmed beard, the master of himself.

Public rooms are rooms open to all travellers, like those of an inn, where they can stay with a roof over their heads, a bed and food.

'What are these rooms like?' muttered the fat Hodja. 'There must be a special window in these rooms, with a grating and a part which turns. The food is prepared behind the barrier, placed on a tray which the woman turns, and the food goes to the traveller. But the woman stands behind the grating.'

'Even here in my harem, there are no gratings and no barriers,' Syuleiman Aga said.

Again they were all silent. So was Karaibrahim. The one-eyed Hodja, after moving his lips for a long time, remarked hoarsely:

'I heard something, Aga, but I did not believe it. You will tell me. It is true that the *djizié* tax is collected by Bulgarians who bring it to you?'

I did not understand the trap, but Syuleiman Aga surely realized at once what the Hodja was hinting at. Nevertheless, he answered calmly:

'It is true.'

The Hodja cried, triumphantly:

'Yet do you know that the *djizié* is a ransom, payment that the unbeliever makes because we have not killed him, because we have left him alive, to sink in error and sin? Do you know that the *djizié* is a punishment for the unbelievers' disbelief? That is why as soon as Islam is accepted the *djizié* is abolished. Yet you collect it through other people. The *djizié* is paid by every Bulgarian, each one for himself. And he will stand before you, and you will be seated. And you will strike him with your fist on his insubmissive neck and shout at him: "Pay the *djizié*, O enemy of the only God".'

The Hodja rose, waving his arm and striking the air with his fist. Saliva flew from his mouth, and as I looked at him against the light it was as if he were emitting sparks and molten iron. Syuleiman Aga slowly wiped his brow with the palm of his hand—the Hodja had probably spat on him.

'I have seen how the *djizié* is collected. At that time the Aga who was collecting it came to me and complained: "Now I shall be bastinadoed, for I still lack two full purses." But when we paid the *djizié*, we gave the official two purses *baksheesh*.[26] Who is the more useful to the Padishah's state?'

Silence fell again. I was the only one who had not spoken. And what was I doing among these people? Why had Karaibrahim brought me? Syuleiman Aga looked at me. The silence grew insufferable. I coughed. To my horror I felt that I was going to speak, what I would say I did not know myself, I did not want us to be silent, that was all. My knees began to tremble, my heart began to beat, the blood drummed in my ears.

'*Djizié* will no longer be collected in this valley. *Djizié* is not paid by Believers. And when I leave this valley there will no longer be any unbelievers in it. Aga, have you read the letters?'

Karaibrahim was speaking. I drew breath, relieved.

Syuleiman Aga merely nodded.

'These letters order the Kaimakam, the *Cadi* and the Aga Syuleiman, son of Daoud, to assist me, Karaibrahim, with all his might, to dispel the false belief of the unbelievers. What has been up till now, will no longer be. There is no use in talking about it. Tell me, Aga, what you think, what will be the best way of saving the unbelievers? For, instead of rejoicing, they will probably persist in their false belief for days and months. That has been the case in many places. But you know your people.'

The time for quibbling was past. All awaited the answer.

'Aga,' said Syuleiman Aga, 'there are fifteen Believers in the three villages. Of them only ten are Turks, the others have seen the truth in their lifetime, and their fathers were, or are still unbelievers. My hodja, too, is called Hassan the son of Velko, and his father is alive. My *bilyuk-bashi* and my treasurer are Bulgarian unbelievers, and my clerk and my tax-collector are Turks. My guards are Bulgarians, my servants are Bulgarians. You tell me, how can we help you?'

Again the burden was cast onto Karaibrahim's shoulders. He quickly rid himself of it:

'Counsel me, Aga. Remember the letters, think, and answer me.'

'There is practically no one but women in the villages now,' Syuleiman Aga spoke slowly. 'The men are shepherds, a few are craftsmen and fishermen. They are all returning from the shores of the Aegean Sea now, driving their flocks. There are five Turks with them. Do you think it is now the time to deal with the women only?'

The one-eyed Hodja licked his dry lips and opened his mouth again. His eye shone feverishly and irresolutely, his lid blinked.

Syuleiman Aga raised his hand to stop him.

'I know what you will say, Hodja. I, too, have heard about that village. The men were with the sheep, the Turks entered in broad daylight and shut the women up in the church. Then all of them went through what the Hodja is thinking of. When the men returned, the women who had been raped themselves forced their menfolk to get themselves circumcised. They say that the circumcised were more to their taste. But I will tell you, Hodja, that together with the sheep of the three villages, three hundred men are on the way, all of them armed. There must be three hundred pistols with them, a hundred guns and two or three hundred bows. Every man here shoots with a bow.'

'Who gave them arms?' shrieked fat Molla Soulfikar Softa. 'You are to blame! It is forbidden for an unbeliever to bear arms, he must not carry a knife, and they have three hundred pistols!'

'They are for the bears and the wolves, Hodja,' Syuleiman Aga told him seriously, but it seemed to me that his eyes were laughing. 'How can the shepherds wander through these forests without arms? Last summer the bears ate forty mules alone; we didn't count the sheep.'

'When are the men returning?' the one-eyed hodja asked.

'Tomorrow they reach Plachliv Kamuk,' said Syuleiman Aga, and he looked at Karaibrahim.

'We are late,' said the Hodja.

'We have come in time,' said Karaibrahim. 'I knew when the men would return. The Aga speaks truly—we shall wait for them. We shall tell them of the mercy which the Padishah has decided to bestow on them, to make them the equals of his Janissaries. They will think it over. Not for long, for a week or two. For the Grand Vizier is at Candia and awaits glad tidings.'

Karaibrahim rose to his feet as a sign that the talk was over. Syuleiman Aga rose, too.

What was the outcome? Everything had been postponed. But what had Syuleiman Aga gained? At first I thought that there was only one choice for him : to submit. Had he any alternative?

Down in the courtyard, the *Bilyuk-bashi* Kemanchidjogli, a real bandit, met Karaibrahim and whispered to him :

'Aga, it smells bad here.'

Karaibrahim looked at him.

'Ya, Allah, it smells bad to me. I am not pleased with this *Konak*. Alas for the road we have travelled,' the *Bilyuk-bashi* exclaimed in annoyance. 'We set out with bags, but they may put our heads into them. Has it dawned upon you that they can slaughter us in a night?'

'We have guards,' said Karaibrahim.

'And why are we all in the *Konak*?'

'If we were in the houses, it would be worse. Don't whine, but keep your eyes open. Now, be off with you.'

Then Karaibrahim gave me a sharp and searching look.

'Do you believe that?' he asked me.

I shrugged my shoulders. Actually, wasn't this Syuleiman Aga's choice? Were there only a few local rulers who had risen against the Padishah's authority? Wasn't his power dearer to him than his peace of mind?

That night I put my pistol under my pillow. One does not dream pleasant dreams with a pistol under one's head—if one does dream, or indeed if one falls asleep at all.

Sixth Excerpt

> I will ask and you will tell me,
> Have you children in your village,
> Have you children to be taken
> To be our young Janissaries?
> We have heard of Janissaries, Dimo dear.
> Where shall mother hide you, Dimo dear?
> In the forest, or the water, Dimo dear?

The very same night of the day on which Manol met Karaibrahim and saw Elitsa, we set out on foot from the water-mill to the village

of Podviss. But we delayed, for Manol wanted to wait for his son
Mircho. And when the boy came, he told his father :

'Father, Turks met me, and one of them aimed at me with his
pistol, but it misfired.'

And though he feared his father greatly, so that he stood quite
still before him, he showed him how he had mocked at the Turks.
Manol said nothing to him.

The dead of night had come, when the light that has gone and
the light that is to come are equally far from man. But we set out,
although shepherds are very superstitious, for Manol was probably
not afraid, as he was walking with a priest. I was afraid, too, and
it was good that a full moon was shining, so that we did not fall
and break any bones on the way. Mircho either ran ahead of us or
lagged behind, like a kid or a dog, and even in the dark he found
mushrooms and put them in his bag. And he laughed and talked,
unable to restrain his joy at seeing his father. Manol said nothing
to him.

We reached the village of Podviss, which is the third and highest
in the valley of Elindenya. The village was asleep, only the river
murmured between the houses. That village was entirely built in a
ravine, for the people had not dared to take any of the arable land
for their houses, and so they had built them on the bare rock. And
it is a delight to the eye to see the houses and barns leaning over
the river, but the yards were small and stony. The river had never
overflowed its banks, because the pine forest above the village drinks
the mountain water and stops the snow. The forest is a forbidden
one, and the sound of an axe may not be heard in it. Only the
shepherds, when they come down in stormy weather, may cut crosses
on the spruces, so that the lightning will not strike them. People say
that when a Podviss peasant once began to cut down a spruce, it
cried out in a human voice, and blood flowed from the wound.
And the hands of that peasant withered. I do not know whether this
is true—people told me about it—but it is true that without that
forest Podviss would drop down into the river. We passed through
the forest along a secret path and suddenly came out just in front
of Manol's house.

The houses and barns are built next to each other, back to back,
so that looking at them from the outside, they look like a long wall.
This is done so that evil men and beasts may not enter the village.
Manol's house was at the end, and, jumping over the wall, Mircho
pulled the bar of the gate out, and we entered the yard. Although
it was night, in the moonlight one could see that weeds were growing between the stones, and that the crane's-bill along the walls
had crept up the stairs.

Then Manol complained for the first time that night :

'The house is crumbling, and there's no one to look after it. A house is no house without a woman.'

Just then the bell of the Monastery of St Elijah was heard again. The abbot was ringing the bell, for folk here greatly fear the dead of night, and the church bell hallows it. Otherwise, the hillmen wait until the cocks crow for the first time.

Manol stopped in the yard and stared at the moon. And I saw that he was smiling.

'That bell is like a man's voice,' he said. 'And even if you're lying on your pallet, as soon as you hear it you know what the weather is like outside. In winter, the snow-covered bell rings briefly with a dead sound—it does not echo long, it rings as if it were cracked. In spring, when the white wind blows, a scattered, anxious tinkling comes to you. As soon as the north wind begins to blow, the sound comes from a distance and is again full of alarm, but the spring alarm is different. In autumn the bell is as pure and clear as spring water. By day and by night the voice of the bell is borne over the hills. It is best heard at midnight—by day its voice is drowned by a thousand other voices. And when it rings for the last time—do you hear it?—there comes a slight quivering, impatient tapping—as if the bell wants to go on ringing.'

When he fell silent, and the echo of the bell still quivered in the moonlight, the fearful and sinister howling of a dog was heard, so that it covered and drowned the silvery voice. A second howl answered it, and the dogs howled so terribly that a deadly pain seemed to reach us in their howling, so that a man's hair stood on end, and cold shivers crept up his spine. Then a third dog howled still longer and more fearfully, so that the moon shone as cold as a dead man.

Manol ground his teeth and put his arm around Mircho, who nestled up against him under his red cloak.

'The Dark Hole,' said Manol.

That was the name of a black and deep pit—a well, or a cave— up above the village, without a ray of light, and bottomless. That was where they threw mad or vicious dogs, or the neighbour's dogs, and the poor beasts, when they realized that they would have to eat each other alive, would howl so that they maddened all three villages.

'Do you hear?' Manol asked quietly. 'Do you hear the howling of Belcho, and Vulchan, and Mecho? There, that was Vulchan again!'

Those were the names of the three dogs, belonging to Sevda's husband, which had been gambolling around us that day. That was why I could not believe it and said so to Manol, and he replied:

'When did she manage to? Who helped her? She may have made the abbot himself help her to push them in. She may have done it alone. She's not a woman—she's a she-devil.'

And he crossed himself. We went up the stairs and quickly entered the house, as if that hopeless howling were pursuing us. Inside, the chill of the grave struck us, for no fire had been lit in the upper room all the winter.

Then Manol lit a fire, and, when the flames blazed up, our hearts were eased, for fire does not only give light, it hallows everything and with fire one drives out the impure forces which settle in a deserted house.

'Father,' Mircho asked, 'why don't you go down into the Dark Hole and take the dogs out?'

'My son,' Manol answered, 'there are caves into which even your father cannot go. And they say that the Dark Hole goes down to the Lower Earth, and that the dogs howl because they see terrible things.'

'I know that if you wanted to, you could go down,' the boy said.

'Go to the barn and fetch hay, so that we can get the pallets ready,' Manol said to him.

Manol's house was big, with an upper and lower floor, it had a window and a hearth with a chimney. Most of the houses were only on one floor, with one room for cattle and folk, and the fire was lit in the middle of the room, and the smoke escaped through a hole in the middle of the roof.

Manol thrust a piece of pinewood into the fire and lit it. The wind blew from many sides so that he had to turn the pinewood like a poker, to guard himself from the flame, which always darted at him. And burning resin fell from the pinewood, and burned in small grains in the ash. When the pinewood burnt more smoothly, Manol handed it to Mircho and said to him:

'Shut the doors carefully, so that you do not pinch any of those that walk at midnight.'

For he was not quite convinced that the ringing of the bell had driven out of the mountain all that was impure.

Then Mircho went out, and Manol complained for the second time that night.

'Forgive me, Father, for being unable to receive you as is fitting, for my home is without a woman. And a shepherd's house without a woman is like a *chan* without a clapper.'

And he turned his head aside. Over there in the darkness Manol's silver *chans* caught the light of the flames.

It was said that Manol had found a silver treasure in a deep cave. And Orpheus had been cut onto each coin—the singer who put the lions and tyrants to sleep with his flute, and went down into the Lower Earth through the Dark Hole. Others said that on the coins there were persons making love. It was said that Manol's foster-father, the *haidout* Karamanol, left his foster-child two saddle bags full of small silver coins, although it was known that Karamanol drank blood, but took no purses. In any case, Manol gave his silver to have white *chans* cast for him in Nevrokop. And there was more silver in them than copper. If his fifty *chans* weighed two hundred *okas* there would still be a hundred *okas* of silver in them.

Never had Manol's *chans* been hung on the necks of goats and rams. It was commonly said that he was waiting to get a flock with fifty bell-goats in it, before bringing out his *chans*. And only the *Yurouks*—whose sheep were common property—and Syuleiman Aga had flocks of this size. It looked as if the forests would never hear Manol's *chans*.

And Manol rose and went to his *chans*. They were next to the wall, hung up in four rows, each one a full chime of thirteen *chans*, arranged on each row from the first tone to the last. Two peeled fir boles had been placed on trestles, four sticks lay from bole to bole, and on them hung the *chans*. And the fire played over them, but they remained mute.

Then Manol began to tap the *chans* with his nail. And they had been silent all winter, so they sang softly and joyfully, like a shepherd's bride, welcoming her husband. And their voices were indeed silvery.

And as I listened, I realized that Manol was making the *chans* sing the song 'I am white, brave lad, so white, I shine on all the world, Karluk was left all alone, for he was covered in mist . . .'

Then with both hands Manol seized the boles which bore his *chans* and began to shake them. And he shook them harder and harder until first the whole house became a bell, and then the whole world became a bell and the moon was beating as if it were a silver clapper.

The voices of the *chans* poured over me like silver waterfalls, and I could not draw breath, and the silver waters passed over me, bearing away whatever there was in me of dark and evil. And I stood before the bells naked and pure, like a nursling. And in that night I understood the story of the *chan*, which made its owner one year younger at every stroke of its clapper. Such *chans* could almost make a man like a babe unborn.

And I do not remember when Manol stopped ringing them. He

stood with his back to me, his arms at his sides, and I was standing facing him. And in the room the spirits of the voices that had gone were borne about.

Manol said:

'You must put *chans* in your churches.'

Mircho came in with an armful of hay, but did not shut the door behind him; he had probably forgotten about the impure forces. And I saw tears shining on his face, so I wiped my own eyes, too. Manol turned and I saw the same expression on his face as when he had looked at Elitsa.

And Manol said also:

'If one *chan* is cracked, if one is out of tune, the whole song will be swallowed by the earth.'

And I realized that he was not speaking only of the *chans*.

Then we sat down at the low round table, covered with all that Manol had taken out of his bag. And Manol complained for the third time that night.

'Round and short is my table, it holds few people. And few of my people sit around it. Yet I would give my soul for a long broad table, for many sons and daughters.'

When, at the end, I made the sign of the cross over the table, Manol gathered the crumbs from the cloth and cast them upon the fire. And he said to his son:

'My son, go and bring me the chest that smells of fresh pine from the saddle bags.'

And Mircho brought the chest. Manol placed it on the table and said:

'My son, kneel down opposite me. The bones of your mother are in this chest.'

The boy was neither troubled, nor did he grow quieter for, since he had heard the howling of the dogs and the ringing of the *chans*, he had been quiet and silent, like a bird before a storm.

And Manol said to him:

'Do you know why we call the Turks heathens?'

'No, I don't,' Mircho answered him.

'There are some terrible, hairy people, with one eye in the middle of their foreheads. They are called heathens. It's a good thing that Our Lord only lets them out on earth for two weeks—one before Christmas and one after. They eat human flesh. Whomsoever they meet, they eat him up. But there is something still more terrible. Sometimes, if they catch somebody, they make him taste human flesh with them. And he, too, becomes like the heathens. You may look at him from whatever side you wish, he looks just like other folk. He has a wife and children, houses and fields, he ploughs and he reaps. He cannot breed sheep, for whoever touches sheep must be a clean man—the Holy King David was a shepherd, and he protects us from the heathen. And the angels told the shepherds first of all that Christ was born. And we, too, protect ourselves with herbs and with knives. A man of this kind, as soon as the special week sets in, turns into a heathen at night and eats people. He may even eat his father, and his children.'

And Mircho said to him :

'Father, but as the Turks are heathens, why do they eat people all the year round? And why is there no end to their week?'

'There will be. Its end may even be quite near. He who has given them power, may take it from them. Listen further. The Turks, as heathens, sometimes, when they catch a man, make him become as they are—and make him, too, eat Christians. And they like best to turn into heathens anyone whom they themselves cannot devour.'

Then Mircho wanted to say something to him, but Manol raised his hand and spoke further :

'Thirty years ago, when I was a boy like you, heathen Turks came to our villages. They were collecting children, to teach them to eat men, to take them to their own land and make Janissaries of them—that is what these heathen are called. Old and young alike wept and wailed. And one mother threw her son down a well. I was an orphan, I had no one anywhere, either to push me down a well, or to tell me about the heathen, as I am telling you now. Everywhere, whenever the heathen set out to collect children, the orphans are given to them first. And that is perfectly right—so that, should they ever return, they would be unable to cut their fathers' throats. Old Galoushko reared me. He had two other sons then—Dobril and Strahin. And I was like a son to him, but those two were his own sons. And their mother was alive—you don't remember her. Old Galoushko gave the heathens his second son, Strahin. And he saved me, for there was no one else to protect me. If he had given me, I might now be returning to the valley, to look for more children, to make heathens of them. How they do it, I don't know, but whoever tastes human meat with them, can never unlearn it. Probably every man is a beast.'

'They may not be coming for children,' said Mircho.

'God grant it may be so,' said Manol, seriously. 'But that is probably what they are coming for, because they are waging a big war, and their heathens are coming to an end. They have taken everything from us. All they can take now is the children. Now listen, and don't speak again. I have two sons—you and your brother Momchil. According to the law, if they are taking Janissaries, I must give up one of you. Momchil is over age, I have only you left to give. But I won't give you up.'

'And I won't give myself up,' the boy cried. 'Even if they catch me, I shan't become a heathen.'

'Hold your tongue!' Manol said to him, sternly. 'You are still very small and you don't know the habits of heathens. And none of us knows the taste of human flesh. It may be very sweet. The important thing is not to taste it. I want three things of you, not four, though they are a heavy burden for your childish shoulders. But have you noticed how in the forest, a young beech tree, as thick as your little arm, will grow next to a huge spruce, so big that two men cannot embrace it? And if you raise your head, you will see that their crowns are next to each other in the sky. That is the kind of small tree you must be, and rise high up, even though your years are but a few.'

'I shall not become a heathen,' the boy repeated quietly and stubbornly.

'Three behests have I for you as a father, and I want you to swear that you will fulfil them. If the Turks do not catch you, you will forget them. But no one knows the ways of the Lord. So, listen! If the Turks catch you, when they lead you out of the valley, you will cross Syuleiman Aga's stone bridge. My first command is, as you cross the bridge, whether you be tied or not, throw yourself into the river. The water will carry you away. It may drown you, it may cast you up alive, but no one will find you, alive or dead, because there is no road along the banks of the river. Have you remembered that?'

'I have, Father,' said Mircho.

Manol was silent a while before uttering his second behest.

'My second behest is, if you cannot throw yourself from the bridge, as soon as you reach the Miloto Gospoli Pass, stop and turn back. Just as if you wanted to see Elindenya for the last time. Turn so that your breast will face the stone crosses. I shall be hidden in the cemetery and will shoot you straight in the heart. You are to stand there and not move.'

'Will you be able to get away?' the boy asked.

'The forest is beside me. And even if they catch up with me, there won't be more than two or three. I'll cut their throats, as a sacrifice for you.'

'And what is your third behest?' the boy asked.

'My third behest is, if you don't throw yourself from the bridge, and if I don't shoot you up at the Miloto Gospoli Pass, as soon as the road grows narrow at the Devitsa,[27] you must jump into the abyss. People can only walk in single file there. If you can manage it, pull someone down with you. The water may drag you along and cast you out alive. My hand may quiver and I may not hit your heart, but you won't come out of the abyss alive. A maiden once cast herself into it, and that's why they call that crag the Devitsa. If a woman could throw herself from it, what is there left for you? Those are they, my three behests as your father. Did you hear them, my child?'

'I heard, Father,' the boy answered.

'And now swear,' Manol said, 'swear on your mother's bones and on this knife.'

And Manol drew out the broad knife with which he had dug up the grave, wiped it on his cloak and placed it on the chest. And when the boy opened his mouth, he stopped him and said:

'Wait!'

And he turned to me.

'Father, you are carrying holy books in your bag, aren't you? Give me one, that the oath may be more binding.'

I answered:

'Yes, I am, but only the Old Testament. And I have Solomon's Ecclesiastes, too.'

'Never mind,' said Manol, 'he was a Christian, wasn't he?'

'King Solomon lived before Jesus Christ.'

'Never mind. The important thing is that he wasn't a Turk.'

And I placed the book of the wise and despondent king upon the chest with the bones, next to the knife, and Mircho swore upon the bones, the knife and the Book of Ecclesiastes, repeating word for word what his father spoke before him. I stood helpless beside them, and it still seemed to me that I was a nursling, as I had felt after the song of the *chans*. And Mircho seemed to me to be older than I was.

At the end, his father raised his hand and stroked his bowed head for the first time since they had met.

We were silent for a long time after the child had repeated his oath, and once more we heard the howling of the dogs. And Manol turned towards the sound and said in a low voice:

'Be silent, cursed souls. When the flocks come, I shall throw you a barren sheep.'

And when we realized that we would be unable to sleep, Manol said to me: 'Father, read something.'

And I fumbled about in the bag.

'No, read from this book,' said Manol, pointing to the Ecclesiastes. 'Let Mircho know what he has taken his oath on.'

And in the light of the fire I began to read Solomon's Ecclesiastes.

'Vanity of vanities, all is vanity . . . What profit hath a man of all his labour which he taketh under the sun? One generation passeth away, and another cometh : but the earth abideth for ever.

'The eye is not satisfied with seeing nor the ear filled with hearing. The thing that hath been it is that which shall be; and that which is done is that which shall be done; and there is no new thing under the sun . . .'

Thus did I read from Ecclesiastes, verse after verse, and with patience. I heard as in a dream the howling of the dogs, until at last I heard the bell of the monastery ringing for matins. And I fell silent. Manol, too, said nothing.

And when I looked towards the window, the night seemed black to me, but when I rose and looked out, I saw—there light was being born, and the new day was coming.

Seventh Excerpt

I awoke, and when I looked through the window I saw only the tops of the trees. I was looking upon them from above, not only because I was on the second storey of the *Konak*, but also because the ground sloped downwards. No earth was visible, only the tops of the trees. A single pale-green meadow lay high up amid the trees. Opposite me the mountain also rose steeply to its summit, overgrown with a forest.

I went back to my pallet and lay down on it again. The tops of the nearby trees, which I now saw, disappeared at the foot of the mountain. But a spruce rose above it and stood out against the sky. The sky was light.

I was alive. A new day was beginning.

I scoffed at my fears of the night. I remembered how I had strained my ears to hear something in the next room—not because Karaibrahim had told me to eavesdrop, but because I trembled for my own skin.

I gazed at the mountains until they grew red in the light of dawn, but not with the rosy light that irradiates the blue summits of the Alps. This mountain gradually grew red, like a baked brick, slightly covered with moss, because the dark green of the forests nevertheless came through.

I rose and went down into the courtyard. I left the *Konak*. A woman was dashing silvery water out of a bucket, preparing to sweep the cobbles. There was a smell of resin, of damp and of cold.

A young cherry tree in blossom stood before me. Down in the
plain, the cherries were already turning red, but here white flowerets
were blossoming. Whether it had rained, or whether it was dew I
do not know, but the tree was entirely covered with drops. A gentle
breeze swayed it, and the drops sparkled. First one glistened, then
another, in various bright colours, all colours of the rainbow, so
that it looked as if the cherry-tree were covered with a silver-embroidered mantle, sewn with beads. There were hundreds of drops,
and hundreds of sparks flashed and went out on the tree.

I fixed my eyes on a drop. It quivered, danced and shivered,
as if it were afraid of being torn from the tree and falling. Yet
perhaps the earth attracted it like every precipice? It was an
enormous drop—now green, now red, now blue.

I was like one bewitched, like a fisherman who sees a pearl
shining in the depths. Involuntarily I advanced towards the tree.
The brilliant flashes vanished. The tree grew grey. I had so far
been looking at it against the sun, and as soon as I changed my
position, it hid its beauty from me.

'Fool!' I jeered bitterly at myself. 'Haven't you understood
that you must not draw near? Nor stretch out your hand? Stand
aside, fool!'

I went up to the tree, seized its slender trunk and shook it. Heavy
drops rained down and filled my neck. I closed my eyes and raised
my hands. The cold drops ran over my lids. It was good.

I drew back and looked at the tree. Drops of water and the tiny
white petals of its blossoms were still falling from it. Bees had come
—they were casting them down.

The scent of a strange weed rose around me. The woman was
sweeping with a broom made of hard green weeds that she had
just tied together. The fresh weeds left green spots on the cobbles,
and raised a light dust and a wild, heady fragrance.

Then I saw the white legs of the woman, who was bending down
with her back turned towards me. I did not see her face. And such
a desire arose within me. I sensed her warm skin, her hair, her
breath, mixed with the fragrance of the weeds, and I desired her so
strongly that I almost wept. There was another person, a woman,
two steps away from me.

I felt the breath gurgling in my throat, and something growled
in my breast. I turned and fled.

When I entered the inner courtyard, a maidservant approached
me and said:

'Come, the mistress calls you.'

I followed her up the stairs, and heard deep moans, like those
of someone in torment. I broke into a cold sweat with fear. And

because I was going up, the moans grew clearer, and I realized that a woman was moaning.

A fat woman was sitting on a low stool on the veranda, knitting something on thick needles with red and yellow yarn.

And the summit of the mountain that was visible through the branches of the plane tree was yellowish red. The woman's garments were those of a mistress of the house.

Yet what did those silk garments look like on her! Oh, how fat Gyulfié was! The silk was stretched over her thighs, and it looked just as if the curved buttocks of her husband's Flemish horse were covered with it. In front she swelled out as if she were holding two sacks of flour to her breast. She had a round face that was uncovered, without any eyebrows, and, as is the case with many fat women, you could not tell her age, because the fat stretched and polished her skin. Her eyes shone, her lips were laughing, her cheeks were pink. It seemed to me that if I were to pull out one of her knitting needles and prick her cheeks with it, a little red stream would come squirting out, as it would from a wineskin full of wine. There was something in her that pressed on her and inflated her wherever it could. She was surely not very old. That was what Gyulfié looked like.

She examined me for a minute or two with her little black eyes, and her lips were still smiling, as if she were thinking of something gay, and were preparing to tell me about it. Just then the deep moans were heard again. I turned—Gyulfié was on the veranda— and through the open door of the room opposite her I saw a woman lying on a pallet with her head turned to one side. Her wet hair shone. The red covering over her belly moved and writhed, as if cats had been thrust beneath it, and were trying to get out into the light.

'Fear not, she is in labour,' I heard Gyulfié's voice saying.

I cannot have looked very well, for she began to laugh. She had a shrill feminine voice and a bell-like laugh.

'You men find it easy to create children, but you're afraid to look when they're being born. She has slept with a man, and now she's paying for it.'

And turning to the girl who had brought me to the veranda, she shouted at her :

'What are you listening for, eh? That's what is in store for you, too! Or do you think I'm blind? Run to the kitchen and bring the best you can find there.'

That is how respect was shown to the servants—they were brought something to eat, because they were always hungry. Gyulfié took me for a servant, and said as much.

'I want to ask you something about your master.'

I really was in fact, a servant. Why was I angry?

'What master are you asking about?' said I. 'I have no master.'

She looked at me unsmilingly, sternly, and perhaps reproachfully.

'What is your name?' she asked. 'I am Gyulfié, Syuleiman Aga's wife.'

'Abdullah.'

'Whose?'

'If I tell you my father's name, I shall tell you many things which I would like to forget.'

'Why?'

'When I disappeared at the Battle of Candia, my comrades-in-arms offered my weight in gold, in my armour and with my arms, as a ransom for me. Seventy *okas* of gold. Is there as much gold in all your mountains? They thought I was dead.'

'And why don't they give at least a half for your living body? The Sultan himself would not refuse twenty or thirty thousand gold pieces.'

'There is no way back for me. My blood flows in the veins of the French King. How can I return with a turban on my head?'

Why did I tell her these things? Could I be asking for her respect? That fat Turkish woman, shining with sweat?

Gyulfié stared at me thoughtfully.

'It does not cost you anything to lie to me,' she said. 'Nothing at all. You might say that you were the King of the Franks in person. What would it cost you? But I think you are telling the truth. Come and sit before me, on that little stool.'

And she stared at me in the same way when I sat down before her.

'No matter if they did offer twenty big bagfulls of gold for you. You haven't a single one now, have you?'

Just then the maidservant brought a dish of sour milk, pilaf, honey cakes and jugs of red sherbet.

'Eat and drink,' Gyulfié said to me. 'This is what masters and men eat here.'

She herself put out a hand and began to cram the small cakes into her little pink mouth one after the other.

'Why do you eat so much?' I asked her.

I did not feel any barrier between us. A secret seemed to link us. It seemed to me that we had grown up together.

'That is all the consolation left to me,' she said, and began to giggle. Then she leant towards me and said quietly: 'There he is —I wanted to ask you about him.'

And red spots appeared on her cheeks.

I turned. Karaibrahim and the local Hodja Hassan were coming towards us. They passed beside us, turned along the veranda and sat down near the parapet which was at right angles to me. When I saw the wandering look with which the fat woman followed Karaibrahim, I began to laugh. I imagined her naked beside the dry and desiccated Karaibrahim.

'He's an Albanian,' I said. 'I have not seen him look at a woman, but when he sees a fat horse, he turns his head aside.'

She had recovered herself, and shook her head.

'It is not nice of you to mock me.'

She did not look much offended. As for me, any desire to laugh left me when it occurred to me that Karaibrahim had come to listen to what I was saying to Syuleiman Aga's wife. If I could be a traitor in his favour, could I not betray him, too?

I saw that the Hodja was holding some sheets of paper in his hands and I heard him say:

'In Prossoina there are 156 homesteads, of which only three belong to the Faithful, and fifteen widows. In Zagrad there are 123 homesteads, of which three belong to the Faithful, and twenty-one widows. In Podviss there are 109 homesteads, not one belonging to the Faithful, and seven widows. In the three villages there are six hundred men between the ages of eighteen and sixty, who can carry daggers.'

The Hodja was telling Karaibrahim about the Elindenya Valley.

Gyulfié said: 'The Janissary has come to watch the Aga's court.'

She was speaking of her husband, the Aga.

'He's not a Janissary,' I said. 'He is a Spahi, an Albanian.'

She shook her head.

'The Aga has learnt that he is a Janissary. He hides it. But he may be an Albanian.'

Karaibrahim was, indeed, leaning against the parapet of the veranda, listening to the Hodja and looking down at the same time. And the Hodja was saying:

'Folk here sow rye, oats, barley and a few lentils. They mow the meadows to get hay for their cattle. The women grow a little flax and hemp. There are many bees, also, for the honey. But were it not for the sheep, they could not make a living. The Aga Syuleiman, son of Daoud, has 7,300 head of sheep, the peasants about 7,500 ...'

I moved my stool and also looked down from the veranda into the courtyard. I was not troubled by the thought that it was not very polite to turn my back on Gyulfié.

Syuleiman Aga was seated on a gaily-coloured rug, next to the huge bole of the plane-tree in the courtyard. Next to him sat his clerk, with a lead inkpot, a quill and paper on his knee. Four men stood before the Aga with their backs towards me. I saw that their hands were bound behind them. The Aga's armed men surrounded them. I heard one of the bound men say in a choked voice :

'I am the son of Vrazhou *Kehaya*.'

'We are all sons of Allah,' Syuleiman Aga said indifferently.

'You say so, because you have no sons,' the young man spoke in the same choked voice.

'That may be so, I do not know. But it is better to have no sons than to have a son like you.'

Gyulfié stirred. She moved up her stool, puffing and blowing, and peered down from the veranda.

'I am childless,' she said quietly.

'What are they trying him for?' I asked.

'He pestered a girl at the spring. He spoke a bad word to her, and tried to take the nosegay from her bosom. Over there, under the shelter, she is weeping on her father's shoulder.'

I looked and saw another group of people on the other side of the plane tree. I saw both Karaibrahim and the Hodja above them. The Hodja was saying :

'People here are not wealthy, but they do not murmur against fate. And they do not envy others their wealth. They do not complain, they do not curse God. Drought, hunger, death—if you pity them for these, they will answer—it's the Lord's business. If fortune smiles on them, their first action is to give a thank-offering—to build a fountain, a bridge, or a chapel. Their greatest hope is that one day they will be able to build a public room.'

Karaibrahim was listening dispassionately to the Hodja and looking down into the yard. I said to Gyulfié, indicating Karaibrahim with a nod of my head :

'The blood of St Bektash cures barrenness.'

St Bektash is the Janissaries' patron.

She shook her head reproachfully, without looking at me; she was looking down into the yard.

I peered down, too. Two men-at-arms were dragging the young man across the courtyard. At first he resisted in silence, but when he was dragged under the dark vault of the gate he began to shout. His voice echoed.

'What was his sentence?' I asked.

'He will be put into a sack and pushed into the waterfall behind the *Konak*.'

'They're going to kill him? For having once put his hand into the girl's bosom?'

Gyulfié looked at me calmly. With her head raised, her double chins were not visible, and her little chin looked like a heart.

'That is what is done here. There are only four punishments. For a lecherous word or gesture, the Aga has men cast down into the abyss. For theft, he hangs men on that plane tree over there. For banditry, he has them shot on the meadow opposite. For cattle that have strayed into another's field, he shoots the beast and has the owner bastinadoed—twenty strokes on the soles of his feet. If this does not please anyone, let him keep quiet.'

I was a courtier, too, and I, too, had judged. But this court gave me a jolt. I did not feel like watching any more, so I drew my stool away and tried to distinguish the voice of the Hodja, speaking to Karaibrahim, among the voices which came from the courtyard.

'If there is bread and salt, the rest is easy, that is what the peasants here say,' the Hodja was telling him. 'And then again, whatever you put into your stomach, it will ask for more. But they delight in fine things, only they won't kill themselves with work to gain wealth. They will not sell their souls for money, and they never deceive you. They will only steal their neighbour's sheep, but as each man steals from the next, in the end they still have the same number of sheep. They mostly put their trust in the Lord and in their own hands.'

A sweet woman's voice made me turn :

'Mistress, mistress !'

A young woman dressed in peasant costume with bare legs and fair hair had come up noiselessly behind me. It was Sevda.

Sevda had a completely youthful face, the face of a girl, but it already had the bloom of maturity. If I had been told at once that she was a widow, I would not have believed it. But there was something in her, despite her youth, which made every man think that he could obtain everything his soul might desire, and that there would still be something left.

Gyulfié turned.

'What do you want?'

'I heard that many visitors have arrived here, so I thought you might be looking for women to help with the work. I'm all alone so if you want me, let me come to the *Konak*.'

'I know what you're looking for. Go to Stokay now : there she is, over there, having her baby, stay with her; after that we'll see.'

'Alas, mistress, I know nothing at all about children !'

'You're not a maiden, are you, eh, Sevda? You'll soon know all about children.'

Delyo, Syuleiman Aga's bodyguard, came up the stairs. He walked and swayed along, so that the boards of the veranda creaked. His silver-embroidered sleeveless jacket was unbuttoned, his red waistband had slipped down and was dragging after him, so were the straps of his leggings. Careless and untidy, he came up to Sevda, squatted down and began to look her up and down with his bold and shameless eyes. She cast a look at him, quivered like a doe who has felt the presence of a wolf, turned and went into the room where the woman in labour was. Delyo turned on his heels and continued to look at her.

I looked at the woman, too, when she sat down beside the pallet. And suddenly—as the light fell upon her—her face changed. Shadows glided over it. They appeared from the white flesh, as lightly as rot appears where soft fruit has been touched with rough fingers—at the spot where the fruit will begin to rot. They appeared on both sides of the mouth, along the nose, under the eyes, where hollows and shadows would in time lie, making the face—now young—depraved and avid. The secret light revealed the future.

As if she had felt my look, the young woman turned to me. The dark spots of bruised flesh disappeared, so did the shadows and the ugly prophecy. The pure face of a maiden was turned to me.

'A beautiful woman,' I said.

'A bitch in season,' said Gyulfié.

'A beautiful woman. If you hate her, why do you allow her in your house?'

'Allah, why? What for? To watch the show. To see how men dangle around her, how they slobber and look like old asses. And in the end, I shall marry her to the oldest and the ugliest, so that she will curse her youth.'

Delyo, who was still squatting, rose to his feet and came up to us.

'Just as you married me, didn't you, Gyulfié?' he drawled.

'Hold your tongue, Delyo. You won't frighten me.'

'Listen, Venetian—for that is what they call you, isn't it? I came here, young and green, and she gave me a grandmother as my wife. I couldn't do anything with her. She has married off all the Aga's men, there's not a bachelor left. She stands watching the *horo*[28] of the lasses and lads. She'll pick a dwarf for a fine young man, she'll give a spindle-shanks to a big stout lass, to chase him with the pillows at night because he's no good to her. And she just giggles. You're a she-devil, Gyulfié, you're no woman.'

Gyulfié giggled.

'I gave you a house, you thankless fellow. I gave your wife a dowry. If you don't like her, cut her throat, Delyo. You've cut the throats of so many.'

He stood opposite her, watching her with curiosity, and swaying, now on his heels, now on his toes. He was smiling and he spoke carelessly, so that one could not tell whether he was angry, or speaking in fun.

'I'll get even with you, Gyulfié, the Lord is my witness that I will.'

'You're to call me "mistress". What have you come for?'

'The Aga said you were to call to him.'

Gyulfié dragged her stool along and without getting up, still knitting—she had not left her knitting for a moment—called from the veranda :

'Speak, Aga.'

I looked down, too, and regretted it at once. Two men were throwing a noose over a thick branch, and two others had knocked the condemned wretch down on to the stones and were kneeling on him to hold him down.

The Aga raised his eyes.

'*Agovitsa*,[29] Kalin *Kehaya*'s son has deserted his bride, have you a lass to give him?'

Gyulfié clapped her fat hands.

'Come up, come ! I have !'

Sevda cast herself at her feet.

'Be a mother to me, *Agovitsa*, do not give me to Shagoun.'

'What kind of a mother can I be to you, you bitch? Do you think I'm as old as that? Fear not, your time has not come yet.'

Down below a woman screamed from the shelter—I did not discover whether it was the girl whose shift had been torn, or the abandoned bride.

Gyulfié sat down; steps were heard on the stairs.

All the while, the Hodja was talking to Karaibrahim. And now in the brief stillness I heard his voice again.

'That is Elindenya Valley and those are her people. What I had to say to you, I have said. Here are the books with the lists for the taxes and the common lands. If you wish, ask what you want to know.'

'What subjects they will make for the Padishah !' Karaibrahim said in admiration.

'They are subjects of the Padishah now, too,' the Hodja answered calmly.

Karaibrahim rose to his feet. So did the Hodja.

'Why do they call you the son of Velko?' Karaibrahim asked.

'In the thousandth year of the Hejira precisely forty-six years ago, I was taken to be made a Hodja. Such was the order of the

late Sultan Mourad the Fourth, may his name be sacred. Children
were to be taken from the Rhodopes, to sow the seeds of the True
Faith afterwards.'

Karaibrahim was coming towards us. The Hodja walked behind
him.

'You speak like a soldier. Briefly, as I like it,' said Karaibrahim.

'I was in the Persian campaign, at the first siege of Candia and
in Hungary. With Syuleiman Aga.'

'You have sown badly, Hodja.'

'Syuleiman Aga did not allow the people to change their faith.'
Karaibrahim raised his eyebrows.

'No, I did not allow it,' said Syuleiman Aga.

He had mounted the stairs and had come up to Gyulfié and me.
I rose to my feet, he signed to me to sit down again. People crowded
behind him.

'I did not allow them to change their faith, because the Pomaks
—that is what the others call the Bulgarian Mohammedans, while
they call themselves "Ahryané"—because the Ahryané draw aside
from Bulgarians and Turks alike. And instead of helping to dis-
seminate the True Faith, they shut themselves up in their villages.'

'When all the mountains have accepted the True Faith, there
will be no one to stand aside.'

'When all the mountains accept the True Faith,' Syuleiman Aga
repeated. 'That is so.'

And he turned to his wife :

'*Agovitsa*, we bring you the bridegroom. Where is the bride?'

His men-at-arms pushed forward a pale young man with an insane expression. His hands were still bound behind his back.

Gyulfié was radiant.

'There she is, in the room. Stand aside, and let the man see his
wife.'

People drew aside, and the lad saw the woman in labour, who
began to scream.

'What is she doing?' he asked, confused.

'She is bearing a child,' Gyulfié said. 'Yet she is unmarried. Un-
bind his hands. I give you a house and a dowry. Come, kiss my
hand.'

But the unfortunate lad, as soon as he felt his hands free, hid his
face in them—he did not want to look.

Gyulfié was laughing.

'You fool,' she said to him. 'Suppose you had married a barren
woman? Or do you want to jump down into the abyss, after
Vrazhou *Kehaya*'s son?'

Just then the branch of the plane tree, which stretched out towards us, began to shake, as if fruit were being shaken down from it. The hanged man was kicking.

The lad fell on his knees, and pressing his face to Gyulfié's hand began to weep.

Syuleiman Aga turned :

'Is there anything else to be tried?'

'Us, Aga, for the meadow.'

Two old men came forward. They were white-haired, but still hale and hearty.

'I remember. Well, whose is the meadow?'

'It's mine, Aga,' said the one.

'It's mine, Aga,' said the other.

Syuleiman Aga said to them :

'I have thought and thought about it, and I have been unable to understand whose the meadow is. Your case is not clear. Only Allah knows who is right and who is wrong. So let Allah judge you.'

He turned to Delyo. 'Delyo give me your pistols.'

And taking them, he pulled the spark-wheel of one of them.

'Here are two pistols. Both are full, but one of them will not shoot. We will blindfold you, and each will take a pistol and put it against the other's stomach. When I say "shoot" you will pull the triggers. The one who remains alive is the owner of the meadow; the dead man has lied.'

The hale old men stood there more dead than alive.

'Delyo, blindfold them,' said Syuleiman Aga.

'I give up my claim,' said one of the old men, his lips were quite bloodless.

'I give up my claim,' repeated the other.

Syuleiman Aga was looking at them, with the two pistols in his hands.

'Curs,' he said, 'so you do not believe that God will show who is the guilty one? You do not believe in God's justice? Or are you both lying? That means the meadow is not yours. Then it is mine.'

One could not make out whether he was mocking them or speaking seriously. They stood there with bowed heads, but sighed in relief.

'Get out!' said the Aga.

One by one, people went down the stairs. The bridegroom remained with his bride, to await his child. Karaibrahim and the Hodja passed on along the veranda. Syuleiman Aga gazed after them. The branches of the plane tree were no longer shaking.

When the Aga was about to leave, Gyulfié caught him by the skirts of his purple garment.

'Aga,' she said, 'do you know that this man here is a kinsman of the King of the Franks?'

I nearly died of shame. Truly, I felt like a man who was lying and boasting.

The Aga gave me a look—keener and more searching than his wife's. I stood there with bent head, and felt my ears grow scarlet. And without raising my eyes to the Aga, I felt that he believed me.

'No king's blood runs in my veins,' he said. 'But my forebears owned these mountains, and three times they rose in rebellion against their tsars. And three times the tsars gave them their daughters to wife, and three times they sent loads of gold and murderers, so that my forebears might give them the keys of the mountains. But this valley is all that is left to me. This whole mountain region is called Slavi's forests after my great grandfather, Slav, and Despot takes its name from his title. I am only an Aga.'

I wondered, as I heard him, that he did not hide the bitterness in his voice. It was not like him.

And Gyulfié said to him :

'Aga, you got up left foot first today.'

Syuleiman Aga said : 'Look down from the veranda and you will see the man I had hanged. For theft. Go to that window, and you will hear the dying groans of the man I had thrown in the abyss. For lechery I condemned them. So that there might be peace in the valley. I cast men into the abyss for lecherous words, and soon in this valley there will be more raped women split in two than there are trees split by lightning in the forest. I hang men for a stolen rug, and soon the houses will gape open as empty as drawn chickens. Robbed. I shoot bandits, and soon there will be more bandits than honest folk. I bastinado for a crushed ear of wheat in the field, and soon the trampled fields will be overgrown with weeds. There are the two men I have had killed. Why do I judge if there will be praise for such deeds tomorrow? Am I a judge? Or a murderer?'

Could I answer him?

He turned and departed.

Gyulfié was shaking her head.

'He grieves for his brother,' she said. 'Syuleiman Aga killed his blood brother so that there might be peace in the mountains. For the sake of order, he sacrificed his brother. And now that he sees what is going to happen, it seems to him that everything has been in vain. That is why it hurts him. That is why he says—and he may feel that it is so—that he is a murderer.'

Eighth Excerpt

Are you sleeping, Milka lé, waken now.
Turks have enslaved our land, Milka lé,
All that was old, Milka lé, they have slain,
All that was young, Milka lé, they've turned into Turks.

Remember all our sorrows, O Lord, because of the sufferings of Thy Son, and repay our enemies with the same evil, that they did unto us, and add unto it, for they laughed when we wept, and shouted : 'Ho! Ho!' and spake : 'Where is your God, that He may save you?' And unto Mehmed Pasha mete out, O Lord, that they slay his sons before him, and afterwards put out his eyes, that he may see nothing more, and may see only that, all the days of his life, which he will spend in darkness.

The refugees came just at *Predoi*—the great feast, when men mark on tallies how much milk every man's sheep have yielded, and by autumn each one expects to receive a bucketful for each *oka* of milk they yield. And they received buckets full of tears.

For the first time since the black plague many years ago, the women and the children did not come out to meet their menfolk at Plachliv Kamuk where they had seen them off in the autumn, so that the joy at the meeting might wipe out the grief at that parting. Bagpipes would skirl, *kavals* play and hands would be stretched out towards the bags of gifts, and yet—when Plachliv Kamuk appeared on the horizon, only Manol stood there, tall and gloomy. When the shepherds found out that there were Turks in their villages, and that their mothers, wives and daughters had stayed at home behind barred gates, the bagpipes, *kavals* and pipes fell silent. But the *chans* rang on, for there was no one to pull out their clappers. And the sheep trotted on as if they were going to the slaughter.

Then the men grew somewhat calmer when they heard that the Turks were staying in the *Konak* and did not stir abroad. How much hope does a man need to warm his heart? But messengers were sent at once, some to Chepino and Yakoruda, and others to Smolen and Raikovo, to find out what had happened in the left and the right branch of the Krustogorie,[30] since an adder had dared to make its nest in its heart.

And *Predoi* came, but no women and children crowded over the meadows, no shouting and singing was to be heard. The men set the dairies to rights, but half of them were in the villages, and the minds of the other half that stayed with the sheep were there, too. The best shepherds drove the sheep over the sweetest grazing grounds and took care lest a twig should frighten them and reduce their milk, yet they did not know who would drink that milk. The ram was slaughtered and its blood flowed under the milking stools so that the milk, too, might flow there in plenty.

Then Mircho ran up, so out of breath with running that he could not speak a word. And Manol waited patiently for him to speak. And the boy said :

'Refugees are coming from Chepino.'

His father made him repeat the same words three times. The boy repeated.

'Refugees are coming from Chepino.'

And Manol realized what these words meant, and what the Turks wanted in the village. He drew the boy to him and only said :

'It is not our children that they want to make into Janissaries, but all of us. Let us see now, my son, whether your father will have the strength to do what he asked of his son.'

And, wonder of wonders, sheep were left unmilked at *Predoi*. The buckets were left empty and the shepherds stood there with their sleeves rolled up, and their lips grew whiter than the milk which dripped from their fingers.

The time had come. The sword that had hung day in and day out over the heads of the Bulgarian Christians had fallen. The second ruin of Rhodopa had come, because the first time the conqueror had robbed us of our kingdom, but had left us our faith and our tongue. He had come to take them so that Bulgarian would only be a name, which would be forgotten after a time. The dark prophecies of captivity and death were coming true, of times when the living would envy the dead.

At the Milky Meadow we welcomed them—the wretched refugees from Turkish captivity and wrath. We stood on the crest and had not the strength to go down to them, and they slowly climbed up to us, sinking up to their knees in the yellow flowers, as if they were not walking along a sloping meadow, but were going up to a steep summit.

And their eyes and our eyes seemed to be dreaming. And they and we wanted to awaken. They wanted to believe that it was all a dream and that in a minute the cock would crow and everything would be over. But the cock did not crow, and they continued to dream—captivity, fires, violence, blood; they heard groans and screams. Such things could not happen waking : it was all a dream and it had to come to an end.

We, too, were dreaming, but it was a prophetic dream. And we saw coming towards us no unknown people, but our own wives, children and fathers. Lo, that old woman was your mother, that woman—your wife, that nursling—your child. Even knowing that they were at home, and you were up on the meadow, what was the log barring your gate, what were the walls, what were your hands and your dogs? And while you were standing there, looking on, might not your dream be coming true down in the village?

And what a spring it was, dear Lord, what a summer was on the way! The lilac was in blossom. Trees and flowers were blooming. The river was filled with the croaking of frogs, the meadows—with the songs of crickets, the forest—with birds' voices, the sky—with the hum of bees and the beating of butterflies' wings. Swallows darted to and fro beneath the clouds, and trout shimmered in the waters.

And the refugees came on, and already we saw the dream in their eyes.

An old woman of a hundred led them, and a child of five led her in turn. The old woman was so bent at the waist that her head was on a level with the little boy's head.

And both faces were next to each other—the face of age and the face of youth—and both were near the ground, just above the tops of the grasses.

The refugees came and sat down, exhausted, at our feet. Only the old woman and the little boy remained standing—the two faces one next to the other. And both looked up at us. And we said nothing, and the child dropped a big grey rabbit, which he was carrying, and the rabbit began to nibble the grass.

'Are you the leader here, you, with the black beard?' the old woman asked.

And Manol answered quietly:

'I am, Mother. What is your name?'

And the old woman said:

'I am Srebra. Granny Srebra.'

Manol's voice grew louder as he said:

'May the hand that has led these people here be golden. Where do you come from?'

And turning to the mute shepherds, he called to them:

'Run to the dairies and fetch the buckets of milk.'

Thus came Granny Srebra, the foundress of Momchilovo, leading one hundred tormented folk.

May their seed cover Rhodopa.

And while we were waiting for the milk, the child made a fire and heated a big stone. The old woman took it and pressed it against

her stomach—and her hands were blacker than the blackened stone.
The child sat down, put his hand on her breast and dozed off. And
his hand lay on the rabbit, which grew still and quiet.

Thus they sat—the old wrinkled face and ragged, scorched
garment, all crooked and broken, like the branches of a very old
oak, and in the middle a warm, clean fruit, smooth and curved,
the child's little round head. Next to the cracked bark and the
crooked branch lay the round warm fruit.

'Does it hurt?' Manol asked.

And the old woman placed her big blackened hand on her heart,
and said to us :

'It hurts more here.'

And she told us of the capture and ruin of Chepino as it has
been set down in other books and chronicles, too.

'When the Turkish Emir Tsar Mehmed, called the Hunter,
began the war in Mora, he sent 105 ship loads of soldiers by
sea, and 150,000 men by land, and then to Plovdiv town came
six Pashas, and passed through Peshtera. And Mehmed Pasha
with many Janissaries came to Chepino by Kostandovo, and
gathered together all the priests and mayors, and put them in
chains and said :

'"Traitors! Ali Osman Padishah loves you, so you pay no
taxes to him. You only help the Pasha's army when there is
need. And we love you like our Janissaries, and yet you want to
raise your heads against your tsar."

'Then Ban Velyo and *Protopop*[31] Konstantin answered :

'"Great Vizier, our lads have been with your troops in Tunis,
in Traboulos and in Missir until recently. What ill have you seen
in us?"

'And the Pasha said :

'"You lie. The Karabash has told me, the black-headed one,
the Bishop in Philibé—the cursed Metropolitan of Plovdiv,
Gavriil."

'And they said :

'"He does not give us orders, but as we do not pay him
tithes, he slanders us."

'And the Pasha replied :

'"You are Giaours, too, are you not? Why do you not pay
him? So you are rebels."

'And he ordered the Janissaries to behead them all. Then a
certain Karaiman Hassan Hodja begged the Pasha to forgive
them if they became Turks. And on St George's Day, Ban Velyo,
Protopop Konstantin, Pop[32] Georgi and Pop Dimiter, and all

the mayors and all the priests of the other villages accepted the Turkish faith. And as there was a great famine, the Pasha left four more Hodjas to make Turks of us, and whoever became a Turk, he was given wheat for food. Those who did not become Turks, some they beheaded, others fled to the forests, and their houses they burnt.'[33]

This was the old woman's tale, and is not the rest written in the Rhodopa chronicles? And is it not written there how Hassan Hodja sent many horses to the town of Pazardjik, and they brought wheat from Beglik Han and unloaded it in the churches of St Petka and the Holy Apostle Andrew in Kostandovo, and he distributed to the houses that had become Turkish, two measures each of rye and two of millet? And is it not known all over Rhodopa how Hassan Hodja, to their shame, made them destroy all the churches from Kostenets to Stanimaka—three and thirty monasteries, and two hundred and eighteen churches? Thus, by the grace of God, were the Bulgarians in Tsepina ruined. And as for the end of Karaimam Hassan Hodja, that will be told when the time for it comes.

While Granny Srebra was relating the ruin of Tsepina, the buckets of fresh milk were brought, and I seized one of them and set out among the people. And when I entered amid their grief, my manhood left me and I began to weep, I, too, like a woman. And my eyes grew misty so that I did not see the horror on their faces, but I heard their words.

'They cut down my husband at my threshold,' one woman said.

'They tore my daughter asunder,' said another.

'My womb burns,' said a third. 'Father, if I bear a Turk, I shall drown myself with the child.'

But one man refused to drink, and said to me:

'My brother has become a Turk.'

One young wife kept thrusting her nipple into the mouth of her nursling, but it threw its head back and cried, for her breast was dry. Then she tried to pour milk into its mouth and it choked.

And I remembered the lament of Jeremiah. Even the wolves give their teats to their cubs to suck, but our mothers had no milk for their children.

Manol picked a stem of grass, dipped it into the milk, sucked it and kneeling down, placed it in the child's little mouth. And it smiled at him.

And Manol clenched his teeth, and bit the grass stem and I saw tears shine in his eyes.

Just then the old woman called me to her, and I asked her:

'Where is your priest?'

And she answered me :

'The priest was the first to deny his faith.'

And, pointing to Manol, she said to me :

'Call that man.'

And she said to Manol :

'May God reward you for the milk and your care. But let three of your men take a bucket each and set out through the forest. Many have been left there. That one over there, lying on his face and refusing to drink, he will lead them, for his wrath will support him.'

And she said further :

'You have fed us, but you cannot feed us until the children grow up to settle the score for their fathers. Tell us a place where we can build a new village.'

Manol shook his head and said :

'There is no room for a village here; even we have built our houses in the gully, so as not to steal an inch of the arable land. All these meadows that you see belong to the *Yurouks*. Yet how can you build a village? Your men are few.'

And he looked at the crowd of exhausted folk, lying on the meadow. Their men were few, indeed, some ten souls, and the refugees must have been a hundred. The others were old men, women and children. And when they built their village, on what would they live in it? If they gathered everything they had brought, there would still not be enough goods for one home.

'We shall live under one roof. There, that one over there has brought a trough for kneading bread. That one has a chain for the hearth, that woman—a black cauldron. The men will scatter to work, and there will be flour for the trough, wood for the hearth and soup for the cauldron,' said Granny Srebra.

And Manol still shook his head, and said once more :

'When they scatter to work, who will build the village? Who will cut wood and bring it down? Who will dig up roots to make fields for the ploughing? You have too few men.'

Then, growing angry, the old woman shouted at him :

'Men, and men. If they were men, they would have defended their villages and not made new ones. And if you want to know, one man is enough for many women. We need women, to bear children and fill the mountains. So that if the Turks kill them, some will still be left. Do you see,' she continued, pointing to the rabbit, 'I have only one little beast, but it's a she-rabbit and bears little ones every month, and in three months her daughters will begin bearing them, too.'

'I dare not ask you to our village, for no one knows what will be happening there,' Manol said quietly to her.

'Even if you asked me, I would not come,' the old woman retorted. 'We are not going to be beggars. I do not want to flee again. And you, Manol, do not be angry at my words, but think of your wife and your children.'

'I have no wife, I am a widower,' said Manol.

'Are you a widower? And how many children have you?'

'Two sons,' Manol told her.

And the old woman was amazed and said to him:

'You, a widower? It is a sin for a man like you to have only two sons. Just look at yourself, what a fine man you are! You must get married and bring joy to a woman. Let her bear you children, so that you may have grandchildren, as handsome as you are. Do you see those women there?' she said, pointing to the refugees on the grass. 'I have ten young widows, don't look at them now, they're not in good fettle. Take a widow, and one that has borne children, so that you will know that your seed will not fall among stones. Whichever one you like, take her.'

And what a mysterious thing is a woman's soul—the woman who was nursing her child with the blade of grass, took and hid her dry breast, covered herself, blushed and dropped her eyes.

'I have made my choice,' said Manol.

I saw that he himself took fright at what he had said. He turned and called to his men to go and bring lambs.

'Today is a great day,' he said. 'Lambs are slaughtered as a sacrifice. We shall eat them together.'

And the old woman retorted:

'Listen, Manol, and do not be angry with me. It is a great day, today. On this day lambs are separated from their dams, and the rams from the ewes. You graze the ewes to milk them, and the lambs to slaughter them. The Turk separates a child from its mother to make a Janissary of him, and the father from his child to make it cut his throat. We do not want sacrifices. Show us land for a village. If you do not know where there is land for a village who will know? If there is none, we shall go on, until we find some.'

At that moment, a shout came from a distance:

'Brother Manol!'

Goran was shouting, from Mount Chernokan, and we could hear it, down on the Milky Meadow.

And Manol went and stood on the crest, put his palms to his mouth and shouted:

'Spe-e-eak!'

The refugees started, and stiffened, so big was his voice.

'What is hap-pen-ing?'

Thus Goran's voice came to us, echoing from summit to summit
like a wave. And we could see Goran in the distant, no bigger than
a thumb. Manol waited for the last sound of his voice to echo
in the sky and fall into the valleys, and then waited a while longer
because he did not know what to shout back. And at last he
shouted :

'Refuge-e-es !'

Now it was a long 'e-e-e' that was wafted over the air, more
terrible and piercing than Goran's shouts that were like a death
moan.

Goran delayed for a moment; probably he was talking to someone, and at last we heard :

'Com-ing !'

Let it be remembered that Manol and Goran spake thus on that
day, on *Predoi*, when the refugees came. From Milky Meadow to
Mount Chernokan, which is at least two hours' distant. When they
raised their hands, their shouts came after that, like thunder comes
long after lightening. This was set down, as it happened, and there
are still those living who remember it.

And Goran ran up, just as the fires were blazing up, and with
him were Sherko and Momchil. And Momchil had his falcon on
his shoulder, the one given to him by the falconers who train the
falcons for the Sultan. As soon as they saw Sharo, the refugees
crowded together in fear, because there is no other dog like him in
Rhodopa. And the three young men stood before the refugees, stiff
and white with pain and fury, until Goran came to himself, fell on
his knees and kissed the old woman's hand.

'Come, my son, carry me awhile,' Granny Srebra said to him.

'How do you wish me to carry you, Granny? On my shoulders or
my back, or in my arms? And where do you wish me to carry you?'
said Goran, through his tears.

'To the *Yurouks*, my son. I want you to carry me in your arms,
next to your heart, as your mother bore you, for nine months on
her heart, and until you were three years old in her arms,' the old
woman replied.

'I shall carry you until you are a hundred years old, Granny,' said
Goran, and wept louder. 'Be my mother, for mine is dead.'

'You do not want to carry me long, my son, for only one year
is left to me to reach one hundred,' and Granny Srebra smiled her
toothless smile.

And when Goran picked the old woman up in his arms, the three
young men set out for the *Yurouks'* dairies, together with Manol
and the old woman's grandchild. I set out with them, too.

Ninth Excerpt

During the night which followed Syuleiman Aga's court, I was quite unable to fall asleep, and I nearly went mad. I kept repeating 'I'm alive! I'm alive!' but I could not rejoice.

The wind had turned and now blew at the windows of my room. During the night I began to hear fearful groans, cries and snorts. Someone seemed to be writhing in his death throes, and someone else was stopping his mouth. I barely remembered that it was the young man who had been thrown into the abyss, and that the sack was smothering his voice. The persons thrown in this abyss, which was not very deep, did not fall into the water, but onto the stones, breaking their bones, and each one died according to his luck—some at once, while others cried for three days. I prayed for the unfortunate lad to die. He cried out more loudly than ever.

Towards morning, I heard an indescribable, long-drawn-out howling of dogs. I thought the devils must be coming for the sinner's soul. Earlier I had pulled aside the window shutters—they did not close like a door but slid along grooves—now I threw my covers over the shutters. I walked up and down the room, and the cursed boards creaked mysteriously beneath my footsteps. Not only was I not happy at being left alone, but I prayed that some living soul would come to me, even if it were only a cat. When I drew away the covers from the shutters the sun was already shining outside. I could barely stand, I was so dizzy. The sun dazed me, just as if I had drunk a jug of strong wine.

Then Gyulfié came to me and asked me:

'Is he dead? One hears nothing in the inner courtyard. If he is dead, the shepherds have returned. Let his father go down and get him out of the hole.'

And again we heard the infernal, bloodcurdling howling, which was driving me crazy.

Gyulfié grew pale and raised her hand—it seemed to me that she wanted to cross herself—then she began to whisper some kind of a prayer against spirits in Turkish.

I quickly closed the shutters, and the two of us were left in darkness. We were looking at each other, while narrow straight shafts of the light, shining through the cracks, cut us into pieces.

'What is that?' I asked.

'The pit. They throw mad dogs down into it, to eat each other up.'

The howling was heard again, long-drawn-out and rising up, and suddenly it stopped with a heartrending shriek, as if the cur had been torn to pieces.

'You had better get out of this room,' Gyulfié said to me, quietly.

She had noticed in the gloom that I was whispering something. I was saying a prayer in French, and it was a prayer to my former God.

'I cannot,' I replied.

'I shall say that I need the room. And I'll tell you something else—it is not good for you to be next door to Delyo. He is a brute.'

Delyo had been a farm-labourer in one of the villages of the plain. In the same village there lived a Turk by the name of Noussouh, who had a beautiful young wife, but was so jealous of her that he always took her with him wherever he went. Once Delyo met Noussouh and his wife in the fields. And he could not help himself, he turned to see her again—for the woman swayed her figure beautifully when she stepped on sharp stones. But it is death to look at a Turk's wife. Noussouh hurled himself at Delyo with a drawn knife. But Delyo took his knife away from him and cut his throat with it. Then he threw the Turkish woman down beside her husband's dead body. He ran away to a second village, and took service as a farm-labourer again. Once he was ploughing a field with a pair of oxen, and when he lay down to sleep, two Turks drove his oxen off. He caught up with them, seized them and harnessed them to his plough instead of his oxen. Until nightfall he ploughed with the two, pricking them with their swords—one of them died, and the other became dumb. When the Turk returned to the village, he was covered with bloodstained foam from his beard to his heels, like a horse. Then Delyo went to Syuleiman Aga and became first one of his men-at-arms, and then his *bilyuk-bashi*.

'They say,' Fat Gyulfié told me, 'that he does not sleep with women like other men do, but only torments them. Men like that are very bad—they are angry with the whole world.'

We were still standing in the dark, and only our eyes shone, like a cat's. Gyulfié whispered, and it seemed to me that she wanted to tell me terrible and bloody tales. Even if I had not asked her about the deserted wing of the *Konak*, she would still have told me about Syuleiman Aga's fratricide—the secret bothered her.

'Very well,' I said, 'give me a room somewhere else, so that I shall not hear these cries and the howling of the dogs.'

I felt like weeping at all these horrors. How had I happened on this valley? Yet I was glad that I was far from Candia.

'I will find a room for you facing the middle courtyard, the one with the plane tree.'

'Oh, no! Is there no room facing the third courtyard, at the other end?'

'No one lives there. The rooms there are deserted, covered with dust. No one has entered them for the last ten years.'

And she told me how Syuleiman Aga had killed his younger brother Hairedin Aga! They were four brothers. Two had joined the army. Syuleiman and Hairedin had stayed in Elindenya. Both married two sisters.

'My sister bore two boys, now they are waiting in Adrianople for the Aga to die, to seize his wealth. For we have no son.'

As long as their father, old Daoud Bey, ruled, the two brothers lived in harmony. Then Daoud died, and Syuleiman Aga began to rule. Those were troubled years; all kinds of people roamed the mountains; every day there were murders, robberies and thefts. And strangers roaming round hired women in the village. Syuleiman took to severe measures and began to kill. There was no *kanoun namé*—no laws, no courts. There was one punishment —death. The shepherds and the *Yurouks* helped him, and peace was restored in the mountains.

Hairedin envied his brother's strength and renown. He could have done the same. Then their mother, Daoud Bey's wife, made Syuleiman Aga give Hairedin three other villages in the neighbouring valley. Hairedin built himself a *Konak*, found a waterfall and a thick tree, and began to throw people down into the abyss in sacks and to hang them—like his brother. Syuleiman Aga was wise and stern, Hairedin was bold. Syuleiman was just, Hairedin was not. Syuleiman was merciful and generous, Hairedin was cruel.

Elindenya grew rich, the other valley was ruined. Syuleiman built bridges and fountains; Hairedin raced horses and went hunting. And he decided to grow rich by robbery. He got together bands of madcaps and went down into the plains to rob. Once he went south with five hundred ne'er-do-wells, but was resisted.

For a long time, Syuleiman Aga wondered what to do. He would hang the ne'er-do-wells, but what of his brother? His men and his mother gave him advice, while Gyulfié wept for her sister. Syuleiman Aga held his peace. On this side of the mountains, in Elindenya, men were hanged for stealing a chicken, on the other —Hairedin hanged men to take their chickens from them.

Hairedin rose a second time with a band of five hundred men, but this time he went north. They struck at Stanimaka, and returned with booty. Not in secret, as they returned from the south, but with bagpipes, shooting and drinking.

Syuleiman Aga got the shepherds and the *Yurouks* together, and attacked his brother's *Konak*. All day long guns were fired, and in the night Hairedin crossed the river and fled. And when from Progledets he watched his *Konak* burning, he said to the only one of his men-at-arms who had followed him : 'All is over—*Eden boulour*—what you have sought, that you will find.'

For three months Hairedin Aga wandered through the forest like a beast, and none would give him shelter. In the end he went down into Prossoina, wild and in rags—and surrendered to his brother, saying to him : 'Do as you will with me.'

Syuleiman Aga set aside the right wing of the *Konak* for him. He gave his brother, men, raiment and money. He gave him his own men and his own raiment. Hairedin dressed himself, trimmed his beard and, as he wore his brother's raiment, and was very like him in face and figure, he became a second Syuleiman Aga, he grew proud once more, and began to meddle in people's affairs and to threaten them. And he whispered to Gyulfié that he would take her as his wife, and that she would bear him sons like his own. Until one day when he drew the pistol from his brother Syuleiman's case, and shot at his breast. The pistol misfired.

(I remembered the trial with the pistols, and it came into my mind that Syuleiman Aga may truly have believed that God would save the innocent man just as He had once saved him, Syuleiman. And I think that Syuleiman shot his brother with a pistol.)

Syuleiman shut Hairedin up in his room, gathered his men-at-arms, and told them that he would give a hundred gold pieces to the man who killed his brother. From morning till night he begged his inexorable men—who was mad enough to kill his master's brother? And his mother and the two sisters, Gyulfié and Hairedin's wife, rolled at his feet, begging him for mercy. In the night, Syuleiman rose and went out.

'No one ever found out how he killed him,' whispered Gyulfié. 'Whether he shot him, cut his throat or strangled him. He washed and dressed his brother's body himself, and bore him out of the *Konak*. He is buried over there, opposite us. Hairedin Aga. All night long we peered out of the *Konak*. The Aga sat beside his brother's body. The dead man lay on his back, the Aga sat cross-legged beside him, staring him in the face. The moon was shining. Next morning, at sunrise, the Aga dug a grave, and dropped Hairedin into it. That is how it was. His mother became paralyzed, and died; Syuleiman gave one hundred gold pieces for his brother's blood to the children. And since then he has not once come in to me.'

As she spoke, Gyulfié imperceptibly came closer to me, step by step, and seared me with her breath. I did not realize that I was withdrawing till at last I found myself leaning against the wall.

The sweat on my back froze. When Gyulfié ended her narration—and she spoke fervidly, in great detail, whispering and languid—I felt her huge breasts pressing against my stomach. I drew back the shutter of the window, and the sun came pouring in.

I could not stay alone any longer. I found Karaibrahim and told him how Syuleiman Aga had killed his brother.

I had not expected that he would be so deeply stirred. I had never seen him in such a state. He walked up and down his room, whispering in astonished admiration :

'*Mashallah, mashallah . . .*'[34]

He was not horrified as I was; he was amazed. It even seemed to me that he was envious. When he saw me staring at him, he said :

'Do you know that the Padishah himself, the commander of half the universe, has been intending to kill his brother these last twenty-odd years, and dare not do it? That is a great thing. All honour to Syuleiman. I did not judge him rightly.'

And at once he went to seek Syuleiman, and I with him. I trembled lest he should begin to speak about the murder, and lest it should appear that I told tales of all I saw and heard, like a woman.

We found Syuleiman Aga with the three hodjas. They were sitting in the *kyoshk*,[35] drinking coffee and talking about the Koran. Syuleiman Aga was stroking a grey tom-cat. I was surprised to see that Sheikh Shaban Shebil, with the terrible sibilant name, with the brilliant eye and the swagger, was silent. The one-eyed and one-armed hodja, who had lost half of his being in battles for the True Faith, was actually fawning on Syuleiman Aga. He was gaping at him, and talking through his teeth, but he was frightened. The hodjas were not attacking now—they were trying to persuade the Aga.

Karaibrahim spoke to Syuleiman Aga, and spoke only to him, as if the other men were not in the *kyoshk*. And he had probably forgotten us completely, or he would not have been so frank.

'Aga,' he said to him, 'after the battle in the Valley of Siophino, before Candia, we lost so many men that the Grand Vizier Ahmed Küprüli gave orders to have them all buried at once. Otherwise the remaining troops of the Believers, noticing how many men had fallen, would grow despondent. And we began to throw the dead and the wounded into the pits we had dug. We were all Janissaries, true men, who had looked death in the face a hundred times. Then I bent down and saw my sworn brother, wounded. They had taken us together for the army, we had shared the same bread. He was my only friend, and I must tell you that I am a man who does not

easily give his friendship. He was wounded in the breast, but with
Allah's help he might have recovered. I wanted to draw him aside.
The Aga saw me. My friend begged me to cut his throat. I dared
not do it. Someone stabbed him with a knife, they cast him on to the
heap of bodies. He was looking at me and he cursed me. And when
they began to cast in the soil, it fell upon his open eyes. We buried
them—the living and the dead. And the soil moved. Has anyone
seen the soil of a grave moving?'

'I have,' said I. I spoke without meaning to. 'There is such a
punishment in my country, women and girls are buried alive,
and when the earth moves, the hangman jumps on it, on the
grave.'

Karaibrahim turned to me, his eyes were fixed on me, but I
realized that he did not see me.

'They jumped on the graves there, too,' he said in a toneless
voice. 'I did not want to say that. They did it out of mercy, to
make the wounded die more quickly. I scratched the earth that
was moving, and they jumped on my hands.'

And he turned his wrists before him, with the palms of his hands
towards the ground, and stared at them. They did not quiver—
strong hands, long, knotted fingers with oblong nails. Cruel hands.

'Then, Aga, I swore on the grave of my friend that Candia would
fall. And when the Grand Vizier cried that Turkey would fight for
a hundred years but would capture Candia, tears came to my eyes.
And whenever I saw the big cross thrust into the earthworks of the
stronghold, I ground my teeth.'

Karaibrahim was silent. We were all silent—Karaibrahim's three
men, surprised at his excitement, for we had never seen him moved;
Syuleiman Aga and his hodja watched him with attentive, vigilant
looks.

'That is why, when I was told that I must come to Rhodopa, I
did not want to obey. I wanted to stay before Candia. Then the
Grand Vizier called us all together and talked to us from his heart
—as I am talking to you, Aga. We are in a bad way. Before Candia
we are in a bad way. Janissaries and the troops from Europe, headed
by the Grand Vizier, are opposite the Panigra Fort. The Egyptian
troops with Ahmed Pasha are before Bethlehem. The Asians with
Kara Moustafa are before Martignano. We took Panigra. And when
the Grand Vizier gave orders to count the troops, we found that
18,000 men had been lost, and the Christians had lost 3,200 men
and 400 captains. Well-nigh all our commanders, our bravest
Pashas, our bravest soldiers, were slain in the very first months. We
used 10,000 pounds of gunpowder every day, and every grain of it
comes from Constantinople by sea, and the sea is full of Venetian

ships and of pirates. In one day 153 of our mines and 183 of the Venetians' exploded. At one moment, when we got up on the wall, three mines exploded, each of forty barrels of gunpowder, and hurled everything up into the sky—men, stones, earth. The earth opens before Candia and the dead cannot even rest in their graves, but fly up in pieces in the air. The unbelievers put Turkish heads into their cannons and fired them against us. And then 16,000 French swine came with their counts and barons—my tongue cannot get around their names. Swollen-headed men, imprudent and proud, but each one of them wields a sword and has a gun which is not fired with a fuse. From the very first day, they began to hurl themselves against us like cocks.'

'Yes, they hurled themselves at us like cocks, and we slaughtered them like cocks,' cried the one-eyed hodja. He—the simpleton—did not realize what was happening and was fired by Karaibrahim's words. 'We slaughtered them and robbed their bodies. Six hundred knights, and one thousand sword-bearers! We took silver saddles, gold reins, buttons made of emeralds, and rings with rubies. The booty was so great that the entire camp looked like a goldsmith's shop! The rich garments were cast straight onto the ground like loads of wood. For one captain's head, the Pasha gave ten piastres, and Küprüli—fifteen. A living prisoner cost seventy piastres. And what boys there were—white, and with various scents, more beautiful than women.'

The one-eyed man smacked his lips. Karaibrahim stared at him, not appearing to realize that he had been interrupted. At one time he understood, made a gesture and said sharply:

'You fool!'

The one-eyed hodja froze.

Karaibrahim continued:

'A letter came from the Sultan, written in his own hand. Each sign, Aga, had been drawn by his holy right hand. And at the top it had the *Tougra*[36]—Mohammed, son of Ibrahim, always victorious. It told us that he could send us no more aid. The Grand Vizier shut himself up in his tent and for three days he ate nothing. His mother—for the widow of the great Mohammed Küprülis is before Candia with her son—his mother placed the mouthfuls in his mouth, and he spat them out and in his grief poured Polish brandy down his throat. And he wrote a letter to the Padishah. He wrote to him that we were within ten ells of the innermost earthworks, that after having passed hundreds of ells of trenches, walls, gunpowder store-houses and mines, Allah could not fail to allow us to pass these ten ells also.'

'Ten ells,' Syuleiman Aga said thoughtfully, continuing to stroke the tom-cat. He spoke for the first time. 'Are they ten ells?'

'They are ten times ten, Aga, and that much again. The troops are rebelling, the Pashas beat the Spahis with sticks. The Sultan secretly advised Küprüli to abandon Candia. And on top of everything a priest came, they call him Padre Ottomano, the Ottoman priest. They say that he is the Sultan's brother, captured as a child, when he fled in a ship from Constantinople. He cursed the entire Turkish army. We are in a bad way. That is what the Grand Vizier told us, and that is what I tell you. And I know that it is so. And he explained to us that the war will be decided not only at the walls of the fort. It is rumoured that risings are being prepared in Albania and in Rhodopa. If that happens—we must not even think of it. Adrianople is only three hours' journey from the Rhodopes. The Sultan is in Adrianople. That is why Ibrahim Pasha himself, the Aga of the Janissaries, the second after the Grand Vizier, stays in Constantinople. That is why I have come here. And I say to you —help, Syuleiman Aga. It is not a matter of three villages. This is the centre of the mountains. There are another hundred villages all around. Mehmed Pasha is to the north. Abdi to the south. Large numbers of troops cannot come here. Once more I say to you— help!'

I do not know what Karaibrahim was hoping for. It was foolish to think that he would touch Syuleiman Aga with the tale of the Grand Vizier's misfortunes. Perhaps he wanted to make him return frankness for frankness. It had seemed to him that he had found a key to his heart, that he had understood what kind of a man the Aga was. But while he was still speaking, particularly at the end, I realized that he had dropped the key, he had lost it and was fumbling to find it. Syuleiman Aga was not merely the murderer of his brother. These tales of the weakness of the Turks before Candia might bring forth quite different fruit, quite different from the seed that Karaibrahim thought he was sowing.

Syuleiman Aga stroked his tom-cat. Suddenly the animal mewed, scratched his hand, and glided across the room. I did not understand why he did so. Perhaps the Aga had involuntarily begun to stroke him too hard?

Syuleiman Aga raised his hand and put his lips to the scratch— it was above the wrist. This gave him the opportunity to remain silent a little longer.

'Aga,' he said. 'I do not know what you thought when you set out for this place. But I do not see where you can begin. Here we are, six men gathered together, not young people any more— let each give you his advice.'

Karaibrahim, who had been standing the whole time, was now

staring at the tips of his boots with bent head. I felt him grow cool, like a branch on which rain was falling. The embers still glowed, but most of the fire had grown grey and was covered with ashes.

The one-eyed hodja preferred to hold his peace. The fat one spoke up :

'There is a most instructive story. It is the work of the preacher Vani, who speaks every day in the Padishah's right ear. The Jews were astir. Then suddenly their new Messiah, a new Jesus, appeared a certain Sabathai Sevi. He sent messages, as in the days of Paul, a prophet of the unbelievers. He said that the Second Coming was at hand. The Jews from the lands of the Germans, from Amsterdam, from Livorno, and from Venice all set out towards him. Ahmed Küprüli shut him up in a castle on the Dardanelles. The Jews waited for the prophecy to be fulfilled—nine months of captivity, and then the chosen of the Lord would emerge, riding a lion with reins made of a seven-headed serpent. The Sultan himself sent for the Messiah. Kaimakam Pasha was with him, the Mufti and Sheikh Vani. The Sultan asked for a miracle—then he would believe. They undressed Sabathai Sevi and left him naked, and on his breast they drew a circle, and the best of the archers stood before him. The Sultan wanted to see how the arrows would rebound from him. Then the Jew confessed that he was an ordinary man. For blasphemy he was to be impaled. Then he accepted the True Faith. And because he gave up his mastery of the whole world, he was given a bag of gold and fifty piastres every month. He is alive to this day. And thousands of Jews accepted the True Faith after him. Why do we not make a saint here? At hard moments people will crowd around him and follow him blindly. And afterwards we shall repeat the wise story of Sheikh Vani.'

'It will take a long time,' Syuleiman Aga said, thoughtfully.

'A massacre !' cried the one-eyed hodja. 'A massacre and fire !'

'We are about a hundred Believers, and there are three hundred men in this valley alone. And they have arms,' said Hodja Hassan, the son of Velko.

They were silent again.

Karaibrahim was the first to speak. The old Karaibrahim, master of each of his muscles and of each of his thoughts. Dry and taut.

'Aga,' he said. 'Can you gather all the notables of the villages? So that I can see them.'

Syuleiman Aga thought for a long time before answering.

'There are no notables here,' he said. 'They are all *rayah*.'[37]

'There is no village without notables, Aga. The better men. In property, name and honour. They are the ones I need.'

'There are no rich men. True, there are better men, the *kehayas*. Those who have more sheep, or more wisdom. But they are the hardest, Aga.'

Karaibrahim gave a crooked smile.

'I can tell you, Aga, that the more a man has, the more he wants to preserve it. But I do not think of that. As we are one hundred and we have five hundred men against us, we shall find the fifty who lead them. Then we shall be one hundred against fifty As for the rest—what is a body without a head?'

The one-eyed hodja said :

'If twenty of you persist, they will overcome two hundred, and if you are one hundred, you will overcome one thousand unbelievers. Allah is mighty and wise. Allah is all goodness and all mercy. Thus is it written in the Koran. And we are one hundred Believers.'

Syuleiman Aga thought long again before speaking.

'I can bring them together. But if they come to the *Konak,* they are my guests. A hair must not fall from their heads. And what use will that be to you?'

'I want to see them.'

'As you insist, we shall think how it can be done.'

'Think, Aga, and tell me. Soon. And remember Candia.'

I hung my cover over the window before going to bed. I was so tired that I fell asleep. I awoke from the cold—it grew very cold at night in the mountains. I was freezing, trembling with cold and with fear that in a moment I would hear the terrible howling or the groans of the dying man.

Whether I really did hear them, or just imagined I did, I do not know, but I heard them. And whether waking or half-asleep, I began to see only lips before me.

I had heard many tales that day. Lips repeated before me stories of harnessed thieves, of the dead Hairedin, of the men buried alive, of Sabathai Sevi. Words, words, words.

Lips, lips, lips. The lips of Gyulfié, of Karaibrahim, of the Hodja. How many lips there are throughout the whole world !

I saw them. And teeth. Gleaming between lips. Mouths like the trunks of elephants, like the snouts of pigs, like the muzzles of dogs. Eating. Sucking, sticking to one, tearing. Everyone wants to eat.

I heard the dogs howling in the pit. The voice of the world behind the window, the world in which each one had to eat up the other, so as to live a minute longer.

I was alive, alive !

Tenth Excerpt

I'll give up my head on the market place,
But not the leader of my flock,
The leader, the finest goat,
The goat that leads my flock—
The goat with the nine bells.

Thus we set out for the *Yurouks*, to beg a site for a village. And we
were silent, for that is a great thing. For in that village folk would
find a roof and a grave, there they would rear their children and
their grandchildren, their cattle, too, and there they would
plough their fields. Or they would not. It all depended on whether
the *Yurouks* would give them land or not.

And we reached the Kosteni Stones. And there the leader of the
Yurouks, the Bey Ismaïl, was holding in his arms a lamb that
had just been slaughtered, and was sprinkling with its blood the
big white stone on which was carved naked men and bunches of
grapes. He held the lamb in his arms like a wine skin, and squeezed
it, and the blood sprinkled the stone like wine, and the red blood
flowed on the stone, as if the white marble grapes were bearing red
wine.

And to one side, on the right of the white stone stood the
Yurouks' mosque, a simple shed made of boughs between the boles
of four pines, where the *Yurouks* of all the families gathered for
prayer every Friday.

And we stood on the left side, until Ismaïl Bey had finished his
sacrifice to the old gods of the land. And he pretended not to see
us. When Ismaïl Bey had squeezed all the blood out of the lamb,
so that no matter how he squeezed it, not a drop dripped from its
neck, he left the dead lamb on one side, and signed to us to
approach. And we bowed to him.

Then Ismaïl Bey advanced and embraced Manol, and said to
him :

'Welcome, Manol *Kehaya*, to my tents. And this day, and tomorrow, and whenever you wish. For, as long as you led my sheep,
not one was lost and the milk flowed like a river, and the wolves
and the bears were meeker than the lambs.'

For Manol had been seven years a shepherd with Ismaïl Bey,
and another seven—his *kehaya*.

And then Ismaïl Bey clapped his hands, and three young shepherds, his sons, came and knelt before him, and said :

'*Bouyur*,[38] Bey.'

And he ordered them to bring a chair for the old woman, hand-fuls of raisins and an orange for the child, and to give a stag's leg to Sharo, the dog, that he might lose the habit of eating Turkish meat.

And why did we go to the *Yurouks* to seek a village? Because the Sultan had given the Rhodope lands to the commanders of his armies, and they, as they could not inherit them, had given them to the Turkish mosques, or made them a pious bequest. And the mosques had given the mountains, the pastures and the waters to the *Yurouks* in exchange for sheep, wool and milk. The *Yurouks* had the right to sell or make a present of these mountains, grazing and waters, if the new owner were ready to pay the same tithes. These *Yurouks* had come from Anadolia, and had settled along the Aegean Sea and they came every summer to graze their sheep in the Krustogorié. They were divided into races, and *odjaks*,[39] and the seventy-seventh and the seventy-eighth *odjaks* came to the Krustogorié, and Ismaïl Bey was chieftain of one of the clans, for the *odjaks* were divided into clans. The *Yurouks*, although they were Turks, only had one wife, and her face was uncovered. And these women, like the Bulgarian women, wore white kerchiefs, which reached down to their waists. They also had great authority, and their husbands honoured them, so that when they set out on a journey, the women mounted the horses, and the young men went on foot around them and served them. Ismaïl Bey's wife was dead, so two Bulgarian women, who had accepted the Turkish faith, served him.

And Ismaïl Bey said :

' Are you well seated, Mother? Did you enjoy your meat, Sharo?' But he did not ask the child, for he knew that the young enjoy everything. 'Now tell me why you have come, for the sheep will soon return for *Predoi*. Today is a great day. The blood of the sacrifice went right down to the earth and the earth swallowed it. You have come in a good hour. May I be able to grant your request, for I see that you have come to ask for something.'

'Ismaïl Bey,' Manol said to him, 'we have come to ask you to sell us land for a village.'

But Ismaïl did not show that he was surprised, only he said nothing, so that Manol had to continue :

'This old mother, whom we have brought, has about a hundred refugees with her. I do not hide from you that Mehmed Pasha the Vizier has driven them out, because they did not want to change their faith.'

'Mehmed Pasha rules in the plains,' said Ismaïl. 'Here in the mountains it is I who rule. And what need Mehmed had to change people's faith, I do not know. A green water-melon is never sweet, even if you twist its stem. A man grows ripe for Allah of himself. As for land for a village, I must tell you that I shall call the clan council together to decide the matter.'

Manol said to him :

'Father Ismaïl Bey, your word is like a rock, or like a big tree— were a hundred souls to gather together, they could not shake it, or uproot it. Do not send us back, for the souls of these good folk are between their teeth.'

Then Granny Srebra spoke, too :

'Tell me, Bey, for you are a wise man, although you are young,' yet the Bey's hair was quite white—'tell me, so that I may know where my bones will be buried.'

And the Bey began to smooth his beard with both hands, and knew not what to say.

'Manol *Kehaya*,' he said, 'I agree to sell you part of the mountain and water for a village. But we stay here only in summer, and these folk will stay here in winter, too. I do not know where the winter is light, and where the snowdrifts gather. And a hoof must be able to reach it. When we choose land for a village with oxen, we let two oxen loose, and where they find shelter, there we build. For a beast, although it has no voice, speaks straight to Allah.'

'Bey,' said the old woman, 'we do not want a village where oxen will seek shelter. Let goats loose, and wheresoever they may go, give us land there. For we are folk that are driven, and we want a village in which our enemies can hear cocks and dogs, yet still be unable to find it.'

'Master,' Yussouf, Ismaïl's firstborn son, spoke then, for he had come up and was standing silently behind him. 'Master, give them Petglassets.'[40]

And Manol's face lit up at once, because only now did he remember Petglassets.

'Sometimes wisdom chooses the mouths of the young,' Ismaïl said, thoughtfully. 'It is true that Petglassets will do for a village. But before we speak further, I tell you, Grandmother, that it is a place both good and bad. A hoof can reach it, and it cannot reach it. It is both hidden, and not hidden. A river flows out of it, the Strouïlitsa, and it is the only one that comes down in spate in these parts. The path to Petglassets runs along it, and when the river is in spate it floods the path. One autumn, the river shut off five thousand sheep in the valley, then snow fell, it, too, melted, and the sheep were unable to get out, and half of them died. There is one thing more—and that is why we call the mountain there Petglassets. The whole place around the old spruce is bewitched. When you say one thing, it answers five times.'

'Even were it to echo ten times, I thank you, Bey, for your good word. As you speak of it, even though I have not seen the valley, it seems to me that it is made for us. But I do not know what you will want for the whole valley, even if you do not graze your sheep in it. For you are a wise man, and I do not believe you will put other sheep there after that winter.'

Thus spoke Granny Srebra to him, and Ismaïl smiled and answered :

'It is true that I do not send sheep there in the autumn, but the valley is big and fine. Manol *Kehaya*, who is buying the valley, this old woman's folk, or you?'

And Manol said :

'I and my peasants are buying Petglassets. But the title deeds you will put in the name of these folk. I do not want it to be said of the mountain that we have taken the morsels of orphans.'

'Manol *Kehaya*,' Ismaïl Bey said quietly and sadly, 'I do not want to call up the evil spirits. But put half the shares in your name, for nothing is known.'

'And do you know something, Bey?'

'What I know, I know,' replied Ismaïl. 'And as I know you, I think that you will come again to ask me for land. Petglassets is enough for five villages even.'

'I shall not come, Father. Where the tree is planted, there it bears fruit, and there its roots rot. Can you move a spruce in the mountains?''

'Men are not trees, Manol. Lo, we, too, have come from Anadolia. And remember—where trees grow, that is where men cut them down,' said the Bey.

'That is so, that is where they are cut down,' Manol repeated. 'Tell me, Father, what you ask for Petglassets, so that we may see if our strength is enough for it.'

Then Ismaïl Bey dropped his brows, and his look grew as keen as a knife, and he said quietly :

'I want your silver *chans*.'

And Manol also drew his brows together and his look grew as keen as a knife. And he said to the Bey :

'Where have you heard my *chans*?'

'I was standing in the mountains opposite your village. And I heard voices coming from your house, as though you had a flock of heavenly birds shut up in it. Since then I have always dreamed of that flock. I have mountains, I have rivers, I have flocks of sheep, I have dogs, I have sons and grandsons, I have silver. But I have no *chans* like those. And when they ring out over the mountains, as soon as my flocks set out for the south to the sea, everybody will cry from a distance "Ismaïl Bey is coming!" Then I can die.'

But Manol held his peace.

And the Bey said further :

'For those *chans*, I will give you Petglassets, and the five summits around it—St Yani, Karachan, Modur, Svetilek and Posestra. With the grazing and the brooks. I will give you the River Stroülitsa up to the Plav, where the branches that it sweeps away gather in the spring. With the fish and the wood nymphs.'

But Manol still held his peace.

So did we. What could we say?

Then the Bey stepped forward and said quietly :

'Listen, Manol *Kehaya*. I asked you for your dearest thing, so that it would hurt you. For a big village needs a big sacrifice. See, I could take the dog for Petglassets,' and the Bey cast an envious glance at Sharo, 'but his mother has drunk Turkish blood. And it may so happen that I shall die before him. I take neither silver nor sheep for Petglassets. I could take a horse or arms, but a horse is food for dogs, and weapons are cold iron. But the *chans* are living, yet they never die.'

And the Bey said that he did not want Sharo for the following reason. Sharo's great-grandmother had belonged to Gordyo Voivoda, who defended Rhodopa against the Turks three hundred years ago. And when in the end they surrounded him in the fortress of Beden, which is above Vucha, the shepherds were accompanied by their dogs. As soon as Gordyo realized that the fortress would fall, he opened its gate one night, and let the sheepdogs out ahead of them. And then the Sultan's Janissaries, who never trembled either at Cherna, or at Kossovo Polé, fled before the dogs, so that the shepherds passed by their fires and were lost in the mountains. Only one dog escaped that night—Gordyo Voivoda's bitch. Since then every bitch bears one dog of that breed and dies, for the dogs are as big as calves. And they are known all over the mountains. And although Old Galoushko's son was called Troshan, everybody called him Sherko, for the last dog of that breed was called Sharo.

But Manol still held his peace.

Then Ismaïl Bey's daughter-in-law, the wife of his son Yussouf, came to us. She held a nursling in her arms. And Manol looked at her, and ground his teeth. And I understood from the look in his eyes that he had remembered the child whom he had fed with a stem of grass.

'Bey, I will give you my *chans*,' said Manol.

And the woman sensed that he had done it when he had looked at her child, and she was pleased and smiled. And pointing with her hand down the mountain, she said:

'I make a gift to you, Manol *Kehaya*, of the meadow for the sick and crippled sheep. When you build your summer huts, you need not ask my father.'

And the Bey, wise as he was, was unable to hide his joy, so that he rubbed his hands.

And he said:

'I will take all the men and women who wish to come to me, at full wages, although they are inexperienced. And until the village mends its fortunes, I will pay them as they will, with sheep, wool or cheese, or with silver.'

And Manol said:

'Divide the land of Petglassets and the mountain into fifty-two shares, one share for every *chan*. Give each family that comes to the valley one share, and the rest Granny Srebra will keep.'

'Manol,' the old woman said to him. 'My son, I know that it pains you. But Petglassets will become the garden from which seed will be scattered all over Rhodopa. And God has made it so that each Bulgarian word that is spoken there will be echoed with five-fold strength. Rejoice, for you have bought one *chan* with fifty-two, but it will speak Bulgarian.'

And Manol said to the Bey:

'Ismaïl Bey, I will give you the *chans* in the autumn, when your flocks set out for the south. Let me listen to them this summer. And I will tell you why I am doubly sad that I am buying Petglassets from you with those *chans*. Come stamp your foot on the meadow.'

The Bey stamped his strong foot, and we heard the earth echo dully.

'Under your feet there is the vault of a fort. Look well at the ant heaps and you will see that deep down from under the earth the black ants bring yellow millet seed. That fort was built by my forebears, and that millet they gathered with their hands that have long since rotted. Granny Srebra, the meadow on which I met you, we call Milky Meadow.' ('May it henceforth be known as Deliverance,' said the old woman. And this has remained its name to this day.) 'From that meadow to the fort there are leaden pipes. We still dig them out, and cast bullets of them. Water flowed along those pipes for the fort. And when at night the flocks gathered there, the shepherds stopped the water and poured their milk into them. And milk flowed from all the mountains in the fort, as it is sung in the songs, and told in the tales. These mountains my fore-

bears bought with their swords, but I buy them with *chans*.'
Thus spake Manol, and after him no one uttered a word.

Eleventh Excerpt

> And at that time we burned in a fire
> And as we burned, we screamed . . . .

And when we had gone up the sloping meadow, which comes after
the spruce forest, we came out on Mount Purvenets in the evening.
And the wind struck in our faces. The red cloaks of the shepherds
blew out and so did my grey cassock, and their long hair and beards.
And those that came out on the summit were Manol, Old Kralyo,
Stan Stan, Nikola Sargoun, Manoush Sekoul, Vrazhou *Kehaya*,
also called Chilingir, Rad Dragoslav, Dobril Groudnik, Stoiko Protsvet and Velko Radouïl. Momchil, Sherko and Goran were there,
too. So was I. And with us went one of the refugees whose name
I have forgotten.

And the wind blew hard, and seemed to push against our breasts
to make us turn back. But we went forward, and when we ascended
the higher of the two summits, Rhodopa lay before us in all its
breadth.

To the south, and to the west and to the north, as far as the eye
could see, the glow of red fires hid the horizon, and separated the
distance from our eyes. The fires were distant, and we could see
only their glow and the red reflections in the clouds, but they were
strong like the mountain and the sky, so that they did not seem
to be the work of a human hand.

The wind blew from the south, and we turned our faces to it.
And on clear days Mount Ipsarion on the Island of Tasos, and the
Venetian fort of Kavala, and Mount Athos on the peninsula can
be seen from there. And sometimes the glitter of the Aegean is seen,
too. And before them are Dranski Koupen and the Koushnitsa
Mountain, Chengenehissar and Koushlar. Now the fires separated
the Rhodope Mountains from the Aegean Plain and the sea.

Then the wind blew from the west, and again we turned our faces
to it. And to the west, the horizon reaches to the crest of the Pirin
Mountains with Eltepé, to Predyal, and to the right as far as the
Rila Mountains with its summits, and Moussala first of all. And
before them are Big Syutka, Mount Srebren and Batashki Snezhnik,

standing along the Batak Ridge, which separates the Beglik. And before the Pirin Mountains are Mount Besslet above the valley of Despotska Soura, and beyond, Videnitsa. Now the wall of the fires separated the Rhodope Mountains from their sisters Pirin and Rila.

Then the wind blew from the north. And there the eye reaches as far as the Balkan Range, from Mount Vezhen to Mount St Nikola, and the highest to be seen is Yumroukchal. Before them is the Sredna Gora with Mount Bogdan, and the Surnena Gora, and at their feet the even Plain of Thrace. Now the glow of the fires separated the Rhodope Mountains from the Old Balkan Range, and from Golden Thrace.

And the wind did not blow from the east, for there rose the Rhodope summit, Mount Possestra, shielding our backs from the wind.

When the refugee from Chepinsko saw the fires to the north, he knelt down upon the rock and covered his head with the hem of his cloak. And he did not uncover his face to look at the flames which were turning his villages to ashes.

But we looked. Ten times more the wind changed, and not once did we let it strike us in the back, and ever we looked, first to the south, then to the west, then to the north. And the wind was warm, and whichever way we looked we saw the fiery ring which surrounded the heart of Rhodopa. There were clouds above us, and between the clouds and the glow of the fires there was a strip of red sky. And there the red moon swayed and poured down its light, for it had risen early and would soon be full. And the fires tried their hardest to reach it, but they only melted it with their breath, while it rose on high and hid in the clouds. And no stars were to be seen.

And Manol said :

'Is this the dawn or the sunset? For beams rise on all sides over Rhodopa. Is night coming, or is the day coming?'

And I said :

'That is in the hands of God.'

And Manol answered me :

'No, it is in our hands.'

And we could not see Aegean Thrace, Pirin, Rila and the Balkan Mountains, but we looked upon the heart of Rhodopa, surrounded by a ring of fires. And there was much to be seen, for Rhodopa is a great mountain, and has a big heart.

Summit after summit, ridge after ridge, followed each other to the south, the west, and the north of us. And in the blue light of evening the mountains looked like a frozen sea, and the pale-green pastures were like spots of foam, and the dark-green forests were like the depths of the sea. And we saw only the crests of the waves, and the valleys and rivers that descended between them we did not see. And high ridges hid new summits behind them.

There is no man who can take in Rhodopa at one glance. There is no summit which you can ascend, so as to see it at a glance. You must walk over it and suffer over it, and then you can gather it in your heart and look at it—but you must have the heart of an eagle. You cannot see Rhodopa with your eyes, you must see it with your heart. With closed eyes, within yourself.

And the shepherds looked at Rhodopa, and I looked at their faces, moulded by the wind. And I saw that their looks were turned inwards. They did not look only on the pale shadows of the pastures and the dark shadows of the forest, they did not see only the crests of waves and abysses, but their feet trod the paths, as they had trodden thousands of times so far, they ascended summit after summit, and peered down into precipices, they crossed meadows on which they knew every stone, and forests in which they knew every trunk. And their feet felt the firm grass, and their brows parted the twigs of the spruces. And their lips were cold with the waters of the streams of Rhodopa, and their breasts swelled with its songs. Its forests were full of trees, from which they whittled cradles for their children, its land was full of the bones of their forebears.

The wind grew stronger, the chirping of the crickets grew more and more anxious, and they hid in the cracks of the rocks, lest the wind should carry them off. And the shepherds stood facing it, and not one blinked, and not one spoke. From time to time a cricket would chirp at our feet, and its chirp stood out against the common lament of the other distant crickets around us, as if a heavy drop were falling regularly upon a river in spate.

And Rhodopa was burning. Her feet were burning, her hair was burning. She was a woman, a mother, that is why the shepherds called her Rhodopa, and were angered when anyone said Rhodopes. For many mountains are loved less than one mountain.

The Balkan is a father, standing straight and strong, as everything manly must. Rhodopa is a mother, who conceives and brings forth, lying on her back, with her eyes on the heavens. A son grieves for his father, but he grieves for him as one grieves for a man. A son grieves for his mother, as one grieves for a woman. And a mother's sufferings are greater.

Yet, were these handsome men the sons of the Rhodope Mountain? Were they not the mountain itself, and was not the fire burning their feet, and did not the black smoke fill their eyes with tears? Be not envious, you other mountains, of their love for Rhodopa, for she is a great mountain. A martyr is the Rhodopa Mountain. Be not envious, mountains, of Rhodopa. She has suffered greatly, and new hardships were now on the way.

And night fell. And the clouds rose on high so that the moon showed itself. The slopes of the mountains opposite grew round and soft, veiled by the light, like a woman's body by a thin garment. Three lonely crooked pine trees stood forward and grew black, and the moon behind them shone forth. A light, white mist filled the valleys and began to creep up the slopes. And all the colours could be seen, as in the daytime, but they were strange and dead. And the men cast shadows as black as pitch, blacker than the shadow cast by the sun. It grew cold.

Then Old Kralyo said:

'Light a fire.'

And the young men made up a fire in a hollow of the rock, so that all sat down around it, and only I remained on one side.

And the fire brought them together and lit only their faces. But their backs were in the shadow. And it came into my mind that the sun and the moon are the light of the world and shine down on everything from on high in the same way, but fire is the light of man, and shines only on his face. And the fire must not become a big one, for then it becomes like the sun. And I wanted to warm my hands at their fire. But Manol raised his head and saw the fires. And their glow had become redder and higher, stirred up by the darkness. Manol said:

'Put out the fire.'

But Old Kralyo said quietly:

'We cannot put out those fires.'

Yet he, too, took a brand and struck it against the rocks and stepped upon its sparks.

And Goran rumbled:

'Look.'

They were all surprised, for it is seemly to be silent in the presence of older folk. And they looked.

And on the lower rock, the second summit of Purvenets, stood three men, and the wind tossed a white, a black and a red cloak, and in the light of the moon we saw that it was Syuleiman Aga with Hassan Hodja and Delyo. He, too, was looking at the fires. And Hassan Hodja's father, *Kehaya* Velko Radoul, was standing beside Manol.

Then Manol began to speak. He spoke loudly and slowly, to be heard above the wind, loudly enough for Syuleiman Aga to hear him. No one was looking at Manol, and he looked at no one, they had all turned their faces to the fires. But the fires did not cast their glow upon us, so that the faces of the men were not red, but as white as marble. And Syuleiman Aga did not look towards us. And Manol said:

'If we hold out until the winter, until the snows block the passes. If we guard this heart of Rhodopa, which is still dark, so that only the sun and the moon shine down on it. By then, Mehmed Pasha will have gone down to Salonika, and made sail for Candia. Then five thousand men will be found, five thousand knives and five thousand muskets which will bar the road to the fires.'

And he fell silent. Then Old Kralyo spoke, with his face turned to the fires, too, in the same way, without looking at anyone, least of all at Syuleiman Aga. And as the moon shone down on him, it seemed as if he were speaking in his sleep. And he said:

'If we live to see the snows, safe and sound, only a few will go down to the south with the sheep. But they will take enough mules to load them with Venetian weapons. With lead and gunpowder. Many a time has Rhodopa risen, and has defended herself against her tsars, bow in hand. Did not Momchil[41] hold a bow? Will we be weaker with muskets? And when the bullets and the powder come to an end, has not each one of us a bow and a knife?'

And Stan Stan cried:

'It is easy to roam through Rhodopa, when she opens her arms to you. It is hard to pass along her paths when her men defend them.

And Momchil said quietly, so that his words should not be heard on the rock opposite:

'Must we wait for the winter? Shall we grow older by winter, and become men?'

And Manol said to him:

'Be silent. Your elders are speaking.'

And Old Kralyo said to him:

'Mehmed Pasha has an army of one hundred thousand in Tsepina. And Tsepina is two days' journey away, and one day along the shortest paths.'

And silence fell on both the rocks of the summit. Only the wind blew, and the crickets chirped, and a bird of the night gave a sinister croak.

Then Vrazhou Chilingir spoke up:

'What of the sheep? Who can feed our ten thousand sheep in mangers throughout the winter? And one hundred villages of three thousand souls each? For the winter pastures along the sea will be closed to our flocks.'

He did not finish, for Stoiko Protsvet cried out, but he, too, looked at no one :

'May our flocks become cured meat. May eagles peck them to pieces. I want to see the faces of my wife and daughters uncovered. I do not want a turban, I want a fur cap. When I die, I want a cross to spring up on my grave.'

And he fell silent. Again no one spoke on the two rocks. They were silent for a long time. And the voice of Syuleiman Aga was heard :

'Well met, Manol *Kehaya*. Well met, shepherds.'

Yet he, too, did not look towards us, but stood facing the fires.

And then Manol said to him :

'Syuleiman Aga, once your grandfather was master of these dark mountains. Cast off your turban, put on a fur cap, and we shall bring you five thousand men, each with a high heart and a knife. Delay until winter, preserve us, think of something. Until these fires die down. And in winter you will become tsar. We shall forget the sacks cast into the abyss, the men you have hanged on the plane-tree, those you have slain on the meadow. We shall forget your turban.'

And for the first time Syuleiman Aga looked towards us. And as their rock was lower, he looked up. His voice came to us weak, and scattered by the wind, although there was between the two rocks a precipice that was only about ten feet wide. And he cried :

'Manol *Kehaya*, why do you remember the abyss, the plane tree and the meadow? Why do you not remember the white cobblestones, the stone bridges, and the fountains with three spouts each?'

And Manol turned to him for the first time, and answered him :

'Syuleiman Aga, do you remember when you built the big stone bridge? The three villages rose to build it, the woman together with the children. All of them, from seven years up and from seventy years down. Only one pot boiled on the hearth of every ninth house, only one old woman was left to rock nine cradles. Syuleiman Aga, did you build Syuleiman Aga's stone bridge?'

And the Aga made no answer. And after staying a little while longer, he turned his back to the wind, so that his white cloak whipped around and covered his face. And he took it down and began to descend the path. And the path wound beneath our rock, so that when he passed by at our feet, Manol bent down, seized the rock with both hands, and called :

'Remember, Syuleiman Aga. The turban or the fur cap.'

And Rad Dragoslav cried :

'The turban or the crown.'

But we could not make out whether the Aga heard them. And he passed on along the path, and his white cloak blew about over the meadow until the forest swallowed it. In the light of the moon, one could see that the trees were green, but the darkness dug black caves next to their trunks. In them Syuleiman Aga was lost, and from the forest came the shrill cry of a bird of prey, awakened from its sleep.

And Vrazhou *Kehaya* said :

'Why did we open our mouths before him? What if he betrays us to the Turks? And if he does not speak, will not the Hodja or Delyo speak?'

And Old Kralyo said quietly :

'The wind dazed us.'

And Rad Dragoslav said :

'The fires blinded me.'

Only Manol answered :

'What will he betray? That we are Bulgarians. Does Karaibrahim not know it? Or has he not come because of this?'

All night long we stood a silent watch on the big summit of Mount Purvenets. And the wind blew on us. And the fires continued to glow.

And when the moon paled, and the sky grew light, there occurred a miracle which I have seen a hundred times and have never been able to understand.

The mountain began to shine from inside. There was no sun to light it, not even one ray, yet the summits began to shine as if a white light were being born in their bowels.

Then the sun shone on us, and it came from Mount Possestra, where there was no fire. After that, it moved down from the summit, and waded into the red sea, so that it, too, became red and fiery.

And Old Kralyo said :

'It is the sunrise, Manol. Not the sunset. You were asking last night, weren't you? There, the sun has risen and will leap over the fire.'

And Manol said : 'May it be so.'

And we all repeated : 'May it be so.'

And we descended from the summit.

[1] *Aga* (T) = master.

[2] *Rayah* (T) = non-Moslem population of the Ottoman Empire.

[3] *Konak* (T) = house of a notable, castle, palace, government building.

[4] *Miloto Gospodi* (B) = The Dear Lord.

[5] *Yataghan* (T) = Curved sword used by Turkish soldiers.

[6] *Haidout* (B) = bandit.

[7] *Sultan* (T) = a Turkish ruler, a higher title than bey (T), also a ruler.

[8] *Yurouks* (T) = Moslem nomad stockbreeders.

[9] *Kaval* (B) = shepherd's flute, usually made of wood, in several sections.

[10] *Chan* (T) = long bells worn by the sheep, which had a smaller bell instead of a clapper. The shepherds chose their bells to make a chime. That is why to this day the bells of the flock make such sweet music in the mountains.

[11] *Kehaya* (T) = head shepherd.

[12] *Plachliv Kamuk* (B) = The Weeping Stone or Stone of Tears, place of parting. The womenfolk usually accompanied the shepherds to this spot and welcomed them home here on their return, weeping with joy or sorrow, hence its name.

[13] *Samodiva* (B) = wood nymph, fairy.

[14] *Baté* (B) = diminutive of brat = brother, usual mode of address to men by their juniors, whether blood relations or not.

[15] *Beiler-bey* (T) = Governor of a province.

[16] *Kaimakam* (T) = Governor of a county.

[17] *Cadi* (T) = judge.

[18] *Akché* (T) = small silver Turkish coin.

[19] *Aspra* (T) = small Turkish copper coin.

[20] *Oka* (T) = measure of weight of over 2 lbs.

[21] *Bilyuk-Bashi* (T) = literally commander over many, sergeant in an army.

[22] *Tsar* (B) = king.

[23] *Kyoshk* (T) = raised part of a covered veranda, projecting over a courtyard.

[24] *Temaneh* (T) = Turkish salute. The ground, one's breast, lips and forehead are touched to do honour to someone.

[25] Where there were no inns, there were 'open' or public rooms for travellers.

[26] *Baksheesh* (T) = Gratuity, tip.

[27] *Devitsa* (B) = maiden.

[28] *Horo* (B) = round or chain dance.

[29] Agovitsa (T) = Aga's wife, mistress.

[30] *Krustogorié* (B) = the cross-shaped forest.

[31] *Protopop* (B) = archpriest.

[32] Pop = Father i.e. Priest.

[33] Granny Srebra's tale is taken, word for word, from Priest Methodii Draginov's chronicle of the event in the village of Korova.

[34] *Mashallah* (T) = praise be to him.

[35] *Kyoshk* (T) = part of a veranda, usually projecting over a courtyard, and on a slightly higher level than the veranda.

[36] *Tougra* (T) = monogram of a sultan with his father's name and the words 'always victorious' interlaced with it.

[37] *Rayah* (T) = Non-Moslem subjects of the Sultan.

[38] *Bouyur, Bey* (T) = command us.

[39] *Odjak* (T) = tribe.

[40] Petglassets (B) = The Valley of Five Voices.

[41] This Momchil was a famous rebel of earlier days.

PART TWO

My Head I'll Give—
My Faith I Will Not Give

First Excerpt

It seemed to me that the *Konak* was like a spider in the middle of a
huge web. We were weaving the web and wondering how to lure the
Bulgarians into it, while they flew about like flies all over the
mountains. The talk was constantly of shepherds, of pistols, of resistance, but nothing happened and it seemed as if everything were
being prepared for an unreal, ghostly enemy. The only shepherd
whom I had seen was Manol—I did not know then that it was he
—up on the pass, with the skull in his hands. I realized that the
flocks had returned, by the sound of bells which came from the
forest one morning. It seemed as if the mountain had, up till now,
been like a flower which had only colours, and had suddenly grown
fragrant. The sound came like a fragrance and made me breathe
more deeply. It would be lost, then reach one sweetly, painfully
quiet, and one tried with all one's soul to catch it, as if rare drops
of rain were falling on thirsty lips, then the bells would begin
to sing with full force. I was already in another room, and the
howling of the dogs was heard only faintly, desperately faintly. On
the other hand, three times a day I heard the bells of the invisible
monastery being rung. I was prepared, I awaited them, I resisted
their voice. I did not suffer.

In the evening I went out in front of the *Konak* and gazed at
the crenellated wall of the mountains. They were alive. The night
was full of movement and invisible life. I saw fires burning, red
under the clear, white stars.

How would we go there? Or did Karaibrahim hope that the
flies would enter the web of themselves?

By day, people were hardly to be seen in the village. Everyone
had hidden. I waited in vain to see the flowers of those wonderful
rugs bloom again on the stone parapets of the humped bridge. The
stone stood there, white and bare. Did the Bulgarians of the valley
already know why Karaibrahim had come? Or did they think that
this was an ordinary Turkish detachment, and were they hiding
from the soldiers? Were they scheming something? Syuleiman
Aga probably had his own men among the peasants; perhaps

Karaibrahim, too, knew something. But I could only guess and surmise.

The little church beside the *Konak*, with the rusty cross on its slate roof, stood silent and closed. Not once did I see anyone enter it. Afterwards I found out that it was a very ancient chapel, in which Syuleiman Aga's forebears, Bulgarian boyars, had once prayed. Syuleiman Aga himself told me that there were ancient mural paintings on its walls.

I circled around the little church like a dog that has been driven out of the home of its former master. Could I go in? I cast the idea aside as madness, but two or three times my heart would begin to beat faster, and my feet would set out towards the wooden door, studded with big nails. I would manage to calm myself, look around, and it would seem to me that everyone in the *Konak* had seen the madness seize me. I awaited in fear and trembling the moment in the evening when Karaibrahim, supposedly among much else, would ask me: 'Why did you make for the church?' Once I saw the door open, and started forwards towards the darkness which awaited me in the church. I barely managed to pass to one side. I saw only the flame of a candle, somewhere at the end. But again I saw no one there.

What was it that drew me towards the little stone house? I was afraid of myself.

I wanted to get out of the web, to see what was happening around us. But when Karaibrahim told me that the two of us were going to ride through the villages, I did not succeed in hiding my fear. It was in the morning, and I remembered how the mountains marched forwards and hung over the *Konak* at night.

'As long as we do nothing to them, the people here will not attempt anything against us,' Karaibrahim told me. 'We shall only ride through, the two of us. Are you afraid?'

'I am,' I replied. 'But I shall come.'

We passed through the first village and left it. We were riding across the valley along the river. We entered the second village, Zagrad. Perhaps it was because I was so tense, and my eyes were constantly turned inwards on myself, so as not to allow myself to make a movement of fear, that I saw almost nothing around us. Nothing that I noted or remembered. We had passed through Rhodope villages of this kind—stone, slates, and wood turned into stone by rain and sun. We met no people. I felt that we were being looked at and watched.

Karaibrahim was silent, and constantly looked about him. There was something in the way in which he sat in his saddle which was different from usual, but I do not think that it was fear.

We passed through the second village, too—a long village, almost entirely consisting of a single row of houses along the road, and, in places, a second, on the other bank of the river.

The river and the road dug into the stone, and at the side marble appeared. Moreover, stones had surely been quarried here. Ragged bushes grew above, the trees had been cut down and one saw the grey patches of fires. The slope of the mountain looked poor and dirty beside the luxuriant forest around it. And down below, to one side of us, we saw the cut marble, white and clean. The sun which fell upon it struck sparks.

I started at the thought that all these mountains had such a transparent, clean and hard heart beneath the grey soil, beneath the grass and the forests. It could not be so, I knew that it was not so.

We entered the third village and left it behind us. The road rose upwards and the river came flowing down opposite us. Karaibrahim stopped his horse and said to me :

'Wait for me here.'

And he galloped on, so that I did not even have time to reply.

I was left alone. The mountain looked deserted. I felt that I had managed to relax. I felt it in a new constriction of my heart.

I went into the forest, jumped down from my horse and sat down on a log.

It must have been beautiful all around me. It was spring. When I remember the beauty of the mountains as I have seen it at other times, I am certain that it was beautiful.

I was a stranger to the forest. I had lost any approach to it. The seeds of its beauty fell upon my heart that had been turned to stone, and died there. I stood amid the forest as if I were clothed in armour made of fear and tenseness.

I had to relax. I had to dissolve myself in the forest. To stand like a tree, like grass, like a wild beast. But no, I was a man, therefore I had to be full of high thoughts, I had to open my soul, to dig up the furrows so that the seeds might sprout.

I listened with my hand on my pistol. And then I heard the strange sound.

Yes, it was a curious sound. Something light was knocking against the branches of the trees, just as if it were raining sand, or as if big scattered drops of rain were falling.

The rustling was mysterious and faint. Something secret was taking place, something that no one was supposed to sense—something covert and invisible, but very potent. There was a constant rustle, but it came first from here, then from there, and always at

my back. But nothing fell to the earth. A sound of that kind was in-
evitably linked with love, with fertilization and life.

To this day I do not know what that sound was. I suppose that
the pine cones must have been dropping their seeds. I say this—
but I do not know.

It was happening above, high up on the tops of the pines. The
tall, slender bare stems, without any greenery, deep in shadow,
rose up and supported the vaults of branches and dark fine leaves,
and the vaults received the sun. The forest was celebrating its
wedding with the sun.

It was just the same in the *Konak*, where there was always a
creaking at night, as if someone were creeping along the veranda
—barefoot, on tip-toe—in order to enter the dark room, in which
his girl, awake, was waiting for him. And the darkness was full of
the bated breath and expectation of young people.

Childish voices were heard. Somewhere in the forest children
were running about. For the first time I was to see children in the
valley. They were probably looking for mushrooms.

I did not think about that, because I no longer heard the rustling.
The distant shouts had deadened the soft, faint patter, but it seemed
to me that it had stopped to wait for the other sound to go away.
Even the childish voices were hoarse and rough for the warm, silky,
sunny stillness of the forest.

And only when the voices had passed on—but they still came to
me from very far away, deadened, soft, and unreal—did I hear
again how the sun's seed was raining over the tops of the pine trees
and fertilizing the world.

I was alive and the world around me was living.

At first I had waited for Karaibrahim as for a saviour. When
I heard the hooves of his horse, I felt like cursing him.

He did not notice my emotion. He rode on in silence, and I
did not feel like speaking either. We had already reached Prossoina
when he said :

'I found a water-mill. There was an old miller there.'

I heard the sun raining.

'Do you know,' Karaibrahim spoke again after a little while.
'He gave me honey, as if I weren't a Turk.'

Again I said nothing to him.

'There was a maiden there, too,' he said.

Absorbed as I was in myself, I could not but see that he appeared
deeply moved. For the second time since he had entered the valley.

'Was she beautiful?' I asked absently.

He looked at me as if I had asked something boundlessly foolish.

'Very beautiful.'

I went straight to Syuleiman Aga. I did not know what I was going to say to him, but it seemed to me that as soon as I saw him the words would come to my lips of themselves.

Abdullah was doing that. The man I had formerly been would never have gone straight to a man to tell him what he thought. To say nothing of the servants who would have gone back and forth arranging the meeting.

Syuleiman Aga was sitting in the *kyoshk*. A flock of sparrows on the plane tree were twittering, just as if a hundred little bells were tinkling on a horse's neck when he was galloping, or as if someone were regularly rattling an iron box full of nails. The tom-cat on the Aga's knees glanced indolently at them. He was wise, and, knowing that he could not reach the sparrows, he did not permit himself superfluous passions.

The Aga rose to greet me. I saw an inscription in Arabic over the door that led to his chambers. I could not read it, and first I asked him to tell me what was written there.

' "Praise be to those who suppress their wrath and forgive men," Venetian, it is not I who thought of this. These words are written on a door in the Padishah's palace—above the door from the harem to the place of reception. The historian Abdi suggested them, but he had probably read them somewhere. Let us hope that the Sultan remembers them.'

There, that was the word that I needed. The key. The Sultan.

'Aga,' I said, 'cannot the Sultan help Elindenya? So that the bitter cup may pass from it. He is near, in Adrianople, and may already be coming this way. They said that he would set out towards Larissa and would pass either through the Rhodopes, or to the south of them. A messenger could go and return in a few days.'

The Aga smiled. His smile was kindly and a little bitter. He did not ask me how I came to be talking thus. His face was open, and I read his thoughts. He did not try to hide them, nor to deceive me.

And that was the triumph of Abdullah. Since I had become Abdullah, I had liked people much better. I liked them more and more, and with some people I simply fell in love, if the word does not strike some as exaggerated. I felt drawn to them, I even wanted to caress them. I liked their eyes, their movements, their speech. I felt the warmth of their bodies, the smoothness of their skin, the quiver of their muscles. And warmth was born in my heart. I liked them best of all because they were alive.

I felt love of this kind for the Aga. He sensed this, and an invisible link was coming into being between us, which neither of us wanted to admit, or put into words, and to which we would hardly be able to give a name.

'Venetian,' the Aga said to me. 'I should be happy if I knew your real name, but in the final analysis any name is good. Do you know the Padishah?'

I did not know him. I had heard him spoken of, but I had not seen him.

Syuleiman Aga invited me to sit down, clapped his hands to have oranges and sherbet brought, and did not speak until they had been brought.

'I know the Sultan,' he said. 'When the weather is cool, five hundred Spahis sleep in the Sultan's tent, to turn the air away from him with the warmth of their bodies. I have slept in the Sultan's tent. Mohammed the Fourth, son of Ibrahim, has but one occupation—he goes hunting. He has hunted here, too, in Rhodopa. He used to say that these mountains were in his heart, and that he would build himself a palace here. And indeed, they are already building—over there, in Despot, where the palaces of my forbears were. We had a hunt for him with the peasants of seventeen districts. Some 30,000 men got together. They wrote down every hare and every partridge they killed, to say nothing of the stags, the boar and the bears. Mohammed sent the Sheikh Vani game killed by his arrow. He shoots with a bow. Once he hit a target on the wall of his tent from a distance of one hundred feet. He was honoured then as Syuleiman the Law-giver was honoured when he had conquered a new throne. His shot was set down in the books on the history of the Ottoman Empire. Mohammed goes hunting, Küprüli rules. It was thus under old Küprüli Mohammed, it is thus under the son, Ahmed. The Padishah is the shadow of Allah on earth, this Sultan is the shadow of the Padishah on the throne. Whatever Ahmed has said, the Sultan will not change. He is compassionate. I have seen him weep when an Indian mahout died. We were out near Adrianople, hunting an elephant, and the mahout was killed. Mohammed does not want rams to be slaughtered as sacrifices for the Lesser *Bairam*.[1] He turns his head aside when he passes by the heads that have been cut off before his tent. But he will not spare Elindenya.'

'Is it true,' I asked, and stammered, 'is it true that he is afraid to kill his brothers?'

The devil made me ask this question. Of course, I was asking because of Syuleiman Aga's fratricide, and not about the Sultan.

Syuleiman Aga took no notice of my ugly curiosity, nor my eager gaze on his face. Or, if he saw them, he pretended that he did not.

[1] For notes see p. 181.

He never batted an eyelid.

'It is not easy to kill your brother,' he said.

Those were the words of Karaibrahim, when he was admiring the fearlessness of Syuleiman Aga.

'According to the law of Mohammed the Second, the Conqueror, the Sultan must kill his brother, so that there may be no threat to his throne. Since he ascended the throne, Mohammed the Fourth has been tightening the strings of fratricide, and has not yet shot the arrow. And this thought torments him by night and by day. As soon as you see his face and his eyes, you will know that he is the prey of nightmares. He has a round, Russian face, the face of a kindly man, and the dark, threatening eyes of a man who fears something and frightens others. And his two brothers are guarded by their common mother—the Validé Khanum—the old Sultana, whose name is Tarkhan. Whether she is a Russian or a Pole I do not know, but she is a Slav. She sleeps before the room of her sons. Once the Sultan entered on tip-toe, with a dagger in his hand. He was creeping towards his brothers. The Validé was asleep. Two slave-girls awoke her with a nudge, for they dared not speak. The Sultana awoke. The Sultan returned, and had the slave-girls hanged. He can do that. But he dare not kill his brothers.'

'Syuleiman Aga,' I said. 'I asked you, for I knew that you had killed your brother. Forgive me.'

'When you see the Sultan, you will understand how easy it is to be tormented by the thought of fratricide. And you will be able to imagine what it will be like if he kills them. They say that his father, Sultan Ibrahim, cursed him when the hangmen were strangling him in the prison, and his son watched them through the window. He cursed him to roam like a ghost, like a wild animal, over forests and mountains and never to find peace. It may be true. I think that it is the terrible thought that drives him. Do you know how he hunts? That is no pleasure, but torment. He rides from morn to night, exhausts his horses, and he is taken down half-dead from the saddle. He is crippled from a fall, and his back hurts him so that his lips grow white. He gave me the golden bow, not because I killed the bear, but because he heard that I had killed my brother.'

Syuleiman Aga rose and entered his chambers. I thought that he had left me, because he had been stirred and did not want to show me this. I wondered whether I should leave. He returned with a golden bow in one hand, and with an old cross-bow, worm-eaten and rusty, in the other.

'This is the Sultan's gift. And I have brought you this because it was taken from the Franks. It may have belonged to one of your forbears, one of those who had castles in the southern Rhodopes. And they, too, massacred people in the mountains. Yet what happened? They are gone, and the mountains live on.'

He held the crossbow pointed at me. There was no arrow in it, yet I felt that something pierced my heart. Syuleiman Aga held the judgement of Elindenya in his hands. At that moment I realized that the valley was doomed. Worms and rust. Syuleiman Aga had given up. Perhaps he himself had not yet come to a decision. But at that moment I understood him. He was consoling me.

'Do you see these mountains around us? If we go up to one of their summits one day, I will show you the boundaries of my estates. Last night I was up on one of the summits. When the Turks conquered Rhodopa, my great-grandfather, a Bulgarian boyar, accepted Islam. Ibrahim Pasha, the Sultan's son-in-law, told him that he would leave him as much land as he could encircle from sunrise to noon. He might go as he wished, on foot or on horseback. The old man set out on horseback, he knew the crests of the mountains and he rode like a madman. Two hours before noon his horse fell. He had to return to the place from which he had set out, or he would lose all. He dashed through the mountains. I know which way he went. I tell you, you could not travel in a whole day over what he journeyed, running, in two hours.'

'And did he die?'

'He lived another twenty years. And as you said—he died. Is it not all one then? He is no longer living. How many men and what men have lived and are gone. What are we weeping over, we small ones?'

I remembered the silent villages, the marble underneath the grey soil, the sunny wedding in the forest. I did not want to resign myself. I asked the Aga:

'And cannot Ahmed Küprüli do anything?'

Syuleiman Aga asked me, as he had asked before about the Sultan:

'Do you know the Grand Vizier Ahmed Küprüli?'

'I do not know him; I have seen him from a distance.'

'I do know him. I saw him when he was twenty-four years old. He looked like an old man even then. He looked like a lost child amid his tall Albanian cut-throats, all dressed in scarlet. Two men supported him under the armpits, so that he would not waste his strength holding himself up. He is small, and bearded, and from the nose up he looks like Mohammed the Second, the Conqueror. Only from the nose up. His father, old Mohammed Küprüli, at seventy-five looked younger than he does. The old man was made of iron. He could neither read nor write. Did you hear what

Karaibrahim said? Ahmed not only pours Polish brandy down his throat, but tries all the poisons in the world. Hasheeshes, opiums, herbs and powders. He has eighty wives, and cannot sleep properly with a single one of them. He seeks new pleasures, and everything is bitter to him. I tell you, he is so desperate that he ought to go somewhere and become a hermit to escape from the world. Yet he is at the head of the biggest country in the world. A desperate man with power is worse than a beast. What hold can you have upon him? What can you say to him, even if you were to go to him before Candia? He is trying to bolster up the Padishah's shaken throne, but that is also a desperate business, more desperate than Ahmed himself.'

Syuleiman Aga sat down with crossed legs, and folded his arms on his breast. He raised his head and smiled at me. I stood before him, holding the cross-bow in my hand.

His eyes were saying: 'If I did not like you, I would tell you that you are a simpleton. You are seeking wisdom, are you not? Go and forget the moments of weakness.'

Syuleiman Aga said:

'Elindenya is a fragment of the Padishah's demesne. And the muddy stream that is lapping at that demesne has risen so high that it covers the mountains, too. See what is happening. Well, only look at the Janissaries, who were the bulwark of the Sultan's power. They are supposed to be like the monks in your orders, who do not marry, do not thirst for earthly goods and fight only for the glory of God and the Sultan. What are the Janissaries today? The Janissaries marry. Their sons enter the *Sandjak*[2] while still in their cradles and receive wages. Any kind of men enter, and the few real Janissaries despise the newcomers. The Janissaries trade and rob peaceful folk in broad daylight. As a Turk cannot be a Janissary, the Turks at first gave their children to Christians, to make Janissaries of them, and then Turks began to enter the *Sandjak* directly. How many were the Janissaries before? A handful of men, an iron fist. About thirty-years ago, thirty thousand Janissaries set out on the Persian campaign. And three thousand got there. And the children laughed at them. What of the Spahis? The Sultan used to give them land for life, to join his banner when he sent for them, and they wonder how they can stay on their farms, and how to leave the land to their sons. From top to bottom everyone lives on bribes. Even Ahmed Küprüli can be bought. They issue false money. The treasury is empty. And the Grand Vizier knows only one remedy: war at all costs. That is what old Mohammed Küprüli bequeathed to him. Fight outside, so as not to fight inside. Where does that leave Elindenya?'

'Yes, Elindenya is a fragment of the Padishah's demesne . . .'

Syuleiman Aga looked at me, with a suddenly changed, sharp look, he said not a word more, rose and went through the door with the inscription.

I waited. He did not come back.

My heart felt heavy as if I had been insulted, but I managed to laugh. Who could insult me?

I had behaved like a child before his father. I had asked for something. How stupid. Abdullah had misled me for the first time. I forgave him.

Second Excerpt

Migrate, you nine villages . .

And on the following day, which came after *Predoi*, Ismaïl led us to the Valley of Petglassets. Only seven of Manol's men bore all the wealth of the refugees. Sherko carried Granny Srebra, and Goran carried a curly-horned ram over his shoulders. And Manol and I were with them.

At one time we set off up the waters of the River Struïlitsa. And then, like a silver knife, the river began to cut the breast of the mountain.

First of all, the cut, fruitful soil was laid bare and the roots of the tree were revealed. They were terrible, writhing and strong, as they passed before our faces, and I understood why the trees reach the sky, while man barely rises above the earth. Then the soil was left above our heads, and there appeared the rocks which uphold the world. And here they were pierced by red veins, as if blood or the juice of red grapes had flowed down them. And at first, here and there along these veins young spruces clung, slender and delicate, like little hairs on a bald forehead, then they, too, disappeared. Only the stone was left. And the rocks rose ever higher and higher above us, and came ever closer and closer on both sides of us. And the sun was lost and the water ran down the stone, so that it became dark and cool, and terrible, and the voice of the waters grew deep and dull. And the bit of soil on which green grasses grew and on which the sun shone, and from which the big roots jutted forth, went high, high above us, and grew slim, as slim as the green colour on the rind of a water-melon, which you can scratch off with a nail, and green will be left only under your nail, and beneath it white will show; this green was left high above

us, and we were in the red heart of the water-melon, in which there
are no longer even seeds.

And I heard the mountain say :

'Crawl, you little folk. Touch my bowels lightly and take of my
strength. For all that your eyes see every day is but the hair of my
head and the nails of my fingers. For young ploughs scratch my
surface to the depth of two spans, and the roots of the spruces reach
down ten feet, and even the juices of the dead only go down as far
as a man's height. Yes, and living or dead, you scratch my surface,
and your graves are shallow, and your bones are laid bare by the
wind and the rain. And the foundations of your villages and your
towns are shallow, and the waters carry them away and the sand
buries them. Go down, down. Here waters flow that are stronger
than those which flow above. Here veins of gold, silver and iron
intermingle. Even if each of you take a full load of them—some
will still be left over for me. Men, touch my bowels lightly, and
take of my strength.'

Yet we grew smaller and smaller, and gave no thought to the
strength of the mountain, but prayed that we might emerge sooner
into the sunlight. Men's shoulders are too weak for the stony load
of the rocks. And even Goran, with his fur cap, his tufted rug and
his shock of hair, grew smaller than an ant, and the ram on his
shoulders was like a millet seed.

And all the time it seemed to us that we were walking along the
course of the river, and that it was flowing ever downwards—yet
it flowed against us, and sprang from the place to which we were
going.

And we raised our eyes upwards, to draw courage from the light
band of the blue sky above us, and from the two edges of the soil
up above, along the rims of the precipice, on which the light fell.
And these green and light rims were like the banks of a deep river.
And I realized that man lives on the banks, and it is not given
unto him to go down to the bottom of the river.

For very fear, the path clung more and more to the left cliff,
and drops from the wet stones began to drip onto our faces. And
the brook Struïlitsa clung to the right cliff, and grew even denser
and denser. And at one place the right rock had cracked, and a
deep hole yawned there—a cave. The brook seemed to lose itself
there, and spread out in a fearful dark-green pool. And green
bubbles rose above the water. It seemed to me that above the roar
of the water I heard its murmur. And I saw that the water whirled
the bubbles to the left. For the first time the dog Sharo growled.

And Ismaïl Bey called, but his voice reached us weak and low :

'That is where the lord of this water breathes. He has the horns of a ram, the whiskers of a sheath-fish, the claws of a crayfish and the tail of a trout. You must know this : when you pass this way, throw him something, if it be only a stone. But it must be heavy and sink.'

And out of his cartridge belt he drew a hammered knife and cast it into the pool and the water swallowed it.

Then, from Sherko's arms, Granny Srebra said :

'May so many men pass this way that their stones will fill this left pool.'

And I said :

'Amen.'

Those were the first words which were heard since we had entered the breast of Rhodopa.

We set out again, and from steadily staring at the water, which flowed beside us, and from its roar, and perhaps also from fear, our heads grew dizzy, and our knees began to give way beneath us. Then suddenly the two walls of the gorge drew together and there was no road before us. And the River Struĭlitsa emerged from under the feet of the two rocks, gathered together.

And Ismaïl Bey set out to the left and was lost in a cave. And as its floor was covered with sand, and its walls were smooth, I realized that water had flowed here a long time ago.

And the cave came to an end and before us spread the Valley of Petglassets. We all gathered before the cave.

And we were blinded by the sun, and our ears were deafened by the song of the crickets, and we smelled fresh honey. So that it seemed to me that there was a wall of light before me, on the left a wall of song and on the right a wall of fragrance.

Ismaïl Bey said :

'Look to the left.'

And we looked to the left.

'These two summits are St Yani and Karachan. Every St Petko's day a ram is to be sacrificed at the big grey stone on Karachan.'

He said again :

'Look to the right.'

And we looked.

'These two summits are Modur and Svetilek. A ram is to be sacrificed there every year on St Peter's Day.'

And he said further :

'Raise your eyes and look before you.'

And we saw one single summit, all overgrown with a forest right up to the top.

'That is Possestra,' said Ismaïl Bey. 'The mother of Struĭlitsa is there. From there you can see the glitter of the Aegean Sea. You cannot see the sea, but its glitter can be seen.'

One hundred pairs of refugee eyes stared at the summit from which one could see the glitter of the sea. For they came from the Northern Rhodopes and did not know what a sea was.

'And all that is between St Yani, Karachan, Possestra, Modur and Svetilek, and that cliff at our backs—that is the Valley of Petglassets. With its pastures, its forests and its waters,' said Ismaïl Bey.

Then I understood that the gleam I had seen in the eyes of the refugees was not a reflection of the glitter of the Aegean Sea. It was their new land. Their children would be born here. Their bones would be buried here. I would stay a while and go my ways, and they would remain here for ever. They and their seed after them.

Ismaïl Bey turned to Manol, and bowing to him, said:

'Manol *Kehaya*, set foot in the valley, it is yours.'

And Manol made Sherko, who was carrying Granny Srebra, enter the valley first. But Granny Srebra told him to set her down, and she stepped forwards in the high grass. No one else had set foot in it before her. There was no path, because the flocks had not entered the valley that spring. And as we walked across the meadows, crickets sprang up at our feet on all sides, so that we seemed to be wading across a river, and raising sprays of water from under our feet. And we walked slowly and solemnly, for the old woman could barely stand on her feet.

After a while we heard a roaring, and when we peered over to the right, we saw from the steep bank how the entire River Struïlitsa fell into a dark hole and went no further. The whirlpool roared and above it rose foam and spray, and in the mist a rainbow appeared. But we did not look long on that marvel, and turned our eyes to the valley, for it was even lovelier than a rainbow.

Sloping meadows ran down to the Struïlitsa, yellow with yarrow and other herbs, purple with clover and thistles, white with ox-eyed daisies and other flowers. Dark-green pine woods surrounded them, and here and there in the meadows rose bunches of dark spruces, so that they made them still lighter and sunnier. The woods rose up to the summits, and wrapped them as if in shaggy sheepskin coats. And only here and there was the fur plucked out, so that other light meadows could be seen. And when we thought to turn back, we saw a straight stone wall, and at its top spruces, small and low because of the height.

And in the middle of the nearest meadow there rose an old, a very ancient spruce, and Manol made for it.

The spruce raised its huge trunk, spreading out thick straight branches, like stout arms. And the small boughs, the leaves and the moss hung in folds, in folds downwards, and not a twig was to be seen above, as if the wide silken sleeves of a green shirt were falling in folds. A soft breeze was blowing, and the trunk of the spruce never quivered, neither did its top even quiver, although it was light and slender, like a peacock's feather on a fur cap. Nor did its outstretched branches quiver, only the green silk sleeves swayed softly.

When we had all gathered beside this wonderful tree, Ismaïl Bey put his hands to his mouth and shouted:

'Mas-ter-er-er!'

And the echo answered:

'Master! Master! Master!'

But the voices came in waves, so that they chased each other and covered each other, and one heard first 'mas', then 'ter', and most often only 'er-er-er' and 'a-a-a'. And the refugees were wide-eyed with amazement.

'We have come!' Ismaïl Bey shouted again.

'We have come! Have come! Come!' answered the mountain echo.

Goran took the ram down from his shoulder, and crossed himself, although he had heard these voices before. And the wonder was not only in the echo, but the very voices that rang and echoed, in a special way, so that a man felt rather strange.

'Under this spruce,' said Ismaïl Bey, 'a ram is slaughtered as a sacrifice every Alinden.'[3]

And he said the word *Alinden*, stressing the 'a', thinking that it was Ali's Day. But our folk, when they say *Alinden*, pronounce it with an 'i', so that one understands it as it is, the Day of St Iliya (Elijah).

And Granny Srebra sat down next to the trunk of the big spruce, between two big roots that stood out, so that she seemed to us still tinier and more shrunken. And the old woman said:

'When I looked, I thought the village would be here, for what could be finer than that the spruce should rise amid it like a belfry? But we cannot allow every word spoken in the village to be heard five times.'

Then Manol silently picked up the hoe, which one of his shepherds was holding.

'Let the graveyard be here,' he said.

And he struck a blow with the hoe. And the earth, which seemed soft beneath our feet, had stones in it, and the echo sent back the blows of the hoe.

'While you are digging the grave,' Manol said, 'the echo will ring instead of a bell.'

I felt fearful, for the first sod broken in this valley was for a grave, and not for foundations.

Ismaïl Bey said to us :

'I have given you the key of this land and its pledges. Do as we have done, for this have our fathers learnt from the folk who once lived here, May the root you strike reach the heart of the earth.'

And he bowed and went away, and his son Yussouf followed him.

And all that day we wandered over the valley, so that we went around the meadows and the banks of the Struïlitsa, until we chose for the village a site that was sheltered, and neither on an even spot, nor on a steep one, and the forest guarded its back, and at its feet there was a spring. And I sprinkled the meadow with a bunch of the herbs that I picked on the same meadow and I blessed it.

Then the axes rang out and the echo sent their ringing back to us. And fires were lit on the meadow to consecrate the wild and deserted land. At one of the fires the ram was being roasted. And Granny Srebra took two handfuls of soil, and cast them over her head, saying :

'Whoever takes a handful of soil from his neighbour, may it be on his head ! For this land has been given to us.'

Then they took the cauldron, blackened from the thousands of fires that had been lit beneath it, and set out to mark the trees on the edge of the forest which guarded the back of the village. And before each marked tree, they stepped on the cauldron and cried :

'May he who tries to blacken the forest grow as black as this cauldron.'

And the forest became a forbidden place, for without it the snows and the waters would sweep the village away.

And at that time the sun hid itself and a shadow fell over Petglassets. Then the shrill chirping of the crickets died away, and we began to hear the lulling, gentle chirping of the black crickets, those little black crickets, who grow black because they breed in the winter beside the hearths, so that their chirping may remind one of hearth and home. And the folk gathered around the fires, and their flames leapt up higher, and the darkness around grew denser.

And when we had broken up the roast ram on the fresh spruce branches, Manol said :

'I give the new village one *elia* of sheep.'

And one *elia* are fifty sheep.

But I took out of my bag the holy books that I had copied, and that I was to give to the monastery, and had never found time to go there, and I said :

'I give you the first holy books, although they are the Old Testament.'

And I remembered that Mircho had sworn his oath on the Book of Ecclesiastes.

'O-ho !' said Granny Srebra, 'We have our own Gospels.'

And out of her grandchild's bag she took a fat Bible bound in silver.

'The child stole it from the church. May it be forgiven him,' said the old woman.

And she began to take out of the bag other little bags made of cloth, and chanted over them, as if she were casting spells :

'Here is a handful of rye, and a handful of barley. Folks' bread is ready. Here are lentils, and here are white beans, for the pleasure of gluttons. Here are oats for the horses. Here is flax seed and here is hemp seed, that we may be clothed like kings. Grow, little seeds, to cover the valley, to drive out the weeds, to rise to the sky, so that we may rise to the moon on you.'

And when she raised one of the little bags and shook it, something rattled inside it, and the old woman grew sad.

'And these are cherry stones for the grandchildren. Why, dear Lord, have you not made the trees to grow as quickly as the grasses, so that even the old people may live to eat fruit from these little stones ?'

And the folk around her also began to dream, their irises wide open in the light of the fire, for the darkness had hidden their poverty and their misfortune. When it was daylight, they dared not say anything, for they saw bare meadows, wild trees, and turbulent waters. But now they began to talk.

'There, my house will be over there, with a garden in front,' said the woman who had fed her child with a straw.

'And at the spring I shall build a white fountain for the good of all,' said the man, whose brother had become a Turk.

'And over the river here, there will be a stone bridge,' the voice of an invisible man spoke in the darkness.

'And right over there, we shall build a church,' said I in my turn.

And Granny Srebra said to me :

'Father, read us something out of the Holy Books.'

I remembered and found the Lord's blessing on Abraham. And I read, and all around me they were silent and listened to me.

'Lift up now thine eyes, and look from the place where thou art northward, and southward, and eastward, and westward:

'For all the land which thou seest, to thee will I give it, and to thy seed for ever.

'And I will make thy seed as the dust of the earth . . .'

Then Sharo began to howl, long-drawn-out and ominously, and went to his master. And Sherko put his arms around his head, and spoke to him caressingly:

'What do your sharp eyes see? What do your sharp ears hear?'

The dog only whimpered.

Sherko raised his head, began to sniff the air and to listen. And he said:

'Cursed be the hand that cast the poor dogs in the black pit. It is them that Sharo hears. They are hungry and afraid. And they are not mad.'

And then they all remembered that behind the invisible rocks Rhodopa stretched far and wide. And the Turks were raging over her, and fires were turning her body to ashes, and a sword was slaying her people. While we sat there sheltered, others were being blown down by the wind.

Manol said:

'Goran, Sherko, cut down pinewood and get ready. This night we return.'

And they left the valley and returned to the great Rhodopa. I with them.

Thus was settled the new village, later called Momchilovo, in the Valley of Petglassets, bought with Manol's silver *chans*.

Third Excerpt

When I opened the door of my room, I saw a light rectangle outlined on the whitewashed wall, and in the middle of it—my shadow. It was still light, and I wondered who could have lighted a fire in the courtyard. I turned, and saw that the moon was shining.

A big full moon was slowly rising over the mountains.

The dogs began to howl. Two cats rushed out, as if they had gone mad, to climb up the plane tree, and when they reached the top they began to mew desperately, because they were afraid to climb down.

As soon as I had lit the candle, I heard a rattling sound in my room, as if hail were falling—but soft hail, like fresh peas. It was moths, swarms of them. I put the light out, but they still knocked against the dishes on the shelf that ran along the wall, on the saddle, the weapons and pistol cases. A pot had been left on the floor, empty and uncovered, and they bumped about inside it—not so loudly, but more frequently. There was an empty basket in the corner—and they bumped into that, too. Yet the room was not very much darker, because the moon shone through the open window.

'Very strange,' I thought, 'if these little insects hide in the daytime and come out in the dark, why do they so madly seek the light? If they need the light, why do they not live by day?'

I went outside and sat down on the steps. A woman was laughing lewdly somewhere in the *Konak*.

News had come that morning that a whole week ago Mehmed Pasha had begun to convert the Chepino region to Islam, and that he would afterwards go down south, along the course of some river.

The moon went on shining, and over there to the north, or a little to the west—I wasn't sure of my bearings—villages were now burning, and people were screaming. Women, who had been violated, lay there with their skirts turned over their faces, children cast themselves down on the dead bodies of their mothers, men, impaled on stakes, roared in agony. I knew that it would happen. It had happened.

As soon as I thought of the stakes, I felt sick, and began to drive these thoughts away from me.

I am alive, I thought. I am alive, I can go and drink cold water. I can go and lie down to sleep. I live.

What could I do? And ought I to do anything? There were Turks, there were also Bulgarians. The former were the stronger, and slew the latter. And again I said to myself that the important thing was to prepare myself, so that when the storm reached that quiet valley, I could remain calm.

And little by little, looking at the moon, I convinced myself that there were no massacres and screams, and no Mehmed Pashas and Chepino villagers. Abdullah the slave sat on the steps and stared up at the white stars.

Then one of Syuleiman Aga's men came to me and told me that the Aga had sent for me. I did not feel irritated, because I was not sleepy, and I was not hungry or thirsty.

Syuleiman Aga received me in his *kyoshk*. He was seated Turkish fashion on big pillows, drinking coffee.

'What would you like?' he asked me. 'Coffee or sherbet? Or something sweet?'

'You sent for me, Aga,' I said.

He smiled at me, as an old father smiles at his grandchild.

'One does not ask thus, Venetian, but one waits, sips coffee, smacks one's lips, until the important thing for which the people have assembled is spoken by the way.'

'What is the use of that?'

'True, what is the use? You may sit at the edge of the *kyoshk* and your feet will dangle from it. I must tell you that to achieve true wisdom, a man must learn to sit cross-legged. Wise men have invented that manner of sitting.'

'I am far from wisdom, Aga.'

'You are far, truly, but you seek it. You are very young. When you grow somewhat older, you may learn something. You are on the right road.'

'And are you wise that you can tell me my road is the right one?'

'I am not wise, but there have been other wise men before me.'

'Aga, if you really want to offer me something, tell them to make me linden tea. But without honey, and tell them not to strain it.'

'There, that is wisdom again. Coffee sharpens the mind and does not let a man sleep. What do you need a sharp mind for?'

Thus we chattered on, the two of us, the Aga and I, idly, and without thinking much, and we felt that we were both enjoying each other's presence, and tried not to remain alone. A talk that sometimes had no sense, sometimes perhaps had much sense, but the words were spoken just so, by the way. Syuleiman Aga led the talk, always mockingly serious, always half-smiling.

Strange, indeed, how my new covering as Abdullah the slave helped me to get in touch with people. Before, such as I had been, I would even have expected to have a chair brought me on which to seat myself. Ten men would have circled around me, and I would have been puffed up with pride, and foolish.

At one time Syuleiman Aga said :

'Tomorrow I shall ask you to go up to a dairy and say a few words from me to a shepherd. A *Kehaya*. Manol *Kehaya*. You will tell him, "Syuleiman Aga cannot bar the road to Allah."'

'Why do you choose me, Aga?'

'Only you of the newcomers speak Bulgarian. And I do not want to send one of my men—the time of parting has come, and now every man must be on one side or on the other.'

'And I am in the middle—is that it?'

'You are not anywhere yet.'

'Listen now, and let me tell you why you are sending me. To tell Karaibrahim. So that he will know that you are drawing aside.'

'Why do you give utterance to what we both think?'

'So that it will be clear.'

'What is clear? Even the Son of your God, Jesus Christ, spoke in parables. There you are, such are the men of the West. Everything must be clear. Is life clear? Or death?'

And the Aga began to talk again. I drank the fragrant linden tea, straining it through my lips and my tongue, as if it were the most expensive of wines, and taking care to leave the leaves in my mouth. Finally I threw the last sips through the window. The drops fell first, then slowly a leaf whirled after them—and the drops and the leaf were black in the moonlight, but in the sunlight they would have been pale-green.

'I may forget to tell Karaibrahim.'

'You will tell him.'

Yes, I would tell him. Could I set out through the forests without his knowing? I was actually a prisoner, and only the attention and the mind of the man opposite me made me forget it.

'That is true. But why don't you go and tell him? Why does a wise man need all this beating about the bush, all this quibbling?'

'Why? The moon is shining and I am in a good mood. That is why I will tell you. Because Karaibrahim is not like you and me. Because he thinks that he can set the world to rights. He and the others like him. He is like a horse in blinkers, he knows the alphabet to the third letter. He does not see the trend of things. He does not know that here we are in the Rhodopes, not in Anadolia.'

'Listen, Aga. Let us talk awhile in the moonlight. You condemn Karaibrahim because he wants to set the world to rights. Yet have you not devoted your whole life to setting one valley to rights? Why do you not leave the profligates to their debauchery, the robbers to their robbery and the rivers to carry away their bridges? Is not that Allah's business?'

The Aga rose, came down from the *kyoshk* and began to walk up and down the covered verandas on which gaily coloured rugs were spread. His steps could not be heard, only the boards creaked slightly.

'Put the light out,' he said. 'Too many insects fly in. Now you listen. What can be set to rights must be set to rights. The shepherd grazes his flock, the ploughman ploughs his field, the Aga looks after his Beydom. This valley was given to me, I set it to rights. As much as I could. And I must tell you—I did set it to rights.'

'This valley is in a mountain and the mountain is in an Empire. And the day has come when the Empire has remembered the valley. From your manner of speaking, you think like a king.'

'And why should I not be a king, even only of a valley?'

'Because you are the emissary of the Empire. Because, if you were the king of these people, you would have been chosen by them, and you would have met Karaibrahim up there on the pass, musket in hand, and would have turned him back. It is so, Syuleiman Aga, and forgive me for the bitter words.'

'A simple man said that to me—he said it to me when Karaibrahim came. He said it rather differently, but the sense was the same.'

I dared not confess to him that I had heard Delyo's words, although I remembered them only now.

'You told me that I was not anywhere. Now you are not anywhere, either. What message are you sending the Bulgarians? That you are abandoning them. It is so. It would not be so if you were one of them. There was order here, Aga, but it was your order.'

'The people heard and obeyed, they were satisfied.'

I was silent. I knew how satisfied they had been. Abdullah the slave could know that, but it was not given to Syuleiman Aga to know it.

'And now the two of us, you and I, will stand aside, Syuleiman Aga, and we shall watch how others slay and hang.'

'I do not mind about the hanged and the slain,' Syuleiman Aga said, dully. 'Let them die. What fine men have died! What fine men died in the past! Why should not these die? I, too, will die. I mind about the order. What is to happen should happen by the law.'

'It does happen by the law, Syuleiman Aga, but not by yours and not by mine. You told me yourself what happens in the Sultan's Empire.'

'I know,' Syuleiman Aga said sharply, and stopped, facing me in the middle of the veranda. The creaking of the boards ceased. The arc of a niche curved at his back, and the gleam of weapons came from it. I regretted my words, and thought that I had forgotten myself. He spoke like a king, and I, the fool, like a jester to whom everything is allowed. It was as if I had drunk brandy, and not linden tea.

'I know!' Syuleiman Aga, the man who hanged others and threw them into the abyss, continued sharply. 'But I know also that Karaibrahim will do no good. You are right that I, too, am nowhere. And the worst is that it will turn out that I have always been nowhere. I am old, I am tired, and I will soon be going. If I were younger—I do not know what I would do. But hear me, you, Venetian with a turban on your head. You said much to me, I will say only one thing to you. The time of parting has come—one will go to the left, the other to the right. No one will remain in the middle or nowhere. And remember—we, two, you and I, will go to one side. Either to the left, or to the right. Or to Allah.'

And turning, he went heavily down the stairs. And from the bottom of the stairs he repeated :

'To the left, or to the right. Or to Allah.'

Every morning I fenced with Karaibrahim. I was teaching him to fight with straight weapons, particularly with rapiers.

I do not remember when I first handled a rapier. Once, years ago, I had devoted all my time to it. It gave me security—I probably needed to lean on something. I went to receptions and ceremonies, I rode to the royal hunt and openly met the looks of the impudent courtiers. 'You may swagger as much as you like, if you dare, come to the lawn behind the Abbaye St Germain, or the Pré aux Clercs, or around the Luxembourg Palace.' Some came. I killed seven. And then they stopped coming. And that was not easy, because it was the day of the rapier. Men fought for the slightest thing, although duelling was forbidden. Or just because of that. When I come to think of it, I have killed people for nothing. Out of vanity. If I knew anything well, it was how to use a rapier. Many of those unfortunate courtiers who hurled themselves against the Janissaries at Candia, knew how to fight with rapiers and that gave them confidence and pride. They thought of the fighting with the Turks as they thought of a duel. God rest their souls.

Karaibrahim had learnt all his life to fight with a sword. It must be admitted that the trained Janissaries—for at that time the untrained ones were three times more numerous—could cut men down amazingly well. Karaibrahim used to say that each pupil of the Janissaries had at one blow to cut through ten layers of cloth wound around iron wire, and the wire together with the cloth. Anyone who cannot picture to himself what such a thing means, had better try it. I have seen a man cut in two down to the waist at one blow. The rapier is not good against such slaughter. But against a good rapier, the *yataghan* cannot help, either.

Karaibrahim was doing well. He was nimble, lean and light, he had iron legs and broad lungs. However, his hand often wanted to slay of itself. In spite of this, I had recently begun to be glad that we exercised—I had to make efforts to overcome him. I was certain that in mortal combat, with bare rapiers, he would be a still more dangerous enemy, because there was in him a will, a fury, and a scorn of death.

When we were putting guards on our points that morning—he fought with a wonderful rapier with the mark of Andrea Ferrara,

I remembered its former owner—I told him about Syuleiman Aga's errand.

Karaibrahim took up his position.

'So the old man has bowed to it,' he said, and attacked. 'I knew he would.'

I was irritated by the confidence and lightness with which he spoke, and with a lower quarte I pressed my point to his throat.

He, too, was irritated—I took care not to anger him. He half-closed his eyes, one of them almost entirely.

'Come back earlier tomorrow, you will show me that position.'

'What will you do now?' I asked, with a pretence of carelessness, as I parried his blows.

'The Grand Vizier is before Candia, waiting,' Karaibrahim said, dryly, and then only the rattle of steel was heard.

We set out for Manol's dairy in the afternoon. One of Syuleiman Aga's men, mounted on a donkey, led me. He looked negligently at my horse, and sought out paths which made me dismount, while his legs swayed on his donkey.

I soon began to think that the cursed fellow was leading me around in various directions, so that I should not find out where we were going. I wanted to tell him that he need not tire himself so much, as I was immediately lost in those spruce-covered ridges and hollows, as like each other as two peas, but I held my tongue—at first I tried to ask him something, but he did not even open his mouth.

We rode almost incessantly through spruce forests. Within the forest, the branches of the spruces began to grow high above the earth, at two, three and even five men's height, so that one went through it as if was a church, on a carpet of dry needles, amid straight branches, under a green vault. But at the northern edges of the forest, on the side of the meadows the branches dropped down to the very earth, bending to the height of the grass, mingling with the flowers, so that the trees stood like a dark-green wall, and neither man nor beast could creep through them.

There was almost no path. And if there were one somewhere in the forest, in the meadows the sun had dried it and effaced it, so that if you did not know where to find it, you would look long for a place where it began again, under the branches of the trees.

The sun never entered the forest. One saw neither the sky nor space. There must have been broad meadows around, because the sound of bells from the flocks reached us, but I saw no flock. The bells rang so sweetly that one seemed to be breathing an intoxicating fragrance. At close range, individual bells could be distinguished, and it was simply wonderful how such an ordinary thing as a bell can sing so differently—like a viola, a flute, or a clavecin. But the big round bells called *hlopki* rang like a company's drums. The bells of the distant flocks blended in a quiet, tormentingly beautiful song, which died away, and then was heard once more. Sometimes the sound of a brook drowned it.

At last we emerged from the forest, and the upper mountain pastures spread before us. The grass grew high, and wet not only the hooves of the horse, but the soles of my boots in the stirrups. And my guide on his donkey was dark to his knees with the damp.

The sun was setting. And again, as on the day on which we had stood at the top of the pass and had seen the valley at our feet, again everything in the mountains was calm and immovable. And quite different. I was inside the mountains.

Summits near me, bathed by the rain. Dark forests, full of dignity and mystery, along flower-covered meadows. The voices of birds, falling asleep. A blue sky, washed clean. An anchored cloud which did not change its shape, lit by the low sun.

We made our way over the meadows, wet with rain, it smelt of damp grass, of hay freshly mown. When the horse trod on an unfamiliar herb, another wild and fresh scent was wafted around us.

The sloping meadows looked pale-green from a distance, but when we drew near, we saw that they were all yellow from the yellow yarrow, with violet islands amid them. And when we rode into them, the violet islands proved to be thistles standing around above the yarrow, and buzzing with clouds of bees. No wonder that my guide's donkey kept stretching his head out to them.

And the crickets were chirping, or rather they were not chirping, but shrilling, so loudly that no separate voice could be heard. The chirping seemed to rise over the meadows with the scent of the flowers.

Some tiny flies kept circling around my head. I waved my hand as I sat on my saddle. A dainty insect lay in my palm, fresh and damp, as if it, too, had been bathed by the rain, with a sparkling little brown body, and transparent, sticky little wings. Two long slender hairs at its back made it still lighter and more delicate. The mere wave of my hand had killed it.

The rest of the winged insects chased each other before me in the air, rising upwards, touching each other and separating.

To one side of the path the grass grew so thick and tall—as if it were a field in which the wheat had shot up—that I could not restrain myself, jumped down from my horse and strode into it. The grass reached up to my breast. I felt myself looking around. I went forwards, I returned—no trace was left behind me. I was looking for a spot. If only I could go into that grass with a woman, cast down a garment and lie down on it with her. Alone in the world.

I mounted my horse and drove it forwards. The guide looked at me as if I were a madman.

'Have you lost something?' he could not refrain from asking at last.

This time it was I who made no answer.

The sun went down. A shadow fell over the meadows. The air grew cold and sharp. Here and there in the forest, which remained on our right, the whole time, puffs of mist appeared. Someone seemed to be lighting fires and the smoke from them rose up—so clearly did one see the hearths from which the mist rose. The trees on this side stood out clearly against the white background, but the ones at the back were lost in the mist. The forest looked as if it were painted on canvases stretched one behind the other.

My guide began to kick and strike the donkey mercilessly. I grew restless. I was expecting something.

When the voice was wafted to me, I realized what I had been waiting for. I had been waiting to hear the monastery bell.

Instead of it came the invisible voice. It was not clear whence it came, but it seemed to be borne all over the mountains. Someone was reciting a prayer.

'Our Father, Which art in Heaven . . .'

The words were different from those I had learnt, but still I could distinguish them. Suddenly I felt that I was desperate. And as the evening hour had moved me, I did not succeed in resigning myself and growing calm. Twice running the mountains had taken me back to the past—with the bell, and now with the prayer. I felt pursued, frightened and wronged.

My guide had stopped the donkey and was listening to the voice, which was calling on God—solemnly, long-drawn out and even desperately. The man was calling so that someone very distant might hear him, telling him something, as if he were in great trouble. And after every verse he stopped as if to draw breath.

When 'amen' rang out over the meadows and the summits, repeated by the echo, my guide turned his donkey. His face was frowning. It seemed to me that he was swearing under his breath.

'Is it over there?' I asked, because I thought that the voice was showing him the right direction.

'We are going back,' he answered gloomily.

And when he saw my amazement, he explained briefly :

'The time of the law is past.'

I must have looked quite dazed, because he grew irritated and at last began to talk :

'And how do you think you will get into the dairy where Manol is? There are half a hundred curs there. In the daytime, when you go near a flock or a dairy, you stand up on the nearest peak and shout to the shepherds. They stop the curs, because the law says they must. By day the mountains are open to everybody. But once the prayer has been said, the curs are set free, and God help the man they meet and do not know. For who goes about the mountains at night except a robber or an unclean man?'

I realized that we had come all the way in vain. If I had been wiser, I would have understood from my guide's excitement that there really was danger.

'And can't we quickly reach the summit from which the voice was heard?' I asked.

'There's a good hour's ride to it,' said the guide.

He drove his donkey on and explained further.

'I made a mistake, because today they read the prayer earlier. They're going to roast a lamb on a spit again. There's an old man, Kralyo is his name, who learnt to read in his youth, and, who knows where he got hold of a fat book, the Bible. Every evening, when the law comes to an end, he reads a few verses. He is eighty years old, and he has barely read half of it. And he always says that God won't take his soul until he has read the whole book.'

And so saying, he fell silent, stopped the donkey and began to cross himself. From the forest before us came the barking of dogs. And to the left of us, where the forest now lay, a huge red moon rose.

'Why have you stopped?' I asked, already irritated by these prayers, these comings and goings and fears.

'They're in front of us,' the man said quietly. 'They're chasing a stag.'

I have been to hundreds of hunts with dogs, I myself had hounds that were known far and wide, and although the dogs here are ordinary sheepdogs, I could tell by their bark that they really were after game.

'So much the better, we'll get through,' I said.

The man raised his hand tiredly and pointed forwards.

'Do you hear? A second pack is coming. It will head off the stag. Once they taste blood, we're done for.'

We stayed on the meadow and listened to the barking of the dogs. It was light where we were, out in the open, but the forest stood back, in impenetrable gloom. Over there, in the shadow, the barking of the two packs met and became an eddy of roars, growls and squeals. The stag was defending himself. Then it grew quiet.

'It's all over,' whispered my guide.

How long we stayed there I do not know. But suddenly a long mournful howl rose behind us. A dog was squatting on a bare hillock howling at the moon.

'They've got wind of us!' cried the trembling man, and jumped down from the donkey. 'He's howling at a man. The moon has maddened them.'

From the forest there came an answering bark. Whether it really was another dog, or it only seemed so to me, I do not know, but shivers went up my spine.

After jumping down from the donkey, my guide curled up at its feet, and covered his head with his cape.

I sat on my horse, and the horse was trembling all over. Who passed on his fear to whom—whether the animal to me, or I to the animal, I don't know, but I was trembling with horror. I took my two pistols out of their holsters, thankful that they were flintlocks and did not have to be fired with a fuse, for I could certainly not have struck a spark at that moment.

The barking and howling died away. I waited.

Then, along the crest of the ridge, against the evening sky that was still light, on the side of the moon, the shadows of the dogs began to appear. They did not bark, only their shadows were visible. They stood out for a moment, and were lost on the dark hillside, which sloped towards me. Then I saw them gliding down. In the half-light it seemed to me that a big animal of some kind, as big as a donkey or a calf, was leading them.

I grasped the reins of my horse, so that it would not take fright at the shot, and fired into the sky. Instead of the echo of the shot, a human cry reached my ears.

'Down! Do-o-own!'

My guide jumped to his feet, and waving his arms like a madman, began to shout piercingly and lamentably:

'Hey! You people! They've devoured us!'

'Do-o-own! Do-o-own!'

Could they see that I was on horseback? Were they shouting to me to get down? Where were they—in the sky?

The dogs came on, we could hear them breathing. The huge dog which led them threw itself down on its breast a few feet away from me. The other dogs behind it, when they reached the same distance, cast themselves heavily down on the ground, too, as if there were a precipice before them. And whenever a dog crept forwards, a brief growl from the leader brought it back.

On the height opposite the moon, where I had seen the dogs coming down, three human shadows appeared. People! May you be blessed! Had I seen my brother, I could not have been more overjoyed. My breast was filled with joy and a reverent fear, just as Christ's disciples were joyful and fearful when they saw their Teacher walking over the waves, and the storm abating before Him.

My guide, who had fallen on his face again, as if he had seen a vision of angels, uncovered his head in fear and trembling and looked up. I could not restrain myself and began to laugh with sheer relief.

The men descended from the sky and were lost on the dark slope, then they came up to us, pushing the dogs aside with their feet. But the dogs did not rise, they only crawled aside. When the three men reached the huge dog, it rose to its feet and took its stand beside them.

'Who are you? Where are you going?' one of them asked.

The moon shone at their backs, so that I could not see their faces. Two of them were taller and broader, and were wearing heavy capes with high hoods. The third, between them, was shorter, and only had his red cloak on, and was bareheaded. It was he who spoke.

'I am looking for Manol *Kehaya*,' I said.

I loved them all three, and wanted to speak to them with warmth and gratitude. Ever afterwards, whenever I met one of them or heard them spoken of, I felt the same warmth within me. And these three were Old Galoushko's sons, the brothers Goran and Sherko, and Manol's son, Momchil.

'What do you want? Where have you come from?' Momchil asked again.

Only now did my guide rise to his feet and answer:

'Syuleiman Aga has sent us. I am one of his men.'

'That is so, I know him,' boomed Sherko, next to whom the dog was standing.

'As soon as you get back, light a candle to the Holy Mother,' Goran said, and the men of the forest said of his voice, that when he entered the hut and said 'Good evening,' the pine torch always went out.

'Be silent,' his brother said quietly. 'One of them wears a turban.'

I had forgotten my turban.

'You really are one of Syuleiman Aga's men, and I know you,' Momchil said, mistrustfully. 'But what of the other?'

I was not angered by his mistrust. The Turks were in their village.

'Syuleiman Aga sent me to give Manol *Kehaya* a message. Do you know him?'

'I am his son. What have you to say to him? Is it important?'

'Whether it be important or not, I do not know, but whatever it is, I will give the message to Manol *Kehaya*.'

'The man is right. Let us take him to the dairy. Brother Manol said that he would return tomorrow,' one of the two, Sherko or Goran, spoke up.

'We had better take him at once,' Momchil said quickly.

'Momchil, your father gave orders that we were to stay up at the dairy.'

'Did he know that a message would come? He didn't.'

And seeing that the two brothers hesitated, he added quietly:

'Goran, Sherko, I have not seen Elitsa yet.'

'All right then, come.'

'Let us pass by the dairy, so that I can take what I have brought for her. So that I do not go empty-handed,' Momchil begged.

We set out across the meadows, we passed by the dairy, where I left my guide with my horse. We set out on foot, and I could not restrain my fear when the huge spotted dog—black and white—ran beside me.

I examined my companions as much as I could. The first thing that struck one about Momchil was the white, bared neck, broad and strong, as broad as his face, with two straight, strong veins at the side. I have seen drawings of Alexander the Great with such a neck. Any head would look small on such a neck. After we set out for the water-mill, his voice was little heard, yet it was soft and quiet.

Few voices would have sounded manly beside those of the brothers Goran and Sherko. All I saw of them that night were two shocks of tousled hair and beards, and two big shining eyes each.

It suddenly grew dark in the forest. The leaves and the earth were black, and melted into the night, and the bare trunks of the spruces caught the light, who knows whence, and turned quite white. And as no knots, or moss, or dry twigs were to be seen on them, they rose in the darkness like white wax candles, like polished marble columns.

We walked along in the darkness and were silent. I realized that my companions were not particularly pleased to be walking through the forest at night. Sherko cut some pine wood from a thick root with his knife, we lit it, and began to talk.

I was not afraid of the forest, I was not alone, I was enjoying my companions. The warmth of the meeting amid the blood-stained dogs was still in me. The path was not steep, it was soft and covered with spruce needles, and one could also walk straight through the forest between the huge trunks. There were no bushes or grass, our footsteps were barely audible, our voices were quiet and calm.

They asked me what I was and whence I had come. I told them about Paris. They began to question me, asking what people there were like, how they were dressed, and what they ate. Then Goran shyly asked me about the women. I praised them—for I remembered them thus at that time.

'Our lasses here are beautiful, too,' said Momchil.

The two brothers laughed.

Then we talked about the armies, about Candia, the sea and the pirates. I spoke modestly, I do not remember often saying 'I' and it was not clear whether in that distant land I had been a soldier or a prince. And these shepherds may have thought that French shepherds looked like me. Why not?

Then at last Momchil thought of it and asked me. I had forgotten about it, or I would not have unloosed my tongue.

'You praise the Franks and their land. Why do you wear a turban on your head?'

I answered him, I do not remember how or what. We did not speak again.

My companions quickened their steps, so that I barely kept up with them, and when we came out on the moonlit meadows, they picked ferns and stuck them in their waistbands. And mist crept over one meadow, so that Sherko stopped and crossed himself, and with two or three strokes cut a white cross on one of the trees. He probably thought he had seen a white *samodiva*[4] dancing. Other crosses were to be seen on other trunks. The dog crept noiselessly through the forest like a ghost—who knows what he was chasing.

Here and there mist rose, like smoke from hearths, and the moon bored white caves through it. It was with relief that I heard distant human voices.

At the edge of the forest Momchil stopped me.

'Wait here,' he said.

Again I remained alone, but down below people were talking, water was murmuring and a fire was to be seen.

Momchil returned quickly.

'The old men have gathered higher up. And my father was here a minute ago. Come!'

We set out across a meadow on which the grass was short, with poplars here and there, and birches, and with marble boulders scattered about. White trees and white boulders. Invisible water rumbled and roared, like a waterfall.

Momchil was hurrying, parting the bushes with his hands, so that we could go straight ahead, not speaking or shouting once.

I realized that he wanted to leave me and go to that Elitsa he had spoken of up on the plateau.

Suddenly he stopped and seized me by the arm. We heard a quiet voice.

Before us, on a small meadow, turned silver by the moon, stood a man, leaning against a white boulder. He was speaking. Then I distinguished a woman standing before him in the dappled shade of the birch, next to its slender white trunk, and listening to him.

The moon was shining straight down on the boulder and on the man's face, making him white and silvery, moulding him out of marble like the boulder at his back.

And on the woman's face the light fell through a net of leaves, so that it was barely distinguishable—veiled and soft like the white trunk of the birch behind her.

The man spoke quietly, and his words could not be heard distinctly, because water was falling somewhere in the forest.

A quiet breeze stirred the leaves of the birch, and the woman's face swayed. The man still stood there motionless.

The woman emerged from the shadow in which she had been hidden, so that the moon shone down on her, too, white and slender like a *samodiva*. She stepped forward and leant her head on the man's shoulder. He raised his hand and placed it on her hair.

A moan, wrenched from deep down between clenched teeth, woke me as from sleep. Beside me Momchil had hidden his face in his hands, and his hands were quite, quite white.

Then I recognized the man of stone. He was the shepherd with the skull in his hands. Momchil's father—Manol *Kehaya*. And I realized that the birch-maiden was Elitsa.

Then Manol came in front of the mill and I told him Syuleiman Aga's words.

'I cannot bar the road to Allah.'

Even as he listened to me, he did not turn his face towards me, but stood a little aside. And he went at once, without replying to me. He did not ask me how I had come, how I would return, or where I would spend the night.

I was left before the mill, full of scorn for myself. I had felt that I involuntarily tried to speak more sweetly, and to fawn on him, I tried to see approval on his face. Yet he seemed not to notice me.

A hard, grim man, perhaps cruel, I thought. Even the features of his face were immovable, as if they were not lit by an inner light, and his movements seemed to me slow and indolent. It did not only seem to me, it was so. Anger was not blinding me. Yet I was angry with him, he irritated me and destroyed my calm and resignation—after a time the same anger turned into other bad feelings. I wanted to stir him and make him hurry.

'And that man has just returned from a love meeting,' I thought. 'Let us hope that she will at least warm his blood.'

And I schemed how I might insult him.

Fourth Excerpt

'Will you give, will you give, Balkandji Yovo,
Beautiful Yana to the Turkish faith?'
'My head I'll give, Voivoda bold,
But I'll not give Yana to the Turkish faith.'

And that same evening, when the notables had gathered at Old Galoushko's water-mill, the man who had been sent to see what was happening in Smolen, returned. And he brought one of the Smolen men—a priest. When he had eaten and drunk, the priest related the following :

'With fire and sword the Turks succeeded and converted to Islam the population of the villages of Viévo, Smolen, Ouporovo, Byala Reka, Podviss, Vitlovo and a small part of the villages of Ezerovo and Belovidovo.

'But the villages of Raikovo, Oustovo, Lower and Upper Gouénovo, Koutlovo, Petkovo, Ochinevo, Levochevo, Peshtera and Ossikovo offered great resistance to the oppressors, and preserved their faith.

'When the terrible conversion to Islam of the Bulgarians around Smolen took place by force, the Turks did great mischiefs. Some of the peasants they converted to Islam, others they slew and others again they drove into the forests. The Turks burnt the Church of the Holy Apostles Peter and Paul, the Metropolitan's House and the theological school. They destroyed all the books, and all that was of value they plundered.

'The Turks wanted to capture Bishop Vissarion, but he, together with many Bulgarians, managed to flee one night, and settled in Raikovo. There many Bulgarians from the surrounding villages also found refuge.

'The people, seeing that their spiritual leader, Bishop Vissarion of Smolen, was among them, took courage, girded themselves for a new struggle against the Turks, and stubbornly defended their faith. Thus he preserved the village of Raikovo and the villages around it from conversion to Islam.

'And in Smolen itself, and in its region, the Turks slew many men, women and children, who would not consent to accept the Mohammedan faith. Many widows with orphans, who were unable to flee to Raikovo, were forced to spend the night in the forests, exhausted with hunger and lack of sleep. The Turkish hordes caught up with them and subjected them to the most foul deeds, which only a Turk can do. These foul deeds I cannot describe—for my jaws grow stiff.

'However, the Turks found a convenient time to destroy Bishop Vissarion, so that there would be none to sustain the faith of the Bulgarians, for they were despondent at the evil that had befallen them. No aid came for them from anywhere else, and only Bishop Vissarion fortified them in faith and hope that this evil would pass and that good days would come again.

'And early one morning Vissarion of Smolen had set out accompanied by ten men of his bodyguard, all mounted and armed, from Lower Ezerovo to Upper Ezerovo. But unexpectedly, between the house on Revacha and the watermill on the Souro, in the valley, a big armed band of Turks and other rabble appeared. After a great and bloody battle they captured the Bishop alive, and the men of his bodyguard. The Turks took their arms, bound their hands behind them and quickly led them off to Smolen, lest a Christian band should catch up with them, to set their prisoners free, and wreak sore vengeance on them.

'In Smolen, on the orders of Abdi Bey, first of all they tried gently and with kindness to persuade Bishop Vissarion to purchase his life by accepting the Mohammedan faith, for they thought that if he consented to this, the other Bulgarian Christians would very quickly and uncomplainingly follow him. But the bishop refused to accept Islam.

'Then the Turks undressed him, left him quite naked and began to pinch him on the body with specially prepared pincers, with which they tore pieces of the living flesh from his body. Bishop Vissarion suffered these infernal pains without taking fright and without asking for mercy. Blood flowed from the body of this martyr. After this, they beat his body most mercilessly with iron sticks, until the bishop fainted. After they had restored him to consciousness, the Turks stabbed him with their knives and cut pieces off his body, put a heated trivet on his head and mocked him. But this was not enough for them. They abused him before everyone and took him naked around the village to make a show of him.

The Bishop suffered this mockery, too, with meekness. At last one of the enraged Turks emerged from the crowd, and with a sharp knife pierced Bishop Vissarion's breast. He fell to the ground and began to pray. The infuriated Turks thought that he was saying something offensive about them, that is why they cast themselves maliciously upon him with stones, mutilating him and crushing his body flat. And the Turks ordered the Bishop's bodyguards to dig a grave in a garden near the place where the young folk dance on holidays in Smolen, and there they buried the body of Bishop Vissarion of Smolen.'[5]

And when the priest had finished his narrative, he drank wine and began to weep. And I remembered of Bishop Vissarion that he had loved to eat and drink, and had a big beard and a big paunch. But he had redeemed his gluttony with his martyr's death. And I prayed the Lord to forgive me for thinking evil of him.

Then Manol shook the priest and asked him :

'Which villages have remained Bulgarian?'

And through his tears the priest repeated their names.

And Manol said :

'Ten villages. Ten, and we three—thirteen. Neither few, nor many.'

Then he said :

'Rhodopa is crucified. Her right hand is nailed down by Mehmed Pasha, her left hand is nailed down by Abdi Bey. At her feet on the Aegean coast, the Sultan's servants are hammering at bridges to that the Sultan's retinue may pass. Her hair in Philibé is glued to the pillar of the cursèd Greek Bishop Gavriil. We must not expect aid from anywhere. We can only hold out, as others have held out, or die.'

I said to him :

'Or flee to Petglassets.'

But he said to me :

'We cannot and we must not all flee. Karaibrahim will then come to the valley. We shall defend ourselves here. Just as the stag turns at bay and meets the dogs and the huntsmen with his antlers, so that the does with their fawns can escape, so we, too, shall bend our brows against Karaibrahim. Let us start.'

And we went to the notables.

Then the foremost men of the three villages Prossoina, Zagrad and Podviss gathered on the meadow above Old Galoushko's water-mill.

And they sat down at a long table, with white cloths spread on the meadow. They sat on peeled spruce trunks, thirty men on the one side and thirty on the other. At one end sat Old Galoushko with his rebeck on his knees, at the other—Granny Srebra. On Old Galoushko's right hand sat Manol—on his left—Old Kralyo. Next to Manol sat the Abbot of the Monastery of St Elijah, next to him the priest of Prossoina.

God forgive me for forgetting the names of Thy holy martyrs. But Thou rememberest them. Their grandsons also remember them, whoever left a grandson. And the mountain remembers them, too. For even their gravestones were not left standing, so that a man might read their names.

Freshly cut spruce twigs were scattered over the white cloths, so that there was a scent of resin. And on the twigs there were goatskins of wine and milk, lumps of cheese and bread. And from the forest came the smell of roast lamb, and boiled ram. A wind was about to spring up, but for the moment only the spring in the mill pond roared, and hurled iteslf tirelessly upwards.

The moon shone over the meadow. The forest was black, so was the meadow, for the flowers had furled their petals. Only the white milfoil shone, as if glow-worms had perched on each floweret and did not blink.

The faces and the hands of the people around the table glowed, too. No flames danced in a fire, no pine torch was burning, but each man glowed himself, like a spruce log on a hearth. Yet a spruce log does not smoke like pine wood, it does not melt like a candle, but glows all night long with a warm bright light, like a star, fallen from the sky.

They were fine men. What thick beards they had, what sinewy hands, what strong shoulders, what hairy chests! Not one was young, and not one ate a master's bread. And not one had stolen and killed, except the sheep of his neighbour, but that is a joke, and whatsoever anyone had, he had won it with the work of his hands, and the labour of his sons. Very handsome were my brothers in the moonlight, with stern faces and firm lips. And no one spoke, and not one put a hand out to the food, for they were waiting for Old Galoushko to begin singing.

The strings twanged softly and suddenly Old Galoushko began to sing :

'Will you give, will you give, Balkandji Yovo,
Beautiful Yana to the Turkish faith?'

And he stopped. They often sing like that in the Rhodopes— they stop, sometimes they take a morsel, sometimes they exchange a word, sometimes they drink wine. And Old Galoushko's song was like weeping, like a lament and an old, long-drawn-out church song.

When I raised my voice in an empty church, it seemed to me that I was singing a Rhodope song.

And Old Galoushko repeated:

> 'Will you give, will you give, Balkandji Yovo,
> Beautiful Yana to the Turkish faith?'

He asked the notables that were gathered together, and fell silent. But his question floated over the table.

Clouds flew across the moon, and it alternately showed itself and hid itself anew. And the faces of the men glowed, or sank into the shadow. Sixty men were gathered here, but each one sat alone, and asked himself. Not one looked at another.

And stillness lay over the meadow. The forest began to whisper, and a wind rose. The spring rumbled; there was a smell of resin and roast meat. And each one knew the answer. For no other answer could be given.

> 'My head I'll give, Voivoda bold,
> But I'll not give Yana to the Turkish faith.'

The moon had completely vanished. The forest was rustling, the young men sat with bated breath around its trunks. There was a smell of hay and snow. And then from a distance the sound of the bell at the Monastery of St Elijah reached us. It was midnight.

And Old Kralyo said:

'Lord God, how have we sinned that Thou hast turned Thy face from us? What have we asked of Thee? Was it wealth, power, or evil for our neighbours? We have only desired peace, to eat the bread earned by our hands.'

And Old Galoushko sang.

> 'So they chopped off both his arms,
> And asked him again and again:
> 'Will you give, will you give, Balkandji Yovo,
> Beautiful Yana to the Turkish faith?'

It was dark. The wind blew like a fire that blazes up a chimney, or casts itself upon a pile of dry thorns. But it was still soft, and the voice of the spring was heard above it.

And when the Priest of Prossoina spoke quietly, everyone heard him:

'Let us ransom ourselves. Let us sell our flocks, our *chans*, our houses. Let us collect strings of gold coins and bags of silver, so that we may pile them before the Aga. Let us hope that he will look at them, and turn his eyes from us. Better to lie naked in our graves, but that a cross may guard us.'

And Old Galoushko sang :

> 'My head I'll give, Voivoda bold,
> But I'll not give Yana to the Turkish faith.'

The young men, whom we did not see, lighted the fires, and there was a smell of resin and incense. And it grew lighter, but with a treacherous, dancing light.

And Stan Stan said :

'They have come for our souls, not for our wealth. And it is known from Holy Writ that a soul is without price. And a ransom for a soul is so great, that each one should refuse to ransom even his brother. How then can we ransom three villages?'

And Old Galoushko sang :

> 'So off they chopped both his feet,
> And asked him again and again :
> Will you give, will you give, Balkandji Yovo,
> Beautiful Yana to the Turkish faith?'

Then we saw blue, but powerless flashes of lightning, for no thunder was heard. The wind came up like pouring rain and began to roar through the forest. The roar of the fountain fought with it, and one heard first the waterfall, then the wind, and both with equally strong voices. A flock of birds, roused from their sleep, flew in alarm over the mountains.

And Granny Srebra cried :

'Let us flee. Even a wolf, when he falls into a trap, will gnaw its paw through. Let us leave houses and fields and hide in the depths of the forest. We shall eat roots and grasses until the storm passes. The torrent rushes on, the sand is left. We'll build ourselves new houses, and gather new flocks, but one's faith is never given back.'

And Old Galoushko sang with all his might, to be heard above the wind :

> 'My head I'll give, Voivoda bold,
> But I'll not give Yana to the Turkish faith.'

The wind made the fires burn brighter, but every flash of lightning put them out. The men's faces grew first red, then blue. The scent of that flower which only blossoms in rain and storm was borne to us. And from a distance the piteous long-drawn-out howl

of the dogs that had been cast into the Black Hole was heard, as
they remembered how they had run against the wind.

And Nikola Sargoun spoke up, and his words were barely to be
heard :

'If all three villages flee, there will be three new villages in the
forests. And as the Turks have come here, so will they go there,
too. If some flee, and others remain, whosoever is left will give . . .'

And Old Galoushko's unrelenting lament interrupted his voice :

> 'So then they put out both his eyes,
> Nor did they ask him again and again.
> They simply seized fair Yana.
> They placed her on a steed so fleet.
> Fair Yana softly to Yovo spoke . . .'

The song was coming to an end, and there was neither an answer
nor help from anywhere. Yet the storm was only just beginning.
And the first roll of thunder was heard, and for the first time the
heavens spoke. But now after the thunder, the wind dropped, and
again the voice of the eternal water was heard.

And then Manoush Sekoul cried in the stillness :

'Let us stand for our faith. Let us stand like the forest, tree next
to tree. And the notables must stand like the trees at its edge, which
drop their branches to the ground. Not one must be cut down, not
one must bow down, for once the storm gets among the spruces, it
will tear up the whole forest. And the whole crest crumbles if one
crag is broken.'

And Old Galoushko, barely spoke the words, but all heard him
for it was still quiet :

> 'Farewell, forgive me, brother Yovan !'

And the grinding of teeth was heard. And Vrazhou *Kehaya*
said :

'Let us stand like a forest . . . No storm will cast us down. But a
forest is burnt by fire, and swept away by a torrent, too, and
lightning can turn it to ashes. If we preserve ourselves from the
storm, who will preserve us from the fire, the torrent and the
lightning?'

Then the heavens were opened, and the rain came pouring down,
and the flashes of lightning followed each other, and thunder echoed
over the mountains. And the forest roared so that it seemed to take
up every roll of thunder from the sky, and roll it over the mountains.
And, at each flash of lightning, one saw how the silver fountain in
the spring leapt up like a ghost with a body of water, which tries at

every moment to leap up to the sky, but again falls heavily to the earth. And its voice was no longer heard.

The fires went out. And in the darkness, the thunder and the roar of the forest, the lament of Old Galoushko was heard, but the twang of his wet rebeck was not heard :

> 'Farewell, forgive me, Yana fair !
> No arms have I to put around you,
> Nor feet to walk on to see you off,
> No eyes have I to look upon you !'

And the song came to an end, and the storm began. The rain splashed like a flood, the storm bent the trees to the meadow. And they tossed and turned and straightened again. But not one of the notables rose to his feet. In the darkness, the young folk, who were on guard around the meadow, wrapped their fathers and grand-fathers in shepherds' capes of felt. In the light of the flashes Goran was seen carrying Granny Srebra back to the water-mill.

Then Momchil bent over Manol and called to him.

'The ram is ready.'

And they brought the boiled ram, and Old Kralyo drew out the shoulder blade, peeled the meat from it and looked at the bone. That is how the shepherds of this region predicted the future : by a ram's shoulder-blade.

The shoulder-blade, still warm, was passed from hand to hand down the table, and each one wiped the water from his face with his hand, and waited for a flash of lightning to see the cross. Sixty times did the sky light up, before the shoulder-blade returned to Old Kralyo's hands. And they all saw that there was a cross drawn on the ram's shoulder-blade. I, too, saw it, although I did not believe.

And when he touched the shoulder-blade once more, Old Kralyo cried :

'Do not rise.'

But no one was rising.

And he said :

'We have heard a song, and seen the shoulder-blade, and told each other our grief. But we must not part without deciding what to do. So let us break up the roast meat on the twigs, and let us think.'

And how much Old Galoushko had sung, and what the time was no one knew. It seemed that a year had passed. Yet it was night.

Then Manol rose and cried :

'Follow me, that I may lead you to shelter. The old men had better return to the mill.'

And no one was surprised, although no one knew of any dry place or cave near by, yet if it had been light, they would have looked at each other, for they all believed that Manol knew from his foster-father of treasures and hidden places in the mountains.

That is why they followed him through the forest, although there was still thunder in the air. But the lightning showed the crosses cut in the spruces, so that their fear was somewhat lessened. And as the pine torches did not burn, and they might have set fire to the forests, each man unwound his waistband, so that the one after him could take hold of its end. And we went thus through the dark for an hour or more. And we went ever upwards.

And when we reached rocks, which we all knew, so that we trod on dry soil, Manol said:

'Light a pine torch.'

And, torch in hand, he divided the bushes, and revealed the entrance to a cave. And again he said:

'Enter, and fear not.'

And the first to enter with pine torches in their hands cried out, and came out again, backing away faster than when they had gone face forwards. I, too, entered.

And the cave was full of dead folk. But dead folk such as one had never seen—neither corpses nor skeletons. And their heads were neither skulls nor faces. They were everywhere in the cave—some lying, others sitting beside the rock. And some lay on their faces right at the entrance.

When we came to ourselves, we saw them in the light of the pine torches. The dead folk had dried up, and their skin was stuck to their bones, but no bare bones were to be seen. Only their white teeth were bare, for their lips had been drawn back, and their eyes had dried up. And their heads were more terrible than white skulls. Their garments hung about them in rags, and would probably have fallen to dust if we had touched them. But who dared to touch them?

Yellow, terrible and silent, the dry dead folk squatted before us. And they were all women. There were children, too, small dry skeletons, sitting and lying beside their mothers. And one of them —almost as small as a kitten, for its bones had been soft—was at its mother's bared breast. And in the lap of one woman there were two.

And Manol said:

'These dead folk have been here three hundred years.'

Yet they had not rotted, for the cave was dry and well ventilated, and the earth was only sand, or God knows why.

And Manol said further :

'They stayed here when the Turks conquered Elindenya. To-morrow, when it is light, you will look down and see your villages. They stayed here, waiting for their men folk, who were fighting the Turks, to return. They waited a day, they waited two days, they waited a week and more. No one came. From here they saw their villages, and the Turks in them. It would have taken them two hours to reach their homes. No one went down.'

And all were silent, but Old Kralyo said :

'Manol, Manol, you brought us here on purpose. But as we have come, let us sit down and talk.'

Yet what could you talk of, when the dead sat around you and were silent, looking at you with their hollow eyes, and their teeth shining in the light of the pine torches, like an open mussel with its mother-of-pearl in the shallow water? They were women, and we were men. And whoever had not been a man, became one that night.

And the council of the notables, fifty men, and fifty dead women and children, decided that we were to defend our faith as well as we could. In that cave, after the mummies were buried, food would be brought, and food would be taken to Petglassets also, and to other places in the forest. But there was not very much food.

And nothing else was decided, for none knew what was to happen. According to what the Turks did, we would respond.

Yet the hearts of all of us were so heavy, and the wind howled so outside, that when we went out of the cave, all began to sigh and moan, as if the bands of a barrel were being broken around their breasts.

And lo, outside the day had come, and the rain had stopped and the sky was turning blue. And the sun rose. But the mists were rising upwards and becoming clouds, and the three villages did, indeed, appear out of the mists, so that the wet slates of their roofs glittered. Then a rainbow appeared in the clouds.

And I thought then, and think now, that those dead folk must have stood in front of the cave and stared down at the slates that covered their homes. And the sun must have shone then, and their eyes, now dry, must have sparkled with tears, and their lips must have been soft and red, and hidden their teeth, and their breasts must have been full of milk, and their warm wombs full of unborn children. And yet they had not gone down. But Elindenya was full of people again.

And I remembered the Lord's words in Genesis, when, after the flood, the rainbow appeared : 'This is the token of the covenant which I make between me and you and every living creature that is with you for perpetual generations : I do set my bow in the cloud, and it shall be for a token of a covenant between me and the earth. And it shall come to pass, when I bring a cloud over the earth that the bow shall be seen in the cloud. And I will remember my covenant, which is between me and you and every living creature of all flesh; and the waters shall no more become a flood to destroy all flesh. And the bow shall be in the cloud.'

And there was a rainbow over Elindenya.

Fifth Excerpt

In the morning I saw Granny Srebra and Old Galoushko. I had gone out, and, as there was no one, I lay down in the clover in the sunshine. The bees were humming around me, it was warm and there was a smell of hay. I dozed off. The voices of two old people awoke me—one was a woman's, the other a man's. I rose and saw Granny Srebra and Old Galoushko.

Old Galoushko the White One . . . He was all white, but not from the flour of the grain which had not become ears, but from age. His years were not so numerous, he could have been Granny Srebra's son, but he was white all over—his long beard, his hair, his bushy eyebrows. He wore a white hempen shirt, held in at the waist —I was told later that many years ago the men in the mountains had worn white clothes. A strange, dreamy smile shone in his eyes and played on his lips.

And Granny Srebra . . .

We realized what a fine woman she had been only after she died—because of the emptiness which she left behind her. We were so used to seeing her trudging along in Momchilovo, helping and comforting everyone, that we thought—it has always been so, and will remain so. People said then : 'If we had known what it would be like without her, and what a fine person she was, we would have taken the best care of her and would have fallen on our knees before her every day.'

And when they saw her shade wandering around the Old Spruce, they were not afraid of her, for her shade was still bent and humble, and while she was still alive, the old woman's sole strength was her spirit.

Such as I saw her on that bright morning, such she remained to the moment of her death. And how could she have aged more?

She always went about bending to the earth, and when she straightened up, she would put her hands to her waist, and raise herself painfully slowly, as if there were a load of stones on her shoulders. A black kerchief, faded with age, was tied around her face, and because she was bent, the thin little braid of white hair would fall forwards. I shall not even try to tell of the kindness and gentleness that radiated from her, so that anyone who was angered or noisy would guiltily bow his head before her. She no longer had any teeth, and the wrinkles gathered around her sunken lips and the dark eyes, full of love. And although every wrinkle spoke of age, there was something childlike in her face.

She appeared to have melted and grown small. Only her busy hands with their knotty fingers had remained big and bony, and when I placed my hand next to hers, palm to palm, you saw that she had a much bigger reach. And one of her shoulders was higher than the other, perhaps because she always leant on a stick or, as she said, because of the heavy baskets she had carried in her youth.

From morning till night she was never idle. But whatever she did, there were three things that were closest to her heart : weaving and embroidery, flowers and herbs, and songs and stories.

When she spread one of her rugs on the ground, it was just as if she had spread out a meadow full of flowers. She herself span the wool, she herself dyed it, with various grasses, barks, leaves and roots. Her delight began with the colours. At times I have woken with a start in the middle of the night, to see her, her scant hair loose over her shoulders, in her white shift, bending over the loom like a ghost. A pine torch would be lit. 'What are you doing, Granny?' I would ask. 'I've thought of something, I'm matching colours,' she would answer. At the end, when her strength left her, she would only do the dyeing and the embroidery, and teach the others. There were piles of cloths with embroidery on them—they were called *zashivi*[8]—and they went from village to village, so that the women might learn how to ornament their costumes. She always let people have them, whenever she was asked for them, and she, too, received from somewhere these wonderful patterns on yellowed, rather dirty cloth.

Herbs were Granny Srebra's second love. For her the spirit of a good or an evil being was imprisoned in every herb, so that before she boiled or ground them, the old woman always talked to that spirit in caressing and moving words. She herself picked the herbs in the valley, but she also had helpers, herbalists, who sought herbs in the forests and mountains, and who afterwards took them around the villages. They all knew Granny Srebra. Each herbalist came about the time of a holiday, so that the old woman would expect them, and prepare to welcome them. 'Branimir from Perin will be coming. He likes hare . . .' But one day old Branimir would not arrive to eat his hare. First one, then another of the herbalists would not arrive on the holiday, having stopped somewhere to rest forever, leaning against his basket of herbs in a sheltered spot.

Granny Srebra kept her herbs hanging in bunches from the rafters, or in the painted chest beside her pallet. Whenever she lifted its lids, strange fragrances would be wafted from it. She used to put herbs and fruits among the garments, too, so that they would smell nice. And her whole room was so beautifully fragrant, with a faded and somewhat sad fragrance, that one began to breathe more deeply and more quietly.

Granny Srebra loved embroidery and herbs, but song was a very part of her. From the moment she rose, until she went to bed, the old woman sang. There was a time when her voice was borne over hill and dale, but in her old age she sang almost without a voice, as if she were singing to herself, as she went about, as she span, as she boiled her herbs. She had songs for every kind of work, but most of all she loved to sing songs about heroes. About old men who had lived long ago, leaving the tracks of their sandals over Rhodopa, hewn out like stone vessels in the rocks, so that rain water would be gathered in them, for the birds of the air to drink. Songs were borne about her like the fragrance of the herbs around her chest. Sometimes it seemed to me that they fluttered about her like birds, and perched on her shoulder, and when she lay down to sleep, they would rest at her head. We could get her to sing all her songs, only there was one which she sang but once a year, at the graveyard, under the Old Spruce—her song about Momchil.

As soon as I shut my eyes and imagine Momchilovo, I see Granny Srebra. When Manol was born, she forgot her fairness and her care to give to each a fair share of her love, and became his slave. 'If Manolcho[7] were not here,' she would say, 'I would never have known what love of a child is.' Yet she had borne fourteen sons and daughters.

There she would be; he would awake in the middle of the night, and see Granny Srebra asleep beside him. She would put out a hand, tuck him up, and gently vanish into the darkness like a ghost. Whenever she saw him at a distance, she would quicken her step, her stick would tap the path more often, and she would hand him an apple, hidden under her apron, or prunes, or a honey cake. There she would be, watching over him, after he had fallen in the Black Hole and hurt himself. Whenever he opened his eyes, she would start, raise her nodding head and ask anxiously : 'Oh! What is it Manolcho?' When he began to see evil sprites and spirits, she would sleep beside him and soothe him—she believed in ghosts, but did not fear them. Everywhere, everywhere, in each of my memories, and in each memory of Manol, son of Momchil, son of Manol, stood Granny Srebra, her love, her kindness and her songs.

I was seeing her now for the first time, such as I remembered her for ever, and Manol, son of Momchil, son of Manol, had not yet been conceived.

Old Galoushko asked me :

'Do you know the man who came to the water-mill three days ago? He ate honey and went away.'

I realized that he was speaking of Karaibrahim.

'I know him. Shall I take him a greeting from you?'

The old man was silent a while, then said :

'No, don't.'

And he asked me :

'Where do you come from, stranger? You do not look like a Turk.'

'I am a Venetian. Since I accepted Islam, they call me Abdullah.'

Then Granny Srebra said to me :

'May you be cursed.'

Those were the first words I heard from Granny Srebra. And as I did not expect them, and the beauty of the morning had opened my heart, they hurt me very deeply. I tried in vain to smile.

Old Galoushko either had not heard the old woman's words, or pretended that he had not heard them. He was somewhat deaf, deafened by the perpetual rattle of his water-mill, and by listening to himself, and not to the world around him.

'Have you ever seen Janissaries?'

'I have,' I replied.

'Is it true that they are fierce?'

'They are called the mad dogs of the Sultan's greatness. And they are, indeed, like dogs, sick with madness, for no one else hurls himself to tear their own kind to pieces, as the Janissaries do.'

'I have a son who is a Janissary,' the old man said simply.

He turned and went into the water-mill.

I was left alone with the old woman. And she was staring fixedly at me with her kind eyes, so that I did not know what to do with my hands. And after she had cursed me, she uttered not a word more. She only stared at me. She looked so kind-hearted and so wise that if I had not clearly heard her curse, I would not have believed that she had uttered it.

Old Galoushko came out of the water-mill, and in one hand he carried a little dish of honey, and in the other a wooden bowl full of red wine.

'Take this, stranger,' he said to me. 'I was not here last night to entertain you.'

I was so unhappy about the old woman's words, and about my own words on the Janissaries, that I did not put out a hand to take the dish. Although his hands were full, Old Galoushko stretched them out to point to something up in the mountains.

'Over there,' he said, 'there is a ruined city, all made of white stones. Mountain folk lived there a long time ago. I have seen their gods, drawn on slabs. They had goats' legs.'

And he began to laugh softly.

'Do you see those hollow logs? Do you know how much water has flowed along them? It flows and flows.'

He bent down and left the little dish and the bowl on a marble stone.

'Do you see these hands? Do you know how much grain has passed through them? Big fine grains. What ears of wheat could have grown from them! But the stones ground them to flour. The rye was eaten by men, and the oats, when it happened to be a good year, was eaten even by the donkeys. It flows, and flows.'

I stood there, surprised and touched. When someone gives a man a push, and he loses his balance, it is easy to shake him afterwards. I felt like weeping as I looked at the old man's dreamy, rather sad smile.

And he repeated quietly, shaking his head :

'It flows . . . It flows . . .'

And as I looked at him, I suddenly felt that everything flows and passes on—the clouds, and the water, and the forest, and even the stones.

Then Granny Srebra spoke :

'Every stone weighs in its place. Have you ever seen a tree bear fruit when it has been moved to another spot, Grandad Galoushko? Wherever the tree's seed falls, there must it strike root, and there must it bear fruit. Have you ever heard of anyone who has written a song in a tongue in which his mother did not sing? When the stallion forgets his kin and mounts a donkey, the mule that is born has no progeny. In the old days, when the Turkish Sultans were wise, they did not allow their Janissaries to marry. And once they married, their wives did not conceive, and, if they did, the children they bore were killed. What is this man that you should comfort him? An uprooted tree, a stone displaced. What do we expect of him?'

'Good,' the old man replied. 'Everything is meted out, according to a man's back. Each is laden according to his strength. If he has bent, that means that God has made his back soft.'

'You would forgive everyone, Grandad. Better break than bend.'

'There must be men. Both good and evil, and God is in men. If there were no men, God would have no place to live. He lives in the grasses, too, and in the beasts, but He acquires his image in men.'

'But the devil lives in man, too.'

'The devil, too, is in God. How can you believe, Granny, that if God willed, He would not crush a devil? For God, the devil is nothing more than a flea is for a dog. It jumps and jumps, but when the teeth snap—it isn't there any more.'

'Listen, Grandad. The way you talk, it would appear that God has also blessed those brutes who set fire to our houses. My head has begun to turn like your mill stone from your words. But I am not much surprised at you, because men are like that—they see the stars in the sky, and miss the spark that will burn their house down. What I know—I know. This is good and that is evil. And what you know is like the mist. You will admit yourself that you do not understand it very well. It spins out like mist, and you cannot see through it.'

While they were talking, Old Galoushko broke off a twig from the willow that stood beside him. And as he spoke he handed it to me and showed me the honey with his eyes.

I, too, looked at the honey. And I saw that the sun had stopped in its middle and had melted it entirely. I took the little dish, and into it, I dipped the twig, which had taken part of the bark with it, so that it was like a little shovel. And when I twirled the twig, I stirred the sun, and raised it to my mouth. I raised it quickly, so that it would not drip, and it shone yellow before my eyes, and I swallowed it. I shut my eyes, and the real sun was shining just before me, so that there was yellow beneath my lids, as if honey, thick and sweet, were being poured into them, as if I myself were full of honey.

I opened my eyes; the sun blinded me. I took the wooden bowl and drank. It was not ordinary wine; there was something rotten and fresh in it. It was made of raspberries. I shut my eyes again—now a red, sparkling juice poured itself under my lids.

'Granny,' I said. 'If I had died, I would not be eating sun now and drinking juice.'

Granny Srebra was still looking thoughtfully at me with her black eyes. She had probably been looking at me while I ate the honey and drank the wine. She shook her head and said:

'His hand is good and rich in lines, yet he has come to do evil. If we do not slay them, they will slay the people in the mountains.'

I looked at my hand, but did not understand anything.

'Granny,' said Old Galoushko, 'the folk in these mountains are like one man. And he is immortal. Two die, two hold out, but it is just as if a big man had cut himself with his axe and his little finger has festered and his thumb has healed. It is so arranged that he always remains alive. What is coming is terrible, but it is not as terrible as all that. And it is not so very important. The mountain does not die.'

That same morning when I ate sun, and had sun under my lids, fate showed me Elitsa for the first time. For in the night I had seen her from a distance, in the moonlight, and I had taken her for a *samodiva*, and not a woman.

She was standing before me now, out on the meadow in front of the water-mill, and I was looking at her.

Always, whenever I want to picture Elitsa to myself, I remember clearly how she looked on three or four occasions. And when I remember other things, she always appears so to me, yet I never thought on a single one of these occasions that I would remember her thus. Only on that first morning, when I saw her, I knew that I would not forget her.

Before me stood the Rhodope Mountain.

On her chestnut hair she wore a white kerchief, like the snow-drifts on the high summits.

Her woollen garment fell in blackish-blue folds, like that abyss of distant pine forest which I had seen from the pass. Green and yellowish red bands, the colour of an orange, interwoven on her apron, like the broad meadows with flowers scattered on them.

The white slippers on her feet looked like fruit trees in full blossom at the foot of the mountain.

And there was silver embroidery on her sleeveless bodice, that looked as if foaming brooks and waterfalls were flowing down the mountain.

Her eyes looked as if they were pierced by light, they were quite light-brown—does have eyes like that—the eyes of the little fawns are darker, they are even black. Her lips quivered, meeting and parting like the wings of a perching butterfly.

When she spoke, her voice seemed to me very deep and very womanly for her girlish face.

'Forgive us, stranger,' Elitsa said to me, 'for not giving you the welcome that was meet. The lamb was a sacrifice, not to be eaten, the bread was not enough for the many guests. Forgive us.'

I did not reply. I only bowed deeply to her, with a bow I had long forgotten, and which I had not made since I had left the Palace of Louis XIV.

'Are there any women like this one in your lands, stranger?' someone asked quietly beside me.

It was Momchil, who had approached with a noiseless step and was standing beside me. Without wanting to, I began to enjoy the sight of him and to delight in him. In the sunlight one could now see that his strong, beautiful neck was dark and tanned. His mouth was wide, with firm and narrow lips. The nose was short and straight, his eyebrows were straight and short. His cheeks were hollow, so that the upper part of his face stood out with its broad cheekbones and high forehead. His hair fell to his shoulders, like his father's, but it looked softer and lighter. Although his face was tanned, one could see that he was pale, and his eyes shone feverishly.

'Our womenfolk are different,' I answered, and added at once : 'No, there are none like this one.'

Momchil was looking before him and not listening to me.

'Elitsa,' he said. 'I am going back to the sheep. Pick a nosegay of crane's-bill for me and give it to me. So that I may put it in a green dish with cold water, next to the door. When I go out and when I return, it will smell of crane's-bill, of a maiden's soul.'

'My nosegay, Momchil, has already been given,' Elitsa replied.

She spoke, and it was just as though she had bent down, picked up a stone from the ground and struck him between the eyes. Her lips were still quivering, and her eyes shone boldly and desperately. But she thought that she was striking him out of the blue, for she knew nothing about last night, and that is why, after standing thus and waiting a while, she dropped her lids in surprise. Her lips were pressed close together, so that even the red line in the middle was lost.

'Then give me a jug of water to drink, and then I will set out,' Momchil said quietly.

'You know where the water is,' the girl spoke hurriedly, then turned and fled.

Momchil and I looked after her.

'Wait for me, I have something to fetch,' he said, and disappeared to one side, but I think that he wanted to remain alone, for he was panting, and was barely controlling something in his breast.

In the clear morning, the meadows and forests near the water-mill looked deserted. It seemed to me that during the night, as I slept in the water-mill, there were a lot of people around me and something had been moving about in the darkness, but now it had gone and was scattered. I watched the water leaping up to a man's height from the earth and falling back again, and thought about its indomitable force. And the water descended from the lake to the mill along a hollowed sloping tree trunk, all green with mould, and here and there, flowers grew at its edge. At the side one saw a slender wooden groove, quite green, too, so that it was lost among the green ferns and the crane's-bill. One could not see that the water flowed along it, so smooth and light was the surface of the stream. It seemed to be ice. But someone had placed a flat stone across the hollowed stem, so that the water dashed against it, and leapt angrily up, just like the spring above—weak, of course, although wrathful. Thus one could drink of the spurting stream in comfort, for it entered one's mouth of itself. If that stone had not been there, one could not have known how swiftly and strongly the water flowed.

I drank, and when I raised my head, I looked at the big hollow tree along which the water descended to the water-mill, and in it, too, the water sparkled smooth and apparently motionless.

I went up to it, stretched out my hand and managed to dip it into the water. It thrust my hand aside, leapt up and splashed me all over.

Momchil returned, restrained, but very pale.

'There are two roads to Syuleiman Aga's *Konak*,' he said to me. 'The one is straight, short and easy. You will go down from here to our village of Podviss, and from there, always keeping to the river, you will pass through Zagrad and reach Prossoina. The *Konak* is above the village. I cannot accompany you along this road, and I do not advise you to take it. Your men are only in Prossoina, they have not dared to go higher up.'

I thought that he did not want to be seen with me, the Turk, passing through his villages.

'The other way goes around, up along the crest. You came by it. If you like, I will accompany you to the pass with the crosses, from which you can see Prossoina.'

'Why should you lose your whole day with me?' I asked him straight out.

'And what should I do with it? Besides, you are a guest. My father's guest.'

Without answering him, I set out in silence upwards along the path that led to the little lake with the spring. Momchil set out after me.

'Wait,' he said to me, when we had walked by the water some ten steps.

He stopped, took a chain of silver coins out of his cartridge belt and knelt down on the bank. One by one he tore off the little coins and cast them into the water. But they did not sink at once, for the water gushed forth from the bottom near the bank, and they whirled like autumn leaves, before turning on their edges and sinking. The bottom was not deep, the water was clear, so that one could see that they did not lie still at the bottom, but that the jet swayed them this way and that, as if a wind were blowing them. And as soon as they lay with their faces towards the sun, they cast a silver sheen on Momchil's face.

He stood up, dusted his knees and asked me :

'When you changed your faith, did it hurt you?'

I nodded.

'It hurts me, too. It is difficult for a man to tear himself away from the old accustomed way. There were a hundred *paras*[8] on that chain, and in a man's heart there are a hundred pains. And when you tear them out, they do not want to sink, but shine at you from the bottom.'

And we set out upwards through the forest.

Sixth Excerpt

I do not remember what kind of weather it was that day. But it did not rain. It was probably fine, as the days before it had been—sunlit and cool, with slight rain after noon.

Karaibrahim's meeting with the notables of the Elindenya Valley took place in the big inner courtyard of Syuleiman Aga's *Konak*. Buildings surrounded it on four sides; on three of them they had covered verandas, on the fourth, the vault of the great gate gaped dark. The notables entered through it, and the door closed behind them.

In the middle of the courtyard, their backs to the gate, the notables stood in a crowd. In the front row stood Old Kralyo, the man who read one or two verses from the Bible every evening in front of his sheepfold. He had put a white handkerchief around his neck—Syuleiman Aga's token that he had sent for them in peace, and would let them go in peace. Behind the old man, who hoped to live as long again as he had lived so far, stood the remaining notables. More than half of them wore the same shepherd's garments, so that they looked like the soldiers of an army : short brown braided jackets, and baggy trousers, white leggings held in place with black straps, and red cloaks. There were no weapons in their leather cartridge belts, nor were they decked with any posies of flowers. The others were farmers and craftsmen, and several fishermen, dressed so that their trade was in some way apparent. There must have been fifty or sixty men.

The Spahis came down the stairs of the right-hand veranda, and after them came their servants. The servants placed cushions on the cobblestones, and over them they spread gaily-coloured rugs, and the Spahis sat cross-legged in comfort upon them. They glittered with gold embroidery, gold and precious stones, and they had decked themselves out with whatever weapons they had. Their moustaches were blackened and curled, they had placed some kind of perfumes under their armpits, so that the whole courtyard was redolent of them. Behind the Agas stood their servants, also armed.

From the left-hand veranda, Syuleiman Aga's men appeared one by one, and they went and stood to the left of the notables. Delyo stood in front of them with shameless eyes, smiling, his waistband hanging loose, and the straps of his leggings untied, his legs wide apart. His hands were at his waist, his thumbs stuck in his cartridge belt, into which were thrust two pistols and two daggers with mother-of-pearl handles. The rest of Syuleiman Aga's men were armed, too. They and Karaibrahim's men numbered a hundred, to each side.

Syuleiman Aga appeared up on the veranda in the *kyoshk* on the right, with his four clerks. Some of the notables saw him, and all turned their heads towards him.

'*Haïrolsoun,*⁹ Aga,' some twenty voices cried, and Old Kralyo waved the white handkerchief.

The Aga merely nodded his head. He sat down cross-legged, and the four men stood behind him. A servant brought a *chibouk*, but the Aga did not take it. He sat there, his chin in his hands, his elbows on his knees.

The curtains of the windows which were above the dark vault behind the notables stirred, as if a wind were blowing. The women of the house were probably hidden there. Some of the Agas raised their heads and began to twirl their moustaches.

A marble fountain flowed between the notables and the Agas. Between the notables and Syuleiman Aga's men, there was a wide circle of untouched grey ash from last night's fire.

There must have been clouds, for no one stood in the sunlight; there must have been no wind, for the ash did not smoke. It must have been very quiet because one heard the clear sound of the water as it fell into the stone trough.

Then, down the central stairs came Karaibrahim in a purple garment, wearing red boots, and a white turban with black feathers on it. He stopped in the middle of the staircase, looked around the courtyard, bowed to Syuleiman Aga, and continued his descent. The boards creaked, his boots creaked, too, and his spurs jingled. Behind Karaibrahim came I, and behind me, the three Hodjas, Sheikh Shaban Shebil, Molla Soulfikar Softa and the Imam Hassan, son of Velko.

Karaibrahim sat down on a carved chair, I stood at his left side, and on his right stood the three Hodjas.

Karaibrahim, emissary of the Sultan, the man who ruined the Elindenya Valley, took his place facing his victims, the men whom he was to oppress, torture and kill.

Sixty pairs of eyes—the notables'—were fixed on Karaibrahim. There was the man on whom their fate depended. And they wondered what he was like, trying to guess his character and his mind. Only Manol had spoken with him, and several of them had seen him on horseback, riding through the villages, while others were seeing him for the first time.

And at that moment, when their gaze was fixed in expectation on Karaibrahim, I clearly saw the essence of what was happening before my eyes, and I realized how vain were the hopes of the Bulgarians and how little difference it made whether Karaibrahim stood before them or someone else.

To all appearances the four walls divided the people gathered in the courtyard from the whole world. But it was not so, and unless one imagined those walls down, one could not understand what was happening in that courtyard.

Behind Karaibrahim stretched a bright shining track—the road of his detachment—like the dry gleaming slime which a snail leaves behind it. This track led to Mehmed Pasha's army, grew wider, set out towards the Sultan in Adrianople, and flowed like a river towards Candia, where the snail's tracks went to and fro to the very walls of the fortress, wanting to pass through them, and covering them with shining slime—just as the spider covers the fly with its cobweb. And Karaibrahim was only a snail, which had crawled farther ahead than the others, he was nothing but the front end of the track, and could not but be cold and slimy like a snail.

A bright track also stretched out behind the notables, like the silken thread which a silkworm leaves. A thread of this kind stretched behind each of the Bulgarians, and the closed gate behind them wove these threads into a silken rope. It was trying to cut them through with its wooden edges, but it only gathered them together. And those threads went far beyond the gate, covering the big mountain, and the plains behind it, going down under the ground, and clinging to the bones and the stones of the ruins. If a man could gather these threads in his hands, and if he had God's power, he would raise the entire Bulgarian land with them, with the roots and the cemeteries, like a big fish in a net of silver wires.

What could Karaibrahim do, but try to cover the mountains before him with his snail's track? What could the notables do, but cling to the silken threads? Both for the former and the latter, the track behind them was like the umbilical cord, along which the blood of their mother's heart flowed to them. Without that track Karaibrahim would have been a bandit, and the notables—outcasts.

But what of the Spahis to the right? They were praying that the notables would resist, so that they might rob them of their flocks and their women folk. Then, not only would they not pay one *aspra* for each *oka* of bread, and three *aspras* for an *oka* of meat, but they would eat only the livers of the lambs, and their heads would lie on the breast of one woman, and their feet in the lap of another.

What of Syuleiman Aga's servants on the left? They were Christians. They were supposed to guard the notables from the side, but actually some of these notables were their fathers and brothers. What would they do? Where did the track behind them lead?

And Syuleiman Aga, up in the *kyoshk*? Until that day he had sat in that courtyard as the all-powerful master and judge. To all appearances a snail's track stretched out behind him, but would he not wish to gather the silken threads in his hand, so that he might raise the whole mountain like a fish? Had he the strength for this?

But behind me there was no track. The track had been cut. Behind me nothing was left, as nothing is left behind a lizard that has passed over a stone, or behind a ship at sea. I was neither on the one side, nor on the other. I needed no one, and no one needed me. I could go out through the gate, and no one would notice that I was not there. And this meant, so I thought, that I was free, without these threads which the men in front of me dragged after them like spiders. And that was why they could not fall, neither could they fly. My loneliness brought me sorrow, but it also brought me freedom. I alone in all that gathering of men could rightly judge on whose side the truth was.

I did not pass any judgement, for both sides seemed to be in the right—Karaibrahim to want their surrender, and they to want to defend themselves.

But while my reason thus divided the men into black and white, and arranged them on black and white squares, and thought that victory would go to the one who played the better game, my heart was heavy. You could not stand in that courtyard, before that expectation, amid that fearlessness, that self-denial, that resignation, amid that cruelty, that avidity, that implacability—and not feel your heart heavy within you.

The first to speak was Sheikh Shaban Shebil, the one-eyed. He took from his bosom a scroll, placed it over his heart, on his forehead and on his lips. He did not open it, but began to speak slowly in Turkish, and Syuleiman Aga's Imam translated into Bulgarian:

'A great mercy has fallen to the lot of this valley. So far the people here lived in homes on two floors. The Believers lived on the upper floor, ate pilaf, and enjoyed the favour of Allah, while the Bulgarians lived on the ground floor in the stables, together with the cattle and the donkeys. They lived like cattle. But the Padishah of this great state, may Allah bless his name, the holy defender of the holy cities of Mecca and Medina, the father of his subjects, and the terror of his enemies, has decided to stretch out his hand to you, and says to you: "Come ye, who are on the lower floor, in the dark, come to the upper floor where we are bathed in the light of the True Faith, so that you, too, may be enlightened, and enter paradise after your death".'

The Sheikh stopped speaking. My heart grew heavier still. I felt what a monstrous and unnatural thing this meeting was, what a monstrous outrage on these men was Karaibrahim's behaviour—sitting calmly before them, and mockingly demanding that they should trample upon their faith. If this was being torn from the mother's navel, if it was birth, then death must also be near, there must be blood, screams, and tearing to pieces, as there had been on the deck of the ship. This thing here was a mockery. Karaibrahim was no lion, but a snake.

'Aga,' Old Kralyo said in a trembling voice, as he crushed the white handkerchief at his throat with his hand. 'With your coming already we realized why you had come. The Hodja's words are unnecessary. We gathered together and decided to tell you. Our heads we will give, but our faith we will not give.'

And he was silent. The words of the Imam, who repeated the same thing in Turkish, died away.

The talk came to an end, but no one made a move to go.

Then Karaibrahim spoke. And, as the Hodja was silent, I had to repeat his words in Bulgarian.

'I had hoped to hear another answer from you. I could have come straight with sword and a brand, and today in the valley there would only have been True Believers—and the dead. But if not today, then in a week or a month, there will again be only True Believers. I have come to do one thing and I shall do it. When I entered this valley, I was met by the ringing of a despised bell.

When I leave, I shall be sent on my way by the singing of a muezzin.'

'If you leave,' said a voice amid the crowd.

I started. A murmur rose among Syuleiman Aga's men. Delyo smiled. The Spahis excitedly asked each other in Turkish what the Bulgarian had said. Syuleiman Aga coughed in the *kyoshk*. Only Karaibrahim never quivered.

'I shall not answer the coward who spoke behind the backs of others. Or it is better that I should answer him. Even if I do not leave, another will come in my place. You have taken in the refugees from Chepino. And that is better, because you have seen that the Padishah is kind to those who are submissive, but fierce to rebels. A muezzin will sing over Elindenya.'

Old Kralyo stepped forward, as white as the handkerchief under his chin.

'Since you speak, Aga, I shall tell you something, although there is nothing to be said, and every word is superfluous. Go, do not stain the mountain with blood, and we shall bless you for ever. We are loyal subjects of the Padishah. We shall not become more loyal if we warp our souls. Or do you believe, Aga, that even if any man were to accept your faith, he would carry it in his heart? What need have you of traitors and slaves? However you may whittle wood, it still remains wood.'

'But it bends. And wood may remain wood, but a head, once cut off, does not grow again. And your shepherds will tell you what loyal subjects of the Sultan they are, for they gave sheep to the Venetian swine. The True Believers are dying under the walls of Candia, yet you play on your bagpipes. Let the same rope link us, let the same faith cover us, let your sons die under the green flag, and then you will not wait for the Venetians, to rise in rebellion, but you will give them poison.'

And again they were all silent. Indeed, there was nothing to be said. The notables stood there with bowed heads, yet they bowed them not in submission, but like rams, or bulls.

Karaibrahim said:

'I give you time until the third day, after the first Sunday, counted from today. If you do not come to accept the True Faith willingly, from that day on my hands are unbound. And as soon as I see you fleeing with horses and household goods, I am free to do what I will with those I capture. Now go.'

'*Sel gecher, Koum kalur,*' said Old Kralyo.

I did not translate his words, but they meant in Turkish: 'The torrent passes, the sand remains.'

Then Karaibrahim rose and went to the circle of ashes. It lay there in a thick layer, even, bluish-grey, and around it there was a wreath of scorched thorns, which had not burnt up. Karaibrahim bent down and picked up a handful of ash.

'Not like a torrent shall I pass over you, but like fire. And what is left afterwards will be soft and warm like these ashes.'

And indeed, the ashes lay there smooth, soft and resigned.

From the crowd of notables Manol came out, bent down and picked up from the earth a handful of scorched thorns.

'And at the side there will still be pieces of wood left, black but not burnt up.'

The thorns, which the fire had not reached, lay in a circle around the ashes—tousled, bristling and insubmissive.

Karaibrahim and Manol faced each other. One holding a handful of ash, the other—a bunch of thorns. And they looked each other straight in the eye. And Karaibrahim, without changing his face, began to curse in Turkish through his teeth.

By force of habit, without thinking, I stepped forward and began to repeat his words in Bulgarian:

'Curs! Sons of bitches! That is why your women bear curs. And curs shall gnaw your bones.'

It would have been comical if it had not been terrible. Karaibrahim cursed in Turkish, and I spoke his words in Bulgarian. But what kind of a curse is a translated curse? That is why I thought of this and fell silent.

Karaibrahim continued to shout. And as soon as I stopped talking, my mind began to work again, and I realized that Karaibrahim was trying to insult Manol, to anger him and make him lose control of himself. The Spahis jumped to their feet and laid hands on their arms. If anything happened in the quarrel, Syuleiman Aga's promise that he would let the notables go, safe and sound, would not hold good. Who could seek justice of an infuriated man?

Manol grew pale. His hands gripped the thorns so hard that blood ran down his wrist.

I looked at Syuleiman Aga's men. Delyo was still standing with his hands at his waist, but he had raised himself on tip-toe, and it seemed to me that I heard him growl. The men behind him stood there with dark faces, and their fingers opened and closed on the handles of their weapons.

I raised helpless eyes to the *kyoshk*. What was Syuleiman Aga waiting for? Yet he sat cross-legged on his cushions, listening.

When I glanced at Manol again, I saw that he was smiling. He was still pale. But his eyes were half-closed and there was scorn in his smile.

And then I saw something which amazed me, and which I did

not believe at first, but it was so. There was a kind of gloomy joy
on Manol's face and on those of several of the Bulgarians behind
him. Lo, something terrible was coming, but it was also great, and
they would be able to measure their strength against it, so that it
would be seen that this strength was also great. Manol despised
Karaibrahim, and regretted that he had not shown himself an
enemy worthy of him.

And as Karaibrahim shouted, the wind suddenly carried to us
the unbearable and desperate howling of the dogs that had been cast
into the Black Hole. They were all howling at the same time, as if
they were somewhere around the *Konak*. And I felt death in the
courtyard.

Karaibrahim fell silent. He was panting. And perhaps he had
shouted to infuriate himself and fan his own anger, so that he
could cast off that sinister calm of something decided or predeter-
mined, which hung over the *Konak*, so that he might feel free, and
possessed of his own will.

The dogs howled and the wind drew their howls out, making
them still more terrible. Manol said :

'Do you hear? You called on the dogs and they have answered
you. You want to turn our valley into a Black Hole, in which we
shall gnaw each other, Bulgarian Mohammedans and Bulgarian
Christians. You are not so foolish as to raise us all to the upper
floor. You want those of us who go up to jump on the heads of
those below us. That is what you want. You want to turn us from
wolves into sheepdogs. To hunt the wolves. Do you want us to
accept your faith? Go, ride over Rhodopa, over the Bulgarian lands,
turn everyone to your faith. Come and say : "There is no Bulgarian
left, you are the last." Then we shall consider whether to give in,
for, if there is no one against whom you can turn our hands, and
make us raise them, we shall not be striking our brothers. Or at
least we shall die without defending ourselves, for there will be
nothing to live for. Go, go, turn all my brothers into Turks, and
then come to me.'

'I shall not leave a single one of your family,' Karaibrahim said
quietly and emphatically, 'who will not draw a cross with his blood
and spit upon it.'

'I have a hundred brothers,' said Manol.

And he opened his hand, so that the thorns fell from his fist.
I looked at it and remembered Granny Srebra's words. He had a
rich and fine hand, with a wide hard palm and countless lines. And
the blood drawn by the thorns flowed over them and filled them.

I looked at Karaibrahim's hand, too. He had dropped the ashes
and they outlined the lines of his hand. And Granny Srebra would

have said that it was a poor hand, for only two lines crossed it and one ran down towards the wrist.

But Manol turned, and entered the crowd of the notables.

'Go,' said Karaibrahim, 'and count ten days from today onwards. And from that day, such things will happen that anyone who merely hears of them will hear a roaring in both his ears. And so much blood will flow, that it will support an *oka* of stone. Whichever faith is the strongest, let it float up.'

'Aga,' Old Kralyo spoke once more, 'what can you do to people who are ready to give their heads? You, master, must know that you can do nothing to men who have decided to die.'

'There are things, old man, that are far, far more terrible than death. You will see them.'

'If there is, indeed, anything I have not heard about, then you will only make death more strongly desired by us.'

I stood aside and listened. To all this great talk of blood and death. The men before me could not understand what their words meant. Death. I had felt it. One does not speak of it. We shall see when they stand face to face with it.

I was right when I thought of the silken thread that lay in their tracks. They did not want to break with their own kin and become their enemies. We shall see, when the time comes, whether it is easier to be your own enemy. Whether the knife in your brother's ribs hurts you more than the knife in your own. Then it will become clear what part of their resistance is simply stubbornness and hard-headedness. It will become clear what is merely slow thinking, sluggishness and a dislike of change. It will become clear which is the stronger—the stake or the fear of God.

Or were they brave because they had the white handkerchief, and Syuleiman Aga's word? And they went out of the gate and went away free to their forests and meadows.

I thought bitterly and angrily.

Did I envy them?

Seventh Excerpt

A lass began singing in the green forest.
Where did a young monk hear her?
Then roundly he cursed the young lass :
'May the Lord kill you, my little lass,
Why did you not sing this morning,
Before I had taken my vows?
And the deuce take this black cassock ...'

The first of Karaibrahim's ten days came. And it began to pass and after it nine more days were left.

And I sat me down on the empty meadow, near the white peeled spruce trunks, on which the notables had sat, beside the withered spruce branches and the charred embers of the dead fires. And the branches had not burned to the end for the rain had put them out. And the fountain in the lake murmured evenly.

Not even if I walked and walked for ten or for a hundred days, could I find help for Elindenya. But my spirit did not remain in one place, and on that first day it rushed around many lands to find an issue, or a friendly hand.

At first my thoughts wandered over Rhodopa. And here I even saw the pine cones along the paths, for my feet had caressed every blade of grass, and every thistle had thrust a needle into my soles. And amid the blossoming grasses I saw woollen overdresses and embroidered smocks, and they were not rags that had been cast away, but dead bodies. I saw roots grubbed up not by the wild boar but by childish fingers. The villages were deserted, the hearths burnt out, there was blood on the thresholds. I saw the bellies of women with child ripped open so that the unborn might be killed in their wombs. I saw women with child striking their bellies with stones to kill the children of strangers. I saw sufferings and blood that were not to be told of. And I was filled with fear and did not want to see more.

Then I heard the even beating of drums and I saw something like a black anthill crawling over the mountain. I approached—it was the army of Mehmed Pasha. I stared at the faces of the soldiers —empty eyes, empty hearts, empty bellies. There were no words which could fill them.

And when I had gone over Rhodopa, far and wide, I fled from

them. I set out to the south and I saw the sea. And over it sailed ships, leaving a white wake behind them. Half the people in them were thinking of Candia and half of booty. I saw Candia, too, swarming with bodies, weapons, soil, worms and smoke, and over the swarm I saw a white line and it was white walls. And when I remembered that they were black with the smoke of gunpowder, they grew black. And on them stood tiny little men, and they were shouting something, probably for help, but I could not distinguish their words.

And I set out to the west, and I walked amid a desert, for I did not know these lands, until I saw something shining in gold and brilliance. I saw the King of the Franks eating and drinking. And because I did not know the faces of the men, nor their garments, nor their houses, I saw only gilded mantles, goblets, white teeth and white flesh. And something hummed like a hive and rattled like a bag of money. And although I cried out, none heard me, and I myself grew deaf.

Then I set out to the north, and travelled all over the long-suffering Bulgarian land. And I saw sickles, and flails, and hoes, and pails, and scythes and dark men working with them. And whoever I called to, looked at me and I fled from his eyes. And still further north, after I had passed a deep white river, and it was the Danube, I saw steppes, and snows and, somewhere far away, men with beards, dressed in furs, and riding on sleighs. And when I cried to them, my cry reached them through the blizzard, and they turned and set out towards me. And they marched and marched, and were coming, and they grew slightly bigger, until my feet froze, and I turned back.

And I entered the Sultan's camp and fell before him to beg for mercy. And I saw spears, and guns and pistols, and daggers and *yataghans*, and red tents, green flags and yellow horsemen. And the Sultan's tent was surrounded with stakes and on them men and heads were impaled. And when I entered, he turned and looked at me, and I entered into him through his dark irises, and heard these words ringing in his head : 'I want to kill my brothers !'

And I found myself on the meadow once more, and beside me stood the white spruce trunks, arranged beside the withered spruce branches. I was exhausted and desperate. Then I remembered the faces of my brothers, how handsome they were and how strong, how their voices rang out through the storm, and how their beards were blown about. And I said to myself : 'Whatever we can do, we must do by ourselves.'

Just then someone touched my shoulder, and when I turned, I saw Elitsa. And she said to me :

'Father, you had dozed off.'

I looked at her. And she was so beautiful that I felt my throat go dry, and my breath stop, and my jaws stiffen. And when I remembered Manol's face as he looked upon her, and I realized that it was not desire that had been in his heart, but pain. For my heart began to ache, too.

And she said quietly to me :

'Father, I have no mother, and my father welcomes both good and evil as things sent from God. Something weighs upon me, and there is no one to whom I can pour out my soul. Hear me, I beg you, and be as a father and a mother to me.'

I looked upon her, and her beauty wiped out the road along which I was wandering, and my heart ached, and I was on the verge of cursing my lot and my cassock. And she said to me further :

'Momchil, Manol's son, and I grew up together. One day, many years ago, we were bathing in the river and we saw that we were different. From that time I became shy of him, and I was drawn to see him. Last spring I found out how children come into the world. And from that day I wanted him to be the father of my children. I was happy to welcome him to the water-mill, and I was happy to go high up into the mountain and see him beside his sheep. When I knew that he was coming, I put on the garments I loved best, when I knew he was listening to me, I sang the songs I love best. And now Manol has come. He looked at me, and I grew mute. He came to me as a king comes to his maidservant, he approached me as the wolf approaches the lamb. He spoke to me, and told me that his house was empty, that his life was passing, that he wanted to have more sons and daughters. And I dropped on his shoulder. And he stood above me, so that I could not go against his will, yet at the same time I stood on high, and he stood beneath me, and looked up. I was like one who was dreaming. Is that love, Father, or magic?'

What could I say to her? What did I know of love and why had she come to me? I said to her, as her father would have said :

'Everything comes from God. Ask your heart.'

And she looked at me with clear, open eyes in which there was no shame and no repentance. And she said to me slowly :

'I know that it is sinful, but if I asked my heart, I would take both of them.'

Then she fell silent, and I saw that Momchil and her brother Goran were coming up from below. Momchil's falcon was perched on his shoulder. And Momchil was as white as a flower. When they stopped before us, he said to her in a choking voice :

'Elitsa, is it true that next Sunday you are going to marry my father?'

And she said to him :

'Why do you ask me?'

And again he asked her, and it seemed to me that he would begin to weep :

'Elitsa, tell me, is it true?'

And they stood one opposite the other, and looked at each other, as if Goran and I were not there. And the falcon on Momchil's shoulder stared at Elitsa, and its eyes were round, wild and cold. Then the falcon shot its head to one side and stared at Momchil's eyes, and I shivered, as more than once before, for it always seemed to me that in a second the cruel bird would peck out the lad's black eyes.

And anger blazed up in Elitsa's eyes, her cheeks and her lips grew red, and she cried to Momchil :

'Do you remember when you came to bid me good-bye in the autumn and I had fallen asleep on the meadow. And my smock was undone and my overdress had ridden up. And you called to me, so that I rose up. Why did you not bend down?'

And he only stared at her, not believing that he heard such words. And she cried again :

'Do you remember when I came to you up above, and we chased each other in the forest, and you caught up with me near a spruce, and my face was burning, and my bosom was burning, and I asked you prettily to let me go. You let me go. Why did you let me go?'

And he opened his mouth and was unable to say a word. And she still cried as if she were about to weep :

'Do you remember, when I told you that evening, when there was no moon, and the stars were twice as many, to come with me to the spring, so that I could fill my jars? And I held you by the hand, and you said to me : "Fear not, fear not." Did it not come into your mind that I go to fetch water every evening without you? Why did you not put your arms around me?'

And only now was he able to say :

'Elitsa, Elitsa, Elitsa . . .'

And she stamped her foot and said to him with hatred :

'Call me Elitsa now, for in a week's time you will call me Mother.'

And when she saw that he hid his face in his hands, she said to him quietly :

'The bird perched on your shoulder, and then it flew away. And it perched on another shoulder. Why are you surprised? There is only one Manol in all the mountains.'

And as Momchil had taken his hands from his face and was
staring at her as though he did not know her, and Goran, too, was
staring at her in amazement, she grew angry again and cried :

'That stone over there—Manol moved it from the door here, so
that I might comb my hair unseen. If you are men, move it that I
may see you do it.'

And Momchil bent over the stone. He bent like a bow and embraced it, as ivy embraces the trunk of an oak, and his white neck
grew red. And the falcon thrust its claw into his bent back, and
often flapped its wings, and shrieked fearfully. And one could not
see whether it was helping him to raise the stone or was pressing
him down to the earth. And Momchil was only able to turn the
stone. And he drew back.

Then Goran seized it, and with a roar, he was able to raise it,
but he dropped it, and the earth shook. And when he straightened
up, breathless, he was barely able to speak :

'He must have been mad when he moved it. And he did move
it, the stone used to be beside the door. Otherwise I would not have
believed it. He cannot have been alone.'

And if one says 'He is not alone,' that is to say that an impure
force had helped him, as the song goes : 'This woman is not alone,
she has given me herbs . . .'

And Elitsa smiled :

'He was not alone, I was with him. And he was looking at me.
As for you, Momchil, since you were not able to raise the stone, no
one knows whether you will be able to have sons as handsome as
your father's—for you are a handsome lad. But no one knows
whether your sons will be handsome.'

And she looked at him with hatred and triumph, then turned
and ran to the door of the water-mill. Momchil drew out his heavy
knife and began to slash the birches around us, so that twigs and
chips flew about. And the falcon on his shoulder flapped its wings
and shrieked again. And Elitsa turned at the door and said to
Momchil :

'You may slash the twigs, but you did not raise the stone.'

And he was shamed and put his knife away. And Manol came
out of the water-mill and came up to us. He said to me, without
looking at his son and Goran :

'Father Aligorko, I am getting married on Sunday, stay on for
my wedding.'

And slowly he began to gather with his sandal the twigs his son
had cut. And when he had got them together in a small green heap,
with the white wood of the twigs standing out like flames here and
there, he said, without raising his head :

'I know, Momchil. But is it not all one whether her children will be your brothers or your sons? They will be of your blood.'

And Momchil said to him in a voice that was not his own:

'Is it not all one to you whether they will be your sons or your grandsons? They will be of your blood.'

And a long time passed before Manol answered. And his eyes still looked down on the little green heap of branches. And when he spoke, he said:

'That is so. But you can plough every field, and wherever you cast grain an ear of wheat will grow. And this is the last field in which I shall enter, otherwise I shall never bend over a plough. And this is the last pasture on which I shall turn my sheep out to graze, otherwise I shall never be able to go up to the high mountain. You have the mountains. For me there is only one meadow. You have flocks—for me there is one lamb.'

And he was silent. And Momchil stared at him fixedly, and so did the falcon, but Manol did not raise his head to meet their gaze. And only when the steps of the two young men had died away, for they turned and disappeared in the forest, only then did Manol raise his head, so that I barely recognized his changed face. Something had opened within him, something had softened, like a lump of soil which has absorbed the warm rain. And he said to me:

'If you and I had not gone to the graveyard on that day, I would not have seen that the roots of the grasses grow even in graves. I thought that I had withered, and yet there was still one blossom on the twig.'

And I thought that he had also seen bones, and a skull, but I did not tell him so. And then he said:

'My wife may have been as beautiful as Elitsa. Do I remember? I do not. Youth thinks of itself. Youth is greedy and insatiable, and does not look at what it holds in its hands. Youth does not understand what is beautiful. Youth does not understand anything. The shadows of sunset must fall so that a man may see how the sun shines on one side of the bole, and on the other darkness is already gathering. The shadows must grow longer, so that a man may see and understand what is beautiful.'

And we both set off slowly downhill through the forest, towards the village of Podviss. And it seemed to me that Manol's steps were heavier than usual. At one point he said:

'Do you know, Father, there is a song: "A widower is like a severe frost—it burns whatever it falls on; a lad is like a fresh dew—all that it falls on sprouts." Can it be true?'

And he walked ahead of me, and his shoulders were broad, and his back was firm. He was wealthy, he was strong, why should I

not tell him the truth? Why should I spare him, when God had
given him so much, and was adding to it?

'Manol,' I said. 'The song goes from mouth to mouth. If it were
not true, someone would have failed to pass it on.'

And he turned and looked at me, and there was a smile in his
eyes.

'Father,' he said, 'you struck me on purpose. And you should not
have done so, for there is another song, and you know it.'

And Manol began to sing softly:

> 'Whoever has mother and father
> Let him sit to his heart's content,
> Whoever has kinsfolk a-plenty
> Let him roam to his heart's content,
> Whoever has a sweetheart so lovely,
> Let him love her to his heart's content—
> For the time of parting has come.'

I had forgotten how Manol sang. He sang most beautifully, just
as if he were speaking and playing his *kaval*, two voices from one
throat. And when he stopped singing, he looked at me again, and
repeated:

> 'The time of parting has come.'

I said: 'I think of nothing else.'

And Manol said:

'Three days after my wedding comes Karaibrahim's day. Do you
remember when they spoke that evening of the end trees that guard
the forest? I am one of them. I am like a spruce and have not the
strength to pull up my roots and set out for somewhere. If there
is a massacre, I shall be slain. Let me have three days. Do not envy
me. And Momchil is like a stag—there will always be a forest and
a meadow for Momchil. Do not pity him.'

And he set off, and I looked at his back.

Eighth Excerpt

When Karaibrahim heard the news that Manol was getting married
on the seventh day of the term he had set, he merely said:

'Allah has taken his reason and will deliver him into my hands.'

Otherwise nothing changed in our life. The men ate, drank, and lay around, and Karaibrahim did not make them do anything, he only checked their arms. I did not know what Karaibrahim intended to do when the tenth day was over, probably he himself had not yet decided. Every day we fenced with swords, and I noticed that his blows were growing careless, and his look was not so keen. It seemed to me that he was not getting enough sleep and was tired. I thought that some woman must be mixed up in it, and Gyulfié told me that every night he dressed himself in shepherd's garments and went somewhere. This showed great daring, for he could have been killed and we might never have found his body.

The day of Manol's wedding came. Gyulfié said that it was right that they should invite Syuleiman Aga, and that he ought to send rich gifts. The shepherds neither invited the Aga, nor did he send gifts.

Then came the night, and from afar the distant playing of bag-pipes could be heard. And those nights were dark, although they were starry; the moon rose late, and the sun found it pale and growing slimmer. I had gone to bed when I was called.

Karaibrahim's men had formed up in one of the inner courtyards of the *Konak*. Karaibrahim, dressed in simple clothes, without orna-ments and feathers, told us :

'This night Allah will deliver the unbelievers to us. In the morning you will awaken beside beautiful women, and I shall give every one of you a handful of gold pieces, if he tells me that his woman has been touched by a man. Go and remove from your garments all that shines—gold, stones or iron. Take the spurs off your boots, and tie your boots around your necks with strings. You will go bare-foot—afterwards you will make the unbelievers lick the blood left on your feet by the thorns. I will lead you along a secret path that I have discovered. If anyone speaks in the forest, in the morning I will nail his tongue with red hot nails, so that he will smell his own roasted flesh. If anyone shoots before I tell him to, I shall cut the thumbs off both his hands, so that he can never again use arms. Go !'

And from afar we still heard the playing of the bagpipes—the Bulgarians were making merry in the village of Podviss.

We crept out through a back door of the *Konak* and sank into the forest at once. Karaibrahim said that Syuleiman Aga had sworn not to let anyone out of the *Konak*, but we left five men at the five gates, with fuses lit, to shoot at any who might try to escape.

The road through the forest was hard. Besides thorns and stones, there were nettles, too. But no one uttered a word. We climbed, we descended, we crawled over rocks. At first I thought that I would follow our road. Vega was low in the heavens then, the North Star

was on our right, Scorpion with red Antares was on our left.
Afterwards on a meadow I saw Vega above our heads, as if we
were looking at it from the bottom of a well with walls of pine-
trees. I saw no other stars.

We began to descend some kind of a slope. And when we had
circled a huge cliff, which hid the sky, fires blazed up beneath us,
and singing and playing poured over us. The reflections of the fires
danced over our faces. We could see people, too, black and small,
dancing around the fires, holding each other by the hands. We
could even see the pipers blowing their bagpipes, but no sound of
human voices, and no playing of *kavals* or bagpipes was to be heard
—the sounds of them all were blended into one.

We stood above them, looking and listening. The people were
either a thousand, or five hundred, and there may even have been
two thousand. Even the most experienced eye of a military commander could not have counted them. They thought that they were
safe, yet half an hour later they would be in our hands.

What would happen if I raised my pistol and shot into the air?

In the distant light of the fires I saw that the smooth muscles on
Karaibrahim's face were twitching. A tooth gleamed under his
moustache. I trembled, for he seemed to have read my thoughts,
and was waiting like a tiger to see if I would do anything.

Karaibrahim said quietly.

'Stop here and wait for me. The path is down below. Let two
men come with me.'

And he disappeared into the darkness.

We waited a long time for him, and the more time passed, the
more it seemed to me that nothing would come of our attack. I
knew enough of the art of war to imagine what it meant for a detachment to run downhill through a forest and to have against them
enemies who knew every trunk in it. And the fires seemed to me to
be farther and farther away from us. There was only one possibility
—to disarm the watchmen silently.

Karaibrahim reappeared without our hearing him. We stared at
him, tensely. He said :

'There are no watchmen. They are mad.'

Sivri, the *bilyuk-bashi*, spoke up :

'That cannot be, Aga. There must be an ambush.'

Karaibrahim repeated :

'There are no watchmen.'

And he was silent a while, as if he did not believe his own
words.

The monastery bell struck midnight.

Karaibrahim spoke again :

'Kemanchidjogli, you will take thirty men and pass to the right of the fires. Bersendjiarab, you will take the other thirty men, and when Kemanchidjogli stops, you will go beyond him and pass beyond the fires. Do not fear—the unbelievers are blinded by the flames and the wine, and it is dark in the forest. Each of you is to take his stand behind a tree. When I come out amid the *horo*, light the fuses of your rifles and jump out into the light—in a chain, one next to the other. And remember—I said before that I would cut off thumbs. Now that I see success so near, I tell you—I will cut off heads. Sivri *Bilyuk-bashi*, you will pick out thirty men with Frankish flintlocks, without fuses, and you will follow me.'

To me Karaibrahim said nothing, but I marched beside him.

With a beating heart I went down towards the fires. I forgot that I was stalking men. The passion of the chase had seized me, and it was just as if I were creeping up on game. And they, poor devils, were singing and dancing. It may only have seemed so to me, but there was something wild and unnatural in their merry-making, in the droning and skirling of the bagpipes, in the playing of the *kavals*, which were raised to the stars. There was something exaggerated in everything, but had not the naked bacchantes torn Orpheus to pieces alive centuries ago in these forests?

We took our stand in a semi-circle around the fires, leaning against the trees. I remember how my heart beat against the reddish-silvery bark of a spruce, and how the tree seemed to quiver at its beats. My cheek was pressed against the same bare bark, and I heard my heart in the tree, and my sweat ran down the bark. I was bathed in sweat from the climb and the strain, my throat was dry, my bare feet were burning. The handles of the two pistols almost slipped through my wet fingers.

Yet the Bulgarians were dancing the *horo*—black, their backs to us, melted by the flames opposite them. At the end of a long table sat Manol and Elitsa, she all in white, he with his red cloak, his hair falling on his shoulders, his face copper-coloured in the firelight. On either side of them there was a barrel of wine, and whoever scooped up the wine and drank it, dashed the earthenware dish down on the ground. One heard the cracking of the dishes amid the skirling and the noise.

I was shivering and frozen with cold when someone touched me. Karaibrahim handed me his turban. I took it.

And he set out calmly through the edge of the forest towards the fires. And his bald skull shone.

Without knowing how, with the turban in my hands, I followed him slowly.

No one looked at Karaibrahim.

And as soon as he reached the linked hands of the dancers, he stopped, tore them apart with a blow of his hand, and with a bound reached the bagpipe players.

With his right hand Karaibrahim wrenched the bagpipe out of the hands and the mouth of one of the players and raised it on high. He pressed the pistol in his left hand to the swollen bagpipe and shot into it.

There was a shot. Not all at once, but trailing off like the air escaping from the pierced bagpipe, the playing and the singing stopped. The *horo* froze. But at one end of the meadow people were still laughing and shouting.

'Stop!' shouted Karaibrahim.

And he cast the empty pistol on the ground.

In his right hand only he held a pistol, his left hand was free. Like a lunatic I passed through the broken ring of the *horo* and stood next to him. He took the turban from my hands and placed it on his head.

There was a drumming in my ears, I felt light and luminous. People stared at us in silence. No one stirred. The last laughter died away. The flames crackled. Manol rose slowly to his feet. My ears drummed still harder. A child began to cry.

Karaibrahim stretched out his left hand, palm downwards, and with a smooth and sweeping gesture made a circle in the air. Indian fakirs probably hypnotize crowds like that.

And suddenly the glowing dots of human eyes, fixed up on us, disappeared. People turned, without a sound, without a noise.

At the edge of the forest, almost in a circle, stood Karaibrahim's men. At both ends of the circle the fuses of the muskets shone like candles; in the middle there were no fuses. The black wide muzzles were turned on us. Around the necks of the Turks hung their boots, one on each side, as if each one were ridden by an invisible demon.

Manol shouted. I did not see him; it must have been he.

That was the moment. The spell was broken. Eyes flashed against us once more.

And who knows what would have happened? Then Old Kralyo took his stand next to Karaibrahim and me and raised his hand.

'Stop!' he cried.

Whoever of the Bulgarians had put a hand to his waistband, dropped it. The moment passed.

Unfortunate wretch, who stopped the massacre on the meadow. Such was your fate—I was to be your hangman, I, the monster who had come from Paris. Why did you do it? If it had happened one month later, you would have been the first to leap at the muskets. You were five times our number. But you still believed in justice of a kind, in men's words, in who knows what. A beast believes only in his teeth and his claws.

And the moment passed. The men were already thinking. They saw the muzzles, as they should have done. If they were drunk, they were sobered. Every man thought that if he hurled himself forward, he would be the first to die.

Karaibrahim won. He was the better player. And the other men were only beginning to learn.

'Aga,' said the old man.

Dignity and strength at least had been left in him. Of what use were they to him?

'Aga, why have you come? There are still three days left.'

Without realizing that I was doing so, I repeated the words in Turkish. I may even not have done so.

'You will spend them in the *Konak*. As guests,' said Karaibrahim with a cruel smile.

And he drew himself up, showing his teeth and growling, his eyes fixed on the Bulgarians around him, like a man accustomed to dealing with men as if they were beasts. He seized Old Kralyo by the arm and thrust him aside.

'Get out! The notables here!'

Three or four of the Spahis jumped forward in the circle and began to stare at the men's faces.

That may have been the second moment when the Bulgarians ought to have hurled themselves against us. And once again Old Kralyo wrecked it.

'Men!' he cried. 'Do not move, lest there be bloodshed!'

Bloodshed! O God!

And like cattle selected from a herd, the Spahis divided the notables on one side, next to Karaibrahim and me. But some of them came of themselves, wiping the sweat from their faces, as they had been doing a minute ago, still holding hands in the *horo*.

'This one, this one and this one!' Karaibrahim was saying, pointing to the notables. He had remembered their faces in the *Konak*. They went next to Old Galoushko and Granny Srebra, but they passed them by.

'Now all the men!'

And several of the Spahis began to tug at the men. The women began to scream, the children shrieked, but the men caressed them in silence and gathered around the fires. The musketeers separated the women from the men, standing in a dense row with their backs towards us. I saw the eyes of the Bulgarians.

Then, and only then, did Karaibrahim turn to Manol.

He was standing at the other end of the table with one arm

around Elitsa's shoulders. The table, with the wedding feast still spread on it, stood between him and Karaibrahim. The flames of the fires had almost died down and had become quite low, for no one had thrown any branches on them, so that Manol looked taller and darker. The muzzle of Karaibrahim's pistol was aimed across the table at Manol and Elitsa.

'Take him! Alive!' said Karaibrahim.

And six Turks, barefoot, bending down, began to advance towards Manol, their arms stretched forward and swaying, like wrestlers.

Manol caressed Elitsa, thrust her away from him and stood there, his arms folded on his breast. But when the six pairs of hands suddenly seized him, he shuddered as if in loathing, drew away and escaped from them. And his arms were no longer folded.

When the Turks put out their hands a second time to seize him, he raised his and struck. He struck three times and three of the men fell to the earth. He struck in silence, as if he were using a hammer once only. He did not fight to get away, he did not struggle, he did not defend himself. He merely raised his right hand and struck. If he had gone berserk, it seemed to me that he would have killed all six. But perhaps his wrath was of that kind, silent proud, and desperate.

The three remaining Turks seized him. One jumped on his back and put his elbow on his throat and his knee at his waist. The other two twisted his elbows back. When they saw that he did not struggle, they relaxed, and he stood between them, straight, bare-breasted, and even his hair was not tousled, but fell well-combed onto his shoulders.

'*Haïrolsoun*, Manol!' said Karaibrahim.

He advanced slowly, straight across the table treading with his bare feet across the roast meat and the bread, lightly kicking the bowls of wine and the water jars. He went up to Manol and took a broad knife out of his cartridge belt. Then several Turks went among the men and began to take from their waistbands whatever arms they found there. In the stillness pistols and knives fell with a rattle. And when they flashed in the firelight, they fell in a heap by the fire—a heap as silent as its owners. And those who searched the notables, dropped their purses into their bosoms.

As soon as the last pistol had fallen with a rattle, Karaibrahim pointed to me and said:

'Venetian, *mashallah*!'[10]

I went up towards him, still dazed as if I had been struck over the head, still feeling that what was happening was unreal and was happening in a dream. Something else ought to have happened, not that. I thought he was calling me to say something to Manol. And

I heard, as I stepped over the grass—and it tangled between my toes like matted hair in the teeth of a comb—what Karaibrahim said:

'What I have said I hold to. Look, these maidens here with white wreaths on their heads are all virgins. Here a maiden is a maiden. Choose first. But do not touch Elitsa.'

I realized that he was making a gift of the maidens he had promised the Spahis. In front of their fathers, in front of their mothers, in front of the men whom they were to marry. What had he to fear? He was the victor.

I raised my eyes and saw girlish faces before me. The fires had died down still further. They were lovely, God, as lovely as *samo-divas*, young, horrified and pale.

I put out my hand and took the nearest of them by the shoulder. I felt her delicate shoulder, the quiverings of her body. She was drawing away, but still in the same silence; it seemed as if that night they had all been struck dumb.

Then the Bulgarians realized what was happening, for at first they had not understood Karaibrahim's words. And a terrible screaming and howling rose over the meadow, a grinding of teeth and hoarse cries. The animals brought to the wedding as gifts and tied up at one end of the meadow began to bellow and to bleat.

And as I stood there with my back turned towards her, I heard behind me Granny Srebra's voice:

'You are no men! You are curs!'

My hand froze on the girl's shoulder.

And something black and terrible flew past me at the height of my breast. It flew past and stuck like a limpet to one of the Spahis who was holding Manol. A second later the man was rolling on his back, his gullet torn out of his neck, open upwards like a fired pistol, and blood was spurting out in bubbles. And the man was howling not through his mouth, but through his gullet.

The terrible dog—for it was Sherko's dog—rose on its hind legs and without jumping fell on the shoulders of the other man who was holding Manol. But he managed to put his elbow over his throat, and the dog tore at his arm.

Manol disappeared. I was looking at the man rolling on the meadow, and the dog was worrying him, and in my hand I still felt the stiff warm shoulder.

I heard Karaibrahim's voice:

'Manol, come back! Sherko, stop the dog!'

Elitsa lay, bent at the waist, across one of Karaibrahim's knees, her flowing hair reached the ground as if it were holding her head up. Her eyes were closed, and Karaibrahim was pressing his pistol to her back.

Manol turned. He had reached the first trees of the forest. First he looked over his shoulder, then he turned his whole body. Sherko was standing beside him. And farther back, almost in the forest, a third man could be seen, pale, wearing a cassock—the priest we had seen at the cemetery with the big stone crosses.

'Down, Sharo!' cried Sherko.

And the dog drew away from the man and went slowly, still growling, to lie down at his master's feet. While he was still on his way, Manol started back, passed the dog and went to the crowd of the notables. But the priest's face and his cassock were no longer there.

'The priest! Hold the priest!'

But the man had melted into the forest.

Mircho came running across the meadow and, pressing his forehead against Manol's hip, he began to sob.

'Venetian, I have seen the one you want. We shall share the women by daylight. Sivri *Bilyuk-bashi*, tie up the notables and the men. The notables' hands and the men's feet. We are taking only the notables and the maidens to the *Konak*. We'll leave the men, the women and the children here.'

'Master,' said Sivri *Bilyuk-bashi*, 'let's cut their throats.'

'They belong to the Padishah's flock.'

'Let's take them all.'

'As soon as the notables give in, they will come to us of themselves. They are shepherds, they follow the rams. Come! Put on your boots (for their boots were still slung round their necks), half of you put them on while the other half keeps guard!'

Just then the Turk whom the dog had knocked over rose from the ground. He drew his dagger and his pistol, and swaying and stumbling he made for the dog and Sherko.

'Come back!' cried Karaibrahim sharply.

The Turk did not hear him.

Then Karaibrahim caught up with him in two bounds, seized him by the shoulder, turned him round and felled him to the earth with a blow in the face.

'This fellow,' Karaibrahim said, pointing to Sherko, 'will breed dogs for us like that cursed cur, such as there are nowhere else in the Padishah's lands.'

Then he pointed to the fallen Turk.

'And this one will not cast lots for the women. He'll take what's left. Come!'

Two men began to tie up the notables, while the others held their muskets and pistols at their breasts. Someone took Mircho and led him across the meadow, and the boy struggled and bit them. It was one of the Hodjas, the one-eyed Sheikh Shaban Shebil. For they were both with us, the accursed men, and, in the forest, besides the pistols, they had held knives in their mouths.

The other, Molla Soulfikar Softa, went up to Karaibrahim.

'Aga,' he said and smiled, 'we are holy men, we do not want women. Give us the boy. One boy for the two of us. We are poor men—half a boy is enough for us. The Sheikh has only one eye, and one hand anyhow, he doesn't need more than half.'

Karaibrahim only waved his hand. I felt I was going to be sick —I remembered the ship.

And Mircho fell into the hands of those two obscene fellows, the Hodjas.

Then Manol raised his head and spoke :

'One thing I will ask you, Karaibrahim, and tell me the truth. Has my son Momchil been killed?'

'What is this man asking?' Karaibrahim spoke coldly and proudly.

'About his son,' I said, translating Manol's words.

'He was guarding the path by which you must have come,' said Manol.

'Tell him that there were no men on the path. His son must have heard us and fled.'

And all realized that Momchil had left the spot at which he had been posted. I remembered the man like a rock and the girl like a birch, and Momchil's face on that moonlit night. And how on the next morning, the silver coins had danced in the spring which did not want to receive them.

Thus in one night Manol was left without a wife and without his two sons.

Karaibrahim and I entered Manol's house, prepared for the first night. We went up the steps. We pushed open the door, decorated with flowers and branches, and went into the upper room.

A float light was shining. No, there were two of them. Only white could be seen in the gloom. Whitewashed walls. A white pallet bed without a cover. A white nightgown hung above it. Elitsa's nightgown. White flowers on the floor.

Who had been at work here? There was no woman in Manol's family.

And, in the corner opposite, a silvery-white gleam—Manol's *chans*.

Manol was to have brought Elitsa here that night. And now Karaibrahim was going to take her away.

Karaibrahim stood in the middle of the room. He seemed thoughtful to me. Perhaps because of the light of the float light, perhaps after the strain of the night's attack. He had relaxed. He stared at the white pallet and was silent.

I shivered at the thought that he might bring Elitsa here, to the pallet prepared by another and for another.

Karaibrahim tore his eyes from the pallet and turned them to the glitter at the end of the room.

'Bells here, too,' he spoke quietly through clenched teeth. He said the words bells in Bulgarian. And repeated in Turkish—*chans*.

He went up to them, suddenly drew his *yataghan* and struck out. There was a loud crash. I grew deaf.

The *chans* crashed to the ground, scores of them at a time, like the ripe fruit of a felled tree. They rolled about.

Karaibrahim struck a second time amid the ringing and the echo. The last pole on which the *chans* were hung fell to the ground.

And in that narrow room Karaibrahim began to chase the *chans*. To lunge at them, kick them and dash them against the walls.

I felt demented. I shrank into a corner and closed my eyes. I dared not flee from the room, yet at any moment Karaibrahim in his fury might cut me to pieces.

I shall never forget it, that battle with the silver *chans*. I did not hear the sound of a crack. They thundered and echoed and crashed. They rolled, they leapt up and struck the ceiling. Their ringing flew around the room like a bird with iron wings, striking me in the face. It seemed as if flashes of lightning blazed up and fell, and struck. For I saw that ringing, brilliant and blinding. Karaibrahim's *yataghan* was like the tiny feather of a white dove against it.

Karaibrahim may have fought the *chans* till the morning. Perhaps he only fought them for a few minutes. At one time he fell—the *chans* had knocked him down and he was rolling amid them.

And when I thought that I really was going mad, the ringing slowly, very slowly died away. A solitary *chan* only was left ringing quietly as it died away, while two or three others barely audibly joined in.

I opened my eyes, expecting to see Karaibrahim stretched out on the ground dead.

He was not there. He had fled.

Ninth Excerpt

Godfather Bogdan, Bogdan,
As you sit eating and drinking
Do you feel really happy?
Come outside, Godfather, and see—
The yard is full of Turks.

The sun rose and set, and night fell, and then another day came. And, day by day, the days given by Karaibrahim for men to take thoughts passed away. And, day by day, Manol's wedding drew nearer. All Elindenya was preparing to celebrate it, for Manol was not going to have a widower's wedding, but seemed to be marrying for the first time.

Why were they doing this? Was it to show that they did not care a fig for Karaibrahim's threats? Or to drown their fear? I do not know, but my heart grew heavier every day and I prayed that that day would come sooner and pass by. And for every day of the week there was some custom or other, and certain songs were sung, so that people had plenty to see and plenty to sing. But while posies were being made and songs were being sung, the men were settling who would guard the paths, they were cleaning their pistols and sharpening their knives. And they led the flocks out to graze in the mountains and milked their sheep. And Momchil put his name down first to guard the most distant path. At last the sun rose on that day, and set. The wedding began.

And after I had stayed and watched the people's merry-making, I could not help myself, and set out towards Zagrad to pass by the shepherds who were guarding the road. This feverish merry-making could not gladden my heart, I did not belong to these parts, I could not understand the men. I was gladdened only when I saw Granny Srebra's eyes as she caressed the cows, sheep and mules that had been brought as gifts, for they were all to go to Momchilovo. And twenty cows, between two hundred and three hundred sheep, and forty mules had been given as gifts.

And as Sherko and I were talking, the dog suddenly began to howl, and seized its master's red cloak, and began to pull him away. And only then we started and heard that the playing had stopped and that stillness lay over the mountain, and while the other guards stared along the road in the darkness with their hands over their eyes, Sherko, the dog and I rushed back to the wedding.

I emerged from the forest and in the light of the fires I saw the wedding guests and around them Turks with muskets. And Karaibrahim stood in the middle.

And six wrestlers, with hunched shoulders were making for Manol. He raised his hand and struck one, so that the man's eyes started out of his head. He struck one, and five hurled themselves at him. He struck the second, so that the man's teeth fell out on to the ground, and four men hurled themselves upon him. He struck the third, so that he broke the man's neck in two, and the other three hurled themselves upon him, and twisted his arms behind his back.

Then the dog flew past the fires and leapt on to Manol's guard on the right side. Manol shook the other two off and lo—Sherko, too, stood at my side. But Karaibrahim's voice was heard, and Elitsa lay on his knee. And Manol slowly returned. But I hid in the forest.

And when I had reached the path up above, I drew breath and called :

'Momchil, Momchil, Momchil!'

And Goran came out of the forest and Sevda was beside him. And Goran asked me, like a man startled out of a wonderful dream :

'Father, why are you shouting?'

And I told him about the Turks. And he suddenly realized that they had passed along this path while he was in the forest. And seizing his huge head in his two huge hands, he ran down the path. And I called to him :

'Come back!'

Sevda was still holding him by the waistband, and he was dragging her after him. Then he turned, seized her neck in both his hands, and pressed her down to the earth. And when he straightened up, he was still folding and unfolding his terrible fingers in front of his face, as if he were still strangling her. And he began to weep like a child, yet it was just as if he were laughing.

I asked him :

'Where is Momchil?'

He did not hear me, so I repeated my question, and then he said through his tears :

'Up there.'

And he pointed to the mountain.

'Come, let us find him,' I said, 'for he may return by another path and fall into the hands of the Turks.'

We set out through the nocturnal forest. And I kept calling Momchil, but no one answered me. I only heard an echo on the meadows, and a frightened bird flapped its wings. My calls returned to me; weak and exhausted from wandering over the forests and the summits, they lay down at my feet, saying, 'He is not there,' or 'I did not find him.' And my voice grew hoarse, and my ears were deafened by my cries, and the incessant chirping of the crickets, so that I said to Goran:

'You call now, so that he may hear you.'

He only shook his head, for he was still weeping and his throat was choked with tears.

Then Momchil silently appeared before us, and furiously cried: 'Be silent!'

And he was holding his hands over both his ears. He looked like one that had lost his wits. And when I brought my face up to his, I saw that he had shut his eyes and kept his lids down with all his might, as if he wanted to close all doors that led to him, and to remain alone. I shouted to him:

'Miserable wretch! Why did you flee from the path?'

He heard me, and dropped his hands for a moment, saying:

'So as not to hear the bagpipes and the *kavals*. And the shouts of the wedding guests.'

And as he spoke, he stopped, listened, and sighed with relief, saying:

'They have stopped. Has day dawned already?'

And I told him, although there was no longer any wrath in my heart, but only pity, for he would have to learn, sooner or later:

'The Turks have captured Elitsa and your father.'

I thought that he would die. That as he stood before me he would grow stiff and turn to stone, and that he would fall like a stone on the meadow. But he drew out his knife with his right hand and thrust it into the palm of his left hand. And he stretched his hand out, palm upward. Blood filled his palm and flowed over between his fingers and dripped to the earth. And one could hear the earth swallowing and drinking it. And in the light of the stars the blood was as black as pitch.

And when the black blood that had over-filled his heart, had flowed out on the earth, and the earth had drunk it up, Momchil turned and gazed at Goran. And the two of them gazed long at each other, and not one of them uttered one word.

Then Momchil backed away and disappeared into the forest. And afterwards we heard him running across the mountain, and twigs broke beneath his feet.

And Goran dashed away on the other side. But his weeping was no longer heard. From Momchil's side nothing more was heard.

And I was left alone, and I sat down upon the meadow, for my shoulders could no longer bear the burden of the terrible days that were coming, and my legs gave way at the terrible road that lay ahead of me : me, and the folk of Elindenya.

And although my exhausted body was on the meadow, and I felt the grass, wet with dew beneath it, my spirit was living through those days to come, and my feet were already treading those paths ahead.

Momchil would wander over the mountains, driven by men and by his thoughts, until he returned to his own folk, or the falcon pecked out his dead eyes somewhere in the wilderness. Karaibrahim would shut the notables up in the *Konak*, and torture them, until he broke their will, or until he killed them. The folk of Elindenya would scatter in the forests; some would move to Petglassets, some elsewhere, others would return to their valley and wind turbans round their heads and still others would not return, and would remain forever in their unknown graves in the mountains.

Many were the paths that lay ahead of the folk of Elindenya, and each man would go his own way.

And my way lay before me. And now I had to rise and go to the Monastery of St Elijah, to tell the old abbot about Manol's luckless wedding. So that he, too, might set out on his way, and with him the brethren of the Monastery. And when they had hidden in the caves, they would wait until the storm had passed, or live like the wild beasts to the end of their days.

Then I had to go down into the black cellar of the Monastery, and, taking in my bag all those old books bound in silver, and those old charters sealed with the gold seals of the Bulgarian Tsars Ivanitsa, Assen and Alexander,[11] I had to set out across the mountains and the fires. I would not be stopped. I had to return to the Monastery on Mount Athos to leave the books and to prepare with the other monks to meet the savage Mehmed Pasha, who was making for the holy peninsula.

I walked all the time along the hidden paths. Already I saw the Turkish camps down below; I hid in the bushes, and the thud of Turkish horses passed me by. And in the light of the burning fires, to comfort myself, I read the words, written in scarlet letters, with which the great Bulgarian Tsars had granted the Rhodope monasteries lands and men : 'I, Assen the Second, son of the old Assen, Tsar and Autocrat of all the Bulgarians and the Greeks . . .' These words were written on the charters. I knew it, and I had to hide these words from the flames which would seize the ancient monastery tomorrow, to blacken its walls, to bring down its roofs, and to melt its bells.

But I would not go straight to the south; I would set out to the west. There, in a village high up in the mountains, in which there was so little soil that folk carried up baskets of it on their mules to bury their dead, there was a little stone house, and in it a white-haired old woman was waiting. And in front of the little house there was an old apple tree, and I had told her : 'Wait for me when the apples of this tree turn red.' And day after day she had watched the white blossoms blooming and the green fruit swelling, and had waited for it to ripen. And she waited for her son. I would lay my head on her shoulder and say, 'Mother,' to her. And for a day or two I would not be the humble monk Grigorii, but would become a man like the others. I would become Nikola, who, as a child, had climbed up that apple-tree. I would chop wood, I would dig, I would climb up on the roof to put in order the old mildewed slates displaced by the snows. Before donning my faded cassock and slinging the heavy bag of books over my shoulder. And the old woman would see me off at the threshold, and would give me a red apple, a symbol of my vow to her.

I would not travel that road. I knew it, as soon as my feet set out along it as in a dream. I travelled it in my heart. I travelled for days and months, but the road which my feet travelled was not even as long as a grain of barley.

I would stay in Elindenya. I knew it, and I felt like weeping.

---

[1] *Bairam* (T) = Mohammedan festival lasting three days, after the feast of Ramadan.

[2] *Sandjak* (T) = Junior School for Janissaries

[3] Ismaïl Bey mispronounced Ilinden, St Elijah's Day.

[4] *Samodiva* (B) = wood nymph.

[5] The narrative of the priest from Smolen is recorded in 'Historical Notes in which are Recorded the Important Events, which Took Place Concerning the Population of the Krustogorié Region.' This document was written in the eighteenth century by monks, who ministered to the population of the Rhodopes.

[6] *Zashivi* (B) = samplers.

[7] Manolcho = Diminutive of Manol.

[8] *Para* (T) = small Turkish coin.

[9] *Haïrolsoun* (T) = good fortune go with you !

[10] *Mashallah* (T) = praise be to you.

[11] All Tsars of the Second Bulgarian Kingdom, 1187-1396.

PART THREE

Manol and His Hundred Brothers

First Excerpt

My name is Slav. Before that it was Abdullah, but I was called
the Venetian. Still earlier, I was a count and bore the name of a
famous French family.

I thank Manol for teaching me what a man's life is.

I thank Elitsa, for without her I would never have known love.

I thank Granny Srebra for teaching me to love songs and helping
me to distinguish poisonous weeds from healing herbs, and evil men
from good ones.

I thank Charles for teaching me to fight with a rapier, and
David for teaching me to ride.

I thank that unknown oarsman who taught me Bulgarian.

I thank my mother and my father. My mother handed me over
to wet-nurses as soon as I was born. My father looked upon me as a
means of achieving his own ends, and not as an individual. Nevertheless, I thank them for bringing me into this world.

I am thankful for having lived, and for still being alive.

I pray fate for one thing only—to help me meet death, as Manol
met it.

I had wealth and I lost it. I could get it back, but I do not want
to. I met great men, and they died. I would give my life, as much
as is left of it, for them to open their eyes for a moment.

Lo, I look at my hand as it writes these words—its brown skin
with black spots and purple veins. I look upon the shadow which
my hand casts upon the sheet of paper. Once my hand was young,
its skin—smooth, its fingers—straight, its nails—pink. When your
hand turns these leaves, mine will have dissolved in the earth, its
bones will have become brown like sticks, such as the bones of
Manol's hands are probably now. And then they, too, will dissolve.

Every evening I undress and examine my body. A long white
beard falls upon my gaunt breast. Are these protruding ribs, the
knots on the knees, the stringy muscles, mine? I lie down and I
know that one night will be my last. I do not believe that I shall
die. But when I remember how many people have died before me,
I almost begin to believe that I, too, will go. I shall surely die on

my pallet, because I have met death a hundred times on the walls of fortresses, on ships, in mountains and forests, and it has always passed me by.

So why should I tire myself watching beside a taper at night, and calling up ghosts, instead of warming my old body in the sunshine by day? Why do I not set about copying Solomon's Book of Ecclesiastes, and sign my name at the end? Vanity of vanities, all is vanity. What profit hath man of all his labour which he taketh under the sun? For there is no remembrance of the wise more than of the fool for ever.

Solomon was alone. I am not alone. As for my body, bodies are the business of the gardeners that fertilize their gardens with them. Not the bodies, but the deeds of men are important. They do not die.

Every morning, before rising from my pallet, and every evening before falling asleep, I lie on my back and call on the names of those that were dear to me, with my eyes closed. First I call the dead, then I call the living. But as many years have passed I become more uncertain whether some of the living should not be among the dead. And as I do not know whether the living are not already dead, I call the dead as if they were living.

Elitsa, Granny Srebra, Manol, Momchil, Old Galoushko, Goran, Morosini, de Beaufort . . .

Then I repeat the names the other way round, so that the last shall be first. I do not do it, so as not to anger them—I think that each of them deserves to be first.

They come from the warm darkness beneath my lids, and their faces bend over me. Sometimes their outlines appear quickly, sometimes I mould their images painfully slowly. At first I chose to see each of them at a significant moment in their lives, and I tried to remember them at the chosen moment. Then I realized that the shades return to memory at the moment which they wish, and I suddenly see them in glimpses that I had already forgotten.

Elitsa carrying water. Momchil eating, Manol smiling. When had that happened?

I seldom speak with them. More often I only call them and let them sink back into darkness. That is enough for me. I am never alone.

I thank Father Aligorko, who taught me to do this that night on the shores of the bewitched lake.

To be a man means to live with people. To be linked with them, to give them the best of yourself. The best in me are my memories. Many people will come to life in them, people who gave their blood while they lived, and who will now give their example.

When I was young, I thought that I was predestined to become a great man, perhaps the King of France. For my family have given my country kings. Whatever happened I never valued, but always waited for the unique and irrepeatable moment to fall from Heaven. I saw myself at the head of countless troops. When I set out for Candia, I thought that the moment had come. And when I was in the *Konak*, I thought that my road had led to it so that I could kill Karaibrahim.

I am now inclined to think that the aim of my life was to write this chronicle of the greatness and the fall of Elindenya Valley. It is time for people not only to act, but also to consider what they have done. It is time for people not to repeat one and the same mistake a hundred times, and by taking note of what occurs around them, to excuse themselves and to be ashamed of being men; they should see the deeds of other men, who lived before them, and be proud that they are men.

I do not know whether I am a French nobleman who remembers that he has been in the Rhodopes, or I am a Rhodope man, who remembers that he has lived in France. Now I am no longer in either of these places.

Up to my fortieth year, I lived at the court of Louis the Fourteenth and considered that that was the essence of my life. I was not a man, but the seed of a man.

At the age of forty I set out for Candia. Twice the French had set out for Candia as if they were going on a crusade, to save the fortress from the unbelievers. They were to fight the Grand Vizier himself. The flower of French knighthood gathered in Candia. The first to arrive were the regiments commanded by the Comte de Tresmes. Then came the Comte St Paul Longueville, the Chevalier de Bandon, the Chevalier d'Harcourt and princes of the houses of Lorraine and Bouillon. Others there were Dampierre, Beauvan, Colbert, the Maréchal de La Motte, Fénelon with his two sons, de Sévigné and another 16,000 soldiers. The fleet was commanded by the Duc de Beaufort and the regiments by the Duc de Noailles. I was there, too.

The deserted streets, over which were scattered cannon-balls and dead bodies, and the bloodstained, ruined fortifications cooled our heated imaginations. But we were Frenchmen, we were vain, brilliant and brave, we had come to fight and not to look on. We glittered with gold, diamonds and gold lace, and also with enthusiasm. In vain did Morosini conjure us not to venture outside the walls of the fortress. He told us that this war was not like others in which we had drawn our rapiers.

We decided to attack the enemy in secret. That fired our imaginations. We wanted to attack 2,500 Turks with 300 knights. That was heroic.

We made our sortie at dawn through a breach in the wall. It would be a sin to say that our men were not fearless. We were more than that—we were demented. We hurled ourselves upon the Turks, but the enemy had been warned. Nevertheless we pressed him hard, we threw him out of the trenches, we hunted him. One fortification fell, then a second, then three more. Morosini was madly firing all the cannon in the fort to support us, after we had disobeyed him and made our sortie. Candia was erupting like a volcano, cannonballs were falling all around. New troops emerged from the fortress. We roared and cut down the enemy. A Franciscan monk, with a crucifix in his hand, led us. The Duc de Thierry and the Lords of Villeamor, Fénelon and Lafontaine gave proof of wonderful courage in their feats. Afterwards they said that I had been the bravest of all. I remember nothing.

From the fortress they saw that the Turks were gathering in their camp to strike us in the rear. With great difficulty we succeeded in turning our maddened soldiers back. One Capuchin friar was astride a cannon, cursing us for abandoning the crucifix. We dashed back, leaving 500 noblemen on the battlefield. Something struck me on the back of the head, and I lost consciousness.

When I came to myself, I found myself cast into the hold of a ship. There were many other prisoners there, and still more rats. No light ever reached us. From time to time, a wave would dash through the boards of the deck and wash away our excrements.

For three days, and perhaps for three years, the ship tossed and pitched without cease, and I was sick without cease. In three days, I turned from a man into a whimpering sobbing animal. Turks would enter, mock me and do with me what they willed. I remembered this later. At the time I swayed, and vomited and wept into my vomit.

On the fourth day we were taken up on deck and they began to impale us—one of their admirals had been killed. I was indifferent to everything.

Then the first inhuman scream rang out. I looked around—and saw the stakes.

I had never seen them. I had heard about them and I thought they were just ordinary stakes. These were like rafters, as thick as a man's legs, and could have been the masts of ships. Their tips shone, roughly sharpened.

I imagined—nay, I felt that stake entering my body. I felt that it was rending me asunder and tearing up my insides. I began to scream.

Someone bent over my head and told me to repeat certain words. I repeated them. I would have done everything. That is how I became a Moslem.

Afterwards Karaibrahim took me as his sword-bearer. I do not know whether he had seen me on the ship when I was not a man. I do not know whether he had not gone down into the hold of the ship to make a mock of me. He behaved well to me, because he was flattered at the thought that a renowned French count polished his sword.

One day Karaibrahim called me to his cabin and there I found an unknown wretch, as thin as a skeleton, with vacant eyes and half-open mouth. I realized that he was an oarsman on a galley. The chains were still on his wrists and his ankles.

Karaibrahim said to me.

'This man will teach you his language.'

I heard Bulgarian for the first time. I had learnt Turkish while I was still in France, from boredom and vain glory while I was waiting to start for Candia. I wanted to question the captured Pashas on life in the harems.

The Bulgarian from the Rhodopes was exhausted to the point of madness and death. He often fell asleep. But sometimes he would begin to sing in a faint, hoarse voice—and I would leave the cabin.

Later the Bulgarian disappeared. Not till we were in Rhodopa did it come into my mind that Karaibrahim had known about the conversion to Islam six months before he set foot in Elindenya.

Second Excerpt

I was placed in front of three maidens. All three were fair-haired and blue-eyed, like three identical fruits on a branch with three twigs. The first was lovelier than the second, the second lovelier than the third, the third lovelier than the first. I had forgotten during the night which maiden I had chosen, and she did not speak up. So the Spahis offered me the choice of the three loveliest captives.

I thought that I was deciding the fate of the three maidens. Then it crossed my mind that I was no better than any of the Spahis.

I felt ashamed of myself and chose the middle maiden. I led her off to my room.

All that day went by in preparations for the night that was to come. Whatever may have been passing in the hearts of the Spahis and the soldiers, not one touched a single one of the maidens. They were keeping the victims for the appointed hour. Karaibrahim forbade them to enter the village, 'for everything there belonged to the Padishh.' But the Spahis had found wine from somewhere, and I do not believe that the chickens and the lambs roasting on the fires were Syuleiman Aga's. Syuleiman Aga did not show himself all day long. Neither did Karaibrahim.

And I did not go into my room all day, either.

Night came. The moon was to rise late. Fires blazed up, drums began to beat, and then in the *Konak* the women began to scream and groan.

I shall never forget what happened that night. I remember what I did and what I thought. I must have been drunk.

I made for my room. The screams, the tears, the moans, and amid them the rude laughter, the jeers and curses made my heart weep. I was maddened by that storm with flashes of lightning; I felt like howling and throwing myself down on the ground. I could not endure this mockery of the human will, this breaking of arms and legs, this breaking of wills. Every room was the hold of a ship.

I felt waves of tenderness pouring over my face. My room was a haven. I wanted to caress, slowly, with rapture, barely to touch human skin, temples, the whiteness on the inside of wrists, the knees and the neck with my hands. I wanted to relax in a woman's lap. To forget. To hide myself.

And from the waist down something was tearing me and convulsing my muscles. And from there a bestial growling and grunting rose towards my breast. I was like a sea above the wavelets of which a warm wind was blowing, and in the dark bowels of which muddy water was gushing forth, trying to reach the surface. The white and black juices of my body were fighting among themselves.

I opened the door of my room. For a moment it seemed to me that it was empty, and my heart was emptied. I raised the pine torch in despair, weeping, relieved. In one corner there was what appeared to be a heap of clothes and two eyes glowed at me, like the eyes of a cat in the dark.

I thrust the pine torch into a ring. I barely managed to fix it there, for my hands were trembling. I crossed the room—my knees gave way beneath me and suddenly cast me up. I knelt before the girl.

She had grown wild. She was ugly. But she would have had to

be a hundred times uglier to repel me. I saw what she was hiding a hundred times more tempting than it was.

Afterwards, after that night, I called to mind her features as I saw them then. Not as I saw them—as they looked. Nothing was left of her beauty. Everything about her had grown sharp, stiff and crooked. But I did not see that face of a madwoman. I saw my dream. Opposite me there was something warm, soft and round. There was darkness, hair, a whisper. Breathlessness, faintness, relaxation.

I spoke to her. In Bulgarian at first. I mixed up my words like a madman, I told her that she was alive. That she was another person.

At first it seemed to me that there was no greater happiness than to embrace that other person, to put the blanket over our heads and warm the darkness with our breath. To get away from the *Konak*, from the mountain, from Candia, from the entire earth, even from the stars. That woman held warmth and darkness in her bosom, under her garments, next to her skin.

She hissed like a cat at bay.

I must have spoken French to her. Surely I must have. I tried to embrace her, to kiss her. She crawled along the wall as if her back was broken. She never straightened up, nor did she run across the room. She did not raise her hand to strike me with a sweeping blow. It was not a struggle, but a kind of groping of blind and paralysed men. I would catch her bare foot and try to put it to my face. She crawled on and kicked me. It was pitiful and humiliating.

I stopped, panting and exhausted. My heart was deafening me.

Outside the women were screaming and groaning. In the next room I heard cries, the falling of bodies and blows.

That was life. Strong and primitive. Mine was shameful.

I seized the girl. I began to shake her. To roll her. And I felt that my fingers were on her neck and my hands were striking her head on the floor.

I was killing her.

I jumped up and ran out. I tumbled down the stairs. No one was guarding the *Konak*. Had there been anyone to lead the Bulgarians, they would have slaughtered us like sheep.

But in the *Konak* the women were screaming and groaning.

The moon was rising. A late moon, reduced after being at the full. It gave forth a strange, weary and gloomy light, as if I were looking at the world through a smoked glass. The kind of light there is during an eclipse.

I walked through the forest, stumbling, waving my arms and

persuading the girl. And a man jumped out from behind a tree. I froze on the spot, my sweat grew icy and I felt that I was wet through.

The man fell at my feet, embraced my knees and began to weep; 'Pasha! Pasha! My daughter!'

Other men jumped out, too, and they, too, lay down on the meadow. I saw in the moonlight that their hair was white.

'My granddaughter!'

They were pleading with me instead of killing me with stones. They appeared to me like new-comers from another land, they did not look like the proud shepherds I had seen at the *Konak* and around the fires at the wedding. They could not awaken.

And from the *Konak* came the screams and groans of the women.

I dragged myself away, kicking hands and faces, as I had been kicked in the room. I came to myself when I heard a brook, and crashed down on its bank; lying on my stomach along the small stream I drank, and dashed water over myself.

Little by little I grew afraid. I heard the distant screams and the laughter, and over them the quiet, indifferent murmur of the brooklet. I retraced my steps.

The forest, lit by the late moon, now looked to me like a cave in which the pillars of the moon beams rose like white stalactites. Mists were rising. It was cold.

I came out onto a broad meadow. The moon hid behind a cloud. In the darkness insects of some kind shrilled on every side, short and sharp, as if a steel wire, stretched taut, were vibrating. A creaking and a ringing. The ringing came from my left, from my right, all around me, never at the same time, and it seemed to me that the same little steel fly was flitting around my head and winding a silver cobweb around me, and cutting my brain with short flashes. The male glow-worms quivered anxiously—disappearing and glowing again, looking for something which they did not find. They left a brief, light trace, and with painful impatience I tried to guess which way they were going, but in the darkness they had changed their direction, and glowed in another spot. There was something incomplete, something that was asking and that was left without an answer in the broken ringing, and the broken flashes of light.

Only in the grass, wet with dew, the fat female glow-worms—heavy, big, wingless—glowed calmly with a cold radiance, waiting to be found.

I reached the wall of the *Konak* and set out along it. Above me cries that were now tired, and moans and panting came from the windows. The moon was rising, and the moonlight grew weaker. I was as weary as if I had walked all night. I was hesitating whether to go in, when I heard the sweet voice of a woman above me :

'Where have you been, Venetian?'

I did not see the face, but I recognized Gyulfié's voice. She was standing at the wooden grating of the window. I was glad of her presence. I heard a voice like a human voice, alien to the madness and the horror of this night.

Silently I entered the *Konak*. There were bodies rolling in the courtyard. It was dark under the plane tree. The fires dying out, the embers glowed raspberry red.

I did not grope about on entering the *Konak* as I had thought I would a minute before. I was looking for someone. There was someone to look for. I went up on to the veranda. It was deserted. A door creaked and Gyulfié called to me :

'Come in.'

It was dark in her room. She asked me again :

'Where have you been?'

I answered :

'Far from the *Konak*. The women screamed and wept.' And I confessed quietly : 'This is no place for me, Gyulfié.'

She took me by the hand, and bringing her lips close to me in the darkness said quietly :

'I want to go and hear something, but I am afraid. Come with me.'

She opened something like a cupboard and we both began to descend a flight of stairs. It was quite dark. I was not surprised because I had been along many secret passages. I groped along the steps with my feet. My right hand rested on a rough wall, Gyulfié held my left hand. The wall was cold; Gyulfié's hand was soft and warm.

We began to walk along a passage. On both sides of us was stone, above us were boards. Over our heads we heard voices, footfalls, snores. I fumbled in my waistband to take out my flint and strike a light to look around. Gyulfié seized both my hands.

'Don't. This passage goes all around the *Konak*, around the outer wall. It passes under the windows, and in some rooms you can enter it through the cupboards. If you strike a light, it will be seen through the cracks between the boards.'

I thought at once and asked :

'Isn't this passage at the same height as the cellar and the stables? Aren't the notables shut up there?'

'Yes, they are,' Gyulfié answered. 'That is why its breadth is lost, and no one realizes it is there.'

'Let us go and hear them,' I begged.

'No!' Gyulfié's refusal was sharp. 'Enough pain. Come.'

We went on. Once Gyulfié stopped. I felt that she was hesitating. Then her voice reached me through the darkness :

'Remember this place. The secret door is here. You are a good man, you do what you can. Those who made it came and have gone. Only I and the Aga know it. If you strike a light, you will see that there is a scorched girder built into the wall. It moves.'

We went on. Once more Gyulfié stopped. I wanted to question her, but she squeezed my hand, to make me hold my tongue. She was listening. It was quite quiet. In a little while she herself whispered to me :

'This is Karaibrahim's room.'

Somewhere above me, quite near, Elitsa was breathing. I did not want to think, I did not want to imagine anything. I was choking.

I heard Gyulfié whisper :

'I was here before, too, but I got frightened. You can't believe in anyone. She never made a sound, yet she was supposed to be water none had drunk from. She should at least have screamed for the sake of decency. There, she's quiet now, too . . .'

I put out a hand to stop her mouth. My fingers touched something warm and wet. She bit me.

And we began to writhe on the cold earth like two naked worms in the darkness of the basement. We were silent. I and Gyulfié.

And that night I realized what an ardent and desperate woman she was.

In the darkness we never noticed when the sun rose. I barely dragged myself to my room.

As soon as I opened the door, I saw that it was dark inside. The girl's body hid the window. She had hanged herself and hung there—long and extended—and the tips of her toes almost touched the ground. She had stepped on my saddle.

I took her down. She was very heavy and was already growing stiff.

It grew light in the room. I saw her kerchief in the corner and threw it over her terrible face. Her fair hair, which I had tousled in the night, showed beneath it.

I knelt beside her. I looked at the body which had maddened me several hours ago.

I did not even know her name. How had she given life up? What had she obtained for it? What was there, besides life, that I did not know?

What was her body worth now? The down on her cheeks, the down under her armpits? The long lashes above the blue eyes?

I thank you—it is all one whether the Lord God of Sabbaoth or Allah—for being alive.

I cast myself down on my pallet. I had no strength to call for anyone. And I fell asleep at once.

I awoke as if someone had struck me. I saw the body on the floor and, stumbling, I dashed out. Elitsa! Elitsa and the stillness in Karaibrahim's room.

I saw Elitsa through the branches of the plane tree, on the other side of the courtyard. She had leant her elbow on the balustrade and was looking at me through the leaves of the tree. I was at once filled with hatred of her. It seemed to me that there was no despair in the posture of her body. Her two braids hung down from the balustrade like two dead snakes. She had even braided her hair.

I wanted to turn, when Karaibrahim's servant dragged himself up to me. He told me, yawning, rubbing his eyes with the back of his hand, and pulling up his baggy trousers:

'The Master has sent for you to fight with swords.'

Even that morning Karaibrahim did not want to give up his fencing.

I went in to fetch my rapier and silently showed the servant the dead body.

We fenced under the veranda, in front of Elitsa. We were both equally bad. It was clear from Karaibrahim's face that he had spent a sleepless night. He was still leaner, and even weary, something quite unusual for him. I need say nothing about myself.

At one time I raised my eyes and saw the two long chestnut coloured braids. I grew ferocious. I may even have growled. Three times I wrenched the rapier from Karaibrahim's hand and cast it ten feet away. And all three times I stood straight, carelessly resting the rapier on the tip of my right shoe, while he went, bent down and picked up his rapier.

And Elitsa looked on from above.

This time I do not know whether Karaibrahim was angry or not. He seemed not to care. He was right. He had Elitsa.

I made off. I turned sharply and began to go up the stairs on Elitsa's side. I could barely breathe with emotion.

Half-way up I drew aside to let one of the girls who had slept with the Spahis pass me. She was only in her white shift, torn and bloodstained, with her hair unbraided. She had the same look in her eyes as the dead body I had cut down from the window. She was dead, yet she was walking.

I waited for her to pass and began to go up the stairs again. I still hated Elitsa.

When I went towards her, she turned to look at me. Her braids glided over the edge of the ballustrade with a rustle, but they did not slip off to the end, and remained turned to one side of her head so that they slightly bent her head.

She had grown thin. I saw a wax-like pallor on her face. Her lips were cracked, but her eyes shone with a feverish brilliance. And they were not like the eyes of the poor wretch who had passed me a second ago. Under her eyes there were blue shadows. That is how a face should look, drawn by a sleepless night full of passion.

She was beautiful, more beautiful than before. She had survived. She was withdrawn. Passionate. I felt like spitting on her. The blue under her eyes looked to me like the traces of a man's fingers. I imagined that somewhere on her white skin, under her garments, there were these blue, shameful stains. I remembered Sevda, the shadows on her face—a soft, handled fruit rotten to the core.

Only now did I see that Elitsa's garments were in order, buttoned and fastened.

She looked at me, turned without bending her head, and slowly made for Karaibrahim's room.

I dared not go back to my own room, so as not see the dead body, outlined by the tumbled garments. And the blue face, all blue, not like the blue under Elitsa's eyes.

In the courtyard I was greeted like a hero. They had heard and wondered what I could have done to a woman to make her hang herself. Their victims had kicked and screamed, they had cast themselves on the floor and fainted, but in the morning they were all alive. The men clicked their tongues and envied me.

What had I done? I had not done anything.

I had killed her. I, the coward, had not even been able to rape a woman. I had killed her. She had waited. And what she had expected and seen was more terrible than anything I could have done to her. If I had gone back to her, she would have been alive. As Elitsa was alive.

I forgot about the dead girl only when Gyulfié came to me in the night.

In the dark I did not see how fat she was. And she was very fat, a perfect snowdrift of flesh. But was it important whether she was fat or not? She was wise, she was kind. When she wanted to, she could caress one like a mother.

In what way was the other one, the dead girl—the stern and lovely girl—superior to her?

In what way was Elitsa superior to her?

Third Excerpt

Three days later, the time allowed to the notables by Karaibrahim ran out. And he ordered them to be brought out from the dungeon into the inner yard of the *Konak*. For three days they had been given neither food nor drink. Syuleiman Aga, who had not shown himself on the veranda for three days, sent a man to Karaibrahim to tell him that in three days even a donkey would die without water Karaibrahim asked :

'Water runs down the walls of the dungeon, doesn't it ?'

'Yes, it does.'

'Let them lick the walls. And no one has died of hunger in three days.'

On the third day in the morning, Delyo asked to enter the dungeon and the sentry did not stop him. He stood in the doorway. holding his nose because of the stench that came from within, and asked in a snuffling voice.

'How many are you ?' And as no one answered him, he was forced to enter the dungeon and pass among the captives who were lying on the ground. He counted them and found that they were sixty-three.

'But you were sixty before, weren't you ? Who are the three new men ?'

Old Kralyo answered him, probably hoping that they would set the new men free, as they had not previously appeared before Karaibrahim :

'There are eight new men, and five of the former ones are not here.'

And he spoke their names. I remembered only one, because he was later among the six first chosen by Karaibrahim. I set it down here, so that his grandchildren may know of him, if this manuscript reaches them. The old man's name was Volchyo Krilatitsa.

I was standing at the door when Delyo came out and took off his sandals which were covered with filth to the top. Old Kralyo could not help himself and asked :

'Why do you ask ?'

'Have you heard hammering over your heads ?'

Indeed, for three days there had been a constant hammering on stone coming from Syuleiman Aga's rooms.

'The Aga has ordered your names to be inscribed on a stone slab. He is making a monument for your grave. If anyone is willing to give up his faith and accept the True One, let him speak up—his name will be effaced.'

Delyo grinned, and laments and curses were heard from inside.

Towards noon Karaibrahim's men brought the notables out into the inner courtyard. The last ten were carried out.

They all gathered in a heap around the fountain. The fountain was guarded by four Turks with drawn *yataghans*. One shepherd—one could not tell whether he was young or old—kept hurling himself at the water, shouting :

'I want water.'

The men pushed him back, and wiped their hands on their clothes in disgust. He would fall, and set out again, now on his feet, now on all fours, still repeating :

'I want water.'

There was no one else in the courtyard besides the notables and the four soldiers. Some of the notables lay on the ground, others stood. Some covered their eyes with their hands and cloaks, for the sun blinded them; others covered their ears with their cloaks, so as not to hear the noise of the water. But all of those who looked about them kept their eyes fixed on the silvery stream of the fountain.

When Karaibrahim began to descend the stairs, several of those who had laid down rose to their feet. And Manol's voice was heard, saying :

'The mountain is looking at you.'

And after him was heard :

'I want water.'

The mountain could not see them—the courtyard was surrounded on all sides by verandas and buildings. And it was better so. What was left of the proud peasants who had stood on the same spot ten days ago? Garments plastered with filth and earth, faces black and green from the slimy dampness which they had licked from the walls, beards, matted and tousled, hands blue from the straps that bound them.

I saw their eyes when I went down to them. They looked gloomy, desperate and wild.

Karaibrahim took his place on the same spot where he had sat ten days previously. He was seated on the same carved chair. He was dressed in the same clothes. Next to him stood I and the two Hodjas, the one-eyed and the fat one. Hassan, the son of Velko, was not there. But now Karaibrahim had covered the lower part of his face with a handkerchief to guard against the stench, and his voice sounded dull and changed, but his merciless eyes glowed above the handkerchief.

I remembered what had happened ten days ago. I also remembered my thoughts. Had the thread that bound these men to the mountain been broken, had they already been left alone? Was their mother's blood still flowing through them, or had their blood been closed in a circle, so that only his own heart beat in every one's breast?

Sivri *Bilyuk-bashi* asked, as he stood by the fountain :

'Aga, shall I bring out that one with the spotted cur?'

'Leave him, he is no notable,' Karaibrahim replied and was silent.

Karaibrahim was silent, so were the notables. Then Karaibrahim put questions, and I translated into Bulgarian. It seemed to me that I myself was putting the questions. Ten days ago I had felt lonely, and I was alone now, but without wanting to, I was already joining the group of men in clean clothes and turbans. For those opposite, the filthy and desperate ones, reminded me of the inferno on the ship. They repelled me, I wanted to get away, or to have them removed.

'Who spoke before?'

Old Kralyo came forward, bent and weak, his white hair and his white beard blackened.

'Old man,' Karaibrahim said to him, 'the ten days are past.'

Old Kralyo was silent.

The voice of the man maddened by thirst was heard :

'Give me something to drink.'

Karaibrahim said :

'Drink from the source of the Pure Faith.'

And I translated.

Then Old Kralyo spoke and said :

'May you be cursed.'

Karaibrahim rose to his feet, and his voice was as calm and even as ever :

'What were these three days of suffering for? What was this stubbornness for? But I forgive you. There, before you, is the fire, the ashes of which I showed you last time. Pour ashes on your heads and let each of you place one of those fezzes and turbans on the ashes.'

First he pointed to the circle of ashes, which I had not so far noticed, then to a heap of fezzes and turbans piled up against the wall. And he said further :

'And your flocks will be yours again, and each one will go to his home, and the blessing of Allah will be upon him.'

While Karaibrahim was speaking, the captives who were standing helped those who were lying down to rise to their feet. And as they leant against each other, clinging to each other, they crowded together in a very small huddle, and not only their hands appeared to be bound, but the whole lot of them seemed to be tangled in a common rope. And the thirsty one kept close to them. They looked like a huge beast with sixty heads and one hundred and twenty feet. Old Kralyo leant his back on them.

Old Kralyo answered Karaibrahim:

'What we had to say to each other, we have said. Do with us what you will. We are in your power.'

And he fell silent. They were all silent, even the man maddened by thirst. Then the sound of hammering on stone came from the veranda and of hammering on wood from the gate.

From above someone called:

'Aga, the *Yurouks* want to enter.'

Karaibrahim shouted:

'Tell that damned clerk to stop, and the *Yurouks* to wait.'

The hammering on the veranda stopped, but on the door men hammered still harder. And the voice from above cried:

'The chieftain of the *Yurouks*, Ismaïl Bey himself, has come.'

Karaibrahim thought for a while, and said:

'Let him enter.'

The gate was opened and into the yard came Ismaïl Bey, the *Yurouk*, on horseback, and after him came his seven sons, they, too, on horseback. With a quick look the *Yurouk* chieftain glanced at the bound notables and saw Manol.

And Manol met his glance, and said quietly, as if in shame:

'Well met, Father Ismaïl.'

'*Haïrolsoun,* Manol *Kehaya.*'

And Manol said further:

'Happy are you, Father Ismaïl, that you have seven sons.'

'Happy are you, Manol, my son, that you have a hundred brothers. How can I compare myself with you?'

Then he looked around, and turning to the servant who had opened the door, he asked the man:

'Where is Syuleiman Aga? Why does he not come out to welcome me?'

And from the veranda was heard:

'I am here, Bey. You are welcome.'

We all raised our eyes, and for the first time in three days we saw Syuleiman Aga. He was dressed in his expensive purple garment, combed and trimmed, but he was pale and had grown thin.

Then Vrazhou *Kehaya* called to him in a trembling voice:

'We are here, Aga! See the state we are in! Did you not throw men into the abyss for a lecherous word? Did you not kill my son? See my daughters, now! A curse upon you, you butcher!'

Syuleiman Aga pretended not to hear him. And Ismaïl Bey, without dismounting, said to Syuleiman Aga:

'Aga, this man here, bound like a murderer, Manol the Hundred Brothers by name, a son without a father, gave me, Ismaïl Bey, his fifty-two silver *chans*, and for them I gave him land for a village.'

Karaibrahim spoke up:

'Where did you give him land, Bey? Where?'

Ismaïl Bey, who had not turned to Karaibrahim, and had not greeted him—for hospitality demanded that Karaibrahim should greet him first—did not turn to him even now. And Karaibrahim grew pale with spite and mortification.

'Ask him,' Syuleiman Aga pointed to us. 'The Janissary before you, Ismaïl Bey. And forgive me, I am ill and cannot descend the steps. If you come up to me, I shall bow to you to my grave.'

'How can I come up to you, since you have not come down?' Ismaïl Bey said loudly in perplexity. 'What is happening here? Are you the master of this house, or these unknown men? And who is the Janissary among them? I do not see him.'

No one answered him.

'Then tell me, you with the tuft of hair on your forehead. Where are my *chans*?'

'Who are you?' Karaibrahim asked him.

'I am Ismaïl Bey, of the seventy-eighth *odjak*. I am looking for Manol's *chans*.'

'We have put the *chans* away. But how am I to know they are yours?'

The *Yurouk* looked around the courtyard and the verandas.

'Is there anyone here to say that Ismaïl Bey does not speak the truth?'

'I will give you the *chans*,' said Karaibrahim.

The *Yurouk* pulled the reins to turn his horse. But he stopped the animal as he was, with his head turned on one side.

'Aga, can I ask you something?' he said to Karaibrahim.

'Ask me.'

'Then I ask you. Why are these men here bound? I know them. Not one of them has stolen or killed.'

'They stand against the will of Allah.'

'Manol *Kehaya* told me that Mehmed Aga was converting folk in the plains to Islam. I said to him: "A green water-melon, even if you twist its stem, will never be sweet." I will say the same to you, that you may remember it, Aga. A green water-melon ripened by force is never sweet.'

The chieftain of the *Yurouks* spoke calmly, but with a kind of carelessness. A more critical ear would have heard scorn, too, in his voice. Karaibrahim was unable to restrain himself :

'Bey, when you entered, I wondered that your garments should be like those of these shepherds, bound in the courtyard.' (And indeed, the *Yurouks* wore garments exactly like those of the Bulgarians, the same leggings and sandals, the same braided trousers, the same waistband, sleeveless jackets and shirts. But they had no red cloaks.) Now I no longer wonder. Remember that the gate is at your back and not before you. And it is easily barred. Why have you come?'

'Young lad, if you bar the gate, my men will bar the passes. You will bar the gate with a spruce pole, my men will bar the passes with iron rifles. Do not try to frighten me, I am old.'

Karaibrahim rose to his feet. Yussouf, the *Yurouk's* eldest son, spurred his horse forwards and came up to his father. The bound Bulgarians began to murmur and stir.

Sheikh Shaban Shebil, the one-eyed Hodja, came forward. From his bosom he drew out a scroll, kissed it and raised it on high to the *Yurouk* Bey. The latter did not stop his dancing horse, and signed to the Hodja to give the scroll to his son. The Hodja kissed the paper again and put it in the young *Yurouk's* hand.

Yussouf read something and nodded to his father. Ismaïl Bey quietened his horse, and during this time, Yussouf kissed the scroll and handed it back to the Hodja. And Yussouf whispered something in Ismaïl Bey's ear.

The Bey bent his head, as if were bowing, then he raised it. He raised his hand, too :

'Forgive me, Manol *Kehaya*, forgive me, you, too, shepherds. Such is the will of Allah.'

He reared his horse up on its hind legs, turned it thus and spurred it to the gate. As he passed by each of his sons, the latter turned his horse after him. And just as he was about to disappear in the dark cave of the entrance, the man who was maddened by thirst screamed :

'I want to drink, Ismaïl Bey. Give me a knife to cut my veins.'

Ismaïl Bey stopped his horse and looked back. He said something to his son Yussouf—what, no one heard. Yussouf dismounted—for the first time a *Yurouk* set foot on the stones of the courtyard— and took down from his saddle a little swollen goatskin. He went back to the bound shepherds and asked :

'Who wants to drink here?'

From the womb of the hundred-legged beast, the man who was maddened by thirst, emerged and opened his mouth. Yussouf raised the goatskin on high and squeezed it. The thin white trickle of milk fell and gurgled in the thirsty one's mouth. The fountain gurgled, too. The thirsty man bowed his head, as if he had already lost his madness, as if he were already shamed. For a second the trickle struck his bent forehead. Then it stopped.

Yussouf dropped the goatskin and asked :

'Is there anyone else who wants to drink?'

But all the shepherds who had followed the white trickle with crazed looks, bent their heads. And the thirsty one, having slaked his thirst, went and hid himself in their midst. They made way for him in silence and in silence again they closed their ranks.

Yussouf returned to his horse, tied the goatskin with a strap and leapt into his saddle.

Ismaïl Bey called from the gate :

'Let no one say that Ismaïl Bey passed by a thirsty man, and did not slake his thirst. If any of you, or your sons, or your daughters turns off the road at my tents, there will always be shelter and a pallet for him. At least Allah does not forbid one to welcome another man under one's roof.'

One after the other, the *Yurouk* horses passed through the tunnel and the thud of their hooves grew dull, then they died away. And the door swung to with creaking at their backs.

And Karaibrahim waited, as if to let the spirit that was left after them die away, too, and said :

'Hear me, notables, who look like scarecrows. You have said your say and I will repeat mine. No man will be left in this valley, who will not draw a cross with his blood and spit upon it. I shall torture you and kill you with fire, water, earth and air. With iron, wood and stone. With sharp edges and blunt ones. Give up your faith now, for from now on the sufferings you have undergone will seem to you as thick as my little finger, and those that are coming will be like my waist. Yes, I promise you that and I will keep my word.'

But the notables were silent.

Then Karaibrahim gave orders to drive that hundred-legged monster back to the dungeon, and left only Old Kralyo in the courtyard. And the old man looked on helplessly, while his comrades were swallowed up by the black door.

The bent old man and strong Karaibrahim were left alone, one opposite the other. And Karaibrahim leant over the old man, like an eagle over a plucked hen. The old man was trembling all over as if his courage had followed the others. I stood beside them,

translating, and expecting every moment to hear the old man say :
'Have mercy, Aga.'

'Come, now, the others aren't here. Change your faith.'

'I cannot, Aga.'

'How so, you cannot?'

'Well, I simply cannot.'

'What if the others change theirs?'

'If the others change theirs? I shall see, Aga. Let me be the last one.'

'Is it not all one, Giaour, whether you be the first, or the last? You will change your faith anyhow. Change it first.'

'What of the others?'

'What do you mean, the others? Did I not tell you? It's all one whether you are first or last.'

'It is not all one, Aga.'

The old man pressed his lips together—you could not have parted them with a knife.

Karaibrahim furrowed his nose, and at the same time his nostrils dilated. Where the outer side of the nostrils touched his nose, the skin grew white. Two white lines curved up around the arch of his nose. Karaibrahim straightened up. I thought he was going to burst. He said to the *bilyuk-bashi*, who was sitting by the fountain :

'Go into the dungeon and find the five oldest shepherds. Let them be six with this one. No, I am not going to butcher them. Shave them, clean them, give them food, whatever they ask for. Let them each ask for one thing. Fulfil their wishes. Then come and tell me you have done so.'

The *bilyuk-bashi* stood there, his mouth agape.

Karaibrahim added.

'Lead out Vrazhou *Kehaya*, too, the one who cried against Syuleiman Aga.'

Karaibrahim went away, and that day I saw him no more. I only heard his voice.

That same day Sevda came to the *Konak*, she had not appeared since the night of the wedding. Gyulfié received her angrily. Sevda was trembling from head to heel, and kept looking around her.

'What do you want? Why have you come again?' the Agovitsa shouted.

'Ask that man to go.'

'He will stay here.'

The woman suddenly burst into tears.

'He comes every night, and goes every night, Agovitsa. He hurts me, he tears me to pieces. I have run away.'

'Who comes?'

'He comes, terrible, hairy, his eyes glowing. He begins to strangle me. "It's your fault . . ." "Because of you . . ." "I have been left without a heart . . ." Then . . . And he only goes away in the morning.'

'Who, you jade?'

'Goran, Old Galoushko's son. Because I lured him away on the night of the wedding, and he left the path. Look.'

And Sevda rolled up her sleeves to show the bruises on her arms. She also undid her shift. I looked, but Gyulfié looked still more avidly.

'If you can't make love,' she said in a toneless voice, 'if you can't make love, why do you take it up?'

'I can't make love, Agovitsa, you say? I? It's that I'm afraid.'

She thought of something, glanced at Gyulfié, grew thoughtful and said :

'I am afraid of bearing his child. Suppose it is as big as he is? I shall die, I shall be torn. Do you know that whatever bitch his brother's dog mounts, dies—her pups are so huge.'

'And what do you want, bitch?'

'Hide me in the *Konak*. Otherwise I'll betray him. I can't stand any more. Let them come and catch him.'

'If you utter one word, I'll tell the Aga to have you impaled. Then your womb will be torn asunder, and your foul heart. Stay in the *Konak*.'

And when Sevda had moved away, swaying her slender figure, she said spitefully after her :

'She is barren, like I am. And she knows it. She said that on purpose to me, about the child, so that it would hurt me. I know her.'

'How can you know, Gyulfié?' I asked.

'I know best by the way she looks at men. She begs everyone for a child. Don't you see what she is?'

I said quietly, feeling no shame in front of her, but in a voice which showed that someone else had said it before me :

'There are three things which are insatiable, four even, that do not say: "Enough!" And the first two are—hell, and an unfruitful womb.'

'That is true! Oh, it is very true! And what are the other two?'

'The earth which is never sated with water, and fire, which does not say: "Enough!"'

'That is also true. But there is something else, as well. I shall tell you what it is—a man's eye that never looks its fill of women and of sons.'

She stood there in front of me, huge, round, her skin shining as if it were stretched on a drum, and her little lips smiling. Suddenly I saw that tears were streaming from her eyes.

'Forgive me, Gyulfié,' I said to her, deeply moved.

I was sorry I had talked to her like a man with a man. I did not want to lose her.

She angrily wiped her tears away.

'And do you know why that jade talked to me about Goran and showed me her breasts? She knows that I am mad about him.'

She, for her part, was talking to me like a woman talks to a woman.

'Many are the men I have met; three times has my womb leapt. And, moreover, only when I looked at them. That is surely how women that are with child feel their babes quicken for the first time within them. One of the men is Manol, the other is Goran, and the third is Karaibrahim. I know that only these men can wake the children within me. But there is no way by which I can woo them.'

And casting me a playful look that sat comically on her round face, she said to me :

'You're not cross, are you?'

She thought she was taking her revenge on me.

Black and terrible pages are coming. I wonder if I ought to write them. I grow despondent. Weariness seizes my hand. My head is heavy, I do not feel like doing anything. How can I pass through that sea of suffering and horror? I look ahead and see the piles of sheets which I must fill with tales of human suffering. When I recall them, all those gloomy days, during which the sun, too, seemed to have been darkened, they pass before me within the space of a few moments only. My memory does not want to delve into them. My heart flees from them. But if I begin to describe them, I must strain myself to draw from the black water of the well memories long drowned in it. For days on end I shall awake, knowing that a day of cruel memories awaits me.

All my wisdom, all my calm, garnered in the hard years of trial, are shaken the moment I remember those days. I know, I know, man is not a beast; that is why I am writing these lines. But there are men who are beasts. Woe unto them, that evil has chosen them to be its beasts of burden. Still—why was all this necessary?

But I must begin. I imagine that I am a pearl fisher. I have brought piles of oysters up from the depths and have let them rot. And I fumble about amid the decaying flesh and the stench with shuddering fingers to find the hidden pearls.

From the day on which Karaibrahim took the starving and

thirsty notables out into the inner courtyard, I lost my balance. It happened suddenly. I felt that something was bearing me along and that I could not stop myself. I was like a leaf in a storm. The wind blew me first to one side, then into a stone, then to another side. Was it a nightmare, was I waking? I could not stop to look around and ponder. Blow upon blow fell upon me, and at once I covered the wounded spot with my hand, and in that time I was struck in another spot.

I was alive, but I did not rejoice. I had only one thought— to hold out. Not to scream, not to tear my clothes, not to fall under the wheel of the terrible cart which was rattling and shaking over Elindenya. Not to make a mistake. I knew that it would end. Sometimes I did not believe that it would end. Only at first, I was able to relax at night with Gyulfié. But that was not a rest.

We were shut up in the *Konak*—we, Karaibrahim's men, the captive women, the Bulgarians in chains. And Syuleiman Aga and his men. The entire *Konak* was under a curse. I was cursed to stay with them. I could not go out and set out over the green mountain, to lie down in the grass. I was cursed. Death awaited me there. I could only watch the sun rising and setting through the window. The green tops of the forest cast a cover over the mountain, under which another life, hostile to mine, seethed and lurked.

All afternoon Karaibrahim's cut-throats busied themselves about the six old shepherds. I remembered how the Roman soldiers had dressed Jesus in a purple mantle. The old men were trimmed and washed like children. They were given food. I watched them eating. Old Kralyo refused. Vrazhou *Kehaya* wept, his tears fell on the plate, but he ate. And the four other old men ate well, without hurrying. The muscles of their temples and chins stirred. They were like travellers, who have stopped for a while, ready to rise and set out on a long journey. They were asked what they wanted. One of them asked to milk a sheep. He was brought a cow. He milked with patient skilful movements, and the hundred men watched him from one side, as if he were working a miracle. Vrazhou *Kehaya* asked to be allowed to shout. He was laughed at. He drew a deep breath and gave such a shout that the water of the fountain stopped running :

'Daughter, where are you?'

From the veranda, as if it came from a deep cave, a woman's voice wept.

'I am here, Grandfather !'

They stopped his mouth, but did not beat him.

The third asked to be led out of the *Konak* to look at the mountain.

The fourth asked to be allowed to put away the bread that had been left on the table.

They went to ask Karaibrahim, and he swore at them mightily.

I do not remember what the fifth asked.

Old Kralyo did not ask for anything.

As soon as it grew dark, Sivri *Bilyuk-bashi* came and said that the old men must go back to the other captives. They were bound and taken away. I thought that Karaibrahim expected the six chosen men to tell the others how wonderful it was outside in the light. But I was deceived.

I was talking to Gyulfié on the veranda. She was sad—she had gone to Syuleiman Aga, but he had driven her away. Men and lights began to stir in the courtyard. New pine torches were being lit. Karaibrahim was preparing to go in to the notables.

I dashed into Gyulfié's room. They looked for me to interpret, but they did not find me. Hodja Hassan was brought. Then I remembered, and entered the cupboard, and groped my way down along the secret passage. I easily found out where the dungeon was. The stones of the wall had purposely been left without mortar between them, so that what happened inside could be heard. Light was now shining between the stones.

I heard Karaibrahim's voice.

'These six men, whom you yourselves chose today, will be the first to die. Every day I shall kill one of them, so that there will be enough to last the whole week. On Friday I will rest. One of them I shall have impaled, the second I shall have cut up in pieces, each piece so small that an ant can carry it, the third I will bury alive in an ant-hill, the fourth I shall crucify on the ground, so that the flies will eat him, the fifth I shall burn alive, the sixth I shall flay alive. I told you— I shall torture you with earth, fire, water and air. With wood, stone and iron.'

The Hodja Hassan, son of Velko, slowly repeated these words.

The notables were silent. Narrow slits of light showed around the heavy stones. I had pressed up close to the damp wall; that was why I froze and shivered.

And I heard Karaibrahim say further :

'And thus, week after week, six at a time. Manol, where are you?'

Manol did not answer.

'Are you frightened, Manol? I shall kill you last. I have been told that a hundred years ago, when Cyprus fell, as Candia will fall, our men flayed a Venetian captain alive, and filled his skin with feathers. And put his clothes on it. And he lived flayed for three days and saw himself in his own clothes. I want to know whether you, too, will live to look at yourself from outside.'

Hassan Hodja repeated the same thing in Bulgarian.

The notables were silent.

Karaibrahim said :

'Only one man at a time will see how each of you dies. So as to tell you about it afterwards. When you imagine what has been, it will be all the more terrible for you.'

And he ordered Sivri *Bilyuk-bashi* :

'Untie the six. Give them dice. Leave them a pine torch. Let them cast lots to see who will die tomorrow.'

The light grew fainter. Only a pale, quivering thread was left, swaying between the stones like a cobweb blown about.

Twice I heard every word of Karaibrahim's. In Turkish and in Bulgarian. Without wanting to, I translated them to myself.

The sound of clanging iron was heard, as the door of the dungeon was closed. Then I heard Old Kralyo's voice :

'Manol, spare us !'

And Manol spoke.

'Why do you beg me? Beg Karaibrahim.'

And the old man said again :

'Manol, have mercy !'

And he began to weep.

Manol's voice was heard, calm and strong :

'If you want to, give up your faith !'

Old Kralyo answered through his tears :

'May you be cursed ! I will not give it up !'

'Why do you curse me?'

'Don't look at me so ! Don't look at me !'

And Manol said :

'The mountain is looking at you.'

And Vrazhou *Kehaya* screamed :

'May you be cursed ! Cursed be the mountain ! Cursed be my mother ! I don't want to die, I don't !'

The cobweb of light was torn. On the other side of the wall the pine torch had burnt out. I waited and shivered with cold in the dark. No one spoke again.

I came out of the secret passage. I pushed Gyulfié aside and went to my room.

At first I lay down on my back. Then I began to toss and turn like a madman. I hated Manol.

I was alive. Yet he prevented me from living.

I wanted to crush him, to twist him, to see him stretched out and pitiful. That fool of a Karaibrahim only knew how to cut throats and butcher people!

The generations of French noblemen who had for centuries tortured, oppressed and crushed human beings and human wills were awakening in me. I shivered as at an irrepressible secret passion, stronger than the passion I had felt that night for the girl who had hanged herself. I struggled with the temptation, I thrust it away, but it rose from the depths. It came from the darkness. I whispered something, twisted and turned and moaned.

I was torturing Manol. He was beside me. He was hanging by his thumbs with weights of a hundred kilogrammes hanging on his feet. His bones were leaving their sockets, his sinews were tearing, his skin was bursting. His body grew so long that he joined the floor and the ceiling. I put wet boots made of straps on his feet. I made him ride on sharp points. I roasted him over a slow fire, bound only by a chain by the waist, and he ran around the stake, and all around him there was fire. I buried him alive, and his mouth was filled with earth. And more, more, more!

That fool Karaibrahim! I wanted to jump up, to open his door, to raise him from the bed on which Elitsa was sleeping with her hair unbraided. I wanted to shout to him how to torture, to seize the pine torch and dash into the dungeon.

A warm human body was writhing before me. And whatever I did to him, someone else wanted to do it to me, and now I, too, was tossing and writhing, for I was defending myself. And I could not tear myself away from the terrible thoughts which shook me like an ague. I cried: 'No! No! No!' And something dark and indefinite was coming towards me.

I did not notice when Gyulfié came in. As soon as she touched me, I cried out. She stopped my mouth.

In the morning, before slipping away, she looked me straight in the eye.

'This isn't you,' she said and shook her head.

It was I.

Fourth Excerpt

May God strike down the cuckoo grey
That its cry was heard before the spring,
Before the spring, before Annunciation,
Luring forth the bandits young and brave.

For one hundred years Syuleiman's *Konak* stood amid Elindenya, its walls shining white, while life for Elindenya's folk was black. In the old days, it was like a haunt of ravens, from which hungry soldiers flew out to pounce on Christian souls as if they were carrion. Now it was white like a serpent's egg in which an unknown monster was being hatched, a monster which wanted to cover the entire valley with its webbed wings.

The folk of the three villages had scattered over the surrounding mountains like hunted birds, driven out of their nests in which only the white egg was being hatched. They stayed in the mountains and waited.

I, too, waited. We were waiting for our emissaries. For down there, in the *Konak*, sat sixty Bulgarians, bound with grief and iron, and they were our emissaries, who had gone down into the monster's lair. And there was no news of them, or from them, not even a word. It was not the enemy who had captured them and driven them off—we had sent them, the mountain had sent them to show Karaibrahim that he would never break our will.

Every day I went up Mount White Head, sat down on the ruined marble walls and gazed at the *Konak*. And afterwards I closed my eyes and began to summon the faces of the notables to my mind. They came one by one, looking as they had done in the moonlight on that night near the water-mill. I would send them my good thoughts, but they would go, as if they had not heard me. And when I opened my eyes, I would see the *Konak*, standing white down below, and even the sun's rays bounced off its white walls. And I knew that behind its walls there was cold and darkness, and in that cold and darkness the notables spent their days.

And we waited for our emissaries. What else could we do? The young people were angry and said: 'Let us attack.' The old only shook their heads. For their fathers had told them what stones they had split and what logs they had brought down when the white walls of the *Konak* were rising.

And as I looked at the *Konak* and the roofs of the three villages,

I remembered the mummies we had found in the cave. They, too
had stood here and had looked at the same slates of the roofs. And
they, too, had waited. But they had not waited to the end. That is
why I did not much like going into the cave, so that I would not
see the terrible faces and the empty eyes.

Two hundred persons were gathered in that cave, most of them
women and children, and the greater part were the wives, children
and grandchildren of the unfortunate men taken away by Karaibrahim. As the folk of that region believe that the swallows do not fly
south in winter, but hide in caves or become bats, they would say,
as soon as they saw a bat: 'Why can't we become like the swallows
or the bats, and awake only when spring comes to the valley and
the memory of Karaibrahim melts like snow?'

But they awoke every morning and wanted to eat. And before
placing a morsel in their mouths, they would run up the steep slope
to the ruined walls of the pagan temples to look down on the
Konak. And it was always there.

Five days passed thus, filled with waiting and grief. On the very
first day one of the girls fell ill with fear and called her friends who
had been carried off to the *Konak*. And her brothers brought up
from the village the chests, filled with her trousseau and placed
them on the sand of the cave, that she might look on them with
delight and think of her bridal days. And she begged her friends to
put on her new garments, and she gave them as gifts to those on
whom they looked well. On the third day she died. On that same
day a child was born, and they brought the shell of a big turtle
and placed the child in it, and when it cried, they rocked it.

After I had read morning prayers to the kneeling wretches—
and I read them up above on the height, amid the ruins of the
temples of the old gods—I set out along the crest of the Elindenya
Valley, to go to the Miloto Gospodi Pass. There I sat amid the
big stone crosses and drew strength from the calm of the mountain.
And on the first day, when I entered the graveyard—lo, the biggest
cross had disappeared. And, long as I sought it, I was unable to find
it. And on the second day, a second cross disappeared. On the third
day, when I went up there after the burial of the young girl, and
was thinking about her sisters in the *Konak*, my eyes were sharpened
by sorrow, I saw that someone had been digging and had afterwards carefully covered with fresh turf the place where he had dug,
so that it would not show.

Someone was hiding the crosses in the earth. They are there
to this day and only they have remained, for later the Turks broke
all those which still stood in the graveyard. And when the sun
shines once more over Rhodopa—may that be soon—let people dig

up the meadow to the right of Miloto Gospodi Pass. And they will find the stone crosses in the earth.

That night I hid in the forest beside the graveyard, in great fear. And in the middle of the night a shadow appeared amid the crosses, and I heard the blows of a pick. And straining my eyes, I recognized Momchil. I rose and called to him, but he began to withdraw, walking backwards as before a ghost, and melted into the forest. 'Momchil,' I called to him, but he did not answer.

And in the daytime, when I was returning, I saw on a meadow in the distance a falcon digging its claws into the eye of a doe, flapping its wings to deafen it and trying to peck out its eyes. The doe was down on its knees, tossing its head but the bird of prey would not leave it. Then, from the forest, a man appeared and the bird rose. The man seized the doe by its forelegs and raised it up. It stood on its hind legs, its hooves on his shoulders, and the two seemed to be staring each other in the eye. Then the doe fell sideways and began to squeal, and I remembered that Momchil had slaughtered the goat thus, when Vrazhou *Kehaya* had defeated Manol. He had raised it onto its hind legs, looked it in the eye and thrust his knife into its heart. I ran down, but the falcon shrieked and flew at me. I covered my face with my hands, and when I took them away, there was neither Momchil, nor the falcon, nor the doe.

Momchil, too, was waiting. He wandered alone through the forests, driven out by the people, and waiting to see what would happen in the *Konak*.

Only one person did not wait to the end, and she was a woman. Every day Sevda came up to the cave and from there went up to Mount White Head, and she always asked me: 'Father, have you seen anything?' And when the Turks came out on the fifth day and went to bury someone alive in the ant-hills above the *Konak*, and we could not tell from afar who it was, she burst into tears and said to me: 'Father, give me your blessing, I am going to the *Konak*.' And she went down. It was not so, no, it was not so. She left on the third day.

And the others waited.

But what would happen if word came that the notables had bowed their heads and spat on the cross? Would these people go down to their villages, so that the men should wind turbans round their heads, and the women hide their faces?

The people waited. They waited in different ways, for every man is different from the other. The wind blew over the mountain, bearing laments and songs, and blowing about the black kerchiefs and the white ones. And the stronger the wind blew, the louder grew the weeping and the singing, and life and death boiled in one cauldron. By day the mothers wept in the cave, their faces hidden in their aprons, by night their daughters filled the forest with whispers. And wedding after wedding took place without the brides being fetched and without festivities, and as many as came to me to be blessed, twice as many married of themselves. But when they returned in the morning, holding hands, they asked first of all, 'Has word come?'

And the children wandered through the forests and began to bring the first strawberries. And they brought basketfuls of mushrooms, so that we made soup of all the various kinds, and some we roasted and others we dried in the shade. But the children, too, coming out of the forest with hats made of ferns on their heads, would ask, 'Has word come?'

One night, when I, too, had returned to the cave, for a cold wind was blowing; the child in the turtle shell began to cry, and its mother screamed. I dared not open my eyes, lest I should see the faces of the dead, but a light showed under my lids and I opened them to look. Someone had thrown dry roots on the fire and the flames leapt up, but the smoke drifted towards the entrance around a man who stood there, that is why we could not recognize him. And he stepped forwards in the light and we saw Momchil. His hair fell over his face and his shoulders, matted and full of burrs like the mane of a wild horse. His face was gaunt, so that his neck looked still thicker and more shapely, like the necks of the folk carved on the marble slabs up above. And his eyes glowed. He said to us :

'I have dug up the grave of Enihan Baba, the conqueror of Rhodopa. Up there, there is a *teké*[1] over his grave, to remind us that the Turkish commander massacred our forefathers and captured their wives. I lit a fire, to consecrate the earth and drive away his spirit, and I dug up his grave. And I did not put out the fire, for I wanted to burn his bones, and to scatter the ash in the wind, so that his spirit would not be able to gather it on Judgement Day. There were no bones in the grave.'

And he repeated :

'There were no bones in Enihan Baba's grave.'

People were waking up one after the other, throwing the rugs off their faces and looking at him. And suddenly he began to shout :

'There are no bones ! There is no Enihan Baba ! Rhodopa has no conqueror. No one has conquered the valley. Yet for three hundred years we have bowed before Syuleiman Aga and three paltry Turks. And one empty *teké*. The mountain has not been conquered.'

[1] For notes see p. 271.

Then one woman was the first to cast something at him. She cast her apron at Momchil, and it spread above the fire and flew as silently as an owl. And others cast things at him, and as the cave was sandy, so that there were no stones, they cast sandals, pieces of bread and fur caps. And one cast a handful of sand. They did not aim at him with strength and spite, but seemed to want to cover him and hide him from their eyes.

And the sand was scattered in Momchil's face and he covered it with both his hands, and backed away from the fire. And the darkness hid him. The people, still without speaking a word, lay down and wrapped themselves up, covering their heads.

On the following day, the children found the body of a fox in the forest. When hunters kill a fox in winter, they skin it, and hang its body on a branch. And there the skinned carrion hangs until it dries and becomes black, for even the hungriest beast will not eat a dead fox. It may hang there for years, for it is poisonous. The children found a black body of this kind, placed it in the rock, and the first bent down, picked up a stone and cast it at the body. And said :

'Cursed be Momchil.'

And the second bent down, picked up a stone, cast it down and said :

'Cursed be Momchil.'

By evening the pile of stones was up to my waist, for the old folk, too, when they passed, cast a stone, only they said nothing. I seized the hands of a wise old man, and begged :

'Do not do this—he did it from great love.'

And the old man said to me :

'Love is one's own business, but standing guard is everyone's. Let him wander, cast out like a cuckoo. You know, Father, why the cuckoo is cursed, do you not? Because one summer it began to cry before the forest was in leaf and deceived the young *haidouts*. They took to the mountain, but snow fell and they were caught by their tracks. Since then the cuckoo has no nest of its own. God has not forgiven one bird, for ten *haidouts*, at that. Are we to forgive Momchil for betraying Elindenya?'

And he cast the stone. But the stone seemed to strike me, and remained a weight on my heart. But that was the fifth day, and when I went up to the ruins, I saw that the Turks were burying a living man in an ant heap. And a fire blazed up in my breast and melted the stone.

If it were true that centuries ago in times of drought, the high priests lit huge fires before these temples to show the clouds the way, so that heavy rains fell—if it were true, then the flames in my breast alone would conjure up such clouds that a flood would sweep away the cursed *Konak*, and all Elindenya, too.

And in the night the man buried in the ant heap rose from the dead and came to the cave. And it was Vrazhou *Kehaya*. The ants had gnawed through the ropes that bound him, and he had fled.

And the news that we had at last lived to see a man from the *Konak* flew over the mountain, so that pine torches set out in the darkness and gathered around a big fire in the ruins. For the folk of the three villages were scattered around in ten and even in twenty different camps, and were now coming together for the first time since the wedding. And when we piled all the torches on top of each other, the flames rose and lit up the white stones and the people's white faces. And Vrazhou *Kehaya* began his tale. He began quietly, but the folk at the back did not hear, and a wind rose, so that he had to shout. And what he told grew still more terrible because he shouted it, and it was shameful for a man to speak such things. And the wind blew the fire and the flames about.

And when I found the strength to raise my head and look around, I saw only white stones around me, and they were rosy from the fire, but I did not see a single erect forehead. And I felt like giving Vrazhou *Kehaya* a push, to make him stop. But I dared not touch him, for he was a martyr.

Then Momchil leapt out of the darkness where he had been hidden, listening; he leapt to the fire and cried :

'Why do you weep, fools? Rejoice that the mountain has borne such men.'

And no one picked up a stone to strike him, although their feet stood on stones. Momchil was the son of Manol.

The following day Vrazhou *Kehaya* gathered his household—and they were many—and went down to Zagrad. And when the people realized that for another sixty days Karaibrahim would kill one man every day, many said : 'Let us go back to our houses, for until then the Turks will not touch us.' Apparently, not one of them thought that the notables might give in, so that each one counted sixty days, one man for each day.

I, too, counted them. And I bent to the earth when I thought that for sixty days we would look down from on high and see a man dying, yet we would not be able to help him. We would not even know his name, so that we could pray for him. And even if we did not see it, we would know that every day one of the sixty would die. That is why I did not go up, but went down towards Old Galoushko's water-mill.

And he was sitting on the white stone which Manol had moved

so that Elitsa might comb her hair unseen. He sat there, swaying backwards and forwards, as if he were weaving on an invisible loom. And his white head swayed like a pendulum. But the spout still roared, cast itself up and fell in the lake. And the wheel hidden under the water-mill turned, so that its walls shook, but the mill-stones did not grind anything.

The old man did not hear me. And when I touched his shoulder and he looked at me, he seemed not to recognize me. I had to shout in his ear all the terrible words that I had heard the night before from Vrazhou *Kehaya*, I had to shout them so that the deaf old man could hear me. And just as last night I had wanted to give the shepherd a push, so someone ought to have been found to push me into the lake, so that I might drown and be silent. But I was silent in the end, for I began to sob with fury and grief. The white old man looked at me as if he knew something still more terrible. The wheel rattled and the stones shook, and my head was dizzy, for I had bent backwards and forwards with the old man.

And he stopped swaying, and I remembered that I had seen a captive bear swaying thus, I do not know whether because of boundless grief, or because it thought it was going somewhere. And the old man seized my bag, but said no word, for he had become mute after the night of the wedding. Happy were those who could weep.

I understood, and I took out the Psalter. For Old Galoushko could not write, but he knew the big letters. I opened the pages of the Alphabetical Prayer and he pointed out letter after letter with his trembling hand, until I read :

'What of the child?'

And he looked at me with such eyes, and asked me with such pain, that it would have been a hundred times better if he had told me anything in the world. And I thought that he was asking me about Elitsa. It was only later that I understood that he was asking me what would happen to the child of Elitsa and Karaibrahim.

Fifth Excerpt

Syuleiman Aga dismissed his men. In the morning only we, the captives and the notables, were left in the *Konak*. Karaibrahim went in to Syuleiman Aga. The Spahis were shouting and threatening the Aga, for they had found the body of one of their fellows, and one of the captive girls had disappeared.

Karaibrahim came out, outwardly angry, but I realized that actually he was glad.

'Aga,' Kemanchidjogli called to him. 'Why didn't we cut their throats? Now they'll take to the forests and become idlers.'

Karaibrahim shrugged his shoulders.

'Fifty more or less makes no difference.'

For, of Syuleiman Aga's hundred men, barely fifty still remained —the rest had fled earlier.

'They are armed,' Kemanchidjogli insisted.

'Better for them to be in the forest than in the *Konak*,' Karaibrahim said and went away.

Syuleiman Aga was left alone. Only the two Turkish clerks and three servants were with him. Gyulfié, too, had only a few women with her, some of them converts to the True Faith.

That same day they brought out one of the six old men and impaled him.

The following day a shepherd from Syuleiman Aga's flock came, and weeping, told him that Delyo had set fire to two sheep-folds—one with ewes, the other with lambs and rams. The two sheepfolds were on two mountains, the one opposite the other.

'When the lambs bleated for their dams, the black earth shook. When the ewes bleated for their lambs, the blue sky was split,' the shepherd wept.

There was an old *haidout* custom: to roast a live lamb on a spit. Whoever could stand its cries, remained a *haidout*. Whoever stuffed up his ears or went away, returned to the village. Delyo had burnt a thousand sheep and a thousand lambs alive. Thirty men had bound the shepherds in the evening, three unbound them in the morning. The rest had not been able to stand the test.

I was standing beside the Aga; I had come to show him that it was all one to me whether he was the ruler of a rich valley, or a deserted old man. It seemed to me that Syuleiman Aga's lips were moving and that he was whispering:

'Why? Why?'

But aloud he said:

'I nourished a wild beast, it was only proper that he should bite me.'

And the shepherd related further that half the Aga's sheep had been stolen by the Bulgarian shepherds themselves, and the two Turkish shepherds had been killed.

The Aga turned to me.

'What have I lived for? I do not grieve that my men have left me. But the peasants? I was the shepherd, they the sheep. I was a good shepherd. I guarded them from wolves, I cleaned the stones from their pastures, I put bridges over the rivers. I milked their milk, I sheared their wool, I roasted them on embers and ate them. I am a shepherd, am I not? They were sheep, were they not? What else could I do?'

And what could I say to him?

The shepherd's lament had barely died down, for he could not forget the burning sheepfolds, when two Tartars came, riding the same horse, and led by one of Syuleiman Aga's men. The horse struck sparks with its hooves, crushed by the double load, and the Tartars waved bare swords, threatening their guide that they would cut his throat. The Aga had sent him to find out what was happening with Mehmed Aga, and lo, he was returning with the Tartars.

The guide first went to eat and drink, but I think that he went to Karaibrahim.

I made as if to rise and go, but the Aga stopped me with a smile. And in the next room the clerk was hammering the inscription on a stone slab, and seemed to be splitting my head.

The guide came—an old, experienced man with crafty eyes. And he began to curse the Tartars who had wanted to take their horses as well, along the secret path, so that they had fallen and risen for three days, and in the end one of the horses had drowned after all, and the Tartars had nearly cut the guide's throat.

I wondered at the Aga, how he could stand the fellow talking nonsense to him, and how patiently he waited for him to tell him the important thing.

But the man, it would appear, was waiting for the Aga to ask him, yet at one moment he said of his own accord:

'Nothing came out of it, Aga.'

'Did you give what I told you to? If they asked for scarlet cloth, to give golden silk? If they asked for white *groshes*[2] to give yellow gold coins?'

'Nobody wanted anything, Aga. They are all like wild beasts. They want blood. And there was nothing to ask about. As soon as I reached the top of Mount Vrushnik everything was clear. To the north everything is burning. Last night I saw a fire somewhere hereabouts, also, so that I feared that you, too, might be burning.'

And he fell silent. The Aga was silent, too. Then the man said:

'But these Tartars have come with good intent, Aga. They bring you good news.'

He fell silent again, waited a while and spoke once more:

'Your brother's sons, Hairedin's whelps, are with Mehmed Pasha. They are undermining you.'

He held his tongue and said no more. He only handed the Aga a heavy bag.

'Here is the gold, Aga. It is all there.'

The Aga nodded, but did not put out his hand, and the man was obliged to leave the gold on the floor. He became confused and went away.

'Send for the Tartars,' the Aga called after him.

And in the next room the cursed clerk was still chiselling the funerary inscription, and hammering as if he were undermining the foundations of the *kyoshk*.

The two Tartars came in, bow-legged, in their sheepskin jackets and filled the *kyoshk* with the smell of sweat and chafed bodies. The Crimean Tartars were allies of the Sultan, and supplied him with fifty thousand light horse. They kept the Muscovites and the Poles in check, while the Sultan held them with his troops in Kaffa and Tana, headed by a *Beyler-beg*[3].

The Tartars handed the Aga a scroll with a letter, and gave themselves airs although otherwise they appeared to be amiable and smiling.

Syuleiman said to one of them :

'Pick that over there up from the ground.'

The Tartar raised the bag and his eyes grew as narrow as slits cut by a razor when he felt its weight.

'Open it,' said the Aga.

For, of course, the Tartars had never thought that there was gold in it.

The Tartar untied it and looked in, while his fellow peeped over his shoulder.

'It is yours,' said the Aga.

And the two, as at a given signal, fell flat on the ground. And as they lay on their faces, one of them said—I did not grasp which one, for the two were as like each other as twins :

'Be on your guard, Aga. I know no more.'

His voice was quiet, and, because his lips were touching the floor, it was toneless and obscure.

They rose and went away, but the Aga was silent for a long time, holding the scroll in his hand. From the next room—but it was heard as if coming from the cellar—came the regular hammering of the chisel on the tombstone. Mentally I bowed to the Aga for not opening the scroll at once.

He rose and passed through a door. On the floor, not the clerk, but Hassan Hodja himself sat cross-legged, carving the marble slab. His beard and eyebrows were covered with white dust. I remembered Old Galoushko, the White One—where was he now, the poor wretch—and his words about the grain which did not become ears. The names of the notables were being turned into dust, yet what ears could have sprung up from their seed.

'Read,' Syuleiman Aga said to him, and handed him the scroll.

The Hodja left the chisel and hammer, wiped his sweaty hands on his hair—he was not wearing his turban—and took the scroll. He unfolded it and began to examine it. Again the Aga did not make him hurry.

'It is for the Cadi,' he said. 'For you, but is written as if you were the cadi. It is from the Sultan.'

I saw the *Tougra*[4] of Mohammed, Son of Ibrahim, Always Victorious, but the man did not kiss it.

He began to read :

'"To the most just of judges among the True Believers, first among the spiritual dignitaries, professing the singleness of God; mine of virtue, wisdom and just decisions for the entire people; heir of the knowledge of the prophets and the emissaries of God; the man distinguished by the great mercy of the Almighty, the Cadi of Elindenya, our Molla, may his knowledge and his virtues multiplied . . ."'

'Do not read further,' said Syuleiman Aga. 'Tell me what it says.'

'It says that for your justice, he rewards you with a scarlet cloth robe, a white silk waistband and a gold chain—a sign—for your neck. You are to go to Adrianople and receive them.'

'What do you say to that?'

'The Sultan knows as much about this letter as his late father.'

'His reward will be according to justice. Read further.'

The hodja began to read again :

'"In no case, however, make it necessary for me to send my sacred order on this question a second time. This you must know, and trust to my holy sign." That is all.'

'"And trust to my holy sign . . ."' Syuleiman Aga spoke the words one by one. 'And what is this about a second order? Who is invited a second time for a reward?'

'That is what it says.'

'Finish the inscription and get ready for the journey. We set out tomorrow. A man cannot escape his fate. Nor his reward. Have you much left to do?'

'I have one more name to carve and below it the words : "The loss was great, but such was God's will. In memory and consolation".'

'We can do without the last words. That is understood. Everything happens by God's will. And what consolation is a tombstone? Whose is the name?'

'My father's,' said the Hodja.

I barely smothered my cry.

'How so, Hodja, is your father among the notables?'

'They impaled him today,' said the Hodja.

As soon as it grew dark, I went down into the secret passage. From Gyulfié's room I took a cover and a cushion, that it might be soft for me on the stones.

Gyulfié was getting the Aga ready for the journey and was weeping. Once he had left, she would remain alone and without support. I was barely able to recognize the artful, shameless woman; tears flowed from her like water from a pierced wineskin, and her flesh hung loose.

Through her tears, she told me that one of her maids had seen Karaibrahim embracing Sevda. And then she had heard that Sevda was mocking Elitsa. She told her that Karaibrahim had promised her (Sevda) *Konaks*—she would only sit there and thread seed pearls. Karaibrahim had told her that white hands and a white face like hers ought not to be burnt by the sun.

'Well, what of it?'

I was sorry for her, and angry with myself for trying to get away from her, but I could not bear such tears.

'What of it, indeed! Suppose she accepts the True Faith? The Aga is going away, Karaibrahim is staying here and Sevda with him. She will rule the *Konak*.'

'Is that where the shoe pinches you?' I thought.

'Never fear, would Karaibrahim exchange Elitsa for Sevda?'

'Dear God, what a fool you are! One would think you weren't a man. Elitsa is clear water, and Sevda is red wine. Who would drink water when there is wine to be had? Were she to learn for a hundred years, Elitsa would never learn Sevda's skill. That bitch was born knowing.'

Would Karaibrahim really leave Elitsa? I hoped so.

When I set off, Gyulfié's plaints turned to spite. Perhaps that was what hurt her the most.

'I have fancied three men in my life, and that bitch is already sleeping with two of them. Do you know what she said to Elitsa? That she would take her husband away—Manol, I mean. Do you hear? And if she does it and sleeps with all three, I shall die.'

Manol was Elitsa's husband. I had forgotten that. What kind of a husband was he, if he had not even touched her?

I was going down to Manol. I loved Elitsa, but now I was not interested in the fact that Manol was her husband. Something far more important was drawing me to Manol and the notables.

I wanted to understand them.

The shepherds possessed a great secret—how not to fear death. I had reached the truth that the most important thing was to be alive, but a man could not rejoice at life as he should, if he remembered and trembled all the time because he would die. But the shepherds were not afraid. Otherwise—how could they hold out? If I found out their secret, if I understood where their strength was hidden, I would obtain wealth a hundred times greater than what I had lost.

And I decided to go down into the secret passage every night, next to the wall of their dungeon, and to listen to what they said to each other. They would open their hearts before their death— for, after all, they did not know that anyone was listening to them. I was not so stupid as to hope that I would obtain their secret easily. Perhaps I would not understand anything. I would have to interpret, to think things over, and to seek. And perhaps it was their strength that drew me to them, and I simply wanted to be near them—the big, handsome, undefeated men.

And so I lay down by the wall and began to listen.

They were speaking of the burnt sheepfolds and cursing Delyo. They did not remember his former misdeeds. The burning of the lambs stupefied them; it seemed to them a kind of a sign, a sacrifice to God. Songs were sung about such terrible crimes, and after the evil-doers had lain ill for nine years, grass grew on their bones, and a snake made its nest in their hair; they saw with their eyes, but could touch nothing with their hands. What vengeance awaited Delyo?

Thank God they did not talk of Velko who had been impaled. Afterwards I realized that they did not speak about the man who had been killed that day. Only the man who had been sent to witness his death would say: 'He is dead.' Or: 'He still suffers,'—and that man spoke no more.

From time to time they laughed. How? Calmly, as if they were at home. Most often they remembered their flocks and their dear ones, wondering what they were doing. There were some who would begin to weep.

I had leant my head against the wall and sat there with closed eyes. It was all one whether I looked or not, for it was quite dark in the secret passage. I would be carried away by their words, not pitying the men, forgetting that they were condemned to death. I no longer knew whether I slept and was dreaming, or whether, waking, I heard human voices. I may even have dozed off, and heard the voices through my sleep.

I started, because the voices were silent. I opened my eyes and saw that a cobweb, stretched between the stones, was quivering in light. There was a light beyond the wall.

I heard Sevda's voice :

'Manol *Kehaya*! Manol!'

And Manol's voice :

'Get out!'

'Manol!' Sevda repeated with a tremor.

'Get out!' Manol repeated coldly.

'Let her be, Manol,' several voices begged. 'Perhaps she brings news.'

'Who can get into this dungeon?' Manol replied. 'Only someone at Karaibrahim's service. What do you expect from the likes of her?'

'Is Elitsa any better than I am? Your Elitsa? Upstairs with the Turks!' panted Sevda.

A cry was heard. Or rather Manol roared, but he must have bitten his lips. And he said in his ordinary voice :

'Go.'

'Manol, forgive me. I will save you, Manol! Not now. I paid the guards. Another evening. Wait, Manol. Put things off, wait.'

And she spoke on, confused and passionate.

Did Karaibrahim know? Had he sent her, to separate Manol from the others? Or had she herself really bribed the guard?

Suddenly the light went out. I heard quiet, muffled voices :

'Lie down here. Here.'

Then I heard the rattle of the chains on the dungeon door and a light showed again. Someone else had entered the dungeon.

Syuleiman Aga. He said to Manol :

'Manol, tomorrow I shall no longer be in Elindenya. I want to set you free. You will take Elitsa and leave the valley.'

Manol answered him :

'I offered you a whole kingdom and you did not give up your faith, although it is not even yours. Yet you want me to give up my faith because of a woman.'

Syuleiman Aga said to him :

'I do not want you to give up your faith. Be what you will. If you like, I will send you your flocks. If you like, in the autumn, when the sheep go to the Aegean Sea, I will order them to separate your sheep and take them wherever you say. Leave Elindenya.'

I heard Manol say :

'What of the others?'

I heard Syuleiman Aga answer him :

'I cannot let you all go. I no longer have the power and the strength. Only for you, can I do it.'

And Manol asked him :

'Syuleiman Aga, would you leave your friends?'

And the Aga was silent for long before he answered :

'I do not know. After I had killed my brother, I would not have left them. Manol, I have never had a friend.'

Manol said :

'Then you will not understand me.'

The Aga spoke quietly :

'Manol, the pine-torch is burning out. No one needs you here. Go out, fight. I cannot tell you more.'

And Manol laughed :

'Does no one need me, Aga? No one? It is not so. We are emissaries here, and the mountain expects us.'

'Then—go back to the mountain.'

'It is waiting to see what we shall do.'

Silence. The light between the stones grew dim.

'Then—fare you well, Manol *Kehaya*. I have not got a hundred brothers, I made a mistake. I shall remember that night on the summit.'

The Aga's voice seemed full of bitterness.

'Farewell, forgive me, Syuleiman Aga. Good luck go with you.'

Manol was bidding him farewell in a calm and solemn voice.

The light vanished. The chains rattled. And suddenly Sevda's unrestrained weeping was heard. During the entire talk she had lain on the ground in the filth, among the bound bodies. She was weeping now, quite without hope, like any weak, helpless woman.

'Did you hear?' asked Manol. 'Get up and listen to me. Find Momchil and tell him that the knife with which I dug up his mother's grave is hidden under the last slate of the roof. The one with the cross on it. Let him cut off Karaibrahim's head with that knife. Then I'll forgive him.'

He was silent and then added quietly :

'From my grave. Did you hear?'

'I heard,' Sevda answered in a trembling voice. 'The last slate with a cross on it.'

'Bend down and I will turn to one side. Take the ring off my finger. And give it back to Elitsa. I cannot do it alone. Pull, pull hard. Get out.'

There was silence. Then Manol spoke again :

'Tell her that I am no longer her husband; I never have been. She must feel free, the ring must not weigh on her. Did you hear?'

'I will give it back to her, Manol *Kehaya*.'

Sevda's voice had grown calm and submissive.

'And if you meet Father Aligorko, tell him to find Ismaïl Bey and

ask him to lend the silver *chans* for one day. When they take me out
to die, let him strike them up on the mountain. That I may hear
them for the last time.'

When the chains on the door rattled, I rose and groped my way
up with outstretched hands, like a blind man. I could not bear any
more.

On the following day Syuleiman Aga set out. He was mounted
on a different horse, not the huge one on which he had welcomed
us. He gave that one to me, together with the rusty cross-bow.

'I give you two things which are of no use at all. I give them to
you only for remembrance of what has been. To remember that
things are different and will be more different in the future. Remember that what is past is past. The egg is broken and the chick
has flown away. Remember, too, what I told you before. The time
of parting has come, and each man will take his stand to the left
or to the right. Where will you take yours?'

'In the middle,' I said.

He smiled.

Besides this, he ordered his clerk to write a deed of gift to the
people of Elindenya. He made them a present of three mountains
and wanted them to be divided into as many lots as there were
families in the valley.

The Hodja, the clerk and three Turkish servants set out with
him. The two Tartars also travelled with them. On the saddle in
front of the Aga two bags of money had been flung.

No one went out to see him off outside the *Konak*. Neither
Gyulfié, nor Karaibrahim.

Syuleiman Aga made his horse circle round the plane tree, then
he spurred it and it galloped at the black maw of the gate. The
hooves made a hollow sound, as they would on a barrel.

I ran up to the window, to watch from there. I found Karaibrahim there.

I was amazed to see that there were people in the deserted village.
They were few, perhaps a hundred souls, and they stood on both
sides of the road. As soon as he saw them, the Aga stopped his
horse, and set out at a walk. We saw his back.

He entered among the people. Not a voice was heard. We saw
sparks flying over his head. The Aga was throwing handfuls of silver
aspras along the road. No one bent down to pick them up.

All along the road through the village, until he was hidden by the
bend, the Aga cast money along it, as if he were sowing grain. I was
about to go, when Karaibrahim tugged at my sleeve :

'Look !'

Only then did I notice that where the road could be seen passing along the slope of the mountain—on the first meadow and then right up on the Miloto Gospodi Pass at the crosses—there were many people. The Bulgarians hidden in the forest had come out to see the Aga. There were women and children down on the meadow, I could tell them by the colour of their clothes. Up on the pass there was only red—the shepherds' cloaks—that was where the shepherds stood. My heart was heavy. I waited painfully long for the little group of horsemen to appear, and then slowly to approach the people.

The Aga passed, and was lost in the forest. And I waited still longer for him to come out on the Pass, alongside the huge stone cross which stood out against the sky. I gazed at the red spot by the crosses and waited. The Aga passed there, too. He stopped there. Then the red spot parted, joined up and disappeared into the green of the forest.

I waited for the Aga to emerge on the other summit, too, on the crest. At the spot where we had seen Elindenya. I thought that he would stop and look, as we had looked then. We for the first time, he for the last.

The horsemen did not stop. They appeared for a moment and vanished.

I heard afterwards that Delyo with two of his friends had stopped the Aga, but Goran had cut Delyo's throat.

Sixth Excerpt

I clearly remember how one by one I mounted the steps which led me to that terrible decision.

I had come to the Elindenya Valley and wanted to rejoice that I was alive; I had not succeeded. I was alive, but I did not rejoice at that. I rebelled against the men who prevented me from relaxing in my swamp, and I wanted to go to their hangmen. I had not succeeded.

Now I was seeking something. I was a man who was seeking. And I had to find what I sought quickly, for there was not much time. I could no longer sleep. My hope was in the shepherds, and every night I listened to their talk, and shivered ten times over, every time I thought I was hearing their secret. When I emerged into the light, my heart would remain empty. It was not that. No, it was not that.

And so, the first day they impaled one man. The second day they buried Vrazhou *Kehaya* alive in an ant-hill. Up above the *Konak* there were huge ant-hills—piles of earth and dry spruce needles, almost as high as a man—and in them lived big black ants with jaws like pincers.

On the third day they buried the third old man up to his knees in one of those ant-hills and cut him up bit by bit—in pieces so small that an ant could carry them.

On that day Sevda accepted the True Faith. At last one person in the Valley of Elindenya had been converted to Islam—the beautiful widow, the bitch of Podviss village.

They veiled two of Gyulfié's maidservants—it would have been comical otherwise for two women with uncovered faces to cover Sevda with a yashmak. They cut off her long fair hair in the middle of the yard and made kiss curls on her cheeks. They placed a red Turkish fez with a string of silver coins on her head. They covered her face.

And they called her Safidé.

Karaibrahim set aside the deserted wing of the *Konak* for a harem. But she always found some reason to pass through our inner courtyard with the two maidservants at her heels. There were one hundred beautiful women in the *Konak*, but we men gazed after the only veiled woman. And Sevda knew how to walk.

Gyulfié hid in her room. I did not want to meet her, but every night I passed beside her to go down into the secret passage. Her face swollen with weeping and her eyes glowed with fury that that 'bitch in season' had captured her *Konak*.

The fourth day came on which they were to burn the fourth old man alive. But they cut his throat instead.

On that day I took a new step towards the great decision.

In the morning the Turks found the *bilyuk-bashi* Bersendjiarab dead in front of the *Konak* gate. He had gone out to relieve himself and the arrow had pierced his throat. He lay with his trousers down and his face in his own excrement.

The Turks were furious. I say Turks, but these men were brutes from ten nationalities and one hundred races. They were growing tired of staying inside the *Konak*; they grumbled and cursed Karaibrahim in secret. But in front of him they kept their eyes on the ground.

Nothing could stop them now. They opened the gate of the *Konak* and rushed into the village. There were madmen there, who continued to live in their houses, hoping for who knows what. About noon they brought in about ten trembling men, nearly battered to death, whom they had caught in the village. They decided to behead them all.

They did not behead them on a block, but made them sit down cross-legged in the middle of the yard. They held a contest to see who could best cut off a human head at one blow.

I looked on. Why? So that I might not be able to forget it later. I was torturing myself. Or else I could not do otherwise.

Finally there appeared a black Arab, who had been an executioner in the Hungarian town of Offen. He made the old shepherd sit down cross-legged, but bound his arms in front, so that the open hands lay side by side between his knees. For a long time, he settled his head as if he were going to shave him, and each time the old man sat submissively in the position in which they had placed him.

Then the executioner said to him :

'Now count up to ten.'

And the old man began to count slowly :

'One, two, three . . .'

The executioner stood behind him, testing the edge of his broad *yataghan*.

'Six, seven, eight . . .'

I thought that the old man would stop counting. Why was he counting? All the men were silent. One could hear the murmur of the water.

'Nine . . .'

The executioner raised his *yataghan*. The flash of its blade glittered in a silver surface, as if a round mirror had hung in the air for a second. It passed through the man's neck and came out the other side—darkened.

The head fell on to the knees, into the open hands, with the neck downwards, and all heard the lips say :

'Ten.'

The body still sat straight. Two fountains of clear, foaming blood spurted up, higher than the executioner's head, and fell downward.

Shouts broke out and hands were clapped. The executioner stood there—stupid, unruffled, with a brutish face and bloodshot eyes—and smiled proudly.

The body sagged, fell on its side and disappeared behind the crowd of Turks who surrounded their comrade. And he was telling them something, still smiling stupidly, as if he did not understand clearly what was happening around him.

'I will kill him,' I thought. 'I will kill him.'

And I felt relief. I was surprised, and listened to myself. I felt easier.

So that was what I had to do. Give a human sacrifice to the demons who tormented me at night. Atone for my sin, for standing aside, while others died in torment.

That night I listened to the shepherds' talk with a calm heart. Then I went to my room and went to bed.

I knew that I would sleep. Tomorrow, in a week, in a month, on the first convenient occasion, I would kill the executioner. The demons believed my promise.

I fell asleep.

On the fifth day they drove four stakes into the earth in the form of a cross and tied the hands and feet of the fifth victim to them. The shepherd lay there naked on his back, smeared with honey—so that the flies would eat him. His lids were kept open by chips so that he would look at the sun.

For the first time I awoke after a decent night's sleep. I had the strength to continue the struggle. I cursed myself for not having thought earlier of offering my tormentors a sacrifice.

Karaibrahim had realized that inaction in the *Konak* was irritating and infuriating his men. It was all right if their fury was directed against the Bulgarians. But it might well be directed against him. And he sent them off to search the forest above the *Konak*. They were to deploy in a line and go up until they reached the meadow. A senseless job, in my opinion, but it was welcome. Karaibrahim stayed in the *Konak*. I was free.

I left the *Konak* calmly for the first time since who knows when and set out along the meadows. Up along the slope I heard the voices of the Turks, who kept shouting to each other, although each of them could see the man on his right and on his left.

I took off my shirt, spread it out on the meadow, and lay down.

I lay on my stomach in the grass. The sun shone down on me. I felt the blades of grass pricking my stomach, wet with sweat. The wind rustled in the tree-tops, and a barely perceptible breath crept over my damp skin. There was the scent of many herbs, but that of crane's-bill was the strongest, perhaps because I was familiar with it.

I lay thus, with closed eyes. The shouts of the Turks died away. I listened to the flies and the beetles. A hundred voices. The hornets had the lowest hum—not those yellow ones, the big ones that look like wasps, but the buffalo flies, the ones that madden the cattle and have green eyes. The mosquitoes buzzed the most spitefully on a high, piercing note. And between these two voices there were a hundred others, but I could not distinguish them. Now two flies were chasing each other, and I became tense as I realized that the fly was not flying calmly, but was looking for something. Perhaps for me. My body attracted it amid the meadow.

I opened my eyes. The shadows of butterflies were flying over a small sunlit piece of earth, covered with grass-stems.

Something was already alighting on me. It crawled over my
back. I raised my hand—sweat was running down my back. It dried
in the sunlight, and gathered down below, in the shade.

Suddenly the crickets struck up. Some were cutting a wire with
a saw. Others were rubbing a comb. Then a grinder-cricket chirped
beside my head. The stone wheel of a grinder began to turn. The
knife touched it. At every revolution it gained speed, and at every
revolution the iron touched the stone, more and more often and
more and more quickly—and the metallic rasping hissed rhythmic-
ally above the grass. It seemed to me that I could see sparks flying
on all sides under the clear sun.

There was a break. A swift, incessant turning. A high sound, then
a quiet, faint, last touch of the knife, the last finishing touch, the
last sparks.

I heard the bees. At a hand's span before me, a big wild bee
perched on a flower. It was black with orange stripes on its belly.
Avid, rough, it trampled the flower with its bristling feet, and
wormed itself into it. It lapped up the nectar, panting and choking,
and flew off, displeased.

And the voice of the other bees, the tame ones—gentle, full of
calm, full of patience and satisfaction.

I dozed off. And I felt myself merging into the earth, growing
into it, with the grass covering me and swaying over me.

Perhaps that was the shepherds' strength? That they merged
into the mountain? That they became part of it—rock, tree, grass?

Something pricked my hand. I raised it. This time it was not
sweat trickling down. It was a fly—big and black. I looked at it in
my palm.

And I saw a black cross on the earth. It was the body of the
crucified shepherd. Flies covered it thickly, one next to the other.
If anyone were to approach it, they would rise in a black, buzzing
cloud—like black smoke.

I lay and listened to the voices of the insects. He was listening to
them, too. They were coming to drink his blood.

Not he, but I lay crucified on the meadow.

My lips were cracking with thirst. If I did not drink water I
would begin to scream. I wanted to rise—I could not move. My
arms and legs were bound to the earth.

I felt such despair that for the first time I wanted to die. Not
only because of what was taking place at that moment. Because of
what was going to happen tomorrow, the day after tomorrow, for
months on end.

My thoughts had found a new way of tormenting me. Every day,
together with the victim whose turn it was, I would be crucified,

cut up, buried alive, or burnt alive. And I would not even be able to die.

I jumped up. How could I allow such a thought? Why didn't I stifle it before it was born? I would no longer be able to vanquish it. What sin-offering would it demand of me?

I went down to the river. I lay down on my stomach and dipped my face in the clear water. I drank and drank, until my whole body grew cold and clean inside. I loved to drink water.

This time the water did not taste sweet to me. The old man lay in the sun, dying of thirst. The cursed thoughts dried up even the last sweetness of life in me.

I saw strawberries on the slope. Time had been passing outside our *Konak* and the fruit was ripening.

The strawberries hung like red drops under their three green leaves. So ripe that as soon as I touched them I did not feel them falling into my hand like a drop of water. And when they were already in my mouth I had to close my eyes, lest the sunlight should efface the subtle sweet and tart taste which melted—like a drop—on my tongue. A drop. A drop. A drop.

The crucified man was dying of thirst.

That evening the Turks undressed the captive Bulgarian women, lit a fire and made them dance naked amid the courtyard, where Karaibrahim had twice met the notables.

The Turks stood around in a circle, watching. Two of them blew *zourlas*[5], two of them beat big drums, while two of them sang *maanehs*[6]. The rest of them clapped their hands.

Only Sheikh Shaban Shebil did not clap. I was standing on the side of his sound arm, so that I could not see that he was one-armed, and his terrible immobility froze me.

It seemed to me that the women, who swayed in the light of the fires, sweating and weeping, were trying with all their might to make him, and him only, clap his hands. And they did not succeed.

I went to his other side. His blind eye was there. Now a blind man was bending forwards like a beast, a blind man was beginning to see.

The sheikh rose and went up to his room.

I watched the Turks. They were clapping and drinking the wine which the Prophet had forbidden. I felt a gloomy joy that the fate of each of them depended on me. In a minute I would choose my victim. They were making merry and did not know that death might go and stand behind each of them. I was certain that I would kill whoever I chose.

Ferocious shouts interrupted the merry-making. The women fell on the cobbles, the Turks jumped up and drew their arms.

Mircho was running around the veranda, and the one-eyed hodja was running after him and roaring. He was running without moving his sole arm, holding his hand to his mouth.

The boy was caught. His eyes and teeth flashed, and he was growling. He had bitten the Hodja's hand to the bone. The Sheikh was crying with pain and wanted to kill him, but without hands, for he could not take his lips from his wound. Blood was trickling down his beard.

Karaibrahim gave orders that the child be cast in the dungeon with the notables.

I went to my room and lay down. I knew whom I would kill. Whom I would sacrifice to my demon, so that he would give me a calm night.

Sheikh Shaban Shebil. The one-eyed, the one-armed.

I will kill you, Hodja.

I could not fall asleep. I had been unable to buy sleep and a calm night. I needed a bigger victim if I wanted to live.

Then came the fifth day of the killing of the old men.

Today I was to be flayed alive—they were going to flay Old Kralyo. Since yesterday, when I was lying on the meadow, I knew that I would go through every movement of the executioner's. I felt the pain to the tips of my fingers, as if I were scratching a rough stone with my nails. I kept folding and unfolding my fingers.

Until tomorrow. I had to hold out until tomorrow. Tomorrow would be Friday, the day of rest.

Karaibrahim came into my room.

'Why aren't you up yet?' he asked.

I rose, and dressed myself. I did not hurry. He waited patiently for me. At last he said to me :

'You will flay the old man today.'

I was putting on my boots. I stood up and looked at him. He was staring me straight in the eye.

The entire game between the Janissary and the French nobleman was a lie and a piece of folly. The fencing, the riding side by side were a lie. It was folly to believe that he respected my former greatness, that he behaved to me as if I was his equal, and that his relations with me were those between equals.

I was a slave. He was the master.

He gave orders and I had to bow my head.

His eyes were icy, it seemed to me that I saw spite and mockery in them.

'You thought that you would stand aside. You thought so, didn't you? No! Come to us, Venetian! Stain your hands with blood up to the elbows.'

That is what his eyes said.

But he did not understand what my eyes told him. They said: 'I will kill you.'

He stood and waited, expecting me to draw back, to beg him to let me off, to humiliate myself. He had decided that what he wanted was to be done, but probably he would not mind seeing me trembling and pitiful.

I said to him:

'Let us go.'

And I followed him. On the stairs he let me go first, perhaps to see whether I was trembling, perhaps because he hated to feel anyone at his back.

I went down the stairs. One, two three. Down. I heard the voice of Syuleiman Aga: 'And you thought that you would stand aside, didn't you? The time of parting has come. Either to the left, or to the right!'

No, Aga, not to the left, nor to the right, but up, or down. The world did not lie on an even plain, on a tray, there was up and down in the world. And now I could distinguish this again.

I was going down the stairs. I saw the courtyard, filled with Karaibrahim's men. And in the middle there was a white spot— Old Kralyo's bare back.

He only said:

'I have deserved it. For stopping the men that night, at Manol's wedding.'

I did my work clumsily. The brutes around me jeered at me.

Every time I raised my head to toss my hair back, I measured the distance to Karaibrahim. He was sitting, one leg crossed over the other, on a costly carpet, five feet away from me. I clutched the razor. An uncertain weapon. I ought not to risk it. Only a jump separated us. I would wait. Not long—until tomorrow.

The old man died. The disappointed men scattered, cursing the dead man.

Farewell, Old Kralyo, you, who read the Bible every evening, and believed that fate would let you read it to the end. You will not do so. You will not stand facing the eternal mountain, under the boundless sky, sending them your feeble human voice.

'I have finished,' I said to Karaibrahim.

He said nothing to me, but it seemed to me that I saw admiration in his eyes. He merely nodded. But when I turned to go, he called after me:

'Take your rapier and come.'

We were going to fence.

Why didn't you kill him on that day? I knew why I was putting it off. I did not want to bid the world farewell. I was not afraid. I wanted to hear the voices of the shepherds once more. To stand on the other side, behind the wall, not like a trembling coward, but as their equal, as their brother, separated from them only by the wall between two cells.

We fought. And every time the point of my rapier, covered by a guard, touched Karaibrahim's body, I saw it sinking into him.

Tomorrow.

And when I raised my head, I saw Elitsa.

I was thankful now that I was not a murderer with my arms bound at my back. I could enjoy the sight of her once more. The joy that the world was beautiful returned to me again, I could admire people once more, feel them close to me and fall in love with them. She called me with an imperceptible nod. I went up the stairs. I did not tremble as on the previous occasion. I did not meet a maddened girl on the stairs. I went up.

I stood before her and looked at her. Her lips glistened with the mother-of-pearl sheen of whitened, bitten skin. Blue shadows made her eyes still bigger. I did not think about the bruises on her body. There were none. She said quietly :

'Kill him !'

I shook my head. Which movement meant 'yes'—a nod or a shake of the head?

She repeated :

'Kill him !'

I could have told her what I had decided. I could have asked her for her gratitude that I would save her. A promise, a hope, which would consecrate my last hours. I would know that it would not come to pass, but I would rejoice.

I did not ask her for anything. I looked long at her and went away.

That evening I went down to the secret passage and knelt beside the dungeon wall. I wanted to beat my fists against the wall, and cry to them :

'Brothers !'

I wanted to tell them that tomorrow I would kill Karaibrahim. That tomorrow Karaibrahim would be dead.

I said nothing.

I heard a child's voice, and started. I had forgotten that Mircho was with them. He was begging Manol.

'Father, pretend to become a Turk. Let them only free you.

Afterwards you will run away to the mountains and kill them all. Father, you must kill the two Hodjas.'

Manol answered him quietly:

'My son, you have seen a fortress. The world is divided by a vast fortress wall. From one end to the other. People stay inside the fortress, and evil attacks from outside. Every man stands at an embrasure on the battlements, and guards one foot of wall. I do not know, there may be great men, commanders, who guard a hundred embrasures. There may be one great commander, who knows what is happening all along the wall. I see my foot of it. I know that I must defend it. If I do not defend it, who will? You must fight, too. Each one in front of his piece. You do not know what is happening around you, at the neighbouring foot. You do not see. You look only in front of you, and strike the hands and faces of the evil men who want to climb up the wall. Perhaps it is precisely at your gateway that evil hopes to pierce the wall. You must fight, and not for one moment must you retreat from your embrasure, consoling yourself with the thought that you will go back to it in a moment. If you move, evil will enter in. And when you die, your body must block up the gateway of your embrasure.'

There was silence in the dungeon.

Then the childish voice asked:

'Father, what is evil?'

Silence. Then—Manol's voice:

'Evil is what divides people.'

A little later:

'Good people.'

I rose and went. Manol had answered me.

A stone on your right, a stone on your left and in the middle— you. Yes, each one of us was standing at a gate, each one was defending a gate through which evil could enter. I had left my gate empty, and now I was returning to it.

Manol, the only thing is that the wall is not straight. You, too, may know, you may not have said it because of the child. The wall winds so that sometimes its embrasures fall one opposite the other. And when you shoot, you kill your brother. The wall winds like a river through a plain. If you set out along its course, along the water's current, you would travel a day, but if you cut across it over dry land, you would get there in a minute. I had long dragged along the low current. I ought to have cut across it.

I lay on my back, and for the first time I did not try to go to sleep. This was my last night. I knew that by murdering Karai-brahim I would condemn myself to death. I, who had understood that the only precious thing in the world was life, was renouncing it of my own free will. Just as the wise man, Abdullah the slave, had replaced the blind French nobleman, so now a madman, a third man, a rebel, was going to replace Abdullah.

It was senseless. It was absurd.

Life renounced itself, and thereby renounced everything, for life was the foundation of everything and there was nothing beyond it. It was senseless, but it could not be otherwise. Better a living dog than a dead lion. It was true, it was wise, but of what use was it since the lion could not become a dog? When you die but do not become a dog? Although you wanted to. The time of parting was coming, when the lions had to die, and the dogs had to live.

A pity that I had been born a man, and not a dog. I could not change it.

In the morning I rose, and carefully examined my rapier—a wonderful piece of steel with the mark of Andrea Ferrara—I flexed it, and waved it. I attacked the wall. The rapier submitted to every command of my will, to every movement of my hand.

I was still alive.

Even the edge of the steel was wonderful. And how wonderful is a living human body, how wonderfully and terribly is man made. I carefully fixed the guard on the point so that it would fall off at any stronger thrust.

I took my stand opposite Karaibrahim. There was no one around us. Karaibrahim forbade his men to watch when he fenced. Perhaps there was, nevertheless, a chance of my escaping after I had pierced him?

I heard a rustle over my head, but I did not raise my head. It was Elitsa; I had bidden her farewell.

We had only exchanged a few thrusts when Karaibrahim dropped his rapier and said :

'The guard of your rapier has fallen off.'

I could have killed him then. I stepped forwards and only rested the bare point on his breast. He understood. He paled, retreated and with a swift movement removed the guard from his rapier.

And we began to fight along the wall, beneath the veranda. And on the veranda stood Elitsa, watching us, as she had done after the first night she had spent with Karaibrahim.

Slowly and implacably I pressed Karaibrahim against the wall. He could have called for help—I think I would have killed him at once if he had.

Suddenly, for the fraction of a second, the silver veil woven by the point of Karaibrahim's rapier was rent asunder and I saw his unprotected breast. A lightning attack, and Karaibrahim would have lain on the ground with a piece of cold iron in his heart. I would have seen the spark of life vanishing from his pupils, seen them grow motionless and his eyes glaze over.

I did not pierce him. I could not. My hand did not make that sole movement. It delayed.

Karaibrahim sensed that death was beside him. He grew quite white. But not the tiniest drop of sweat appeared on his face.

For a second time the veil was torn, and for a second time I delayed and in a second the veil was closed.

The third time I understood. I could not kill him.

Then I grew pale. And I sweated. I began to defend myself. Karaibrahim's eyes began to sparkle. I always look at my opponent's eyes to guess his intentions. I have never come across such keen, hard eyes.

I was in despair. I felt like dropping my rapier. I could have burst into tears. Not that I feared death; I feared my helplessness. My arm grew weak.

I retreated, stumbled and saw the green leaves of the plane tree above me, the blue patches of sky between them and Elitsa's face. I had fallen. In a second Karaibrahim's face hid them. He was standing over me, as if he were bending over a well, and I were lying at the bottom of it. My body grew soft. My knees were spread out, the stones pressed on my elbows. I did not feel the cool chill of iron.

Karaibrahim drew back. I saw Elitsa turn and disappear. And her braids slid over the balustrade of the veranda, like two snakes, following their mistress.

I heard Karaibrahim's voice:

'Rise!'

He was looking at me with curiosity. No one would have guessed that he had been almost dead a minute ago. He called two Turks, pointed to me and said:

'Shut this man up in the room next to mine. One is to stand at the door on to the veranda, the other—at the door into my room. Guard him. I will come.'

He was going to the big Friday prayer meeting.

I followed my guards. I would remain alone for a while so that I could think.

I had flayed the old man in vain. I had dishonestly bought a peaceful night and that rest, lying on the meadow—I would not kill the executioner with the *yataghan* and the one-eyed Hodja. I had no right to stay by the wall last night, and to think that it was a wall between two cells in which brothers were shut up.

I was worth nothing. I was good for nothing. I had been unable to put out my hand and pierce Karaibrahim through. Why?
I had to think.

Seventh Excerpt

> Two young madcaps loved each other,
> From their childhood to their youth.
> And the time came for their wedding.

And the sky grew dark, so that it was blue, and looked as if it were bruised. And the rain came pouring down and white flashes of lightning blinded us.

And Momchil and I hid under a spruce at the edge of a broad meadow. The rain came down, and every drop was as heavy as molten lead, and struck the earth, as if someone were hurling it down on the earth with tears and fury. Then hail began to fall, too.

And while I was shivering with the cold, and the water was seeping through the spruce branches, so that it ran down my hair and my beard, I was glad that I breathed the air of the mountain. For neither rain, nor hail reached the poor prisoners in the *Konak*.

Momchil said to me :

'Father, let me light a fire, so that we may warm ourselves.'

And I merely nodded, for there was neither warmth nor fire for the poor prisoners.

The hail stopped and the sun shone. Then the meadow stretched out before us, all flooded, as if silver had been poured over it. And it glowed so brightly that my eyes began to hurt. Only where there were spruces a dark stain was left beneath them. And it was not from the shade of the spruces, but because under them it was well-nigh dry.

But it was still raining from the wet trees. The drops fell from branch to branch and from there on to my hair, and from my hair on to my shoulders, running down from my hair to the tips of my fingers, so that they dripped on the earth. And the entire forest was full of a whisper, as at the time of the ripened cones, when the seeds come pouring down from above. But now the earth, too, was whispering as it drank the watery seeds. And I remembered how the earth had whispered on the day, when Manol and I had entered the graveyard with the stone crosses.

And Momchil said :

'They have forgiven me. Yet they have not forgiven Momchil, but Manol's son.'

He still fled and hid from the folk.

And I said to him :

'Look!'

Over the meadow, blazing with silver, a woman was walking, as if she were floating over a lake, all black for the sun was behind her. And Momchil grew pale, wanting to flee, and said to me :

'Elitsa is coming.'

I seized him by the arm and stared, but I was unable to distinguish anything in the sparkle of the wet meadows. And the woman came steadily on towards us.

And Elitsa came and stood before Momchil beneath the tree. And I held Momchil's arm, but he no longer pulled away, only his hand grew as cold as a dead man's. And the eyes which looked upon Elitsa were full of horror.

She stood before us, and big icy grains of hail shone in her hair, as though she had woven pearls into it. And she said :

'I am pure. I am as my mother bore me.'

There were blue circles under her eyes, and her lips were white and bitten. And Momchil said to her :

'Get out of my sight.'

And Elitsa said :

'Every night Karaibrahim lay on the other pallet, on the other side of the room. He lay on his back and stared at the ceiling. And I lay there, listening to his breathing. He did not go to sleep. Neither did I sleep. And as I waited for him to rise and come to me, I got ready to die. But he did not come. And all the nights in the *Konak* passed by thus.'

Fury and hatred began to flash in Momchil's eyes. And he said : 'Be silent!'

And he whistled to call his falcon, which had hidden somewhere from the storm. Elitsa repeated :

'I am as my mother bore me.'

She put her hand to her breast and drew out a folded white kerchief.

And as she unfolded it, we saw the flash of a knife.

'Sevda let me go. She had been to Manol, and he told her where he had hidden his knife. I went and took it. If you kill Karaibrahim with this knife, Manol will forgive you.'

And she handed him the knife. Then we saw that on the white kerchief two gold rings were left shining one beside the other, bound by a chestnut lock of a woman's hair. And Momchil stared at the rings.

'Mine. And Manol's. For Manol sent my ring back to me.'

Then Momchil hid his eyes with his two clenched fists, and in his right he held his father's knife. And he said quietly:

'Go.'

And Elitsa asked him still more quietly:

'Momchil, have you no faith in me?'

And he, still pressing his fists to his eyes and forehead, replied:

'I do not believe you.'

Tears swam in Elitsa's eyes, and they shone, like the meadows flooded with molten silver. They shone and lit up her thin face. And she seized Momchil by the wrist, near the edge of the knife, and quietly said to him:

'Come.'

And she dragged him after herself into the forest.

And when the sun was setting, I made for the cave. And on a sloping meadow there was a rock which the snows and the ice had torn from its bed, when they were sliding down in the spring. The rock leant forward, as if it were preparing to overturn, and behind it there was a deep pit, its empty bed. And the grass that grew there was dark green, such as one never saw elsewhere, for it grew straight up from the open bowels of the earth.

On the green grass lay Elitsa's red and yellow apron that she had cast aside. And it seemed as if a fire were burning on the grass.

Here the two young people had lighted a fire, to warm their hearts, so full of cold. And the rock had moved to open the earth's womb, so that Momchil's son, the grandson of Manol, might be conceived in the very heart of the mountain.

And as I gazed on the fire of Elitsa's apron, I did not see when Momchil and Elitsa came and stood before me, hand in hand. And there were no longer any tears in Elitsa's eyes, but they shone still more brilliantly than before.

And Momchil said to me:

'Father, bless us. Let us two wretches come together. She—forever blackened in the eyes of men, for no one will believe her, as I believed her. I—forever blackened in the eyes of men, because for love of her I forgot my duty. Bless us.'

I blessed them. And they were so happy and beautiful that my heart began to ache again.

And I went downhill. The steep path along the gully had become a brook, and the water was flowing and flashing amid the stones. And as I kept my eyes on my feet, and the water kept flowing, the flashes of light danced before my eyes and I grew dizzy, and did not know whether I was walking, or whether the path was running beneath my feet, or the brook was dragging me along. But on that day, so full of flashes of light, I was not able to forget the brilliance of Elitsa's eyes.

And when the path reached the river, and the brook poured into it like the waving tail of a white horse, lo—I saw Goran catching fish in a pool. I gazed and I saw that the foam whirled from right to left. Pools like these are called left pools. Folk think they are bewitched, and cast into them anything magical which they may find, so that it was strange that Goran should be catching trout in a left pool. I wanted to pass him without speaking to him, for he did not hear me because of the noise of the water, but I bethought me of Elitsa. Was she not his sister?

And as I was going down to him, he drew out a quivering fish, unhooked it and began to measure it with a stick to see how long it was. As soon as I touched his shoulder, as he was squatting with a pile of silver fish speckled with red before him, he jumped to his feet, startled, and grew pale, then red. And I said to him:

'Rejoice, Goran, for your sister Elitsa has returned.'

He seized me by the waist as if I were a small child, lifted me up in his joy and whirled me around in a circle. But when he let me go, I saw that his eyes were still sad. And Goran asked me:

'Father, why do they all blame Momchil for leaving the path, but no one blames me? Was not I, too, on the path? Or am I not worth as much as he is? Tell me.'

And I said to him:

'He did it for himself, for his love, but you were lured away, Goran. That is why.'

But he shook his head and said:

'When Momchil fled, so that he would not hear the bagpipes, he thought that he was leaving me on the path. When I followed Sevda, I saw that the path was left unguarded.'

And he stood with bowed head, but I saw his eyes, for, although he was bent, they were a span above my head. His eyes were very sad. I asked him:

'Why do you catch fish in a left pool?'

And Goran grew very red again, and answered me:

'I have made up my mind to catch a fish as big as this stick.'

And he showed me a stick as long as an ell, adding:

'Fish as big as that are caught in the bewitched pools. If I could catch the master of this pool, he would help me.'

And as the thought came into his mind, he jumped up nimbly, stirred the fire, and hung several fishes over it. And the remaining trout he threaded on a twig and handed it to me, saying:

'Sit down and eat, Father, you are hungry. And give these fish to the women in the cave.'

I said to him:

'Come and bring them.'

But he shook his head and answered:

'There is no longer any time.'

And after we had eaten of the white flesh of the fish, from which arose fresh steam, I rose and wiped my fingers on the hanging boughs of a spruce. And they were wet. Goran, too, rose after me, and as soon as he seized a taller branch, and began to rub it between his hands, he suddenly dropped it and began to weep. He sat down beside the dying fire, over which smoke rose, hid his head between his knees and wept.

I was silent. And he said to me:

'Father. On the day on which Syuleiman Aga departed, I wanted to see him, but far from the other folk. And when I had gone up the Maiden, I saw that Delyo was waiting for him in ambush with two other bandits. And I said to him: "Are you not ashamed, having eaten his bread for ten years?" And he said to me: "Shepherd, go your ways. If the Aga were not already near, I would have a bullet for you, too." And I said to him: "It is easy to talk, pistol in hand." And he cast aside the pistol and drew his knife. And he said to his associates: "Stand aside and watch me slaughter this ram." And we fought. And he jumped about like a weasel or a squirrel. And his knife was the longest, only I have longer arms. And his associates asked him, 'Delyo, shall we shoot him?' and he swore at them. But when I pressed his neck against a tree stump, he cried: "Ha!" And he surely wanted to say "*Haidé*!"[7] but nothing more was heard, for I cut his throat! And the two bandits shot at me, but they missed me, so they fled into the forest. And as my hands were bloodstained, I stretched them out to wipe them on the branch of a spruce. And when I felt the thick leaves on my fingers, I remembered how I had cleaned my fingers from the grease of the roast lambs, and how happily I had straightened up with a full heart over the bones I had gnawed. Now I was wiping off human blood, and I wept. And the other day when I stroked a dog, its fur seemed to me just like a spruce branch, its hairs were just like the spruce needles, so that I did not seem to be stroking it, but to be wiping blood off on its back. I cannot touch a spruce again, Father. I have come to hate spruces, for such bloodstained fingers are wiped on them that I cannot touch them. And what use is a forester without the spruces? That is why I wept just now when I touched the spruce branch. And they have stolen the spruces from me.'

He continued to weep. But I had to go, so I stroked his hair. And I started when I felt his stiff hair beneath my fingers, and said in a trembling voice :

'God be with you, Goran. Come to the cave.'

He did not answer me.

But when I was already up on the crest, I heard his voice coming up to me from below :

'God be with you, Father.'

I never saw him again.

Eighth Excerpt

I did not think about anything. I stood at the window and looked out.

Karaibrahim did not come that day. It rained, and then cleared up. The sun shone. Evening came.

I did not sleep all night, the second night running. Karaibrahim did not come home all night.

Day dawned. And the sun rose again.

The forest opposite was bathed in sunlight. I saw the light brown and yellow trunks of the spruces, as straight as pieces of taut string, cutting the green wall here and there. It seemed to me that the forest was embroidered in green yarn on rough cloth, like the Gobelin tapestries on the walls of my castles, and that the tapestries had worn away here and there, so that the fabric and the warp of the foundation had shown through. Were not the trunks the foundation of the forest, too?

Tapestries. What foolishness predestination is. This morning I had been sure that I had left the castles and the tapestries, that I had gone down into the inferno of the ship and had accepted Islam only because I was predestined to kill Karaibrahim. But I had not killed him.

He would come in a little while. I did not know whether he would ask me anything. I did not think of what I would answer. I did not think about anything—I gazed at the forest on which the sun was shining.

I heard voices, speaking under my window. Gyulfié's voice and a man's.

From the time spent in the secret passage, I had grown accustomed to listening without looking. Now I peered down from the window. The man was Goran, Old Galoushko's son, that huge Bulgarian who had taken me to the water-mill.

Goran was begging Gyulfié to let him into the *Konak*. He held several big trout in his hands—I had never seen their like.

Gyulfié's voice was as sweet as sherbet. I could not see her; she was speaking from a window nearby.

Goran was one of the three men who made her womb quiver, wasn't he? And wasn't Goran Sevda's lover who strangled her every night? That was the person whom the young man was looking for.

I knew that Gyulfié would not miss the chance of revenging herself on Sevda. But she also had something else in mind.

She would quickly console herself if I disappeared from her life. Our love was barren. I was pouring pails of water into a bottomless barrel. Fate had seen to it that I should not succeed in binding myself to the world, that I should remain alone, that I should leave nothing behind me. It was better so.

Yes, Gyulfié would let him into the *Konak*. She would say that she had wanted the fish. But she wanted something in exchange.

'Why, what can a woman as old as I am want?'

He looked at her. I could not see her, but I knew what he saw—he was looking at her as if he were seeing her for the first time. And how he understood, and how amazed he was at first, just as I would have been amazed, if I had been told at my first meeting with Gyulfié what would come to pass between the two of us.

Goran bent his head.

'I am wretched,' he said quietly.

Gyulfié sang from the window :

'You'll get over it. And throw away whatever you have with you. A pistol, a knife. Otherwise you will be stopped at the gate.'

The dirty slut.

Once more I gazed at the green tapestry of the forest as one stunned.

The howling of a dog was heard. I started, for I thought that the dogs in the Black Hole were howling. But the dog was barking in the courtyard.

Suddenly I remembered that Goran was the brother of Sherko, who was shut up with his dog Sharo in the dungeon of the other inner courtyard. The dog had got wind of him.

Goran was the brother of Elitsa. Goran might not be coming for Sevda. His sister and his brother were here.

I had not much time to think and to be agitated. I heard Karaibrahim's voice in the room next door. He was talking to the Turk who was on guard at the door of my room.

I heard him sit down on the little three-legged stool by the fire-place—it creaked. It grew cold at night, and fires were lit in some of the rooms. Karaibrahim did not come in to me on purpose —he was torturing me.

I felt ill. I sat down and began to wipe the sweat from my brow. I had not expected to meet Karaibrahim thus—with blue lips and trembling.

In the room beyond, Goran's voice rumbled out:

'Are you Karaibrahim?'

Goran spoke from the threshold of the door leading on to the veranda.

'Who are you?' Karaibrahim asked dryly.

'Goran, Galoushko's son.'

I heard Karaibrahim rise to his feet.

'Get out!' he said sharply.

Steps moved across the room. Karaibrahim had sent the guard at my door, not Goran, away.

Goran rumbled:

'It is you I was looking for, Karaibrahim.'

Heavy steps moved across Karaibrahim's floor, from the veranda to the middle of the room. I glided noiselessly to the door of my room—Goran's steps would have drowned even the walk of a bear. The boards creaked, so did the ceiling.

A short cry, full of astonishment and pain made me draw back from the door.

Something heavy fell in the other room. The next moment I hurled forwards and pushed the door with my shoulder. It was un-locked and I shot into Karaibrahim's room, almost losing my balance.

He lay on his back, a red line cut his bald skull and his face. His eyes were full of horror, his mouth agape as in incredible amaze-ment.

Goran, who was bending over him, straightened up and looked around. He looked like a madman who had suddenly been startled. His face was insane. I did not move, as though it were possible that he might fail to see me. In his hands he held a big knife. He was staring at Karaibrahim, at me, at the window with the forest showing through it, at the gutted fish on the floor, in which he had hidden his knife.

His look fell on the hearth. The embers glowed red. He jumped towards it. And as he stood with his back towards me, I saw him thrust both hands to his breast. A groan was heard and he fell with his face in the fire.

Karaibrahim moaned and turned on one side, with his face

towards Goran. I knelt beside him. He turned on his face. I shook him by the shoulders.

He whispered with his face on the boards:

'Is he alive?'

There was a smell of burnt flesh in the room.

I jumped up and with difficulty pulled Goran's huge body aside. I turned him on his back and shut my eyes. From the strength of the blow, or from the fall, the knife was buried in his breast up to the hilt. His face was burnt.

I went out on the veranda and began to shout like a madman.

There was a thudding of feet, shouts, curses. The howling and barking of dogs, blows on a door. The prisoners were knocking.

Karaibrahim lay there with his eyes shut. His whole face was cut in two, so was his breast. Perhaps he was dying.

Sevda came flying in, looked at Karaibrahim, looked at Goran, swayed and fell heavily on the boards.

Bending over Karaibrahim, Sivri *Bilyuk-bashi*, the cut-throat, was asking him:

'Who was it, Aga? His face is burnt.'

I understood why Goran had killed himself over the fire. Otherwise the Turks would have revenged themselves on his sister and his brother, who were in their hands.

Still with his eyes shut, Karaibrahim said:

'I do not know.'

Gyulfié was reviving Sevda. She was asking her something in a low voice and was smacking her face, pretending to be restoring her to consciousness. Then she turned to me and said helplessly:

'She is with child. Did you hear? That bitch.'

And she began to cry spitefully, as if Sevda had deceived her.

Like a swarm of wasps, which fly out of their nest when someone throws a stone at it, the Turks dashed out of the *Konak*. They were maddened, so that they forgot that this might cost them dear. They put a watch on Prossoina and flew on horseback to Zagrad. They reached it, but they did not manage to reach Podviss. Distant shots were heard.

They caught about three or four hundred men. I was amazed when I found out how many fools had stayed in the two villages. But when I saw Vrazhou *Kehaya*, I started—I thought he had risen from the dead. Either he had been taken out of the ant-hill, or Karaibrahim had let him go. They shut the prisoners up in one of the inner courtyards. Shouts and screams were heard—the new prisoners were shouting, the raped girls were screaming, the notables in the dungeon were shouting. The Turks were shouting, too, and firing their pistols.

Five Turks were killed that day. The rest did not sleep all night. The fat Hodja—Molla Soulfikar Softa—came out on the veranda from time to time, saying that Karaibrahim was on his death-bed. If he died, the Turks would kill all the others.

In the morning Goran's body was placed in the square in front of the *Konak*, and they began to make people walk past it. One after the other—old men, old women, women with nurslings in their arms and children clinging to their skirts. Gloomy men. Then the notables, dirty, smelly, looking like shadows. Then the girls, the solace of the executioners.

They looked at each other and barely knew each other. They sobbed, their voices choked. Not one clear cry was heard on the square. A father saw his daughter, defiled by the Turks, a child saw its father, his hands bound behind his back. They uttered no sound.

On his back, his huge hands stretched out, lay Goran. With white hands and a black face. The knife still stuck out from his breast.

One by one the Bulgarians walked past him. That is how the living bid farewell to their dead in their coffins, in the middle of the church. Everyone kisses his crossed hands then, but now everyone kissed his open palm with a glance.

'Who is he?'

'I don't know.'

A blow. The stricken man fell to his knees. Another blow. Another body stretched out on the ground.

I did not translate, they understood each other. I was swaying with lack of sleep, my head was bursting. Instead of a turban I had tied a wet towel around my head. And those people. It seemed to me that it was one and the same man who passed a thousand times and always said one and the same thing.

They all knew him. And if anyone did not know his name, he had learnt it during the night, when the Bulgarians whispered among themselves, crowded together in the yard, in expectation of death. They were silent. So was I.

They walked past; they passed one after another and bent over the black face.

Somewhere at the end of the crowd a confused babble of voices arose. The Turks ran up; in a silent row the Bulgarians tried not to let them through.

Old Galoushko came out on the square. If up till then there had been a stifled whisper, now all was silent.

Slowly, step by step, the old man crossed the square and stopped

in front of his son's body. He knelt down beside him, looked long
at the burnt face and rose to his feet. He stretched out his arms,
opened his mouth two or three times, but no sound came—I did not
know then that he had become mute.

Then he spoke:

'My son, Goran.'

A woman burst into tears with pain and fury. They thought that
the old man was mad. They were amazed that the man who had
lost his speech with grief, should have recovered it in his new grief.

Old Galoushko said:

'Cry out, all of you, that the mountain may hear his name. Why
do you hide it? If we all die, who will tell of him? Let the mountain
remember it.'

He turned to Sivri *Bilyuk-bashi* and said:

'Take me to your chieftain.'

I stepped forward and said:

'Karaibrahim gave me orders that anyone who recognized this
man should be taken to him.'

Karaibrahim lay on the pallet in the same room in which Goran
had wounded him. He was wrapped up in a light coloured rug—
that kind of rug is called Sunrise, because red flames, which gather
in a fiery ball, are woven into the centre of the white wool. It
looked as if the blood from Karaibrahim's wound had seeped
through the rug. A fire of spruce roots full of resin, burned in the
fireplace, so that it smelt of the forest. Through the window one
saw the bright mountain. At Karaibrahim's feet sat Sevda, beside
the fire sat the two Hodjas, next to the window I saw Kemanchidjogli. Karaibrahim lay with his face to the wall.

Old Galoushko advanced softly, as if he did not want to wake
him up, bent over him and called him:

'Strahin! Strahin!'

Karaibrahim quivered—barely visibly, like the eyelid of a man
who is pretending to sleep. But he did not turn.

The old man said again:

'Strahin! My son.'

Sevda rose to her feet, white and terrible, the kerchief which she
held before her face to keep it veiled, fell from her hand. She retreated backwards, groping for support. She leant up against the
door, pressed against it and began to look for the latch. She was
unable to go out, because the door opened into the room, and she
did not think of moving aside. And she stayed then to hear.

The Turks had not understood anything as yet, for Old Galousko
spoke in Bulgarian.

I was not surprised. I had guessed it when Karaibrahim had

refused to give Goran's name. After all, the man had told him what it was, hadn't he? Karaibrahim did not know that I had heard Goran's words. I gathered the broken and scattered bits one by one, I remembered incidents, talks, individual words. The entry into the valley, the ride to the water-mill, the saving of Sherko. Karaibrahim was a Bulgarian. I knew that he had not touched Elitsa.

'Strahin,' the old man said, quietly.

Kemanchidjogli roughly pulled him back. Karaibrahim turned then. I saw his face. The tuft of hair on his forehead had been shaved off. The knife's edge had slipped along the skull, cutting a shallow line, but a green balsam, spread on it, marked the wound across the whole face, broad and terrible. I barely recognized him.

He made a sign that he wanted to speak. They placed pillows at his back. He said, gasping and stopping after every word :

'Kemanchidjogli, Sheikh Shaban Shebil, Molla Soulfikar Softa. I am a Janissary from this valley, Elindenya, from the village of Podviss. This man is my father. The man with the dog, shut up alone is my brother. And the girl whom I took from the wedding is my sister.'

He stopped. He half-closed his eyes and the green stripe across his face grew dark, for he had become quite pale. When he opened his eyes, he collected his strength and said :

'Shut the old man and the girl up with the man and the dog. Wait until I recover and take my vengeance. Do not touch them.'

The Turks looked at one another. Kemanchidjogli said :

'Aga, you are speaking Bulgarian.'

I had not noticed it. During my entire stay in the valley, while I interpreted, Karaibrahim had understood every Bulgarian word. I remembered that when he had entered Manol's house, he had said 'bells,' and not '*chans*'. Now, in his fever, he had involuntarily spoken in his mother tongue.

Karaibrahim was unable to repeat his words in Turkish and became unconscious.

The Turks looked at me. I was the interpreter Abdullah once more. Could I lie? Could I try to save the old man and his children? Karaibrahim might die before he came to himself.

He opened his eyes.

I repeated his words in Turkish. He closed his lids as a sign that it was so.

Old Galoushko was taken to his son Sherko. He was welcomed by the joyful barking of the huge spotted dog.

They looked for Elitsa but did not find her. I was the last man who had seen her standing on the veranda. Karaibrahim was unable to say a word; he was delirious, tossing and turning on his pallet.

Karaibrahim lay in the stable, beside his horse. When he was better, he had himself taken there. He said it was warmer in the stable. And darker, and that the light hurt his eyes. But I think that he went, because his horse was the only being left in the world that was close to him. He boasted of his solitariness, but he probably used to tremble at night. As soon as he was left alone, he used to talk to his horse in a changed, caressing voice, begging it to stretch out its lips to him, promising it a golden saddle and silver hooves. But the horse was frightened by the smell of blood and snorted, and when the bandages of Karaibrahim's wounds were changed, it would neigh and kick the thick boards of the stables. This was strange, for war-horses get used to blood.

Karaibrahim forgave me. He said to me:

'You cannot kill a wounded man, since you were unable to kill a living one.'

And he tried to smile. The green line of the blow, across the forehead, past the left eye, along the nose, across the lips and the chin—made his smile crooked and terrible. He had had not only the tuft on his forehead shaved off, but his moustache as well.

'I ought not to have made you flay the old man,' he said. 'We leaders ought not to soil our hands with petty things.'

He wanted to draw me to him again, to make me feel his equal. He trusted no one—not a single one of the Turks around him. But he thought that I would serve him faithfully. But I remembered his eyes—when he ordered me to flay the old man, and when we were fighting with rapiers. And I knew that as soon as he had recovered, he would kill me.

He kept me in the stables with him for days and nights at a time. He talked to me of his years in the Janissaries' school. He made me look after his horse. That was no burden to me—I was glad to touch that clean and noble animal's silky skin and trim body.

One day Elitsa was brought in. Two Turks were holding her.

Karaibrahim raised himself on his elbows and managed to sit up. One could not tell whether he was glad or angry.

'Where did you catch her?' he asked.

'She came herself, Aga.'

Karaibrahim dismissed the Turks with a sign. He was silent and waited.

Elitsa fell on her knees on the packed earth of the stable.

'Brother, forgive our father.'

Karaibrahim threw his head back, stretched his neck and began to laugh. His Adam's apple moved up and down as if he were swallowing with difficulty and choking. Then he began to cough, and put his hands to his breast, where his wound was.

'Why didn't my brother realize that I was his brother?' he asked. 'Why didn't his blood speak? And if he did realize that he was my brother, was he not the first to raise a hand to kill me? Or is the blood tie so weak that a man cannot tell his own brother, or was Goran so strong that he overcame it? If the first is true—what is it worth that a man should value it, if the second is true—am I weaker than Goran?'

'Brother!' Elitsa said to him. 'If you had not felt the blood tie, you would not have let me lie beside you untouched.'

'I did feel it. And this blow had to come to cut the link between me and my kin. Everything is written. My being taken from this valley, my becoming a Janissary and returning again to the valley to force it to the True Faith. This blow, too, was written and measured. Allah himself raised my brother's hand, to punish me for thinking of sisters and brothers and not of him only. He has punished me severely, but he has not killed me, and with that same blow he showed me that a strong man is alone.'

'Manol is not alone,' Elitsa said proudly. 'Is he weak?'

Karaibrahim answered at once, as if he had thought long about this and had only been waiting to say it:

'The shepherds are sheep. They have lived so long with their sheep that they have become like them. They are rams at the most. Wherever one sheep goes, the others follow it. You have separated a sheep from the flock, haven't you? Is it easy? It isn't, it's difficult. What the others will say weighs upon them. They put their heads together like sheep at noon. A strong man is alone. Forget Manol.'

'I am not Manol's wife. I am the wife of his son Momchil. And I am with child by him.'

Karaibrahim raised himself from the waist upwards, moved away from his pillows, then sank back on them.

'I promised Manol,' he said, 'to make every man of his family draw a cross with his blood and spit upon it. I must get to Momchil.'

And as he spoke, he thought of something and smiled with the sound part of his mouth.

'Bear your child. I will let you nurse it three years. Then I will take it, I will wait for it to grow and put it in the school of the *adjemi-oglani*, the school for Janissaries. Do you know how one becomes a Janissary? Digging in the market gardens, hunger, floggings, cuttings with swords. A single shirt in the year, a single towel, which is taken in a dark room so that you cannot choose? Your son will become a good Janissary.'

'I will strangle him,' Elitsa said simply.

'You will not have the strength to do that.'

'I am your sister, am I not? Come, send me to my father and my brother. Kill me with them. But if you want to destroy Goran's whole family, kill yourself, too.'

'I have no family. I have the *odjak* of the Janissaries. You are not a man, but a woman and have no soul. Your fate is to bear soldiers. Venetian, take her to the harem, to Safidé.'

When we went out, I saw that Elitsa was weeping. I felt pity, tenderness, the desire to touch her, to press her head to my shoulder.

She raised her wonderful eyes to me, swimming in tears, and said :
'He is my brother, but you ought to have killed him.'

'Why did you come?' I asked her.

'Could I not come?' she said in reply. 'Please do not tell my father and my brother.'

I returned to Karaibrahim and found him talking to his horse. I stood beside the door. He felt my presence and told me to come in. He seemed quite gay and softened to me.

'Look,' he said to me. 'What rafters there are on the roof, what girders hold the roof up. Two men could not reach around them. And the steps above are made of whole hewn logs. And the stones of the wall! What mangers, what space! You could tie an elephant up here. When I was a child, I longed for this *Konak* night and day. I gazed at it from top to bottom, I was always around it. You can't understand that, you've been in the *Konak*. I am its master now. Unfathomable are the roads of Allah.'

He fell silent, and spoke once more :

'When I saw the knife above my head—and I was not prepared, for he was my brother—I thought that I was dying. But the knife saved me. Do you remember the tuft of hair on my forehead? All my hair had fallen out, only it was left. That is how my love of my family had been left in me. I could not rid myself of it. My heart was filled with faith in Allah and hatred of the unbelievers —but my father and my brothers stood aside. Now I have seen them. And the knife cut off my tuft. When I pass my hand over my head,' and he suited the gesture to the word, 'I do not feel anything anywhere. When I look into my heart, I see only faith and hatred. I have been saved.'

The Bulgarians taken in the villages were shut up in the inner courtyard with the plane-tree, as if they were in a sheepfold. The

gateway with the tunnel, the stairs and all gates were barred with
thorns and iron, and guards had been placed on the verandas. On
the first day, when they were thrown bread, as it is thrown to dogs,
the men fought for the pieces, and the Turks laughed at them. On
the second day no one bent down to take the bread. Some men
passed around, collected it and took it to the oldest, who divided it.
Every day some of them died, but we did not take out their bodies.
The others prized up the cobble stones and tried to bury them. We
stood on the verandas above their heads and looked at them; they
stood down below as if they were in another world. Karaibrahim
had given orders that not one word was to be exchanged with
them.

I now went down more rarely into the secret passage to the imprisoned notables. Gyulfié would not let me into her room. She
did not weep; she only stared in front of her and kept repeating:

'That bitch, Sevda, is with child. I told you—Karaibrahim or
Goran. Only Manol is left.'

She grew thinner and her skin hung in folds, like a rag. I had
no need of her.

I no longer had such a need of the notables, either. The Turks,
fearing Karaibrahim, dared not kill them, but every day they would
drag out some ten or twenty men and beat them almost to death.
They gave them twenty blows each, and as Sheikh Shaban Shebil
said, 'they struck ten times and counted one.' In the secret passage
I heard the beaten ones receive the newly beaten ones in turn. I
heard Mircho crying. And I heard Manol say:

'The mountain is looking at you.'

I realized that it all had to do with brotherhood. These men
were brothers of the men in the valley and of the men in all the
Bulgarian lands. They wanted to remain their brothers, and did not
want to raise a hand against them. And if one thought more deeply
about it, it was clear that to have a brother meant that you were
a man. And brotherhood was not one blood. Karaibrahim said that
to be alone meant to be strong. In my opinion, one should rather
say—to become a brute. A man does not live alone. Alone or two—
that was the choice. Alone or with the others, with men. Karaibrahim was fighting to remain alone—to break his link with other men.
The shepherds were holding out in order to remain together.
Karaibrahim had reached the end of his road. Would the shepherds
reach the end of theirs, too?

New Turks arrived. One day frequent shots were heard coming
from the mountain. We dashed out. Dark cloudlets of smoke rose
beneath the summit of the mountain, where the stone crosses were.

A black crowd of people was coming down. I saw that they were Turks. They were not defending themselves from the shepherds, but were shooting at the sky, in joy at arriving.

Two hundred regular troops and three hundred mounted auxiliary troops arrived. *Bashibazouks* and mounted irregulars, *akindjis*, as they were called. Three hundred hungry brutes, each with an empty bag at his back and a rope wound around his waist. They had come to rob and to bind men. The notorious Karaiman Hassan Hodja, the man who had destroyed Chepino, the friend of Mehmed Pasha, was at their head.

Karaibrahim ordered us to put him on a litter and carry him out in front of the *Konak* gate. He wanted to see the reinforcements arriving.

The Karaiman was half-mad. He could not speak one word like a human being, he only yelled. The veins of his neck were always swollen, his face was always scarlet, and his eyes looked as if they were about to crawl up onto his forehead. He waved his hands, stamped his feet, and flung himself onto the floor. At first I thought he was drunk. He had brought a dervish with him, who spent hours whirling around, so fast at that, that the skirts of his robe stood out straight at the sides like a mushroom. They said that he had whirled thus in front of the Sultan himself.

Life in the *Konak* began to whirl like the skirts of the dervish's robe. The *Konak* was too small for so many men. That same night they cast aside the thorns and began to drag out the women and children from among the captive Bulgarians. I went to Karaibrahim. He said to me:

'The seas are deep because they receive all rivers, even the muddy ones. Commanders are strong because they do not reject anyone, even robbers. With the help of these men I shall become master of the mountains. I have stayed in the *Konak* long enough. Let them frolic a while. Once I get on my feet, I'll master them. Send for the new Hodja.'

I do not know what they talked about. The Hodja emerged somewhat subdued. The following day a big group of them left for the mountains. It was said afterwards that they had gone to the pit with the mad dogs. They were no longer to be heard.

'They still growl and bark, Aga,' Kemanchidjogli said to Karaibrahim. 'There are two or three of them and they are weak. We threw them a sheep with poison for wolves.'

The howling would stop at last.

The following day almost the entire *Konak* was emptied. Over five hundred armed men set out for somewhere, Karaibrahim in their midst on a litter. Six bearers carried him on their shoulders.

The Karaiman rode on the backs of Bulgarians. He had chosen five
of the stronger men, mounted them, kicked them with his heels,
and stabbed them in the ribs with a dagger. And the poor wretches
climbed up with that black tick sticking tightly to their backs.

Old Galoushko, Sherko and the spotted dog, led on a leash, were
with us. We advanced slowly. The Turks scattered throughout the
forest, searching every gully and every bush. When we realized what
we had set out for, even the fat Hodja grew pale and went to
Karaibrahim.

'Aga,' he said, 'do you know that it is written in the Koran:
"The son, even though he be a believer, may not kill his father,
even though he be an unbeliever"?'

'I know,' Karaibrahim answered through his clenched teeth.
He, too, was pale, perhaps from the pain of the jolting litter. 'But
he can so arrange it that another will kill him. I do not intend
to kill anyone. Be gone.'

I walked along, and although I was already sure where we were
going, I did not want to believe it.

The Black Hole, into which the mad dogs were thrown, was
under high rocks. A dark opening five or six feet wide, and a stone
wall above it, overgrown with wet brown moss. There were ruins
on top of the rocks.

When we got there, Karaibrahim sent a detachment up to the
summit and said to Karaiman Hassan Hodja:

'We shall leave a hundred men there. These rocks guard the
roads from the other end of the valley. There is water up there.'

I went to the hole and peered in. I expected to be choked by a
stench. But there was no smell. One could see nothing. Only darkness.

The hole did not drop straight down like a well, but began
with a steep slope on which a man could not get a foothold. After
that the rock broke—and one could not distinguish what there was
down below. I shouted. No one answered. I understood why the
dogs remained alive, and did not fall to their death at once. Surely
there must be a slope to the very bottom, steeper or more gentle.
The Turks scattered around the surrounding rocks and stony
meadows, and formed a wide semi-circle around the hole and the
little group of men left in front of it. Rocks rose steeply on the
fourth side. And there on the summits around it, other groups of
people could be seen. They were the Bulgarians, who were watching
us at a distance.

A wind was blowing, the sky looked as if it had been swept,
the dog howled. A bare crest stretched out all around us, deserted
and wild. Karaibrahim ordered us to set his litter down on the

ground, and leaning on his elbow, said to his father and his brother :

'Since my return to this valley, my ears have been deafened with talk of brothers, of Bulgarians and of loyalty. Go down into the Black Hole and remain alone there with the dog. Then we will see whether it will remain true to you. And if you eat it up, you will remain one against the other. We will see then whether man is a brother to man.'

And he dropped back onto his pillow. His voice was weak and the wind scattered it.

Old Galoushko, the White One and Sherko did not reply. The wind blew the old man's white beard and his son's black hair about. Karaiman Hassan Hodja said :

'Accept the True Faith.'

Again they did not speak.

Then Karaibrahim gave a sign. Two men with forked sticks, pressed down the dog's neck on both sides, and began to push it to the edge of the Black Hole. The dog tried to turn its head and bite at the sticks, it growled and howled, scratching the rock with its four paws, full of strength and fury.

When its head hung over the hole, it began to whimper in horror. A sharp squeal, a howl—and the dog vanished. His body could be heard striking against the rocks. It squealed, howled and barked and its voice sank ever deeper down. A roar, a thud, a squeal, a thud. At the end a desperate, piercing, helpless howl was heard. From the bottom.

For the first time we heard Sherko's voice. He stepped forward as he was with his hands bound at his back, leant over the opening and shouted :

'I'm coming, Sharo !'

The wind made his hair stand on end, as if the breath of a giant came up from the cave. A pitiful whimper replaced the howl. It was no longer the huge spotted brute that was down below, but a small puppy that was groping about.

Sherko stood on the edge of the precipice looking down. At his back two executioners approached him with quiet, stealthy steps.

They did not push him in. They tied a rope under his armpits and began to drop him down. The huge pile of wound ropes was unwound and grew smaller. Sherko's voice, which rang out at first, grew fainter later, but was still heard clearly encouraging the dog. The man, too, reached the bottom. The rope was a double one. They left one end of it loose and began to pull. Now the white rope, which had vanished into the darkness, was coming towards us. It was endlessly long, and took an endless time. It did not quiver, nor become taut, nor was it shaken. There did not seem to be anything at the bottom of it. Or else there was a corpse. The dog was silent.

Now only Old Galoushko was left at the mouth of the pit. Small, white-haired, bent, his bound hands at his waist at the back, as if he wanted to straighten up. Above him rose the rocks, crowned with the white ruins. Turks were peering down from there.

Were those the rocks he had shown me on that happy day at the mill, when I had eaten sun and honey? And he had said : 'It flows, it flows.' And he had spoken of the gods of the dead folk, who had built the ruined temples to gods with goats' feet. Our gods had paws.

The end of the rope appeared and lay on the rock.

Karaiman came forward once more :

'Accept the True Faith.'

He said it reluctantly, only because it had to be done, certain that he would hear no answer. He did not even expect one. And hurried to draw farther away from the open maw of the mountain.

Old Galoushko did not quiver. I remembered that he had grown somewhat deaf from the rattle of the water-mill and the roar of the water. I said to Karaibrahim :

'He is deaf.'

The wind was growing stronger. The fat Hodja made for the old man, but when he approached the edge, he squatted down and began to rest his hands on the smooth rock. He reached Old Galoushko, rose to his feet—a huge ball beside the thin old man—and shouted in his ear :

'Accept the True Faith.'

And squatted down again at once.

Old Galoushko was staring down into the abyss with an anxious, helpless expression, such as one sees on the faces of the deaf when they are trying with all their might to hear something. He started, but did not see anyone. The fat man tugged at his leg. The old man dropped his eyes and saw the squatting fat man at his feet. He understood, but only shook his head.

Molla Soulfikar Softa crawled back on hands and knees.

We were silent. The wind howled among the rocks.

Karaibrahim said :

'Drop him in.'

And when he saw that the two executioners were lifting the end of the rope, he added :

'Untie his hands, and give him a dagger.'

The old man took the dagger. He stared at it, not knowing what to do with it. His white garment quivered over his body, blown about and stretched by the wind.

'I don't want the dog to eat him up,' said Karaibrahim in a tone-less voice.

And Old Galoushko, the White One, the singer of the mountain, went down into the lower earth, as another singer of Rhodopa, called Orpheus, had gone down centuries ago, when those stones up on the summit had been gathered together in well-built white temples. And the rope returned to us once more.

We listened. I looked at the dark opening with the same expression on my face as there had been a moment before on the face of the old man who had disappeared. I still saw him at the edge of the abyss.

There was nothing. The wind howled.

Shots rang out, faint and scattered. While we had all been looking at the pit, the Bulgarians had come up just behind the Turks. They had done so, not to attack us, but drawn by the terrible deed at the pit. They did not even shoot in return. They turned tail, dashed up the slopes, and disappeared.

We left the pit so quickly that we, too, seemed to be fleeing. The wind met us, making us bend and turn our faces aside. We did not look one another in the eye. We were like the silent crowd which returns from the cemetery, after hearing the soil rattle on the coffin. But a dead body is always left in a grave, while living people had been left in the cave. They were alive, down in the bowels of the mountain in the pitch darkness, amid decaying bodies. How long would they live?

I was alive, but I did not rejoice.

And when we were already entering the *Konak*, the wind brought to our ears the long-drawn-out desperate howling of a dog.

The Turks up on the rocks would not spend a merry night.

Ninth Excerpt

On that day the sun was shining over the mountain. But it was not just an ordinary sun, it was a storm and a whirlwind of sunshine. The wooded slopes that faced the sun, so that its rays fell upon them, were crushed, buried and smoothed out by the light. No hollow was to be seen, nor any shadow, and the trees rose straight, like a wall painted green. And the slopes that were on one side, so that the rays flew over them, looked like green drifts piled up by the wind, broken by the blue shadows at the edges of the spruces with pale-green crests. That is how a storm piles up snowdrifts in winter and breaks them up, so that it buries the mountains. Only here and there could one see the clear blue shadows of the forest on the meadows—on the side which was facing the sun, while on the other side, the forest melted into the meadow. The whole mountain seemed to be covered with gold dust, and gold dust was borne over the forests, as if sunny snow were falling.

On that day, the notables of Elindenya Valley were slain. They were brought out of the dungeon, and tried to keep their eyes open to see the sun, but their lids fell of themselves, to preserve them from the light. They were asked if they would accept the True Faith. They were silent. They were asked what was their wish before their death. They said :

'Kill us in front of the *Konak*, and not amid four walls. Kill us on the square in front of the mountain.'

And Karaibrahim said :

'So be it.'

I no longer interpreted, for he spoke Bulgarian. I stood on one side and looked on. But Karaibrahim had already decided to behead them in the square, so that the Bulgarians in the mountains would witness the execution, and he had even sent them word of this. Five hundred Turks were posted in the end houses of Elindenya with their rifles aimed at the forest, to intercept any bold spirits who might try to hinder the massacre.

Sixty executioners had been sharpening their black knifes on black whet-stones since the day before. They cut down the solitary spruce which stood in the middle of the square, and hewed its trunk to make a block. They even dug a runnel to carry away the blood.

The notables came out with their hands bound behind them, and Karaibrahim had ordered them to be strapped together two by two, so that they walked in couples, their backs slightly turned to one another, for they could not move their arms. Only Mircho was bound separately and walked beside his father, like a calf, bound only by the horns, running to the slaughter-house after the big bull, well-roped and chained.

And when they passed through the dark cave of the gateway to emerge on the square, Karaiman Hassan Hodja said to the shepherd beside Manol :

'Change your faith and in half an hour you will be eating pilaf, and after many years your soul will go to paradise. But the others will roll in the dust without their heads.'

The shepherd answered him :

'When that water stops flowing, I will cease to call myself a Bulgarian and will become a Turk.'

He could no longer see the fountain, which flowed in the middle of the inner courtyard, but he heard its song.

Karaibrahim lay on the litter near the double file of the men condemned to death, and heard his words. He ordered Kemanchidjogli, who was standing beside me, by the litter :

'Before the sun sets, let that fountain be walled up.'

And from the darkness came the shepherd's ringing voice :

'You will wall up the fountain, but the springs in the mountains you will not wall up.'

The men were arranged in the middle of the square in a ragged, yellow-faced, bloodstained file. Some were barely able to stand, so badly had they been beaten. Their feet were covered with wounds, their faces were wounds, their hands were wounds.

On one side stood the sixty executioners with the black knives in their hands. They stared at the notables and each one seemed to be choosing his victim.

From the gateway Karaibrahim appeared in his litter on the shoulders of six wrestlers, stripped to the waist. His litter was placed on a scaffolding so that he might see from on high.

Karaibrahim was silent, leaning on his elbow on a red cushion. The green stripe of his wound cut across his face from his turban to the collar of his garment.

From the *Konak* two men appeared, holding the big marble slab on both sides.

Karaibrahim said :

'On this slab Syuleiman Aga had your names carved.'

And turning to the half-naked wrestler beside the scaffolding, he ordered : 'Take a hammer and break the slab.'

The wrestler spat on his hands and raised a heavy hammer. He struck the marble three times before the white stone cracked.

Three times the echo brought back the ringing blow. I raised my eyes to look at the mountain, which responded to the blows, as if the hammer were striking its marble flanks.

The edges of the forests above the meadows near Prossoina were lined with people. There were Bulgarians on the meadows amid the forest; Bulgarians showed black beside the crosses up on the Pass. It seemed to me that there were people even on the trees along the crest. I had never even thought that so many people lived in Elindenya. They had probably come from other villages, too. Between the silent crowds and the end houses of the village lay the pastures, mown by the sun, and the Turks aimed their rifles at them. From below I could see the Bulgarians ranged on the high places very well. From above they, too, saw the square, as if it lay in the palm of their hands.

A hundred times the wrestler struck the tombstone, before he broke it into pieces. And the more he broke them, the more the fresh, clean pieces of marble grew, catching the mad sun, so that the white pile of shards sparkled more brilliantly in the middle of the square.

Three times the wrestler's hammer stopped. His whole back was shining with sweat. And three times Karaibrahim said:

'Go on.'

When the blows no longer rang, but crunched, as if a strong beast were breaking bones between its teeth, Karaibrahim said:

'Enough.'

The wrestler dropped the hammer and wiped his brow.

Karaibrahim said to him:

'Bend down, take the stones and the dust in your hands, and scatter them at the feet of the shepherds.'

And the wrestler scattered the pieces and the dust of the slab, on which their names were written, at the bare feet of the condemned.

And Mircho fell on his knees, hidden behind his father's back, and leant his head on his bound hands.

Then Karaibrahim said:

'Manol, come forward.'

The file did not move.

Karaibrahim said:

'Manol, I am not going to flay you alive. I shall behead you with the others, for I owe you great thanks.'

And straightening himself up on the litter, he said slowly:

'I thank you, Manol. I have to thank you for a good deed you did me. If my father had given you to the Janissaries, you would have had the best share—the glory and the arms. And I would have followed the sheep and smelt of wool and cheese.'

Then Manol spoke up and answered him:

'I thank you, too, Strahin, for becoming a Janissary instead of me. The best share fell to my lot—to follow the sheep and to smell of wool and cheese. I thank you, Strahin, for becoming Karaibrahim, and not I.'

He was silent, and then I said to myself:

'I thank you, Manol for letting me meet you on my way, so that I could understand by your stature how great a man should be. And when I tried to stand beside you, I straightened my crooked back and my crooked soul. You showed me that besides life there is also a man's life. I thank you, Manol, for having made me a man once more.'

In the meantime Manol bent over his shoulder and said something to Mircho, who was kneeling behind him. And the child, probably encouraged by his father's voice, rose and stood beside him.

Karaiman Hassan Hodja—the master of Chepino, who rode men —stepped forward and opened his mouth. He wanted to invite the notables once more to give up their faith. But Karaibrahim signed to him and he drew back.

And Karaibrahim looked at the executioners. They began to pull hairs from their beards and test the sharpness of their knives on them.

Then Manol spoke again:

'Strahin,' he said. 'Come and let me tell you something. But let no one hear.'

There was a whisper among the Turks, who had gathered there. Some of the notables raised their heads—for from the very beginning they had been looking at the soil that was to receive them. But the Turks stirred, not because they thought that Manol was frightened, but because to the last man they knew the tale of Manol's foster-father, the bandit, and thought that Manol was now going to reveal the whereabouts of a big treasure, to ransom himself. And they all stared at Karaibrahim.

He answered:

'I cannot get up, Manol, and you will not live till I recover. Tell the Venetian, and he will tell me.'

And I went forward a few steps. But Manol shook his head and quietly asked his son something. And the child answered him, and I saw that blood was running from his mouth. And as I was already near Manol, I heard Mircho's words:

'The one-eyed man.'

But Manol shook his head, and I heard his words:

'He has only one hand.'

'Let that one, the fat Hodja, come.'

The fat Molla Soulfikar Softa rolled past me, trembling with greed. He stopped in front of Manol, but stamped his feet impatiently on the spot.

Manol stared him in the eye. Then he suddenly raised his left hand and brought it down on the Hodja's shoulder. While he had knelt at his father's back, Mircho had gnawed through the ropes of one of his hands.

With his left hand Manol pressed the Hodja down. His knees bent and he fell backwards onto the ground. Manol raised his bleeding foot and put it on his throat. But he did not press it down at once—he bent down and spoke quietly to the Hodja. It seemed to me that he was saying name after name.

For several seconds no one moved. Then a bestial roar broke

out, and men foaming at the mouth flew past me, knives in hand. But the bound notables hurled themselves at them as if they were going to fight. They wanted to save Manol from the knives. And five feet away from me, the Turks began to cut down the defenceless Bulgarians.

I shut my eyes. I pressed my lids down. It was just the same as if I had left them open. I saw everything. And perhaps they were open?

I saw knives flashing over the multitude of people. I saw the blood put out their glitter. I saw streams of blood spurting up from the swaying forest of bodies, towards the sun, as if red flames had blazed up. And the Bulgarians died under its unfurled red banner that seemed to be tossed by a storm.

I kept my lids firmly closed. But it seemed to me that I was going in under that red coverlet with open eyes, that I was crawling among arms, legs, knives and bodies, and reaching the Hodja's face with its eyes starting out of their sockets, and seeing Manol's lips as they moved. The bleeding heel pressed the fat throat down, and from above came the words : 'For Mircho. For Elitsa. For Old Galoushko. For Sherko. For Goran . . .' And the heel came down lower.

I saw and I heard.

Over the whole mountain a terrible, long-drawn-out cry rang out :

'A-a-a-a-ah !'

The mountain seemed to be ablaze with cries. The Bulgarians were shouting on the slopes around us and the echo was deafening me.

Then the *chans* rang out like a silver avalanche, which came rushing down the mountain. More terrible than on that night when Karaibrahim was defending himself against them. Manol's *chans* were ringing.

After that, frequent shots pierced the dense clouds of shouts and ringing like flashes of lightning. The Bulgarians were attacking Prossoina.

And above everything, amid everything, amid the shouts, the ringing, the echo and the shots, I heard the sinister rattle of knives. Iron striking on wood, striking on flesh, the breaking of bones like the breaking of wood. And the spurting of blood.

I lived through it.

The shouts died down. The ringing died away. The shots ceased. Only from a distance came the clear, purified ringing of the Monastery bell. It was tolling.

One upon the other the massacred Bulgarians lay rolling on the square. I did not hear whether anyone was groaning. I had grown deaf, my eyes were blinded with light, I felt as if I had risen from my bed after a severe illness, from my death bed.

The executioners began to pull the bodies about, to cut off their heads. Karaibrahim wanted to send them to Mehmed Pasha. They drew aside the fat Hodja with the broken neck. Then amid the dead, Mircho rose up with his hands bound behind him, looking around like a madman. His father's body was drawn aside, and the child came out from under it, for Manol had lain over his son and had protected him from the blows.

As he stepped across the bodies, the one-eyed Hodja made for him, knife in hand.

Karaibrahim's voice was heard :

'Back. I forgive him, let him go !'

The Hodja stopped.

Karaibrahim said :

'If you want to, take him again !'

The one-eyed Hodja turned and spat. Someone cut the bonds on the child's hands. Mircho was kicked out of the heap of corpses. But he stood on one side, staring, and never moving.

Karaibrahim called from his scaffolding :

'Bring him to me.'

And he said to the boy :

'I promised your father that I would make every member of his family draw a cross with his blood and spit on it. Come !'

The child wiped his mouth, bloodstained from gnawing the ropes, and possibly with his father's blood, and drew a cross on the dusty earth.

He tried to swallow, but could not. His throat was dry.

And he spat blood on the earth.

Tenth Excerpt

> Only Manol, blessed Manol,
> Only Manol got through,
> One hand he untied,
> Selim Hodja he caught,
> By the throat he caught Selim Hodja,
> And down on the ground he pressed him
> Speaking his last word to him :
> 'Lie here, you bloodsucker,
> I'll at least die together with you.'

When the news came that Karaibrahim was going to behead the captive notables in front of the *Konak*, I went to the *Yurouk* Ismaïl and telling him Manol's last words, I begged him to give me the *chans*. And he said to me :

'I shall come myself.'

And he did this not because he feared that his *chans* would be lost. He wanted to see Manol's death. And with him came many other *Yurouks*, too.

We stood on the edge of the forest and hung Manol's silver *chans* between two young spruces. From above the square looked like a round silver tray, placed at our feet. And the sun glinted off the white cobblestones and the whitewashed *Konak*, and the roofs of the houses, so that it blinded us.

And we saw how the poor prisoners came out, how they took their stand on the square, and how their executioners stood opposite them. And from above we saw Turks lying in the houses at the end, hiding behind the stone walls, and the muzzles of their rifles shone in the sunlight. But the flames of the fuses were practically invisible, because the sun was so strong.

And I recognized Manol, although it was not near, and I saw the child Mircho beside him. And afterwards I could no longer distinguish him, but saw only a file of men, for my eyes were filled with tears. And the whole world turned to silver, as if the silver *chans* were swaying before me.

So I said to myself : 'Priest, you must strike the *chans* when they begin to behead the first man, for you may miss Manol.' Yet was it not all the same who down below was Manol, and were not other notables, but a few of his thousand brothers?

All around the people began to murmur, and as I was weeping,

I asked them what was happening, and they answered me that down below a man was going up to Manol, but I did not understand anything. Then I saw—and it would have been better had I gone blind—how a swarm of black crows cast itself on the notables. And the red rug of the men's blood was spread on the square.

And I struck the *chans*. And I shook the spruces as if they were the pillars of the gate to salvation, and I struck the *chans* with a bleeding forehead. And they rang and rang, and I became a child once more, and passed through the darkness of my mother's womb. And Elindenya was no longer a valley, but a silver lake. And I always went back, to the first day, when the earth was deserted and unordered, and God's spirit was borne over the waters. And I knew that that spirit was the ringing of a Rhodope *chan*.

And someone seized me by the shoulder and said to me:

'Father, stop. They have slain them.'

I awoke; I heard a cry, the mountain echo and shots. I saw nothing, for I was weeping. And I heard that the people beside me were weeping, too.

Thus all the notables died like men. And if each of them had had a sin, and even if he had had a great sin, the glory of that death would not have let the stains of their former life appear. And the light of their last day is so brilliant that we cannot distinguish the stains of their former days. And nothing more was remembered of them; it was only remembered and said: 'He died on the cobblestones of Prossoina, at Manol's right hand.'

For, indeed, only then can it be said how much a man is worth, when it is seen how he dies. You may cheat anyone, only death you cannot cheat.

And in the gully, into which they cast their beheaded bodies, where their blood flowed and their flesh melted away, dark-green grass shot up the following year. The grass all around was light-green, and looked still lighter because of the yellow flowers growing in it, but not a single flower blossomed on the dark-green grass. Even when in the autumn the other grass withered, dried up and was gone, the grass growing on the graves remained fresh and juicy. And it was seen from a distance like a dark shadow on the slopes.

Until the snow covered it.

Eleventh Excerpt

A new group of Turks arrived, fewer this time—about a hundred men. With them came Hodja Hassan, the son of Velko. He held his wounded shoulder, and from time to time looked at his hand, and the blood on it. And he kept repeating :

'It was Stoiko, Stoiko. And he knew me. He was aiming at me.'

He could not believe that a man of the valley would shoot at him, Syuleiman Aga's Hodja. He did not understand that he had passed over to the right, as the Aga said. As they were riding along the Rock of the Maiden, a band of Bulgarians had attacked them, and ten men had fallen into the abyss with their horses.

Syuleiman Aga was dead. But before he died he had seen Manol's head. The Hodja told us the following about the Aga's death and his last meeting with Manol :

'When Syuleiman Aga and I reached the Philibé, we were told to go to Adrianople. And on that day the heir to the throne, Prince Moustafa, son of Mohammed, was to be given his first lesson. Syuleiman Aga was asked to the ceremony, which was a very great honour and unexpected.

'There gathered at the place for the Divan, the *Mufti*, the *Kaimakam*, the favourite Vizier, the *Nishandii*, the *Defterdar*, the Sheikh Vani, the *Cadi-askers*[8] and other shining lights of the Sultan's power. Syuleiman Aga was there, too, and I with him. And when the Heir to the Throne Moustafa entered, the Sultan rose, went to meet him, and kissing him on both eyes, placed him beside him and seated him. The Preacher Vani read the sacred words : "In the name of God, the All-merciful and All-forgiving." Prince Moustafa said the first four letters of the alphabet. And with that his first lesson came to an end. And the Sultan began to reward his courtiers one after the other, particularly the learned men, and with his own hand he pinned on his son, the Prince, an ornament with plumes and precious stones. That day Syuleiman Aga did not receive a gift. On leaving the place we all walked after the Prince, and there were gold and silver coins spread on the path. There was a great banquet, after which, in the Garden of Fountains, the Sultan talked with his more intimate courtiers about the Koran and the Prophets. And he was so moved that he took the robe from his back and made the *Mufti* a present of it. And Sheikh Vani moved him so deeply that the Sultan forbade his men to turn their horses into the peasants' fields, as they had done hitherto. In the meantime, the other courtiers walked up and down, with nothing to do, and foretold that as the Sultana Rebia Gyulnoush—the Spring Garland of Roses, a Greek—came from Candia and the Sultan possessed her, it was a good sign, and it was right that the Sultan should conquer Candia itself. Syuleiman Aga and I talked of Elindenya.

'The following day, the Sultan went hunting outside Adrianople. On the third day he received Syuleiman Aga in his tent together with other Spahis. With us there were also many envoys from distant lands. We passed by the Sultan's forty-two horses, each with its gold saddle, and past the guardians of the gardens, leaning on sticks and wearing red caps, which hung down their backs.

'There was a small square in front of the Sultan's tent, surrounded by flags and by poles on which human heads were stuck.

'The Sultan sat surrounded by mutes and dwarfs. His throne was made so that he could lie on it, and his feet he put on a purple cushion. And the throne itself stood on a raised place, like a sofa, at the height of a man's waist. The Sultan wore a red and gold garment, buttoned with diamonds across his breast; he had three ornaments with plumes and precious stones on his turban, two standing upright, and the middle one lying backwards. The diamonds cast such flashes of light on his face that he could barely be seen, just as one cannot see the forest, when it lies facing the sun. He was given books and gifts, and each object the secretary took, and handed it to the *Kaimakam*, who handed it to the favourite Vizier. The Vizier placed the gifts on the sofa on which lay the throne. The Sultan did not touch a thing.

'Then came Syuleiman Aga's turn, and the Sultan mercifully condescended to recognize him. He even became animated and began to ask about Rhodopa, about the game and most of all about the bears. And he said that on the way to Larissa he would pass through Rhodopa. And the Sheikh Vani ventured to say something which I did not hear. Then the Sultan made a present of an expensive *kaftan*[9] to Syuleiman Aga.

'As the Sultan was leaving his tent, lo, black slaves advanced towards him, and poured forty-three heads out at his feet from goats' hair sacks. And an emissary said that the Vizier Mehmed Pasha—may his seed be cursed—sent his Commander the heads of his enemies.

'And Syuleiman Aga and I at once recognized the head of Manol as it lay at the Sultan's feet. Manol's eyes were open. And we recognized other heads, although they were cut about and salted.

'Then the Sultan said :

'"May the man who kills an innocent man be responsible in this world and in the next."

'And the historian Abdi at once wrote his words down. And the Sultan said further :

'"I do not want my men to satisfy their passions, when holding in their hands the power that I have given them."

'Abdi wrote that down also. And the Sultan said it, standing face to face with Manol. And everyone can read these words in Abdi's chronicle. Then Syuleiman Aga looked at him and said :

'"These heads here are all those of innocent men. And none of their murderers will be punished."

'The Sultan said nothing. And Abdi wrote nothing down. But Syuleiman Aga squatted down before the heads, and looking upon them, he spoke the names of the dead notables half-aloud. And as soon as the Sultan's suite had passed on, I said to him :

'"Madman !"

'And he answered me :

'"Fool ! Do you think that I have been sent for to be given a *kaftan*? What is written will be."

'And in the night two executioners entered our tent, a Gypsy and a Jew, and tightening a strap around Syuleiman Aga's neck they pulled on both sides until they had strangled him. The Aga was on his knees, holding the strap with both hands and looking at me. I stayed on the pallet opposite. And when the Aga died, he was thrown out of the camp to be eaten by the dogs. And on him was the *kaftan* that the Sultan had given him.

'The following day I asked to see the Sultan, but he had shut himself up with Abdi. The Sultan turned the leaves of the annals of Ottoman history haphazard, and Abdi read him about the feats of his forbears.

'I returned to Philibé, but for a long time I could not enter the valley, for I was told that the Bulgarians were guarding the passes.'

When he finished, Hassan Hodja begged me to unwind the turban from his forehead. His right hand was wounded.

I asked him :

'What are you thinking of doing, you madman?'

He did not answer me; he stood there with his uncovered head and listened. We looked down from the veranda and saw that they were casting the household goods out of Gyulfié's rooms. She was kneeling on the veranda, striking her forehead on the boards and weeping :

'Is there no man to give me sons? Why have I no sons?'

Syuleiman Aga's brother's sons had come, Hairedin's whelps, and were driving her into a narrow little room on the ground floor.

Hassan Hodja turned to me and said :

'I am old, and I can no longer return to the God of my fathers. And I do not want to serve a god who makes men gnaw each other like dogs. I am going to Karaibrahim and the *Karaiman* to tell them so.'

They hanged him on the plane-tree.

[1] *Teké* (T) = Moslem shrine.
[2] *Grosh* (T) = silver Turkish coin worth about one-fifth of a gold franc.
[3] *Beyler-Bey* (T) = head bey.
[4] *Tougra* (T) = monogram of a Sultan with his father's name and the words 'Always Victorious' interlaced with it.
[5] *Zourla* (T) = primitive oboe.
[6] *Maaneh* (T) = Turkish folk song, sung slowly to a long-drawn tune with many flourishes and grace notes.
[7] *Haidé* = much-used expression all over the East, meaning Come on !
[8] Dignitaries of the Sultan's court.
[9] *Kaftan* (T) = richly ornamented garment.

PART FOUR

The Time of Parting Has Come

First Excerpt

> Do not plant a big vineyard,
> Do not build a tall house,
> Do not marry a handsome wife,
> Do not rear lovely children—
> That you may live in peace,
> That you may have no trouble.

There once lived a man in a village below the Pirin Mountain, and his name was Dobrin. He was a merchant and had three sons. His youngest son was called Nikola. I was he.

And when I was twenty years old, lo, one evening we were waiting for our father to return. And the dog began to howl terribly, so that we went out at the gate. A man was coming towards us along the road, crucified and bound with chains on a wooden cross. And the cross did not touch the earth, so that the man could move his toes. And thus, toe by toe, he was walking along the road, and each of his steps was as much as the breadth of a thumb. That man was my father. And behind him, at the end of the road, torches shed their light, and Hafouz Bey, the Janissary of the village, stood there, laughing.

And our father saw that we were coming, so that he lost his strength and fell on the stones as if he had been cut down, and his arms were stretched out and bound to the cross. His chains rattled fearfully. Tears blinded me, and I cast myself at the flames of the torches. But my two brothers knocked me down, and as they had nothing to bind me with, they bound me with the chains, taken from our father, and they were still hot.

The Turks had made black chains red hot, and had bound my father with them. The scars of the red-hot chains wound around him from his shoulders to his knees, strongly welded, link by link, as if the chains still hung on him. And from that day on, he tore his clothes, and remained naked and tried to scratch off the terrible scars with his nails. And he screamed :

'Take off the chains ! Take off the chains !'

And all this because with his own labour and the labour of his sons, he had built a two-storey house.

And we, his three sons, heard the cries of the madman all day and all night, and as we could not endure it for pity and for shame we left that house. Our poor little mother, plunged in grief, was left with our father. And the madman screamed:

'Take off the chains! Take off the chains!'

And with towels and herbs she tried to wipe away the terrible scars. But the chains remained.

My first brother set out along the current of the river. He became a merchant and began to turn Greek. My second brother came out on to the bank. He became the abbot of a monastery. The third brother—and that was I—set out against the current of the river. I set out to revenge myself on Hafouz Bey.

And the Bey left a trail of tears in the villages along the River Mesta, entering each of them and taking the boys to make Janissaries of them. And I went after him, following his bloody tracks among the villages.

And I saw sufferings and horrors, so that I was ashamed to tell them of my grief. For the chains that bound me were scars, and the same chains burned the flesh of people.

One man said to me:

'They took my grain to the last handful, and now my children are starving to death.'

One girl said to me:

'Two of them sat on my arms, a third sat on my head, and the fourth drew my knees apart.'

One old woman told me:

'I had three sons and three daughters. They sold all six as slaves. And they opened my sons' mouths to see if their teeth were sound, and dug their fingers into my daughters, to see if their flesh was firm.'

Then there was a drumming in my ears, and I understood my first truth.

And it was that all over the Bulgarian lands, whosoever spoke Bulgarian suffered and groaned under the heel of the Turks.

And I grew desperate, and went to the monastery to my brother.

In the monastery I found old books and charters, and read of former centuries and battles. And I saw on the gold seals the heads of terrible tsars, with beards and crowns.

And when I set out from monastery to monastery, everywhere I dug out of the cobwebs and the dust old memories and ancient glories.

One monk said to me :

'Lo, with this parchment Tsar Assen[1] granted our monastery three mountains, three rivers and three villages.'

And the parchment was all tattered.

A second monk said to me :

'Lo, with this sword Tsar Simeon[2] pursued the Greeks as far as Constantinople.'

But the sword was rusty.

A third monk told me :

'Lo, this is the ossuary with the bones of the warriors who fought the Turks on the borders of our lands.'

And the bones were a huge mound.

Then there was a drumming in my ears and I understood my second truth.

And it was that now we might be suffering, and now might be slaves, but the Bulgarians, too, had once had a kingdom and had been free and strong.

And when my blood began to boil, I remembered the Bey and set out to look for him.

We got together a faithful band and we took to the forest. And a strong detachment caught up with us, and captured our *Voivoda*[3] Goran.

When they led him out to the gallows, I, too, came down to the village, and mingled with the peasants. And I saw my Bey beside the gallows, mounted on a horse and all gleaming with gold.

And Goran walked to the gallows in a white shirt, singing :

'Since the day began, mother mine so dear to me, since dawn
    was breaking
Since that moment, mother mine so dear to me, an army's been
    marching.'

He was singing about an army, yet he walked alone, and bound. And all around the peasants were silent.

I looked around and saw a thousand Bulgarians and ten Turks. And I thought that the Bulgarian army was there, but it had no horses and no spears.

I cried out with all my might :

'Brothers, we are many and the Turks are few. Let us set the *Voivoda* free !'

But the people drew away from me, as mud withdraws from a stone that is cast, and as folk flee the plague. And I was left alone, in the middle of the square, with my arms hanging down.

And the Bey bent over me from his horse, and his sword fell like lightning on my head.

They hanged Goran, but I remained alive. And from that day on, besides the invisible scars of chains all over my body, I also bear the scar of a sword, hidden in my hair.

When the sword was falling upon me, there was a drumming in my ears again, and I understood my third truth.

And it was that we might suffer, and we might be slaves, and we may have been free, and may have had our own kingdom, but we were not yet awakened, and were not yet ripe for freedom.

And my brother the monk said:

'Touch your head now, and admit that the people are mud. And stay in the monastery.'

I said to him:

'Man is made of mud. Goran, too, used to be among these same folk. Will the day not come when they will all become Gorans?'

And he said to me:

'Madman!'

And I said to him:

'Deserter!'

And he drove me out of the monastery. Thus was I left without one of my brothers.

I went to the other, and his house was a rich one, but in it they spoke Greek. As soon as my brother went out, his wife and child began to speak Bulgarian to me. And his wife was Tsveta who had once given her nosegay to me, and not to my brother. Then the child went out, and Tsveta began to weep, and said to me:

'Nikola, my child is becoming a Greek and is forgetting our tongue.'

I left her some of the holy books that I carried with me. The book was written in Bulgarian. And I understood that I was left without any brothers.

From that day on every winter I stayed in a monastery and copied holy books, and also various other histories in our tongue. And as soon as spring was on the way, I would set out over the lovely, suffering land of Bulgaria, and leave the books in our tongue with village priests and in the monasteries. And I would return with a bagful of coins.

I saw my brothers only once more, and that was at my father's deathbed. Twenty years had passed since we had left our father's house, and for twenty years the madman had repeated:

'Take off the chains!'

And our poor mother rubbed the scars, but they would not be wiped away.

We looked at each other, we three brothers now grown men, over the body with the scars of the chains. And we were no longer brothers. We were strangers to each other, God forgive me—they were enemies.

And in the *Konak* Hafouz Bey, now an old man, was waiting, for he remembered that one of the sons of Dobrin had once raised his head against him.

The first to go in to him was the merchant; he gave a handful of gold coins and said :

'It was not I. I think of the gold. It was my brother.'

The second to go in was the abbot, and he, too, left a handful of gold coins and said :

'It was not I. I think of God. It was my brother.'

I was the third to go in. The Bey was sitting at a table and staring at me. And he had purposely left his *yataghan* on one side, so that I could reach it. But I clung to my bag with all my might.

The Bey said :

'Is it an honour for me to wreak vengeance on a monk, who is not even a man any longer? Give me your bag.'

And he took the handful of coins from it, but the books in the Bulgarian tongue he left. The fool, he did not know that one day they would set fire to his roof.

I went out, and I saw that the sun was shining. And the Pirin Mountains rose above the village, and the snow sparkled white upon its summits. And in our courtyard the blossom on the old apple-tree shone white, too.

My mother said—and her bowed head was white, too :

'My son, set your bag aside and stay with me.'

And although my heart wept, I replied :

'Mother, the seed is in the bag. The furrows are waiting for me.'

And she said to me :

'My son, are you a sower? Or a harvester?'

What was I to answer her? The harvest was still a long way off. But before the barns are filled, there is land and seed. And I knew that there would be those who sowed with tears, and others who would reap with joy. Yea, those who went out with tears, bearing a measure of seed, would not be those who would return with joy, bearing their sheaves. And I thought that I was not even among the sowers.

I said to my mother :

'Mother, I am the guardian of the measure of seed.'

And she said to me :

'Guard it.'

She blessed me and gave me a sprig of apple blossom. And she begged me :

'When the apples ripen, pass through the village.'

And the mother remained at the end of the village on the road, and the son left, and vanished like seed into the black fields, into the mountains, into the sky.

And the son bore the seed over the lovely, sorrowful land of Bulgaria. For the Bulgarian word lived in the books, and as long as there are words of one's own, there is a people, and seed for freedom.

Many times was there a drumming in my ears, and many were the truths I learnt. I learnt them from simple ploughmen and hewers, from mothers that had suffered and from the little children. And from the Monk Grigorii I became Priest Aligorko. And I needed no other reward.

Some kissed my hands and said to me :

'We thank you for feeding our souls !'

Others threw the books in my face, crying :

'We do not want books, give us bread !'

And when I said to them :

'Patience.'

They would say :

'Have we not got it? We do not want your comfort.'

Thus the years passed by, until fate sent me to see the destruction and the glory of the Elindenya Valley. And then my road became so steep that I lost not only my soul, but my name also. And now, when I see the grave before me, and when I want to entreat you— you who come after me— I do not even know by what name to call myself.

Remember with kindness he who has penned these lines.

Second Excerpt

> Stoyan came out before her
> As a greyish white eaglet
> And stroked her with his wings.
> His mother knew him not,
> And plucked out both his wings.

Thus the time of waiting ended and the time of deeds came. And a great pride and a great sorrow filled the folk who were waiting around the Valley of Elindenya. The brave rejoiced when they saw the response of the notables, and the fainthearted became despondent when they realized that there was no other road before them but patience and suffering. And indeed, who would pass over the bodies of the notables to go down to Karaibrahim and spit upon the cross?

We had sent emissaries, we had awaited for them—and lo, they had answered us. Not a sound was heard from a single one of the fifty, but their answer was heard, just as if they had shouted it from Mount Purvenets.

Then Mircho ran up, covered with blood and tears, and told us of Manol's last moments. And we all wept and were amazed, and that tale took the life of one hundred young shepherds. And many people heard Mircho, for the various camps of the refugees had gathered in only two places—in the cave beneath the Thracian shrine, and in the forest above the pass with the crosses. Mircho came to the pass.

Then came Momchil, who wandered around the *Konak*, and his face was still gaunter and wilder. And folk drew aside, some to leave the two brothers alone, others because they still could not forgive Momchil.

And the two brothers stood opposite each other, and they had not seen each other since the night of Manol's wedding.

And Momchil said:

'Is it you, Mircho?'

And Mircho asked:

'Is it you, Brother Momchil?'

He said 'brother,' and not '*baté*'[4], as if those days in the *Konak* had made him his brother's equal.

And he told him of the death of their father. And of gnawing the rope, and how his teeth had broken, and how he had whispered to his father: 'Only the left one.' And Manol had answered him: 'Rise! Even one hand is enough for these men.' And how his father's heavy body had pressed him so that he had lost consciousness. And when he had finished, he was silent a while and added:

'I spat on the cross.'

And Momchil said to him:

'Tell me a second time.'

And the boy again told him about the rope, and about Manol's proud words, and how he had choked the Hodja. And again at the end he added:

'I spat on the cross.'

And after they were silent a while, looking each other in the eye, Momchil begged in a toneless voice:

'Tell me a third time.'

And when Mircho had ended once more with his spitting on the cross, Momchil asked him :

'Did you not hear my father say anything?'

Mircho shut his eyes, trembled, as if he were again in the row of the children of death, and said, as in a dream :

'When he put his heel on the fat Hodja's throat he spoke names. He spoke your name, too. When he fell on me, it seemed to me that he said but one word. He said : "The *chans*". And perhaps he did not say anything, but I heard the *chans* ringing. I don't remember.'

Momchil said :

'Do you remember him speaking my name, too? And Elitsa's name? Was not Elitsa's name the last on his lips?'

Mircho was trembling harder than ever, and pressing his eyelids with all his might, and opening his mouth wide, he said through his tears :

'He was calling you. He was calling you, and me, and Elitsa. And the others who were dying around us. And at the end he was not calling Elitsa. He only said "The *chans*".'

And starting of a sudden, he opened his eyes, looked about him like a madman and began to cry, and covered his face with his hands. But he did not press his head down on my shoulder, nor on his brother's, he wept alone, standing in the middle of the meadow. I put my arms around his shoulders, and they were hard, and did not relax. And I said to Momchil :

'Let him be.'

And Momchil said to me :

'Did you hear, Father? Elitsa once told me that there was no other man like Manol all over the mountains. That is so. If he were alive, I could still hope to reach him. But he has died, and has fled high up, right into the heavens. I was unable to surpass his life, and can I hope to surpass such a death? He is so high up that I cannot even raise my head to look at him.'

Then he said further :

'He gave me Elitsa, also. If he had not set her free, she would have been his all her life. Who would leave Manol for Momchil? Elitsa did not come to me of herself—he sent her to me.'

But I did not listen to him much, and did not understand his grief, for all around us in the meadows and the forest there was weeping, and a grief a hundred times greater than his.

For the time of waiting had come to an end, and the time of deeds had come. A hundred young shepherds agreed together and swore to form an armed band and avenge Manol. Many of the Elindenya folk set out for Petglassets, others set out for who knows where across the forests, still others pottered about up and down like blind men, not knowing what to do. And there were many women without menfolk, many children without fathers, and many a maiden without a sweetheart. Where could they go? And they remained on the meadow, waiting for who knows what, just so that they might look down from above on the roofs of their houses. And perhaps the Turks would leave suddenly, just like that, before the snows fell?

What of the flocks? The white and black ewes, the yearlings, the curly-horned rams? The big goats with the silver *chans*, the brown cows with the black round bells, and the strong donkeys? The ewes' milk had run dry; they had to gather the male and female flocks together, so that the empty wombs would be fertilized. And then the flocks had to set out for the south, as soon as the first rains fell, and the new grass along the shores of the Aegean Sea began to sprout. Who would lead the flocks away? Who would go down from the mountain, leaving wife and child here? Were they to set out with them? Down in the plain, fires were burning and Turks were waiting, weren't they? And if they waited for the first snow, the dear flocks, the white flocks, the black flocks would lie down on that cursed snow and would become carrion for the wolves, the eagles and the crows.

Who would sit down to listen to Momchil's grief? I saw that more and more people were disappearing into the forest, and each one was thinking of himself—that was why I stood beside the path, saying:

'Brothers, remember the folk in the cave.'

For since the Turks had gone up to the ruins above the cave, the women and children inside it could only come out at night, and only in the forest at that, and the path upwards along the rocks was guarded by the Turks. I had come to the people at the pass to ask for food, and it so happened that I saw Manol's death. That night I had to go back; I did not think, in the general distraction to beg *Yurouk* Ismail Bey to open his bags, and he had left unnoticed with the *chans*. That year had been a good one for the *Yurouks*. Their flocks would be doubled now, without their ewes having lambed. For many were those who sold a sheep for a handful of grain, or hired themselves out as slaves with the Bey, together with their dogs and their rifles, and they would preserve their flocks which had already become the Bey's, simply and solely to have someone to protect their families, for the *Yurouk* Bey did not bother about faith and turbans.

And so, I stood at the edge of the forest, begging for the poor wretches in the cave. And some gave a hard crust, a lump of cheese, or a piece of meat, and others gave nothing. But even those who bent down to leave something before me, and those who passed me by, did not raise their eyes to look at me. Could I be angered with them, as I had neither kith nor kin, and these folk would be also putting out a hand tomorrow and begging for their children?

And it seemed to me that the priest of Prossoina was going among the people and whispering something to them. It also seemed to me that he was persuading them not to give anything. Did he, by chance, think that I would flee with the bread? Let us hope this was not true, otherwise it would be a great sin.

And when I had filled a whole sack, I sat down to gather strength, and to wait for the sun to set, so that in the half-light I might try to go down to the cave unnoticed. A baby was screaming and crying beside me, and beside it its mother screamed and wept, too. It had been born here, in the mountain, poor little creature, and would have to die before it knew what it was to have a roof over its head. It would not see smoke-darkened rafters, it would only look at green branches, before the black soil covered it.

I asked its mother :

'Where is your husband?'

And through her tears she answered me :

'He has gone with the band.'

And as I had no strength to rise and move away, I thought to quieten the little one, and spoke to it, and sang and caressed it. And all that was left of it was an open mouth : it screamed with all its might, and although it had no down on its little head yet, tears flowed from its eyes. If there was nothing else, there were tears in plenty in Rhodopa at that time, as many as the brooks and rivulets that flow through it. And the child gasped, and grew quiet, all black and red.

And from the forest came Momchil, without my hearing him, and he came and knelt beside the child. And he said to me :

'I will play to him a while.'

And he put out his hand and took his *kaval* from his waistband. I recognized it, it was his father's iron *kaval*, made out of the terrible musket of the bandit Karamanol. And Momchil crossed his legs and began to play.

It seemed to me that the sound of voices on the meadow grew quiet. It seemed to me that even the forest fell silent. And I remained thus, on elbows and knees, bending over the child, for I dared neither sit nor stand up. And I listened to the *kaval*.

And the child heard it, closed its mouth and opened its eyes. And it looked around with the black, wise eyes of an old man, and slowly sought the song with its eyes. And the blood withdrew from its little face, the wrinkles melted away, so that its little face grew clear and lovely. And a smile curved its little rosy lips, like the gentle rays of the sun, which were just dying away over the tops of the spruces. And the child closed its eyes, and peace spread over its little face. It was not asleep. It was listening to the song.

And Momchil played.

Suddenly the mother screamed, so that she turned me to stone; she dropped the child on the meadow and jumped back like a beast on all fours, and her look was wild like that of a madwoman. And she cried:

'It is dead! It is dead!'

Momchil jumped up, too, and, trying to break the iron *kaval* over his knee, he only bent it and struck it on the ground, and he cried:

'That is all I am good for: to kill children.'

And he hurled himself into the forest.

And I set out for the cave with the heavy sack over my shoulder, and I could already see the faces of the children, who would open it and thrust their hands in it, as if I were bringing them Christmas gifts. It was growing dark, when on a meadow Momchil's falcon appeared out of nowhere. I recognized it, and it flew at my face. Remembering the blinded doe, I dropped the bag and covered my face with my hands. And I saw through my fingers that pieces of bread and cheese dropped out. At first it hurt me, and then I grew angry. And the bird still hurled itself at me, flew off, returned and shrieked in an ominous way. From time to time it perched on a branch, but again it flapped its wings and hopped along. It seemed to me that it had lost its wits or was mad.

And although it did not touch me, and did not even scratch me, the falcon's madness passed into me, so that I bent down, picked up a broken branch and began to stalk it. My mouth was dry and my hands were sweaty, and in my heart there burned a thirst to kill. I had seen much blood, and I, too, wanted to kill. And when the falcon flew at me again, I waved the branch and felt the wood strike something soft, as if it were ripe fruit. And the bird shrieked pitifully and fell to the earth, fluttering its wings and turning round, like a hen whose head has been cut off. I advanced to step on it and crush it, and to feel its body becoming pulp. And in the half-light I saw blood on its feathers.

Then a red veil blinded me. And I remembered how many years ago, I had crushed the head of a viper, and when I had seen its blood and its writhing body, I had fled. And afterwards on a narrow path I had met a man, and my hands had wanted to push him down, so that I could see his head being crushed on the stones.

And the falcon managed to get on its feet and to drag itself across the meadow. I followed it, to kill it, but when I passed the sack with its spilled load, I was ashamed. I stopped. The falcon stopped, too. And I was amazed why it did not flee to save its life, but turned to look at me, and shrieked.

And when I made for it, the bird dragged itself forwards, too. When I stopped, it stopped, too, and turning its open beak, blackened with blood, it shrieked and called me.

Then I realized that the bird was leading me somewhere, and when we left the forest, so that the stony meadow, still light, stretched out before us, I understood where it was leading me. Opposite me rose the rocks and the ruins with the Turkish guard on its top, and under these rocks was the Dark Hole.

And bending down, I seized the wounded falcon and thrust it under my cassock, so that I felt two hearts beating, its heart and mine, and the falcon's blood flowed down my breast. The bird felt that I had understood where I was to go, thrust its head out of the opening of my cassock and shrieked anxiously, impatiently and pitifully.

I was already running over the stones, and the perpetual wind on these summits was blowing my cassock about. I had forgotten about the Turkish muskets, and my horror of the Hole. I ran and wept.

And when I got within about ten steps of the rocks, so that the terrible well into which the mad Karaibrahim had cast his father and his brother, gaped before me, I stopped. And I saw a rope lost in the darkness above the precipice, and its end was wound around a rock. Momchil had gone down into the hole to seek Old Galoushko and Sherko.

A black and ill-smelling cloud hangs over this hole, as if a terrible dragon lived and breathed in it. And the name of this cloud is fear and horror. They say that a Demon lives in that hole. They say also that the Plague lives there. They say that Orpheus went through it in order to go to Hell, seeking his wife. And as long as the Elindenya Valley remembers, and as long as mad dogs have been thrown into that cave, no one remembers anyone else going down into it except Syuleiman's Aga's great-great-grandfather.

And this great-great-grandfather was a poor shepherd, and his only wealth was a dog. But an evil neighbour cast the dog into the pit. Then the shepherd killed his neighbour, set fire to his house and his own house, and settled at the mouth of the pit. And building himself a hut there, axe in hand he prevented anyone from approaching the pit, lest he should throw a mad dog into it. He roamed through the forest, shot game and cast it in to his dog. The rains washed him, the wind dried him, his hair reached down to his waist. Three times men bound him, and threw a beast down into the pit, to kill his dog, so that his reason would return. And the first time they cast down a mad dog, and the shepherd's dog killed it. And the second time they cast in a lone wolf, and the dog tore it to pieces. And the third time they cast in a bear, and afterwards only the howling of the dog was heard, and the peasants gave it up, and let the madman go. They said that a man might well go mad for such a dog.

And after some years had passed, maybe three, maybe five, maybe even seven, one day the madman tied a rope around himself and let himself down into the hole. He reached the bottom and saw his dog, and in the darkness to the left he saw a pile of bones, and in the darkness to the right—a pile of gold. And a hundred eyes shone in the darkness before him, and growls were heard. The shepherd threw them a bone from his bag, and the eyes went out, and the sound of a fight was heard, and howling and the grinding of teeth. And the shepherd passed, filling his bag with gold on the way. He wandered through endless caves, in which streams fell and shadows roamed, and in the end, he reached another well, and at the bottoms of it there were two rams, the one white and the other black. If anyone fell onto the white ram, the beast would take him up to the world he knew, but if he fell onto the black one, he went to Hell. But the shepherd, even if he had jumped on the white ram, had no way of clinging to its fleece—in one hand he held the bag of gold, and in the other—his faithful dog.

Then he pushed the dog into the well, and it dug its teeth into the black ram's neck. And while the black ram, together with the dog, fell towards Hell, the white ram stood there alone and the shepherd jumped on his fleece. And the white ram brought him up into the world and this was at the gorge of the Struïlitsa, beside the hole from which the river emerges. And that the river flows long under ground when it is lost in the Devil's Hole of Petglassets, is known to all, for if it goes into the hole muddy, it comes out still muddy a whole day later in the gorge. And that it flows through secret places is known, for it drags along skulls and gold coins, so that before it was called Struïlitsa, it was known as Murtveshnitsa.[5]

Thus, by sacrificing a faithful soul, Syuleiman Aga's great-great-grandfather won his wealth, so that he became a Bulgarian boyar and later a Mohammedan. And after him no man has been found to go down into the Black Hole, although piles of gold awaited him there. But Momchil went down, and not for gold, but for love of his wife's father. And perhaps for something else, too.

And I seized the rope, and the rope stretched like a cord. I pulled it, and felt that something heavy was tied to its end. I collected my strength and daring, so that, clinging to the rock, I bent over the abyss and peered in. And although night had already fallen around me, nevertheless, the darkness of the hole was twice as black. And it was different. I called. And such an echo answered me that I nearly fell into the hole. Then I pressed the wounded falcon to my breast, to feel another living heart lying next to mine, and I began to pull the rope. What could be tied to its end? A bag of gold, the head of a dragon, or a human body?

And I did not find out, for no matter how I laboured, I was unable to draw out the load. Only from below there came such a moaning, which crept up the dark vaults, that my strength deserted me completely. And I dashed towards the forest, towards the other folk. And the falcon, as soon as it understood that I was fleeing from the hole, began to peck me with its bloody beak, so that I left it on the rock, to shriek over the abyss.

How I got together four men, how we returned without a torch, and how we seized the rope—only I know. The falcon was not there.

And after we had pulled and pulled, we got Momchil out with the rope tied under his armpits, and his head fallen on his breast. The wounded falcon flapped its wings on his shoulder, for it had gone down into the darkness to its master. We thought that Momchil was dead. But only one of his legs was badly broken, and his head was cracked.

While the four men were carrying Momchil on branches placed on their shoulders, he came to himself, and asked where the falcon was. And I was holding it tightly to my breast.

Pine torches were burning on the meadow. And when they placed Momchil on the ground they thrust the torches into the earth around his pallet. And faces began to emerge from the darkness, bending over him, and disappearing into the darkness. And he could not understand why so many people came and were silent.

Then a white-haired old man said :

'To such a father—such a son.'

And Momchil realized that they were bowing to him. And he said, and in his voice there was pain and bitterness :

'Why do you look at me? I have done nothing. I have never done anything. I am cursed. If it had been Manol, you all know, Manol would have gone down.'

And the old man said to him :

'If you had got down, we would have known that it was possible to go down. What daring is it to do something that can be done?

But you tried to do something that cannot be done. Therefore we bow to you.' And weeping, I returned to the forest to pick up the bread that had been spilt.

Third Excerpt

> I'm alive, I'm in great pain—
> With heavy chains upon my feet,
> A lighter chain around my neck,
> And handcuffs binding both my hands,
> They want to make a Turk of me.

And as we sat in the cave beside the fire, a young man came in to us, who was the seventh son of Vrazhou *Kehaya*, and he bore on his shoulders a slaughtered ram. Yet what is a slaughtered ram for one hundred and fifty hungry throats?

And dropping down beside the fire, the young man said:

'I passed by the Dark Hole. And out of it came an old woman as dry as a cast-off lamb's skin, with red eyes and fingers like an eagle's claws. And I knew that that was the Plague.[6] And she stopped me and asked: 'Whither are you going?' I did not answer her, for I knew that she would follow me. And she smiled and said to me: 'Go ahead of me.' And I set off, and heard her steps behind me. It was just as if a hoofed animal were walking behind me. And when we reached the entrance of the cave, she seized me by the shoulder and looked in. She looked at the wasted children, the women without breasts, the bony old women. And she began to shed tears of blood, turned on her heel and vanished into the forest.'

And all that were around the fire began to weep and tear their hair. And they said:

'O God, the Plague took pity on us. When will You, too, take pity on us, O Lord?'

And they looked to me, for I was the servant of God. They waited for me to speak a good word to them, as if I could speak with my Master. And I looked at them, and I saw at their backs the dried-up dead with the white teeth and the eye sockets from which the eyes had run out.

I asked the shepherd:

'Have the flocks set out?'

And he answered me:

'Most of them have gone. And they took the *chans* off their big goats, so that no sound should be heard over the mountain. And not only did they fear lest the Turks should hear them, but they said: "No song may now be borne over the mountains." Where there were five shepherds, there is one only now, and of five sheep only one is left; the others are in the flocks of Ismail Bey. But up on the heights about ten flocks are still about, waiting. And they, too, have no *chans*. Father, have you seen a flock without *chans*? It is as if it were dead.'

I asked him:

'Did Ismail Bey hang Manol's *chans* on his sheep?'

And the shepherd, shaking his head, answered me:

'We waited to hear them, but they have not been heard. They said that he had buried them in the earth.'

And I looked at him—half man, half goat, with his hair curled in ringlets, with a mouth as swiftly moving as a rabbit's muzzle—and I smelt his smell of wool and milk. The Plague had appeared to him, not to me. And I asked him—the child of the mountain:

'Tell me something more.'

And he understood that I was asking him what to do, so he answered me:

'Have patience.'

And crossing himself, he left the cave. And I remained with another hundred and fifty women, children and old folk. And they all had their eyes fixed on my lips and hands, as if I could do something. I have always stood in the middle, among other folk, I have not led, and I have even not spoken first. But the end trees had fallen, so that the wind had reached the trees in the middle of the forest. And looking ahead I did not see another's back, and the wind was beating me in the face. And I felt at my back the breathing of one hundred and fifty mouths. There was no Manol, there was no Old Galoushko, no Old Kralyo, there was not even Momchil and Goran. But even had they been with me, it still seemed to me that they, too, could not have done anything.

Above our heads, in the rocks on the heights, there were Turks, guarding the only path upwards, towards the pastures. Before us was the forest, but, even through it, Turks often called to each other and shot, for they felt that there were people hidden there. No matter how little we believed that they would find the cave, we were losing our last strength in fear and expectation.

But more terrible even than the Turks was the winter. It was still far off, but lo—when I went out of the cave one morning, I saw on the opposite slope what looked like a burning fire—the red leaves of an ash-tree. It looked as if a fiery beast had trodden there, and left its tracks. Autumn had come. And its breath began to light fires first here, then there in the dark forest, the red fires of the ash-trees, the orange fires of the maples, the yellow fires of the meadows full of ferns And afterwards the beech-trees blazed up, too, with brown, red and yellow flames, each tree like a bunch of flowers. And the leaves of the remaining trees grew light and clear like the waxen face of a man about to die. In the summer one could not see where the broad-leaved trees hid amid the pines and the spruces, but now the autumn had set fire to them, and they began to burn like the signals of a sentry giving the alarm. And they cried 'Winter is coming!'

But whither could we flee?

The song birds flew away, and one now heard in the forest the voices of birds which either twittered like orphans, or wailed like widowed folk. But it may have been that we only heard them so. In the meadows there appeared the autumn crocuses that we call 'mend-your-sheepskin'. But what sheepskins had we to mend?

The shadows fell ever longer and ever blacker over the mountain. And once at noon, no matter how hard it tried to leap up, the sun did not manage to peep over the steep north slopes before us. Then an old man of a hundred said:

'When the Black Hollow remains in the shade till next spring, you must expect rain.'

And the hungry child began jumping up and down, crying: 'We'll go and pick mushrooms.'

But I wondered what would await us when the sun hid behind clouds. So far we had frozen at night in the icy cave, but in the daytime the sun had revived us. And it shone more strongly even than in summer so that it burnt our faces and our hands. And if a man may look at the summer sun, the autumn sun will not let you raise your lids to its face. But should the shade of a small tree, as slender even as a man's thumb, fall on you, that shade is cool on your body, and cuts you in two, just as if a cold knife were touching you. What if a shadow should fall everywhere?

And it fell. Low clouds crept up so that the heights were melted and drowned in it. It seemed to me that now the mountain reached the sky. And I wanted to set out upwards and melt away so that I, too, would vanish. Mists rose from the valleys to meet the clouds, then clouds and mist joined hands, so that the mountain vanished. And rain began to fall.

The women and the children and the old men looked at me, and I said nothing to them.

The mountain was silent, lulled to sleep by the rain. Everything grew still, dozed off and began to dream in broad daylight. But we did not even sleep at night, so that we would hear the steps of shepherds who brought us crusts of bread. And we heard the rain falling over the world.

At night we heard the song of a distant, lonely *kaval*. I knew that Momchil was playing. I would come out in front of the cave and listen to the sweet lament, and the cold drops ran down my face like tears. Otherwise, nothing was to be heard. The mountain had become mute, like a *chan* whose clapper had been torn out.

Then one day the *chan* began to ring. Shots rang out one after the other, many shots, and the whole mountain began to sway. We had forgotten that in the autumn the mountain is like silver, and a man hears an echo in places where in summer no one answers him. The shots came from afar, but for that reason they were clear and light, so that there was no threat in them, but only joy. And we all ran out to listen to the distant echo, and it seemed to me that the earth shook under my feet.

For three days the mountain echoed. Then the shots died away. A last shot rang out and wandered long over the mountain, but no other was heard to welcome it. We waited, and heard only the rain falling.

In the night that followed the third day, footsteps came. Six blood-stained shepherds brought three of their wounded fellows and told us about the battle at Vissyak.

About three hundred years ago, at the same time of year, from the tenth day before St Dimiter's Day to the fourth day after it, the last defenders of Rhodopa met the Turkish troops with the Sultan's son-in-law, Ibrahim Pasha, at their head, at the rocks of Vissyak. For fourteen days the Bulgarians held out, curved in an iron hoop, and the Turks attacked on three sides. And in the middle of the hoop stood ten thousand women and children. No shots rang out then, for men had no muskets yet; only the clang of iron, the hiss of arrows and human cries were to be heard. On the fourteenth day the Turkish commander, the Sultan's son-in-law, Ibrahim Pasha, was himself struck down. And on that same day the Turks ascended Vissyak. The heroes whom they captured, together with the captive women and children, were assembled on the meadow, where the two rivers, whose deep gorges cut the grey crags of Vissyak, flow into each other. All the men that wore waistbands were slain there, but they let the women and children go—the women with Turkish seed in their wombs, the children with the mark of shame on their brows.

Ibrahim's widow, the Sultan's daughter, Aishé Sultanié, built a mosque on the grave of the Turkish commander, and for three hundred years since then, twenty Turkish soldiers, each of whom had to have three wounds on his body, guarded the mosque and Ibrahim's grave day in and day out.

This mosque was set on fire by the hundred shepherds who had sworn to hold together on the day of Manol's death. They slew the Turks and raised their banner on Vissyak. They had grown tired of wandering over the forests and summits. But the Turks crawled up to them on three sides—from Posechishta, Klokotnik and Pressloup—and for three days they climbed up the stone screes, and rolled down together with the stones. On the third day, the powder came to an end. Then the arrows came to an end, too. Then the knives were broken. Of one hundred young shepherds, nine fled from Vissyak through Burtsé, Dobristé, Doubakan and Kapnik. The six carried the three. They brought them to our cave.

And the steps of the six shepherds died away, for they were in a hurry to find their living and wounded comrades, and we did not hear any other human steps.

Hunger came, but it treads noiselessly. It went through the cave, so that a young woman would beg, asking:

'Has no one got a little crust of bread to put under my child's head? He is ill.'

For a crust of bread is put under the pillow of the sick, so that the blessing of bread may fall upon them. And it would have been better for the child to have put the crust into its mouth.

Then they began to look for gold coins, to put them in the mouths of the dead nurslings, the unchristened children, so that when they went to Heaven, they might buy a place in paradise. And whosoever had any, gave the poor mothers a gold coin, for he knew that even if he had a bag of gold, he would still not be able to buy a handful of grain.

And we did not sleep at night, but wandered through the forest seeking hips, and blackberries, and whortleberries and haws. And each one rejoiced when, in the darkness, thorns scratched his outstretched hands, for blackberries, hips and haws have thorns. In the dark the children found mushrooms.

Two or three times we found squirrels' nests, full of hazel nuts, and the hazel bushes had already turned yellow and were picked clean. And if there were a hazel nut beneath them it would be hollow, for the squirrels and the mice had cast it aside. In the dark we set traps, but nothing was caught in them, for life seemed to have fled from the forest. And everything was done in the dark, always at night. For in the daytime we could only stand at the opening of the cave, sheltered by the overhanging rocks. Otherwise the Turks would have seen us.

Then we began to eat the resin of the spruces and the pines.

Resin flowed from each cross carved in the trees. And we broke off the tree's already hardened yellow blood, or dug out the foaming white resin of the fresh wounds with our knives, or gathered the new light sap with our fingers. And some placed their lips straight on to the bark, as if they were kissing the holy cross. When we had exhausted the crosses, we ourselves began to peel and cut the bark of the trees, so as to gather resin.

And it was bitter, that cold blood of the holy forest. So bitter was it that the bitterness no longer left our mouths; even when we ate something else, and it, too, seemed bitter to us. And bitterness seeped into my heart, and even my brief dreams became bitter. And I dreamt of hens, clucking over the eggs they had laid. And of farmers, taking honeycombs out of their hives. And of butter, melting over the fire. Was that a dream? Were not the eggs, the honey and the butter over there, across the forest, and could we not go down through that forest to them? And the mothers' milk would flow again, and the lips of the children would grow red, and the old folk would straighten up a little. And I dreamt that the people wanted to set out, and that I stopped them.

Suddenly one day the sun shone. The sky spread over us; clear and clean, a white cloud floated over the mountain. And we all gathered in front of the cave, to warm ourselves in the sun. And down below at our feet, behind the forbidden forest, the wet roofs of the village of Podviss shone. And the people looked at them, and many were able to recognize their homes.

And I remembered the morning when we had first emerged from the cave, after the gathering of the notables in the night. And I remembered the oath we had sworn, to endure to the end. I turned to the dark maw of the cave, and it seemed to me that I saw the dried-up dead coming out of it and standing behind us living ones, so that they too, might warm themselves in the sun. How many times had they come out in front of the cave to look down on those shining roofs, which were once their homes?

I saw them, coming out of the dark, but they did not blink in the light as we did, for their eyes had run out. And they did not weep as we did, for their eyes had run out.

I looked once more towards Podviss. And I remembered that morning when I had thought of the cloud and the rainbow. There was a rainbow over Podviss then.

But now there was none. The cloud had come, and in it there was no rainbow, although God had promised that there would be a rainbow in the cloud and that would be His covenant not to destroy all that had life. There was no rainbow.

God was with those who wandered in the wilderness in a solitary way. Hungry and thirsty, their soul fainted in them. Then they cried unto the Lord in their trouble, and He delivered them out of their distress. And He led them forth by the right way. Oh, that men would praise the Lord for His goodness and His wonderful works to the children of men. For He satisfieth the longing soul and filleth the hungry soul with goodness.

Thus sings the psalm of David. And we were hungry and thirsty.

Others sat in darkness and in the shadow of death, because they rebelled against the words of God . . . They fell down, and there was none to help them.

Then they cried unto the Lord in their trouble . . . He brought them out of darkness and the shadow of death and brake their bands in sunder. Oh, that men would praise the Lord for His goodness!

And we were in the darkness and in the shadow of death, although we had not rebelled against God, but believed according to His word. Why did He not save us?

God saves those who have lost their reason. He delivereth them that go down to the sea in ships. He turneth the wilderness into a standing water and dry ground into water-springs, and there He maketh the hungry to dwell so that they may prepare a city for habitation; and sow the fields and plant vineyards which may yield fruits of increase. He blesseth them also, so that they are greatly multiplied.

Why did He not give us—not fields and vineyards—but only a handful of grain and a bunch of grapes? And why did He let the children we had borne and reared, die?

And when I started, I looked around and saw that the eyes of the folk in the cave, wet with tears, were fixed in me. And I understood that I had spoken in my daze. And behind them I saw the eyes of the dead that had run out. And one old woman asked:

'Father, does not God see?'

What could I answer her? What did these folk want of me?

And I dropped down the steep slope and knelt before a big spruce, on which a cross had been carved, and began to pray for forgiveness that ungodly thoughts had crept into my soul. And I prayed to the tree for every tree is a temple of the Lord. And when I raised my head, I saw how the slender boughs of the spruce came out on all sides from the round thick bole, like the spokes of a wheel. And it seemed to me that the wheel of the spruce began to turn, and I heard Old Galoushko's eternal words: 'It flows . . . it flows . . .'

And I understood that the world goes on and turns, and that one dies and another is born, and woe unto him that falls under the wheel. And the spruce was still turning, and I understood that on that long road and in that river God does not look after each living being, but it looks after itself, and God looks after the way and the river, and only He knows whither the wheel is turning and whither the waters are flowing. And perhaps I should have seen more in my daze of hunger and revelation, had I not heard a human voice calling me.

And I was being called, for a woman was dying. She was dying although she was young, for she had given her every mouthful to her child, which was now falling upon her breasts. And what had she gained? Two or three days of daylight for her son. In two or three days he, too, would die.

And she lay before me, a living skeleton, and from her skull, the bones of which were visible, a wealth of shining black hair sprang, falling like a waterfall, each hair shining in the sunlight. Thus the tallest grass grows over graves.

And as I bent over her, and looked at her hair, I felt myself rejoicing. She was dying, but I remained alive. The sun was shining all around, the stones were being warmed, the sky was blue and the air clear. She was dying, but the sun still shone and the sky was still blue. She was melting away in the clear morning, but I remained, still gathered in a living body, and I could warm myself in the sun, and look at the sky and drink the air. And I felt such exultation that I closed my eyes, so that the people around me might not see them singing.

When I opened them, I saw opposite me the slope of the mountain. Never is it as beautiful as it is in the autumn, when the leaves die. And like the dead woman's hair, each dying leaf shone, and was flooded with colour. Only the pine-trees stood dark and green, untouched by decay and winter. But people were not pines.

That night I fled from the cave. Looking back today, I see that I fled not to save my life, but because I thought that no one could help the folk in the cave. And since I stand before the grave and have no one to deceive, neither people nor myself, I say and write that if I could have done anything for them, I would have stayed in the cave. I had grown proud, and considered myself the leader of these people, and it seemed to me that it was I who kept them in the cave, and my cassock, and that without me they would have sought ways of salvation. Had I been one of those who had others ahead of them, I would have stayed.

But whether I fled for myself, or fled to rid them of myself, was all the same, for flee I did.

And as in those days my heart was not so fearless, I did not admit to myself that I was fleeing, and within myself I swore that I was going to the Bishop in Xanti, to beg him for help.

Fourth Excerpt

I gave up my faith, *djanum*,[7]
I gave up my faith,
My tongue I gave not up, *djanum*,
My tongue I gave not up.

And when I came across a dead man, and his big sheepskin coat lay beside him, I took it and hid my cassock under it. And the weight of the coat—for it was all wet with rain—bent me almost double, and its cold pierced me to the marrow, but the warmth of the new body warmed it.

And step by step, bent under the sheepskin coat which warmed, but also weighed heavily upon me, I climbed up Mount Purvenets, and looked out from there. The sun was shining, mist lay in the valley and only the summits rose around me. And it seemed to me that Rhodopa was like a rose in bloom. Yet, like a tiny insect, I had to creep out of it, to climb every petal of its flower and to go down into the darkness between every petal, until I reached the sea, which washed its stem.

Then I set out across Rhodopa. But I did not set out along the roads that I knew, for they led to Vissyak, and I feared lest I should come across the bodies of the slain shepherds, and see their open eyes.

First I went through that part of Rhodopa which is like a soft, warm woman. And each fold and every valley wound like the curve of a woman's waist, and probably naked maidens once ran over these meadows and around these straight trees, and Orpheus played on his pipe. But now the wide meadows were deserted, and only a cur followed me all day long, ten feet behind me, and neither barked, nor lagged behind. And when I stopped, it stopped, too. All day long, as I walked, I heard its steps at my back. And an eagle circled above my head.

Then I entered endless forests, and they had grown over curved sloping hills. And grass grew among the trees, not like in the forests of Elindenya, where only dry pine needles lie on the ground in the dark.

And the trees were huge and old and between them there were no slight and slender saplings. And they passed slowly beside me, each like the other, until I began to imagine that they were marching, while I was standing still in one place. Yet no, it was I who walked, and they that remained in their places, and in my heart I prayed to them to pull up their roots and set out with me. For, if they wished, they could do it; they stood beside the path like men, and I seemed to see their eyes, with half-closed lids, calm, dark eyes. Was it not Manol who once said to me that he could not pull out his roots, and set out to flee?

Nothing living moved in the forest; only once I saw white down floating over a meadow, and thought it was butterflies, but it was dandelions.

I picked and ate hips and they were as red as blood. I found cranberries, and they, too, were red as blood. I filled my hands with haws, and they were as red as blood. Only once did I see a wild pear tree and bright fruit on it, but when I went up to it, I saw that it was its leaves which had caught the light.

When the sun began to set, heavy clouds, like black puffs of smoke began to come up from the east. And suddenly it grew dark, and at that moment I entered a dark sleeping wood, and I could not see its end. Fallen trees blocked my way, thick moss swallowed the sound of my footsteps. And fear entered my soul, and now I prayed that the silent cur might run behind me, that I be not alone. Then my feet came upon a path. Blessed be the feet that made it. And I understood that there is no wilderness in Rhodopa where the foot of man has not been set, for it is a mountain made for men.

And the path took me out upon a meadow, which, although it was night, shone like the open shell of an oyster. And I raised my eyes in thankfulness. And through the mist I saw pale stars, and rain fell upon my brow.

Suddenly it seemed to me that I had lost the way in the darkness and that I was going back to that cave full of wretched people. And my heart was filled with senseless joy. And when I dropped down on the meadow, so as not to walk anywhere any more, I began to weep. But I wept in silence, for all around there was stillness.

Never again would I see the pale faces of those that were doomed to die. I gave way to my pain, and began to call those faces one after the other, and to speak with each of them, and to caress and comfort them. And I remembered them, as one remembers the faces of the dead. And I knew that I had not lost the way, but had all the time been heading south, farther and farther away from the cave.

And above me, from the sky, came the sad cries of the wild geese, like the farewell of lost souls. And the birds were flying south.

In the morning I entered the other Rhodopa, which is like a proud and gloomy man, and where inaccessible and terrible gorges cut through the steep and bare crags. But the stubborn pines grow over the crags and at the bottom of the gorges flow deep and narrow rivers.

The mist, which crept down below in the gorges, began to rise like dough in the bread troughs, and poured over the mountains. Nothing could be seen now, neither the depths below, nor the heights above, only two feet of a wet path.

Then I heard the blows of an axe. As I trembled, walking along the narrow path suspended above the invisible abyss, I heard the blows of an axe coming from somewhere on high. And leaving the path, I began to climb up the rocks in the mist, towards the invisible man.

Up on the meadow I saw a man's shadow cutting down a tall tree. The blows of the axe ceased and I heard my heart beating like thunder. And when I felt that I was running, I slackened my pace and went slowly up to the man. And, on seeing me, he dropped his axe to the ground and leant upon it with both hands. And his face slowly floated out of the mist, as if it were floating out of milky water.

And I said :

'Well met.'

And he smiled so that his teeth flashed, and, throwing the axe aside, he came to meet me. And he said to me :

'Welcome.'

And I took out my hands from under the wet sheepskin, that he might see that I bore no arms. And the man asked me :

'Whence have you come?'

I answered him :

'From the north, and I am going to Xanti.'

And he looked me over well, and saw that I carried neither bag, nor arms. And he said to me :

'You have set out on a long journey and will lose the way in the mist. Honour me, and stop to rest in our village.'

And when I agreed, he untied his ass and collected his ropes, which were scattered over the meadow. I asked him :

'Why do you not finish your work?'

And he answered :

'I had thought of finishing another piece of work today, but I decided not to. And when I saw you, I realized that I had made a mistake.'

And I saw that the tree he was cutting down was one of Manol's trees, growing at the edge, and supporting the forest. And I was unable to restrain myself and said to him :

'Man, why do you cut the trees at the edge? Will not the wind get into the forest and blow it all down?'

But he smiled once more and said :

'Go into the forest !'

And when he saw that I was making for it, he stopped me with his hand, and said to me once more :

'Do not go in, for you cannot do so. Our forest is so dense that if you cut down a tree in it, it does not fall to the ground. Its brothers, the other trees, hold it straight with their shoulders until it rots.'

I remembered the cave. And I was silent all the way to the village. And the path was narrow and wet.

And then out of the mist rose the first stone houses of the village. And the village was scattered over a steep gully, so that the path wound ever upwards and stopped at every gate, like a child that is asking for something and does not find it. The man said to me :

'Our village is small, we have no public room. Honour my house.'

And we climbed ever upwards, and at our feet ran a muddy stream of water. I asked him :

'Why have you built your village here?'

The man answered me :

'We are settlers. And when the village was being founded, the eyes of the people were misty with tears, so that they did not see where they were laying the foundations of their houses.'

And I thought that they had fled from the plague and had hidden in these gullies.

When we went into his house, there was no one there. But there were live embers on the hearth in the middle of the room. The man said :

'The women and children are out in the fields. Sit down, while I make up the fire.'

When the fire blazed up, I cast off the stranger's sheepskin coat and was left in my cassock. The man looked at me, but said nothing. And taking a pot of groats down from the shelf, he poured the porridge into a bowl and gave it to me. Then he placed a flat tile on the fire and said :

'We'll mix the dough and bake a griddle-cake.'

And he sat down opposite me on a three-legged stool, and looked at me across the fire. And I ate like a hungry man. And the man said to me :

'Forgive me, stranger, for asking you, for one does not question a guest. But what is your name, and from which village do you come?'

I answered him:

'My name is Nikola and I have come from Elindenya.'

And I trembled when I spoke my worldly name, which should have remained hidden by my cassock.

And the man asked me:

'As you journeyed over the mountains, did you not pass through the village of Strazha, and did you not meet a man there of the family of Sakalovs? And are there already Turks in the village?'

And when he saw that I shook my head in denial, the man sighed and said:

'This morning I was to have set out for Strazha.'

Just then the door opened and a woman stood on the threshold in a white kerchief and a black dress. And when she saw me, she cried out, and raised the end of her white kerchief and covered her face to the eyes.

The bowl fell from my knees and the morsel stopped in my throat. I understood that I had entered a Mohammedan village. And I rose to my feet and shook the crumbs from my skirts.

How was I to know that I had met a Mohammedan? He was bare-headed, he spoke Bulgarian, he wore Bulgarian clothes. And his house was Bulgarian. If there was a mosque, I had not seen it in the mist. I could have eaten and drunk and left without realizing that I had been in a Mohammedan's house.

But the man raised the bowl I had dropped, and as he poked the fire, he said to me, without raising his head:

'Why have you risen? Or does not my house please you? Or does my bread taste bitter to you? And do I not speak Bulgarian to you, just as you do?'

And I remained standing, so that the man said:

'The whole village is full of Christians who have fled from the Turks. And tomorrow my house, too, will be full. Besides you, there are two more priests in the village. Sit down and eat.'

And I sat down and took the bowl from his hands. And he sat opposite me and began to speak, and the woman entered with her face veiled, and began to move the pots and pans on the shelves. The man said to me:

'My name is Ahmed Sakal. That is why I asked you about the Sakal family in the village of Strazha. They are my kin. Once, in the days of Sultan Selim the Cruel, there was a big village up on the plateau, and it was called Patleino. When the Sultan began to pull down the churches in the Bulgarian lands, and Turkish troops entered Patleino, only two brothers were left of the Sakal family—Yassen and Spassen. And Yassen accepted the True Faith and settled in our village, which is called Pleshak, and Yassen took the name of Hassan. But Spassen fled, and settled in the middle of the forests in the new village, which is called Strazha. And of Patleino only the foundations were left, and now we call that mound Cherkovishteto.[8] But both brothers kept the name of the family and called themselves men of the Sakal family, although some were Mohammedans and the others—Christians. And they honoured one another and visited one another at weddings and baptisms.'

And the man pointed to the corner of the room, where there lay a well-filled sack. And he asked me:

'Do you see that sack?'

And I answered: 'I do.'

But I did not understand what he was driving at.

And the man said to me:

'The fields of the Sakal family remained in the land of our village, Pleshak. And both brothers divided them, and the first Hassan paid the full price for Spassen's share. But in the middle of the field, there grew an apple tree. But you, as you have journeyed across Rhodopa, you must know that land can be divided, but the tree upon that land is not divided. And the tree remained the property of both and its fruit belonged to both. Every year the Mohammedans of the Sakal family pick the fruit of the tree and divide it in two. And when they have filled sacks with half the fruit, they take it to the village of Strazha, to their relatives of the same Sakal family.'

I asked him:

'How long is it since the division of the village?'

And he answered:

'A century and a half. One hundred and fifty years.'

It was as if he had said 'yesterday'. For one hundred and fifty years the Mohammedan Sakals had passed along the same path to carry the common fruit from the tree they owned in common to the Christian Sakals. The hands of the first Hassan, which had first reached out for this fruit, had long since rotted, and of the mule on which he placed his sacks of apples, not even the hoofs remained. And yet the feet have not forgotten the path.

Then I shook my head and said:

'The apple tree will soon fall, for it is very old. And there will no longer be common fruit.'

But the man smiled once more, in his own fashion, so that all his teeth flashed. And he answered, through his smile:

'My grandfather planted a new apple tree. And my father planted one, too. I, too, have planted one. The new trees already bear fruit. But the old apple tree is still there. Even if it should fall—what of it? In the sack there is already fruit from our trees.'

And I said to him :

'Three of them are not common property.'

But he answered :

'Am I not my father's son? Is not my father the son of my grandfather? We are all one blood. And the trees are of one root, that is why they are common property.'

And rising to his feet, he bowed to me and said :

'Forgive me, but I must leave you. When I saw you, I remembered that Sakal of Strazha may set out in the forest, too, without a bag or a crust of bread. A week ago Turkish troops passed this way, led by the Bey of Pashmakli. He wanted us to set out with him to turn the Bulgarian villages to the True Faith. But our men answered him : "How can we raise a knife over a man who begs me not to in our tongue? And may we not unknowingly, slay the children of our fathers' brothers?" Even the hodja did not set out with the Bey. Not one man of Pleshak left the village to set out and attack the Christian villages. But many went and brought their Christian friends and relations back to their houses, until the storm passes. I, too, intended to go, but I was not much afraid, for Strazha is in the midst of forests. But when I saw you, I knew that I should not tarry. I am setting out for Strazha.'

And he filled a gaily-coloured bag with bread, and took me to the barn, where it is sweeter to slumber in the scent of the fresh hay, listening to the song of the rain upon the stone tiles. And I begged him to give me one of the apples from the common tree. And when I held the smooth warm fruit, it seemed to me the same as the apples of our tree. Our apples were already ripe, too, and my mother was looking at them and waiting for me to return and pick them.

All night long I lay in the barn wide awake. And although I had a roof over my head, I seemed to be amid the mountain, amid the faint and sweet smell of the forest herbs, and the song of the mountain was with me, too, for the rain did not stop all night. I heard the muezzin's voice, still lost in the mist, singing : 'Allah il Allah.' And it reached me as Old Kralyo's voice had reached me from the top of the high mountain. And at first it seemed to me that it was Old Kralyo's voice, and then it seemed to me that I myself was crying out. And I also heard a girl's tremulous voice begin to sing beyond the wall : 'I am white, I am white,

young hero, I am shining o'er the whole world . . .' And I remembered that Manol had made the *chans* sing the very same song
on that night when Mircho had sworn his oath on his mother's
bones. And another woman's voice scolded the girl, saying to her :
'Be quiet, the man of God is sleeping yonder.'

I was not asleep.

The earth could be divided. But the fruit of the tree remained
common property. And Christians and Moslems all ate of it. The
fruit of the mountain was not divided, it fed them all equally.

And when I had met the man, I had not known whether he was
a Moslem or a Christian. I realized that he was a Bulgarian. He
spoke Bulgarian, he wore Bulgarian garments, he lit his fire in a
Bulgarian house.

And when the Turks had tried to lead him out to attack Bulgarian
villages, my man had not gone, for he feared lest he might slay
his brother. For he felt that faith had not changed their blood, and
that his brother remained a brother.

The apple was common property.

And as I grasped the smooth, warm fruit tightly in my hand, it
seemed to me that I was grasping the answer to my anxieties and
questions. For I had given my promise to my mother with an
apple, that I would return to her every autumn. And this apple
was not divided, but bound Moslems and Christians together, for
they all remained Bulgarians. And Rhodopa remained a Bulgarian
mountain.

What did Manol use to say? That he did not want to become a
Janissary who would slay his father. That he did not want to raise
his hand against his brother. These folk had accepted the True
Faith and they had not become Janissaries, and they had not raised
their hands against their brothers. And the girl sang the same song
that Manol had sung.

Lord, Lord, where then is Thy name? And is it not all one to
Thee whether they call Thee Allah, or Christ, and art Thou not
only in the heart of every man, be he Moslem or Christian, but also
in every tree and in every little herb? And art Thou not, O God,
the Lord of the quick, and not of the dead? And did the wheel of
the spruce tell me true, when it told me that Thou lookest to the
end of the way, and not at its meanderings and that Thou lookest
where the river flows into another, and not through what its water
flows?

Why, then, did Manol and the others die? Ought they all to
have spat upon the cross, as they would have remained Bulgarians?
And did the Turks care much about Allah, if they wanted sheep
dogs and soldiers for the Sultan?

The mountain was not a courtyard, surrounded by a wall, but a Bulgarian stronghold with nine rows of walls. And by spitting upon the cross men withdrew from the first wall, and retreated. And there was one wall less to the heart of the mountain, but another eight walls were left. And by dying at the first wall, Manol and the others had held back the enemy and showed us how to die, but living defenders also had to be left, so that they would go back and defend the remaining eight walls. And if the first wall was called the Holy Cross, the second one was called the Common Tree, the third—the Common Song, the fourth—the Common Raiment, the fifth—the Common Past, the sixth—the Common Tongue. Yet were not the walls not nine, but a hundred? And in the innermost one, behind one hundred shells, was the kernel, from which the Bulgarian Rhodopa sprouted eternally, and, no matter how much she was cut, a Bulgarian tree always sprouted from the kernel.

And I remembered the pine-trees on the mountain slope opposite the cave, which the autumn was unable to set afire, and the trees remained green, until a fire turned them to ashes. I remembered also the trees with the broad leaves, which turned red, but in spring they would put out leaves and be green once more. And if Manol and the others were like pine-trees, I would become like a beech-tree. Better that the autumn should turn us red—for after the winter comes the spring—than that the fire should turn us to ashes, for after a fire only grasses grow.

And I fought long, long with my God, Whom I had so far served and the struggle of Jacob, who had fought with God and overcame Him, was as the struggle of children, compared with my struggle, until I overcame God in my heart, and said Allah to Him, and not Jesus. And I said it through laments that echoed over the whole mountains, so that it deafened me, yet better laments and tears from living eyes than the eyes of the dead in the cave, which had run out.

And I set out in the morning, back to the cave, clutching in my hand the apple from the common tree, the sign of the promise that faith would not divide brother from brother and Moslem from Christian and that we would all eat the fruit of one and the same mountain and would call ourselves Bulgarians.

The mist had risen, and the sun shone over the world.

And in a day I covered the road which it had taken me one day and one night to travel, but the wet sheepskin did not weigh on my shoulders. And I had not the heart to pass through Vissyak, but I went round it. And in the forest below the Dark Hole, I met a herd of deer and a pack of wolves running towards me.

And when I went up to the meadow, lo—the eternal wind met me. But I no longer covered my face with my hand to protect myself from it, and it seemed to me that it was a faithful dog, which was rubbing against its master's knees in its joy, so that it blew my cassock about. I looked and I saw that, up on the shrine, there were no Turks.

And I stood on the rocks above the sacred forest with the crosses in which no axe might be heard.

The forest was not there. The forest had been burnt down and the smoke from a thousand huge trunks rose from the mountains, as they burnt out like the fires of thousands of sacrificial altars. And the ashes between the trunks were white, and the trunks were black and a thin wisp of smoke rose from each one of them. And the flames could not be seen, for, after the fire, rain had fallen, as if the high priests of the dead Thracians had once again lighted their pyres so that they could call the clouds.

I set out across the ashes, and my feet sank into them, and the streams of smoke wound around me like the stems of a ghostly forest. And between these pillars of smoke I saw far, far away, for previously the spruces had shut out any view. From time to time my foot would step on a live ember, but it did not hurt me, for my heart hurt me far more. I found the cave with difficulty, and after wandering over the place where the fire had raged. There was neither road nor path, and everything looked different and terrible.

The opening of the cave had been blocked up, and before it lay a huge mound of grey ashes. And when I went up the mound, I sank up to my knees into the ashes, so that they burnt my feet, for the overhanging rocks had not let the water fall on to the pyre. And if the ashes of the place where the fire had raged were hardened and furrowed by the rain, the ashes in front of the cave were warm and as soft as the little hand of a child.

A wall of stones rose at the mouth of the cave, all red from the fire. And when I struck it with my knife, lo, the red crust broke off and inside the stone was as white as mortar. And with tooth and nail I tore out a hot stone. And when the stone fell noiselessly in the ashes at my feet, a black hole gaped in the wall. And in the wall I saw a yellow hand, and on its nails I saw blood. And putting out my fingers, I seized the hand. It was cold. I had come too late.

Fifth Excerpt

Summer was over. Autumn came to the mountain.

The sun shone with a clear bright light, which made my eyes ache very quickly, and afterwards my head began to ache, too. The Valley of Elindenya was like those ornaments that are made of coloured glass on which crystals are poured. The air was so clear that if I stretched out my hand, I could touch the mountain. Over there where there used to be two colours, ten blazed up; in the sun it grew twice as light, and in the shadow—twice as dark; on the verandas it was warmer, in the rooms it was colder.

Long, black unfamiliar shadows fell over the mountains; they no longer edged the rim of the forest as they had done before, but lay and weighed upon it. And they were not soft and warm, like the long shadows of a summer sunset, but were sharply outlined, and pitch-black, like the shadows of a moonlit night.

The blue-black steel of the pine forests grew rusty here and there, from the beech-trees whose leaves had turned red. But only in the lower parts. Up on the summits the dark wall rose untouched by the autumn and by decay. And as the sun did not rise high enough to shine on the steep northern slopes, the forests on them did not cast off the purple, black garment of the shadow even at noon.

I gazed at the mountain and thought of Elitsa.

I gazed at the mountain and blinked as I exposed my face to the rays of the sun. My forehead and my lips burned. I wanted to forget the poor wretches shut up in the inner courtyard of the *Konak*. Karaibrahim still delayed and would not fix the day on which they were to accept the True Faith. He was waiting for something, perhaps for the snow.

Gyulfié came and stood beside me. She was wrapped in a kerchief up to her eyes, so that she looked quite unfamiliar to me. It was, indeed, wondrous how people who had joined their bodies, could become such strangers to each other. I had reached the heart of that woman, and now, if anyone had told me so, I would not have believed it.

'Do you see that mountain?' Gyulfié said to me. 'It has a hundred colours now, but tomorrow it will have only one. White. If snow falls, the mountain will be locked.'

I shivered and thought that snow might also bury Elitsa.

'Why do you not go?' Gyulfié asked me. 'You remember where the secret passage is, don't you? The shepherds will take you to the sea, the fishermen will take you to one of the Venetian islands. This is no place for you.'

It seemed to me that she was driving me away. Not only had we become strangers to each other, there was even hostility between us. I looked her in the eye. How light and living her eyes were, but there was a flash of hardness in them. She had been humiliated, and she was now fighting to get to the top.

'Am I in your way?' I asked.

She shook her head. Wrinkles gathered in the corners of her eyes, and I knew that under the kerchief dimples had now appeared on her plump cheeks.

'I am going to drive these curs out of the *Konak*—whether you are here or not.'

She was speaking of the sons of Syuleiman Aga's brother, Hairedin.

'And I shall bear sons of my own,' said Gyulfié.

Perhaps she had cast me aside as an unnecessary object, because I had not fulfilled her hopes. I said to her :

'Manol and Goran are dead.'

And she answered me :

'Karaibrahim is Goran's brother.'

I remembered how I had laughed on the day when I had imagined naked Gyulfié and naked Karaibrahim beside each other. I did not even smile now.

'If you are hoping to marry Karaibrahim, why should I not marry Elitsa?'

Gyulfié shook her head :

'Karaibrahim is not the same, but Elitsa is the same.'

She was still wise and observant, this fat woman, although earlier her wisdom had been a mouth that laughed, while now it bit. I felt angry with her.

'Momchil is alive, and Sevda is alive, too.'

Gyulfié gave me a surprised and haughty look, as if she had not expected such stupidity from me.

'Sevda is not the same, either. She still flaps about in her slippers and rattles her bracelets around the *Konak*, but she is not the same. Before she was the kind of woman who, if you said, "Good evening" to her, would answer, "Tomorrow evening". Now she says,

"Good night," and looks for a place in which to lie down and go to sleep.'

'When Karaibrahim rises from his sick bed, we shall speak again.'

'When Karaibrahim rises from his sick bed, Sevda will have a belly like a cow in calf. Goran's son will surely be as big as his father.'

'It may not be Goran's son, but Karaibrahim's,' I said.

'It is not,' she said to me.

But I felt that there was no certainty in her voice. And that instant's hesitation brought me close to her once more, so I asked her quietly and kindly :

'Gyulfié, is Sevda ill, by any chance?'

And she answered me in another, a changed voice :

'You will be blind for ever, Venetian. And others are blind, too. But I do not blame you. When a big pine tree is cut down in the forest, and it crashes down on the meadow, so that the earth shivers, who looks at the little spruce, barely a span high, which the pine-tree has crushed with its trunk? Manol fell and crushed Sevda. She had hoped that he would open her womb, and now he is not there.'

'Gyulfié, why do you talk to me only of wombs and fertility? If it is a question of a child, Sevda is carrying it already. Goran and Karaibrahim fathered it, not Manol. It turns out that there was nothing for which Manol should have crushed her.'

'When I say womb,' said Gyulfié, and dropped her eyes, 'when I say womb, I am thinking of the heart, too.'

And she turned and went back into the *Konak*. I was astounded. She was courting Karaibrahim not only out of self-interest: she loved him. Perhaps he had stirred her before; now she was already falling in love with the new Karaibrahim. Where I had seen only a crack in the marble sculpture, a woman's love, like the seed of a spruce, saw a slit in the rock, and hoped to thrust its root in it.

There was a beautiful Rhodope water jar, as green as a lizard. I used to fill it with wine for Karaibrahim. Suddenly I began to find a little red puddle around it in the mornings. I turned it right and left; it was quite sound. And it held the wine. I thought drops must slip down it. But it always leaked a little. One evening I knocked the goblet against it. And then I heard that it rang false, as if it was cracked. I examined it again. And I saw high up, under its mouth, a barely visible crack.

I did not throw it away. I used to tap it with a finger and rejoice at the exhausted, hollow sound with which it responded. And I filled it only up to the crack, so that it would not leak.

Karaibrahim was like that jar. He himself may not have known it. I knew it, and so did Gyulfié. For me the scar of the wound on his face was the crack in the marble face. For Gyulfié it was a place in which she could take root.

The only thing that used to make me feel respect for Karaibrahim, and even stand in awe of him, was that I thought I saw before me a man hewn out of a single piece of marble. He was cruel, he was dry, but he was made of marble. There was neither fear, nor self-interest, nor any other petty feeling in him. I felt that he was stronger than I was, that he was superior to me. Now the marble was cracked.

Was it fear of death? Had he been thinking of death since the moment in which it had touched him with the tip of his brother's knife? I think that he was unable to endure the weight of his father's and brother's hatred.

Two or three days after Old Galoushko, Sherko and the dog had been dropped into the Dark Hole, and no sound was heard from there, Karaibrahim ordered ten starving sheepdogs to be thrown into the pit. And once more the terrible, desperate howling of dogs, which were tearing each other to pieces, was borne over the mountain. To avoid hearing them, I used to fill my ears with wax at night. Afterwards Karaibrahim ordered poison to be thrown to the dogs, so that at last they were silent.

And once, when I was talking with him, he answered me absently and confusedly. I thought it was due to his illness. At one time he seized my hand and said :

'Do you hear?'

There was nothing to hear.

'The dogs,' said Karaibrahim.

Then I realized that he had grown deaf, for his ears were still full of wax, like mine yesterday. He used to stop up his ears so as not to hear the howling of the curs, who were perhaps tearing the body of his father to pieces. And his fear was wreaking vengeance on him by making him hear those howls, even when they had died away. Yes, the marble had cracked, and Karaibrahim tried in vain to fill the crack with wax.

Ten armed soldiers now stood on guard over Karaibrahim, day in and day out. They let almost no one into his room. There were cocked pistols under his pillow, and he checked them a hundred times before me, to see if they were in order. Whenever he went out in his litter, his guards ran around him with drawn *yataghans*, and searched the smallest bush. The new Karaibrahim began to think about money. Perhaps Gyulfié really did love him, and her womanly heart was really filled with pity when she saw the strong man lying there wounded, but she would never have been able to reach

Karaibrahim's bed, if he had not had certain interests in mind. I was sure that Gyulfié, too, was thinking in the same terms.

What had Karaibrahim won so far? The commanders valued him for his iron hand and his iron heart, but what did he get in exchange for them? He had been stabbed, and might have been crippled for life. So far he had been worth as much as his sword. If he could no longer raise it to the glory of Allah, he could only sell it, and, together with it, his horse and his gilt saddle. And he would get a handful of gold coins for them barely enough to keep body and soul together.

But if he married Gyulfié, he would get the *Konak*, the gold, the mountains and the flocks. He would become a second Syuleiman Aga. That is why Gyulfié bound his wounds, trying to bend over him as low as she could, while he pretended not to notice.

I used to respect and admire him, now I despised him. I had been a fool, a fool who gaped open-mouthed at men who were supposed to be strong, because I myself was as weak as a woman. Without the smooth shining surface of the marble sculpture—with that false, hollow ring of a cracked thing—cruelty and heartlessness made Karaibrahim a common bandit. Truly, why had I not killed him?

It was not only because of Elitsa that I stayed in the *Konak*. I also stayed because of the list of those people whom I had sworn to kill. Now Karaibrahim's name was also on the list, after that of the one-eyed Sheikh Shaban Shebil. The name of the cut-throat with the *yataghan*, the former executioner in Hungary, had already been crossed out. I had killed him in the forest, when we were out once looking for men that had fled, and shots were fired from somewhere so that we took cover among the trees and cast ourselves down. I aimed at his shining skull—his turban had rolled off beside him—and shot him. When he was raised up, his mouth was full of dry leaves, and his feet had ploughed up the earth, as if a pig had been looking for truffles.

I was stalking the one-eyed Sheikh, and waited for Karaibrahim to get well. And I tried to meet Elitsa. I do not know what I hoped for. I wanted to be near her and to see her.

I saw her every day when she came out onto the veranda. She still looked sad and stern, but sorrow had not crushed her, and she was proud and straight. She wore a black kerchief as a sign of mourning for her father and her brother, and the kerchief framed her face, making it whiter and more beautiful. I often talked with her now, and successfully hid my emotion and the wild beating of my heart. She never spoke of Karaibrahim, or of the murdered men. Once only she mentioned that she was expecting a baby.

I had asked her how she had the strength to hold herself so proudly and so straight. She answered me :

'You are a stranger and you don't know. There is a song which runs : "Two big pine trees grew up next each other, And between them grew a slender spruce-tree. The two pine trees grew high in the heavens, sheltering the spruce, their little sister . . ."'

She did not sing the words, but chanted them, and—strange— I seemed to hear the song. My head began to turn. But she was carried away by her sorrow and her memories, and did not notice my appearance. And she said to me :

'They have cut down the pine trees; the spruce, their little sister has been left alone. Against the evil storms and icy winds.'

After a short silence, she added :

'I must think of it, too.'

And she placed her hand under her heart.

Of Momchil she never once uttered a word. She did not say: 'Is he not in the cave?' when the Turks set fire to the forest above Podviss, and smothered the unfortunate refugees in Cheleveshtnitsa. She did not say : 'Isn't he on Vissyak?' when for three days we heard the shots echoing over the mountain, and afterwards the Turks brought in one hundred heads, stuck on poles. Why should she speak Momchil's name before me, before a stranger? She probably thought of him day in and day out. She had heard that no fire could touch Momchil and that no bullet could reach him.

We all believed that it was so.

No other name was mentioned as often as Momchil's.

This is when and how he was first spoken of.

Always, when we changed the watch amid the ruins of the Thracian shrine—and this watch guarded the paths above Podviss— a musket, hidden in the rocks would be found to shoot at us. Not that it often hit the mark, but it is not very pleasant to be going along expecting a bullet to whistle past you out of a clear sky. That is why we began to change the guard at night. Already we went along the hidden paths as expertly as the shepherds, for we had walked them a hundred times each.

One night, as we were going through the forest, word was passed quietly from mouth to mouth that the first scouts had found a split stick thrust into the meadow, and that there was a letter in it. Kemanchidjogli and I were walking in the middle of the detachment, so we hurried forward. And Kemanchidjogli was one of the *Bilyuk-bashis*, Karaibrahim's right-hand, and could not stand me. I, too, hated him, as I hate all stupid, cruel and covetous men. We reached the meadow and took the piece of paper out of the stick.

'Read!' said Kemanchidjogli.

'Light a pine torch,' I said.

The pine blazed up and I read on the paper:

'Kemanchidjogli will die here!'

And beneath, these words:

'Momchil.'

'Put out the light!' I cried.

And Kemanchidjogli's face was in front of mine. And I heard the crack of the musket and then the hiss of the bullet. A black hole gaped in the middle of Kemanchidjogli's forehead. I did not hear the bullet strike the bone—I was looking at the man's eyes. And they, too, looked at me, a watery blue, full of fury. Then they stopped looking. They were still before me, a handspan from my eyes, opened, fixed, but they no longer looked. They were empty. Dead.

I could not move. The pine torch went out, the eyes disappeared, and I cast myself down on the earth. A moment later Kemanchidjogli's body fell on top of me.

After that terrible night we often found the bodies of Turks. On some there would be a frost-bitten maple leaf, yellowish-red, and a maple leaf looks like the trace of a bloodstained hand. Nowhere did we again hear Momchil's name, but the Turks stubbornly repeated:

'It is Momchil.'

And when, in the night, the song of a *kaval* would be heard above the *Konak*, they would all say again:

'It is Momchil.'

They brought out several of the peasants from the enclosure in the courtyard—they wanted the men to hear the *kaval* and say who was playing it. And they said to Karaibrahim:

'We have heard it for the last three nights. It is Manol's *kaval*, made of the muzzle of a musket. It is an iron *kaval*, not a wooden one. Manol's son is probably playing it.'

'And what is he playing?'

'He is playing a lament for a little lost sheep. He begs it to return. He weeps, for fear the wolves have eaten it.'

I do not know whether Karaibrahim stopped up his ears with wax again. But he hated the song of the *kaval* more than he hated the howling of the dogs. The *kaval* infuriated him; he could not sleep at night, and he would fall asleep only towards morning. He promised handfuls of gold to the brave fellow who would dare to set out through the forest and silence the *kaval*. No one could be found to do this, and I doubt whether Karaibrahim himself, had he been well, would have set out.

The invisible *kaval*, possibly without meaning to do so, maddened the Turks and mocked at them. If Karaibrahim had been strong, as he had been before, he could have got the upper hand of the *kaval*. But only a strong man endures defeat with a smile, and admits that he has been defeated. That he is weak. The weakling foams at the mouth. Karaibrahim did not want to admit his impotence. We dug holes and placed traps in the forest, as if the *kaval*-player were a wolf. In vain. Against our will and against our reason, we waited for the *kaval* to begin playing every night.

And they were clear autumn days and clear nights, and not a twig quivered in the forest. And every voice was borne in the air like a bird that had been set free. It seemed to me that if I shouted, my voice would be heard as far as the sea. And the song of the *kaval* cast a spell over the whole mountain.

Once, as I was listening to the *kaval*, I heard a man's dying cry. At the gate of the *Konak*, we found the watchman slain with a knife. An outspread maple leaf had fallen on his breast. But the song of the *kaval* never ceased.

I said to Karaibrahim :

'Either Momchil kills, or he plays the *kaval*. There cannot be two Momchils. Has Manol perchance a hundred sons, Momchils, as he had a hundred brothers?'

And Karaibrahim looked at me and said quietly :

'Why should he not have?'

It began to rain, and mists fell. The wind did not blow. In the mornings the mists would rise and break away from the valley, hanging in rags over the mountain, under the clouds, like grapes from a pergola, or like the udders of white cows. At night we shivered with cold. Autumn was burning the last broad leaves of the trees. Only the bristling, grim branches of the pines, the spruces and the fir-trees were left. Fires blazed up in the *Konak*.

In the courtyard, the captive Bulgarians began to die. The captives buried the bodies in the courtyard, prizing up the cobblestones and digging the earth with their nails, for they did not have even one knife.

I asked Karaibrahim :

'What are we waiting for? They will all die.'

He pointed at the mountain.

'All of them at once. The feast must take place, it must be a big feast. When snow falls on the summits, the fugitives will come down to the village of their own free will.'

They did not wait for the snow. I do not remember who cried out first, but a moment later all of the men were crowding out on to the square in front of the *Konak*. They could not believe their eyes.

From the mountain, along the road from the meadow with the stone crosses, came a crowd of people. The Bulgarians were surrendering to Karaibrahim. They knelt and accepted the True Faith.

Many of the Turks jumped on to their horses and dashed out to meet them.

And lo—they appeared, coming up the hill, a long file of ragged, exhausted, yellow-faced people. Two priests walked at their head. One of them was the priest I had met on that first day in Elindenya, standing beside Manol. The priest, who had appeared at the edge of the forest on the night of Manol's wedding and had disappeared afterwards. That priest, who looked young when his eyes were open, but became an old man when he closed them.

I have never hated Karaibrahim so much as on that day. His face was arrogant, his lids half-closed. Now one of his eyes was not tightly closed, as if he were aiming at something. The game lay shot down at his feet.

'Why have you come, priest?' he asked, when the long file had turned and stopped at his litter.

And Karaibrahim lay on one side, biting his nails.

'We have come to bow down to God,' said the priest.

'To which God, you cur? Measure your words.'

'To Allah. The important thing is to believe in God.'

'Where is Momchil?'

'He has stayed in the mountains.'

They were shut up in the sheepfold, in the same inner courtyard where the captives brought in earlier were. And such a wailing and weeping arose that the guards on the verandas began to shoot, and their muskets spat lead into the boards of the ceiling.

'Silence, you uncircumcized!'

They shot at the ceiling, not at the people. After all, they were tomorrow's subjects of Allah.

I went out of the *Konak*. I gazed at the mountain, sunk in mists. I felt like weeping. Never had the mountain seemed to me so sad and orphaned. It had been mute before, the *chans* and the birds had long fallen silent, but I had known that fearless and living men wandered over it.

Then I saw the church. I strode forward, took one, two, ten steps. I did not stop. I knew that if I did not go into it today, I would never go in at all. Tomorrow they would pull it down. The last moment was running out, and I must not miss it. I knew that if I did not go in, I would feel a coward for the rest of my life.

I opened the door. The church had no windows; light entered it only through the door.

It was in semi-darkness. At the end, The Last Supper came floating out at me, as if from a sea of mist, over the altar gates. Faded, soft, radiant. No, there was another light, too. A slit in the left wall cast a curtain of light in front of the wall painting.

Christ and the Apostles were having their supper. They really were. The narrow windows, painted at their backs, were open and light—open to the world. They opened on to somewhere outside the church and rays of light came pouring down from them. Real windows. And the people around the table were alive, too, dressed in shepherds' garments and red cloaks, and there was bread, and onions before them. Christ was wearing a red shepherd's mantle, too. I knew that in the goblets there was not wine, but milk.

Christ was to be crucified on the following day. The Apostles were to be scattered all over the world. Hardship and death awaited them. Yet they all ate with concentration, calmly, absorbed in themselves, and a soft light emanated from the windows behind them.

I slowly shut the door, as if I were being careful not to awaken someone. My heart was full of peace.

That evening Karaibrahim said to me :

'You went into the church.'

'I did. I wanted to see it, before it was pulled down.'

We spoke no further. The Turks were feasting and singing.

And in the middle of the night, the *kaval* began to play. And when one of the drunken men broke the wooden grating of the window, and shouted from it, shaking his fists at the mountain, a bullet struck him in the throat. And the dead man hung down from the window.

The *kaval* did not interrupt its lament.

Sixth Excerpt

> If only, mother, you'd bury me,
> I'd go down to my grave alive,
> And you, mother, press down upon me
> Stones that are heavy and big . . .

And when I saw the mouth of the cave walled up, and realized that the folk inside it were dead, I passed once more through the burnt forest, and my head whirled, like the trunks of the forest, from the smoke. And the world swam before my eyes, all the more so since I was looking at it through my tears.

I went to the folk at the Pass.

And afterwards we learnt how the Turks had found the cave, which is now called Cheleveshtnitsa. A woman, maddened by hunger, set out with her child of two, to look for mushrooms, and the Turks caught her. And they beat her to make her tell them where the cave was, but she only wept. Then they stripped her child naked and placed two bare knives against it. But she did not move, and only lost her wits completely, and screamed for help. And the folk in Cheleveshtnitsa, hearing her voice, and recognizing it, thought that she had met a wild beast, and came out to help her. The Turks saw where the cave was, surrounded it, and called to the folk inside to surrender. And the three wounded shepherds still had a handful of gunpowder, so that they shot from inside and killed the first Turk. And the Turks piled spruce branches at the mouth and set fire to them, and the smoke was drawn inwards, but only screams were heard and no one came out. Then they walled up the mouth of the cave, and the folk inside heard the stones rattling and wept, but no one came out. And the Turks built a huge fire at the mouth of the cave, and the mad mother with her child of two cast herself into it, wanting to get in to the others. And no cries were heard, for the fire rose to the heavens. Whether the Turks were maddened by the flames, so that they set fire to the forest, to burn the crosses on the trees, or whether the fire at the cave leapt from tree to tree, was never known, but the Turks barely escaped from the burning forest alive. That is how one hundred and fifty innocent souls perished in the Cheleveshtnitsa Cave.

When the folk at the Pass saw me coming out of the forest, they thought they were seeing a ghost, for they knew that I had been in the cave. And their eyes were still red with weeping, as if they themselves had suffered the smoke from the fire. They had watched the fire from the Pass. And as they touched me, they rejoiced and cried to me:

'Is it you, Father? Where have you been?'

And I said to them:

'I was deep in the forests, and I saw a sign. And God Himself said unto me: "Go, give yourselves up to the Turks and accept their faith. For it is all one whether I am called Allah, or Jesus. Only have a god".'

And an uproar arose, and some wanted to kill me, and others defended me. And Momchil, who lay beneath a tree, tried to rise, but fell back because of his broken leg, and cried with all his might:

'Stand aside that I may shoot him!'

And when the folk drew aside, I saw him lying on one side at the end of the lane formed by the two human walls. He was leaning on his left elbow, and in his right hand he held a pistol. And as handsome as an angel of vengeance was Momchil, with fiery eyes, sunk beneath straight brows, with a wide mouth, and tightly compressed lips, and gaunt cheeks, sunk in two straight furrows on his face. And the two veins on his strong neck beat, and from the bandage on his head blood dripped.

And I said to him:

'Kill me, but let the folk go down to the villages. Every god is a god of the living, and those who go down into the grave do not praise any god.'

And his two black eyes pierced me, and the black eye of the pistol was fixed on my forehead. Then all three eyes were closed, and Momchil struck the pistol on the ground and began to weep. And he cried:

'Why did you take me out of the Hole?'

And he begged me:

'Father! My father! Father! The others!'

I said to him:

'Glory to Manol and the others, but some must be left alive to tell of their deeds and to honour their memory.'

And the people hurled themselves at me from both sides, some with open arms, others with knives. The priest of Prossoina saved me, crying:

'Stop! How can you go against God's will! This is a holy man!'

And I saw that he was trembling and wanted to save his own miserable life.

And after us two priests, two hundred souls set out from the camp on the Pass, and one hundred saw us off with wailing and curses. And brother parted with brother, and sons with their fathers. I led the renegades. And someone shot from the Pass, and killed the last in the file. But me he was unable to kill, for I went first.

And as we staggered along the road downwards, we looked on the earth. And my gaze glided up the straight pine-trees, and my spirit set out after my gaze, so that my back straightened, and I began to walk as straight as a pine-tree. And the folk, seeing this, took heart, for they thought that a man could not go to his shame with his head raised.

And as I looked at the pines, on a high tree that stood at the meadow above Prossoina, I saw a cross cut into its bark, like the crosses in the holy forest of Cheleveshtnitsa. And I turned off the road, and placed my lips on the cross, as if I was sucking the resin of the tree. But the folk understood me, and each of them passed and bade farewell to the cross, and the mothers lifted up their young children.

Since that day I have not kissed a cross.

Seventh Excerpt

The time of parting had come. The time of birth, of the rending asunder and the blood, of the screams and the convulsions. The time of death, for where there is a birth there death also stands near.

It was not only those five hundred souls, shut up in the *Konak*, who were being reborn. Together with them scores of generations were also being born, generations who would set out along the road chosen by their forbears. Or scores of generations were dying.

Each had to pass to the left, or to the right. Not one was left in the middle. In the middle, like a rock, stood Karaibrahim, and like a river they came towards him, and divided into two streams—the left went to the block, the right one—to the turbans and the yashmaks.

During all the time that I was writing this chronicle, I kept thinking that I would have to describe that day, too. I drove it out of my mind; I did not want it to come to me prematurely. Perhaps I ought to have written its history the very first time that it came back into my memory, and not have driven it out. And as I wrote of the horrors in the *Konak*, I had to leave myself strength for that day, too.

I take up my pen now, and I see that that day stands before me pale and tired. My heart refuses to go back to the square, amid the two currents of the river, amid the screams of the birth. The day of parting stands before me like a forest on a clear sunny day—the sun shines so strongly that the forest is hidden by a veil of mist. And why should I approach it to enter the dark forest?

The day of parting was sunny and fine. One of those sunny days on which the sky is so clear that you wish there were at least one cloud in it. And the night before it had been clear, with a new slender moon. In the morning the forest and the meadows were silvery with hoar-frost. And as soon as the sun came out, the rain-pipes under the eaves of the *Konak* began their song, as if spring had come. The hoar-frost was melting.

I took and broke off a green leaf from the flowers which Gyulfié had placed on my window-sill. Silver hoar-frost had covered the entire leaf. Not spring, but winter was on the way, and snow would soon be falling.

In the middle of the square, a framework of beams was erected, and on it Karaibrahim's litter was placed. In the front row stood the two Hodjas, on both sides of the framework stood rows of Turks, their unsheathed *yataghans* in their hands. And the square was surrounded by *yataghans*. The curtains at the windows of the *Konak* swayed—the Turkish women were stealthily peeping out from there. The wives and children of the *bashi-bazouks* crowded around on the side where Prossoina lay.

I looked at the mountain. Not a soul was to be seen on the meadows. In the shade the slope seemed to flash with fine silver, in the sunshine the slope burned in autumn colours.

Then the gate of the *Konak* was opened, and the Bulgarians began to come out through it—ragged, dirty, and pale amid the sparkling clarity of the morning.

The first to pass to the right were the two priests. I do not remember how they were forced into the True Faith. Perhaps I was looking the other way.

Then Vrazhou *Kehaya* took his stand in front of the Turkish rock. I was looking at him.

He was small and thin, and had grown still thinner in the *Konak*. The two Hodjas, the mad Karaimam Hassan Hodja and that snake, Sheikh Shaban Shebil, stood before him staring at him.

Vrazhou *Kehaya* began to grow smaller. He grew smaller before my very eyes, as if he were made of hoar-frost, so that I involuntarily glanced down at his sandals, to see whether there was not a pool beneath him. I had seen a man appear to melt before me on another occasion, as well—he was a condemned man, who had heard his death sentence.

Karaimam Hassan Hodja said :

'Repeat after me—Allah is great and Mohammed is his Prophet.'
Vrazhou *Kehaya* repeated :

'Allah is great, and Mohammed is his Prophet.'
Karaimam Hassan Hodja said :

'From now onwards, your name is Abdullah, or Allah's slave. Pass to the right.'

Vrazhou *Kehaya* glanced to the left, where the executioners, stripped to the waist, stood leaning on their *yataghans*. Before them stood the white block, cut for the notables. But as they had been beheaded standing, no head had as yet been laid on it.

And Vrazhou *Kehaya* went to the right, where there rose a red heap of fezzes, a white heap of turbans, and a black heap of yashmaks—all brought on mules by Karaibrahim Hassan Hodja.

After Vrazhou *Kehaya* came his family—sons, daughters, daughters-in-law and grandchildren. The hands of the women were free and they carried nurselings and young children. The hands of the men were bound. And their bonds fell only after they had uttered the magic words :

'Allah is one.'

Afterwards, several smiling Turks, with shears in their hands, seized the dazed men and cut off their hair and beards. They placed fezzes on their heads and wound turbans around them. But no one laughed on seeing their carelessly trimmed beards, and their faces, which looked like the backs of mangy donkeys in spring. For there were eyes in their clown-like faces.

And the women put their children down, or handed them to one to another, and put on the black yashmaks. And a pitch-dark shadow lay on the wonderfully-coloured soukmans and aprons, on the flowered meadows, on the green forests and brooks, on the autumnal mountains.

I raised my eyes and looked at the mountain. I expected to see that a shadow had fallen on it, too. But it sparkled with hoar-frost and blinding brilliance—in a hundred colours, and strong. There was no shadow upon it. And through the clear air, over the square flew white scaly seeds, caught up by an invisible breath, and I did not know whether flowers or weeds would sprout from them in the spring.

And the women raised the ends of the white kerchiefs, and covered their faces. Never again would the sun see them. Never again would folk delight in their beauty. And from many varying faces they became one face. Looking at the faces, one forgot that they had blue, black and brown eyes. For, as on the men's faces so in the women's faces, one saw only their gaze.

The children were the only ones who did not understand what was happening, and they tried to pull the kerchiefs off their mother's faces. They did not know, poor things, that at that moment, their fathers were putting turbans on the boys' heads, too, and their mothers were veiling the faces of the girls.

I watched the gate of the *Konak*. I was waiting for Elitsa to come out.

I heard one of the half-naked executioners say :

'Put a blanket on my shoulders. It's cold.'

I heard the one-eyed Hodja say mockingly :

'He is numb with too much joy !'

And Karaimam Hassan Hodja shouted :

'Say : Allah is one.'

In front of the two Hodjas stood Vrazhou *Kehaya*'s youngest son, his hands bound at his back. And he held his tongue. His eyes were dark and huge.

Vrazhou *Kehaya* went up to him, trembling with a terrible foreboding. And he said to the lad:

'Say it, my son—Allah is one. Say it, my son!'

He was not speaking, he was weeping.

His son turned his head slowly to him and stared at him. Then he spat on his father.

To spit on someone in the face of death shows very great courage, for everyone's mouth goes dry at that moment. Many can cry out, but few can spit.

The entire square gasped with one breath. And Vrazhou *Kehaya* fell on the cobblestones and began to writhe, as if a poisonous snake had bitten him.

The lad turned his white face to the Hodjas. He was swallowing, as if he were getting together enough spittle for them, too. The Hodjas stepped back a pace. The young lad's lower lip cracked, and big drops of clear blood fell on his breast.

Karaimam Hassan Hodja cried in delight:

'To the block!'

And that lad was the first who turned to the left, to the block. He set out alone, although two Turks seized him by the armpits.

Vrazhou *Kehaya* tried to pass on his knees between the Hodjas and to reach his son, but he was unable to pass the invisible line, which divided the square to the left and to the right. The Hodjas kicked him fiercely, his sons drew him aside. But he shouted:

'I did it for you, for you!'

And the executioner's brief gasp was heard, as when a woodman's breath leaves his breast, when he raises his axe and brings it down. Then an inhuman shriek rang out, but it was cut short, and hung over the square. After that nothing was heard, for the entire valley rang with cries and laments. Who knows why, the Turks shouted, too, and rattled their weapons. I raised my eyes, and I saw that Karaibrahim had opened his mouth and was shouting. I did not hear his cry.

I was silent.

From that moment onward, whatever happened on the square was accompanied by an incessant weeping and wailing, which rose and fell, subsiding and bursting out with renewed vigour, but never ceasing. Anyone would have gone mad, not only I. Why was this happening? Where was it happening? Was it happening, or was it just a nightmare?

Faces came towards me, a river of faces. And they were just about to crash into the rock, on which I was standing, when they divided into two rivers. The one would turn to the left, the other to the right. Sometimes ten would swim along the right river, one after the other, sometimes three would set out one after the other along the left river. I did not know them. When the notables had been brought out for the massacre, I had looked at their faces, and had tried to recognize which face bore which voice, and whom I had heard speaking in the dark. I did not know these people. But I tried to tell by their faces from afar who would sail down which river.

I could not tell. Perhaps they themselves did not know that the river would drag them to the left. And on the bank stood their near ones, calling to them, entreating them, cursing them. In vain.

You, who read these lines, go out on to a crowded road along which many people are coming. Let them be coming from a celebration, or from market, or work. But they must all be coming towards you, and you must divide their stream with your breast. And whoever passes on the side of your heart, you must know that in a minute he will be disgraced, and the one who passes on your right side, in a moment he will be thrown down on the ground and his head will be cut off. You may not know what a massacre is. Think of it.

Look at their faces, their eyelids, their lips. The tiny sparks in their irises, the wrinkles at the corners of their eyes, the down on the tips of their ears. Look at the women, their faces and their bodies. In a moment the body will be hidden under the yashmak, and the face under a white kerchief. And you will never see it again. And the faces that turn to the left, in a moment they will be separated from their bodies and will turn to dust.

Look at the faces coming towards you, and love them.

And I looked. And I loved those that went to the right, because that was my road, but I loved more those who went to the left, for I had not the strength to pass along that road.

And then I felt that I was beginning to stir, like a piece of ice that had so far been firmly bound to the shore, and now the movement of the ice was sweeping it along. And I felt that something was stirring within me, that something which makes the tame ducks flap their wings in spring, and try to fly, when they hear the free and mournful cry of their wild brothers coming from the sky.

I was praying with all my might. I prayed to my reason, my heart, my legs:

'Stop! It's madness! Don't move! Stay where you are!'

And they wanted to swim down the left river.

I no longer looked at the faces which the big river was dragging along to the rock. I looked at those who had been cast on the right by the waves.

One of the priests, the one whom I did not know, was kneeling on the cobblestones, praying. He was surely praying to his old God, but who would bother about him in that madhouse? I looked at his face and wondered that he had not come on the very first day. He was a coward and a glutton. His flock had held him back by his cassock, because they had thought that it was holy, and he had pulled away, trying to flee. And he had thought that he was leading them behind him.

The other priest, the priest from the upper graveyard, the leader of the newcomers, looked like a suddenly awakened corpse. He had brought these people, and as they had come down from the mountain, it meant that they had agreed to give up their faith. Yet now, faced with the block, they refused, drew back and set out along the left stream. He had thought that they were a flock of sheep, bleating after him, and that they would go whither he led them, since he had taken their sin upon his own shoulders. But they set out along their own road, they separated from the flock. They were, indeed, born for a second time, to die at once, but in those ten steps to the block, they became individual people, not sheep, but men.

And I saw how he was preparing to advance, to cross the line and pass to the left.

I said to myself—I swore:

'If the priest goes to the left, so will I.'

The priest remained on the right. I owe my life to him.

And the river brought more and more new heads and faces. And there were always some who went to the left. Karaimam Hassan Hodja was shouting like a madman:

'Allah is one!'

Then he would turn to the sweating executioners and squeal:

'Count the heads! Count the heads! These are Manol's brothers. Manol had a hundred brothers, hadn't he? Count up to a hundred and there won't be any more.'

But there was no end to Manol's brothers. Some let the river bear them along—calm, absorbed, strong. Others were dead beforehand, and what was to happen on the block did not touch them very deeply. Still others wept, cast themselves on the ground and tried to cling to the earth with their teeth. They even jumped up from the block, screaming: 'Allah is one,' and then knelt and offered their necks to the *yataghan*. I do not know how many they were, but the last ones trampled amid heads and bodies to reach the block.

At the end a bent old woman straightened up. She tore her smock across her bosom and drew out her dry breast. And she chanted:

'Eleven sons have I suckled, and you have slaughtered them all. Out of eleven dead throats I curse you, and add mine—the twelfth.'

And stretching out her yellow breast to Karaimam Hassan Hodja, she cursed him :

'May you be impaled, and scream for a little water. May you drink water, and may it run down the stake.'

Her head was cut off, too. The Karaimam merely said :

'I did not know that Manol had sisters, too.'

But I saw that he was frightened.

I remembered the old woman's words.

The gate of the *Konak* stood there, black and gaping. No one else came out of it. Elitsa did not come out.

Through that same gate they drove back those who had passed to the right side. They separated the men and circumcized them. The heads and bodies were left on the square.

And the sun shone just as clearly and blindingly as ever.

Eighth Excerpt

> Then did he light four fires,
> And got together, collected,
> The ploughs of his nine sons,
> The distaffs of their nine wives,
> The cradles of his grandchildren.
>
> Then did he lift up his voice, lamenting
> Burn, you household goods,
> That I may no longer see you,
> That my pain be unending.

Thus did I become only Ali, instead of Pop Aligorko.

And on the following day, after they had circumcized us, Karaibrahim called us together and said to us :

'Now you are already like us. Set to and pull down with your own hands the temple of your old God, and raze it to the ground.'

And Karaimam Hassan Hodja said :

'Two hundred and eighteen churches have I seen newly-made Moslems pull down with their own hands. Yes, and now I shall see them pulling down the two hundred and nineteenth. And whoever does not put out a hand to remove a stone from its walls, it means that he has accepted Allah only by word, and in his heart he is on the side of the old God. Therefore I shall cut him down.'

And we got together about five hundred newly-made Moslems, men and women, around the big stone church, which stood below Syuleiman Aga's *Konak*. And we stood in a circle around it, like a herd of jackals around an elephant, and we dared not bite it and tear it to pieces. And this was a big church made of stone, and its foundations are to be seen to this day.

Then I came forward, saying to myself: 'May the sin be on my head, for I have no descendants to follow me.' But aloud I said: 'Give me a ladder.'

And two men, put up a ladder to the roof, with trembling hands and drew back. And I went up the ladder and stood on the stone tiles which covered the church. I expected the roof to crumble and earth to swallow me up. But it did not crumble.

And I saw that there were swallows' nests under the eaves, though they were deserted, and it came into my mind that, in the spring, the swallows would not find their nests. And I remembered the words of the Psalm: 'And the swallows find shelter for themselves beneath the eaves of Thy house, God of the Mighty.'

And when I looked down from on high, I saw a wide circle of yellow faces, lifted up to me, and they looked to me like dead men, risen from their graves. But it seemed to me that they were waiting for a miracle. And the faces of the women were covered, so that one saw only their eyes, as if of the whole face only the gaze were left.

Three little stone crosses stood on the crest of the church roof, at an even distance from each other, two at each end and one in the middle. I passed over the tiles, which rang beneath my footsteps, and three times I bent down to raise the three little stone crosses. And I held them close to my breast, so as not to drop them. When I had raised the third, I stood at the edge of the roof, and cast all three down at the feet of the Bulgarians, who stood around the church. The crosses fell on the earth and did not break, for it was soft with rain. No one bent down to break them, but all looked up at me.

Only then did my eyes look beyond the circle of yellow faces, and I saw the circle of the Turks, like a second wreath of thorns made of *yataghans* and axes. And Karaibrahim was half-lying on a litter, and four Anatolian Turks bore it on their shoulders, so that the monster might look upon my foul deed.

And when I was standing on high, I saw that the top of an apple tree reached me, and there was a red apple on its top. All the apples had been shaken down, only this one was left, because it grew at the top. I had seen it the day before; then it had been very high, but now its warm glow was at my hand. And I stretched out my hand to pick it, for my stomach ached, as if I had not eaten for a year, and it seemed so empty that I felt I should never be able to fill it. As soon as I put out my hand, I felt on my breast the hardness of the other apple, the one which the Bulgarian Moslem had given me—the apple from the common tree. I took it out and bit into it, and bent down with my mouth full and thrust my fingers around the edge of the first tile. They were huge tiles, and heavy, too, and all green and covered with moss. And they seemed to have been stuck one against the other by the years, like the scales of a fish. And making a strenuous effort I got the tile up. It was very, very heavy. It seemed as if I were raising a tile not from one roof but from the roofs of one hundred churches, of all the churches in Rhodopa into which I had entered to light a taper and to pray. I was tearing down one hundred churches, and to all the hundred I prayed that they might forgive me.

And I saw a little yellow spider running over the damp furrow of the tile I had lifted, then it dropped into the open hole on a thread of cobweb. And as the sun was shining the little spider suddenly sparkled like a transparent yellow drop. I gazed after it.

And I saw beneath me the altar of the church. And a ray from above penetrated the darkness like a hand, falling on to the picture of the saints of the Last Supper. Never until that day had a ray of light fallen upon their faces, but only the glow of tapers, for light entered the church from the door, and there were no windows at the side even. Their unknown artist had painted them in the light of a taper. And now the ray fell upon them, the curtain was torn asunder, and the dark blood of the sacrament, enclosed within the four walls and the roof, was running out through the fresh wound.

I was unable to lift the tile, I only turned it over, and it rolled off the roof. It fell on to the stones and was broken into pieces. And when I bent down to raise the second tile, and there was a bright light before my eyes and I felt dizzy, I saw next to the rafters which held the tiles, a roll of yellowed parchment. And without even thinking, I took it and hid it in my bosom, where the apple from the common tree had previously lain.

And after the second tile, I fell to my knees with exhaustion and said :

'Let other men come up, too, for the tiles are heavy.'

And more men came up, so that soon only the blackened rafters were left like the skeleton of a fish that has been eaten up. And we came down from the roof. In the meantime, four men took off the oak door of the church, all covered with nail heads, and they were barely able to move it. And it was all the heavier for being full of lead bullets of the heathen who had shot at it for days to break it down. Not one bullet had passed through the wood. And the same four began to break up the stone framework of the door with hammers, while I stood aside and prayed, I knew not to whom—to the air, the sun and the mountain—that I might remain standing and not fall in front of all that multitude of people and especially not in front of the Turks. And I saw that my hands were wet with sweat and yellow, but no one looked at me for they were all yellow, as if they had been poisoned by some herb.

Then the whole fourth wall of the church caved in, and the two side wings and the altar were left. And people were just beginning to pull down the two walls, and already more people had gone forward, since there was now more room, when the voice of Karaimam Hassan Hodja was heard, crying:

'Stop!'

Then he said to Karaibrahim's bearers:

'Bring the Aga up here.'

And Karaibrahim was brought up facing the church. And Karaimam Hassan Hodja called me, and, grinning fearfully at me like a monster with bared teeth, he said to me:

'Slave of Allah, go and break up those images, before which you have knelt.'

And he pointed to the paintings in the church, and they covered both walls and the altar.

And I slowly passed through the church and looked around. One wall was lit by the sun, but cut by the shadows of the rafters, as if the saints were looking out through the bars of a prison, but the other wall was in the shadow. Yet I could not recognize a single face, although I had stayed in that church for hours, and stopped at each image with a taper in my hand. I used to admire and wonder at the skill of the long dead icon-painter, but now his skill was killing me. For it was not the faces of saints that looked at me from the walls, but those of living people. No, they were not living people. They were the ghosts of the dead, and it seemed to me that I recognized Old Kralyo and the other notables who had stood at the mill on that night.

And now it was not a thousand pairs of eyes that were looking at me, as they had looked when I was up on the roof, but only the ten Turks, standing at the gaping wall at my back, and yet it seemed to me that more people were looking at me now.

Little by little I passed through the whole church. And I stopped at the altar.

There on one side stood Jesus Christ. And his beard was black like Manol's, and his eyebrows were frowning like Manol's, and his hair fell like a shepherd's locks to his shoulders. A red shepherd's cape covered his broad shoulders, and his sinewy right hand was raised, bare to the elbow. I could not have stood his look, but fortunately his face was turned to the left.

On the other side of the altar stood the Archangel Michael, the Angel of Death, for the church bore his name. And as I dared not touch the Lord, I set about the saint. Yet he had straight brows, like Momchil's, red wings and red boots, and his garment was green. And I covered his eyes with my left hand, as if I were leaning against the wall, and with my right I wanted to tear the garment at his breast. And I expected that my hand would wither. It did not.

But although the colours looked faded and old, the plaster did not yield to my fingers; only a little green came off under my nails, as if I had scratched a water-melon.

Then once more I passed slowly down the church and went to the Turks. They looked at me in the way that wolves look at a lamb, and waited for a sign of rebellion. And I saw that they were glad.

I said to them :

'Give me a knife.'

And Karaimam Hassan Hodja handed me his *yataghan*. But I did not take it, for I remembered the hundreds of innocent souls whose blood that *yataghan* had drunk. And the black Turkish priest would have cut me down with the same *yataghan*, if Karaibrahim had not leant out of his litter and handed me his dagger. And he said to me :

'Go !'

His dagger was fine and sharp like the tongue of a snake, and had not two, but three edges.

With his dagger I began to break up the murals in the church.

But first of all I pricked out the eyes of the archangel; then I put down the dagger and began to tear with my fingers. The plaster broke like the bark of a pine tree.

Then, from under my fingers, I saw two new eyes fixed upon me. Under the image of the archangel, there were old paintings. I broke them up, too. A man's hand appeared, holding a sword. I broke it up, too. A new sword appeared, red and bent like a flame. Under the sword a child's lips smiled.

The wall paintings were immortal. No, they were mortal, but they did not want to die. I seized the knife and began to stab with it. The plaster came pouring down and dust rose. My lungs were choking, my eyes were filled with the stinging dust, my knees were giving way beneath me. One more blow and I would have dashed out, to run away.

Then suddenly a big piece of the plaster came away. Before it had crumbled in scales, now it fell like a panel over a treasure house.

The sun shone down on a piece of white marble, on which a naked woman had been carved. A mysterious smile appeared on her beautiful face, and she held her high breast with both hands. From the nipple of her breast ran milk, and pouring like a stream over the marble panel, it fell into the wide-open mouth of a naked man, kneeling before her. And the man had the legs of a goat, the teeth of a wolf and hairy pointed ears.

That was Rhodopa, giving suck to beasts and men, gathered together in one body.

And drawing breath, I fell forward upon the slab, and the point of the dagger struck the woman's breasts and broke. And the point fell with a clatter at my feet and shone like a dead beetle, and was buried in the pile of plaster.

Leaning my forehead against the cold stone, I saw at my feet rags of mantles, bits of eyes, lids, fingers, pieces of swords and goblets, I saw the entire pile of broken up paintings. I had broken them up, but I could not pierce the marble panel.

Then I straightened up and felt the firmness return to my knees. Thousands of such panels were scattered all over the mountains. Those that were buried in the soil would see the sun one day. They are immortal. For no one can efface the image of the mountain. And if I, a worm, had managed to gnaw through one tree, other trees would grow up. And if the faces of these people lay in pieces at my feet, new people would be born with their faces, and their faces would be more wonderful.

And when I returned to Karaibrahim, I gave him the remains of his dagger and said to him:

'Aga, your dagger broke.'

But he neither answered me, nor did anything to me.

And as I watched the others breaking up the murals and secretly wiping away sweat and tears, pretending to be tired, and pretending that the lime had got into their eyes, I stayed in the sun, gathering my strength, for there were eight more walls to the heart of the Bulgarian stronghold, and defenders were needed for them.

When the men began to pull down the stone walls of the church, Karaimam Hassan Hodja gave orders that each stone was to be passed along from hand to hand, and that the last one in the row was to throw the stone into the river. That is why there is a pool in the Elindenya River below the *Konak*, and the biggest trout breed there. And when the foundations were razed to the ground, and one saw the forest opposite across the place where the church had stood, Karaimam Hassan Hodja passed by each of us and looked at our hands to see if they were soiled with mortar. And he said to us: 'This mortar is like the blood of the bull of sacrifice you offer to Allah.' He did not look at my hands. Yet I wanted them to be red with his blood.

That is how we tore down the church of Prossoina, on the eve of the Holy Sabbath, so that only its foundations were left showing. But when we began to tear down the supporting wall, which held it up on the steep bank of the river, we tore out only three stones and stopped. For the stones were larger than oxen. And all wondered how the men of old could have built with such stones. But Karaibrahim mercifully allowed us to stop.

And the sun set, and we all expected that we would be allowed to go to our houses, and I awaited to see what more would happen to me. But we were shut up in the inner courtyard of the *Konak*.

And on the next day, Karaibrahim was brought out on to the balcony in his litter. And getting his strength together, he clung to the wooden parapet and raised himself up. And he said to us:

'Turks will settle in the village of Prossoina, to help you until you have more firmly learnt the True Faith.'

And there arose a great wailing, for many of the people were from Prossoina.

And Karaibrahim said also:

'The people from the villages of Zagrad and Podviss will now go and each, with his own hands and the hands of his children and his daughters-in-law, will destroy his house. Let not one stone be left upon the other of those hearths at which you have sinned night and day against Allah. Then you will build new houses in a village but it must be within sight of the *Konak*.'

And when he ceased speaking the wailing died away, for folks were dumb with pain. They wept before, but now they were silent. I was the only one who was not crushed by the terrible news—for one thing, I had no home of my own, and, for another, I remembered the story of my Mohammedan Bulgarian about the ruin of the village of Patleino, and the founding of the two new villages of Strazha and Pleshak. And only when we set out in a terrible file along the road to Zagrad and Podviss were the mouths and the eyes of the wretched ones opened, so that lamentations fell from their lips and tears from their eyes. But those of Prossoina who had wept before now said: 'Better that there be a Turk under my roof, than that I should destroy it.'

And we began first to pull down Podviss. And I remembered the wet roofs we had looked down on from the Chelevestnitsa Cave, and raised my eyes to the rocks. They seemed to have come down just over the village, and rose still higher, for there were no huge fir trees to hide them up to their middle. And from the devastated place smoke rose here and there, as from an incense burner.

And Karaibrahim and Karaimam Hassan Hodja and many more Turks came with us. Karaibrahim in his litter, and Karaimam Hassan Hodja on the back of a poor wretch, who had been caught in front of the *Konak* the night before. And when they saw the finest and biggest house, the Turks stopped and Karaibrahim asked :

'Whose is it?'

Vrazhou *Kehaya* answered him, looking as small as a well-chewed morsel. He wept and said to him :

'It is mine, Aga.'

And Karaibrahim pointed to the house and said :

'Begin.'

And when he saw that many stepped forward, Karaibrahim stopped them and said :

'He alone.'

But the folk said :

'We are the sons, daughters, daughters-in-law and grandchildren of the *Kehaya*.'

And Karaibrahim allowed them to pull down the house. And there were three houses in one yard, and since they stood on high and the yard had a low fence, we watched what was happening from the road.

The *Kehaya* went heavily up and in the yard he stumbled and fell, and remained on his knees. And he drove the women away and said something to his sons. And they began to carry things out of the three big houses.

And they piled three pyres before Vrazhou *Kehaya*. On one the ploughs of the nine sons, on the second the looms of the nine daughters-in-law, on the third the cradles of the forty grandchildren. And the *Kehaya* took pinewood and lit three fires. And when the three fires blazed up, he fell on his face in the yard and wept.

Afterwards they tore down the roof, but the walls they left standing; they only set fire to the barn. And thus, house after house, we tore down thirty houses in the village of Podviss. And of every three and four houses we tore down only one, for none of its folk had remained among us—some had fled, others had been slain. And we tore their houses down. And each man took out of his house what he could carry.

That evening we went back to the *Konak*, and for the first time folk wrapped themselves up in rugs, but we had little room, because of their household goods. And the Turks, although we were now of one faith with them, took what they liked, and carried it to Prossoina. The Prossoina villagers, of course, took nothing out of their houses.

On the third day we tore down the village of Zagrad. And when, on the fourth day Karaimam Hassan Hodja led the people out to tear down the Monastery of St Elijah, I said to him:

'Aga, give me two guards, and let me go around to look for a site for a new village.'

And he smiled and replied:

'A strong tree will strike roots even on stone. And you are strong in your faith.'

I said to him:

'In a fine village there are hens, and sheep, and cows, too, Aga. When you come to visit us, let us have something with which we can do you honour. But in a bad village there are only hungry curs, howling.'

And he let me go.

For three days the people tore down the Monastery of St Elijah, for it was as big as a fortress, and for three days I wandered over the mountains around us. But wherever I looked, I had to see Syuleiman Aga's *Konak*. And I sought well and carefully, and ever wiped the tears from my eyes, for I remembered the words of my man in Pleshak: 'The village is as you see it because the folk could not look around owing to their tears.' I could not choose a better place than the old graveyard with the stone crosses, which our folk had broken with hammers. It was sheltered, and the sun shone on it, and you could see the *Konak* from it. And the bones of our forbears would be beneath our feet, and those three huge crosses, which Momchil had buried.

And when the folk returned with torn hands, and told me that the monastery bell would no longer be heard, I led them to the meadow with the graveyard. I had not laid a stone for a hut of my own, yet my life so ran that I founded two villages—the one in Petglassets, the other above Elindenya.

And when I stood on the meadow, with the silent crowd of people at my back, my hands hung as if they were broken, because I could not take a bunch of herbs and bless the village. But I remembered how we had made the forest a forbidden place, that no axe might touch it, and I said:

'Is there a blackened cauldron?'

And one was found. And we set out again along the huge trees, as if we were going past the pillars of a church, and again I heard the old words:

'May he that raises his hand to blacken the forest grow as this cauldron.'

We were Moslems, yet we spoke the old words. And we were going to found a village, like the refugees had done, only instead of a church we would seek a site for a mosque. And we would be born and we would die here, in our village, as the Christians were being born and dying in Petglassets.

And fires blazed up, as on that memorable night, only at first no one spoke, for they were afraid, because they were beside the old graveyard.

I said to them :

'The whole mountain is a graveyard, and every day you walk over graves. So many folk have lived here, and they have all died. And if you do not step on a bone, you still step on a dead man, although he has become soil and grass. Is it not all one whether the dead died yesterday or a thousand years ago? And is it not all one whether he has left a cross, or a stone, or a spruce above his grave?'

And still folk tried to be as close as possible to me. They did not speak much, because they did not know what to call each other. For they had new Turkish names, and no one knew the other's name, and forgot even his own new one. And men would ask :

'Vidoul, what is your name?'

And the other would answer :

'Mehmed.'

And the former would call to him :

'Metko, bring wood for the fire.'

And the Turks who had been set to watch us, beat us over the head, if they heard a Bulgarian name.

But I tried to get away on one side, and kept touching my breast, where I had hidden the roll of parchment that I had found under the roof of the church. A week had gone by since then, and I was still unable to remain alone, to see what I had found.

And when an opportunity offered itself, I lit a pine torch, and slipped into the forest. And I had just taken out the roll, when lo— out of the darkness came Vrazhou, and with him one of his sons. I cursed him in my mind, but he came to me and handed me a heavy sack. And he said to me :

'Father, the holy vessels of the Monastery of St Elijah are in here—chalices, censers and dishes. They are made entirely of gold and silver. You know best what to do with them.'

He did not wait for me to speak, but turned and disappeared into the darkness. I bent my head over the roll, and felt that there was someone beside me. I raised my eyes—it was Vrazhou *Kehaya* again. He said to me :

'Father, it wasn't the ants that gnawed through my bonds on that day: Karaibrahim let me go. He wanted me to bring the folk back to the village. Father, will God forgive me?'

I looked at him. I did not hate him. I asked:

'Which God do you want to forgive you? The old one or the new one?'

And he seized his head in his hands, swayed and left me. But I heard his voice coming from the darkness. And Vrazhou said:

'Son, you will go to your brother Iglavin, and tell him to take that big goat, with which I got the better of Manol, God rest his soul. Take three more rams. And when you have driven them to the Monastery that we pulled down, you will come and tell me.'

And his son asked:

'What do you want the goat for, Father?'

And Vrazhou said, so quietly that I barely heard him:

'I shall sacrifice it amid the ruins.'

Then his son burst into tears, and began to beg:

'Father, Father, don't slaughter it. There is not another goat like it in all the mountains.'

And Vrazhou *Kehaya* shouted:

'Hold your tongue, cur, son of a cur. I would have slaughtered you, as Abraham was ready to slaughter his own son, but the goat is dearer to me than you are. That is why I shall slaughter it.'

And as he shouted, he began to weep, and only repeated:

'Oh, God! Oh, God! Oh, God!'

Until I no longer heard his voice.

But my pine-torch was burning to an end, so I lit a fire. And in the light of the fire I saw the treasure that I had saved from the church.

For those were the chronicles of the Monastery of St George, of which it is known that it had stood over a deep abyss at Djinevra, and whose bells are still to be heard on stormy nights, warning men of the abyss. And the Monastery was destroyed a century and a half ago when, in the days of Sultan Selim the Terrible, the Turks had imposed their faith with fire and the sword.

Twenty-seven monks, some of whom had not even left their names, had set down for three hundred years all that had happened in Rhodopa—from the time of Ivanko, the murderer of Assen, who had built castles in these places, and from the time of Slav, Kaloyan's boyar, to the destruction of the Monastery. And only one hundred sheets were written, each monk having written three or four. And my heart wept, desiring to know better what had happened in Rhodopa, and what manner of men had lived here.

And on that night, sitting beside the fire, I decided to be the twenty-eighth monk. And I decided to write in detail the story of the destruction of Elindenya, so that those who come after us may know what manner of men lived in Rhodopa in those days, and not forget their deeds and their death.

Ninth Excerpt

> Everything comes out of the earth,
> Everything is a flower in bloom—
> A white rose and a red one,
> And early green basil—
> Yet I shall go down into the earth . . .
>
> Where was it ever heard,
> E'er heard or seen . . .

And as there was no time to hew stones and build walls, we set about cutting down the forest and erecting huts. The women, on their part, dug trenches into the earth, and often brought out human bones. And some of the skeletons had no heads.

On the very first night, the dogs began to bark, and I realized that men had come to the camp, but no one sought me out. Afterwards I found out that Momchil's *haidouts* had come and had brought a skinned ram. And my heart ached, for they had not asked for me, so that there was no hope of ridding myself of this torment and these sufferings. But it may have been all to the good, for I would have time to write the story of the destruction of Elindenya.

In the morning, mounted Turks came to us, twisted my arms behind my back, and cast a rope over my neck. And tying the rope to a horse's tail, they led me to Karaibrahim.

And before I went in to him, they searched my garments all over with their bloody hands three times, so that I shivered with disgust. It was well that I had left the parchment up on the meadow, otherwise they would have found it, for they would have found even a needle. And when they had made certain that I bore no arms, they said to me :

'Go in to the Aga.'

And Karaibrahim lay on a pallet, and at his head was Karaimam Hassan Hodja, the accursed, while at his feet was Sheikh Shaban Shebil, the one-eyed.

And Karaibrahim said to me :

'Last night Momchil came to the new village.'

I replied :

'Momchil lies up in the mountain with a broken leg.'

But Karaibrahim, and Karaimam Hassan Hodja and Sheikh Shaban Shebil opened their mouths and began to laugh, and they laughed long and loud. Then Karaibrahim bared his teeth at me and shouted :

'Hold your tongue, priest, do you not fear the rope? I thought to make you Cadi of the village, yet you lie to me. Last night Momchil killed one of my men.'

I repeated :

'Momchil cannot walk.'

And he fixed his snake-like gaze on me, and the scar of Goran's blow pulled his mouth into an evil, crooked smile. And he hissed :

'Last night Momchil came to your village. Where did he go?'

I realized that there was no use trying to convince him, so I said to him :

'Even if he did come, I did not hear his coming. But he would not come into me, unless he came knife in hand, because I brought the folk down to the *Konak.*'

And the three wolves put their heads together and said something to each other. They believed me. And Karaibrahim straightened up from the waist, dropped his feet on the ground, and said to me :

'Listen, priest. I am leaving in three days, and I do not know when I shall return. And before leaving, I shall turn my head back to see what I have done. What I came to do in Elindenya, that I have done. From now on, no *chan* will be heard over the valley—a muezzin will sing instead. There is only one thing that I have been unable to do, I admit it—to catch Momchil. As a flea jumps over a lion's back, so Momchil jumps over mine. And you must know that even a lion raises his paw to kill a flea. I am strong, that is why I admit it—I want to catch Momchil.'

And when he stopped speaking, he nodded to the one-eyed Sheikh, and the man handed him a green bowl. I saw that there was wine in it. And I grasped from the one-eyed fellow's dexterity, and from the trembling of Karaibrahim's fingers that the bowl was often raised to his lips. Karaibrahim drank, and said to me further :

'Go to Momchil, and tell him that I am leaving. If he comes to me of his own accord, I shall let Elitsa go, and with her his child in her womb. Let his mother nurse him and rear him as she will—with Mohammed or with the cross. Otherwise I shall take Elitsa with me, and shall make a Janissary of his son. And even if twenty years go by, I shall incite him to come to the Rhodopa and kill his father. And if he has died, to desecrate his bones. If he does not want to come, tell the men of his band that whoever brings me Momchil's head, I will fill the same bag in which he brings it to me with gold. And I shall give him Elitsa as his wife.'

I looked him in the face and saw that his eyes were red at the edges and bloodshot. And I thought that the wine would either kill him or drive him mad. And I said to him :

'What if I do not go, Aga?'

And he laughed and said to me :

'I look at you and I see through you as through a cloud. Priest, men like you once lived in these mountains. And when their enemies defeated them, they asked for fifty children as a token that they would not break the peace. And your men answered. "Let us give you a hundred men." They were afraid that the enemy would corrupt their children. I look at you, and I see that you are think-ing : "Better for Momchil to die, than for the son to kill his father." It may even happen that you will bring Momchil's head. Now go.'

And I left the room and I heard Karaibrahim call after me :

'Tell his band that I shall give my horse to whoever kills Mom-chil.'

And the two Hodjas cried out in amazement and grief :

'*Aman ! Aman !*'[9]

They cried mercy for the horse, but had not thought of asking for it for the thousands of martyrs who died before their eyes.

(These are the words of Father Aligorko, but he speaks of himself as if he were an onlooker.)

Momchil lay on the grass; Father Aligorko came up from below. And Momchil held the injured falcon in his hands, and his leg was tied to a freshly peeled pine stick. All around stood the ten *haidouts*, all wearing black *yamourlouks*[10] thrown over their shoulders, with shaggy caps of wolfskin, and bushy brows, drawn together in a frown. They were leaning on long rifles and bare swords, and looking at me. Next to Momchil knelt his little brother Mircho.

And this was taking place on Mount Purvenets where, in spring, the *haidouts* gird on their cartridge belts and swear an oath; where in summer the shepherds play their *kavals*, and court mischievous spirits; where in autumn the winds blow hard, uprooting trees; where in winter the snows lie white and sparkling; where at night wolves gnash their teeth and howl terribly. It was not spring, yet the *haidouts* were on the summit. It was autumn, yet no wind blew. And winter would soon be coming, so that the snows would fall white and sparkling.

When the priest stopped in front of Momchil in silence, the latter thought a little, and said to him :

'False priest, if you have come to die, go.'

The priest said to him :

'Karaibrahim sent me, to tell you that he is leaving in three days.'

And Momchil dropped the falcon and seized his head in both hands. And he only said :

'He is leaving.'

And the falcon croaked, and tried to beat its wings. Momchil dropped his hands and said :

'Speak on.'

And the priest said to him :

'If you go down to Karaibrahim of your own free will, he will let Elitsa go to rear her child as a little Bulgarian.'

And he tried to rise, and even stood up alone, but fell to the earth. And he dropped straight down, like a felled pine, for he could not bend his broken leg. And with his face in the grass, he cried :

'I have a son ! I have a son !'

And Mircho took the falcon in his arms and pressed it to his breast.

The priest said to him :

'You have not, but you will have. Listen further.'

And his men raised him like a child and seated him. And his face was wild with joy.

The priest spoke on :

'If you do not give yourself up, Karaibrahim will make a Janissary of your son. And even should twenty years go by, he will incite him against you, to hunt you all over Rhodopa.'

Then Momchil grew quite pale and began to tremble, and the *haidouts* about him ground their teeth. And they cried with one voice :

'Momchil, we shall all give our heads, but we shall reach Karaibrahim. If we get only to within a hand's breadth of him, may there be a knife in that hand, afterwards let them cut us to pieces alive.'

Momchil was silent, and the priest told them :

'A camel will pass more easily through the Needle's Eye than a needle will enter the *Konak*. Not so much as a needle can you take as far as Karaibrahim—to say nothing of a knife. One hundred men guard him and they will undress you three times before you see Karaibrahim's face.'

They were silent, and the priest said to them further :

'And Karaibrahim ordered me to tell you that whoever takes Momchil's head to him, he will fill the bag with Momchil's head in it with gold. And he will give him Elitsa as his wife. And, in addition, he will give that man his horse.'

And they tried to laugh, but it was as if they wept. And Momchil was thinking something, and asked the priest, and the priest felt mistrust and suspicion in his voice :

'Tell me, Father . . .' (O God, reward him in heaven for calling me 'Father' once more!) . . . 'Tell me, Father, why does Karaibrahim give even his horse for my head?'

The priest knew that he would ask that question and decided to tell him. So he said :

'Because, of every Turk they find killed, they say that Momchil killed him, and they do not believe that you are lying wounded in the mountains.'

And Momchil slowly looked at the *haidouts* around him, and, one after the other, they stopped laughing and bent their heads. Now Momchil began to laugh. And his laughter was the most like weeping.

'I am cursed,' he cried. 'I am cursed to do nothing. I did not get down into the Hole and I have killed no Turk. I only play the *kaval*. And you dishonour me, and shout over the mountains that Momchil is wreaking vengeance on the Turks. Why do you dishonour me? Why do you make a mock of my crippled legs?'

And the oldest of the *haidouts*, whose temples were already touched by hoar-frost, bent over Momchil, and said to him :

'Forgive us, Momchil. But each of us does what any of us would do. And you did what no one has ever done. That is why we chose your name. And it is better for folk to think that one man wreaks vengeance, for one name is easily remembered, and a hundred names are forgotten. And when a hundred men are gathered into one, his forehead touches the clouds.'

Momchil said not a word, and all were silent, and at last Momchil said to them :

'Go into the forest, and when the shadow of the Big Rock on Purvenets covers the Little Rock, come up to me.'

And they set out, and the priest was going to follow them, but Momchil said to him :

'Father, you stay.'

When the others had passed on, he said to the priest and to Mircho :

'Let me put my arms around your shoulders, so that you may take me to the Big Rock on Purvenets.'

And they took him up. And he lay on his face in the short grass, and looked forward over the mountain stretched out before him.

And down below, along the sloping meadow, someone was slowly coming up. And when he drew near, they saw that he was a little shepherd. And he begged Momchil:

'*Baté* Momchil, I am going south. Let me bring my herd past you.'

And Momchil smiled at him and said:

'Why do you ask me? Let it pass.'

And afterwards he asked:

'Are you leading the last herd?'

And the boy answered:

'The last. Snow will fall in three days.'

He was looking at Momchil with big, bright eyes and it was clear that he did not believe in Momchil's injury. And he probably thought that as soon as night fell, Momchil would jump to his feet, and perhaps turn into a grey wolf, and slip down into the valley to tear Turks to pieces.

And the herd set out below them, below the Big Rock. And when he saw that Momchil had shut his eyes, the priest shut his, too.

And the herd was passing in the gloaming, like a rain cloud, and the thudding of their little hooves was like heavy drops of rain falling, and the shaking of the heavy fleeces was like the rustling of leaves under the rain. And from time to time bleating was heard, but no *chan* rang out.

The priest heard Momchil say:

'Rain is falling from above, and everything is rising towards it. Everything comes up from the earth, everything is a flower in bloom, and a white rose and a red one, and early green basil. Yet I shall go into the earth.'

And the priest started, and opened his eyes, expecting to see meadows in full bloom. And the herd ran beneath him like a white river, and the earth was not to be seen, and the white backs swayed like waves. And everything swayed before his eyes, and it seemed to him that river, and mist, and cloud flowed beneath them; and afterwards it seemed to him that the waves stood in one place, and the rock was swaying and was making for somewhere like a ship. And the priest seized the big boulder that stands leaning on two smaller boulders on the rock itself.

And he said to Momchil:

'Momchil, you speak of spring, yet winter is coming.'

And the priest glanced around at the dark forests and the yellow meadows of ferns, and the red meadows of beeches, maples and ash-trees. But Momchil did not open his eyes, and said to him:

'Whether it be winter, or spring—it is life.'

The last sheep were passing, so that the thud of the hooves were heard still more clearly, and there was a smell of grass and dust, as there is after rain. And the sheep passed on. The voice of the little shepherd was heard :

'Farewell, *Baté* Momchil. Until the spring !'

Only then was a dog's bark heard.

Momchil opened his eyes, and called quietly to the boy :

'Fare you well, little shepherd !'

And looking around, he saw the priest and Mircho beside him, and said to them :

'Are you here? Go down, and come back with the shadow.'

And Mircho still held the injured falcon in his hands. And the falcon flapped its wings, so that it fell on Momchil. It clung on his right shoulder with its crooked claws, and it, too, began to gaze at the mountain stretched out before us, over which it would never again be able to fly.

Thus the injured Momchil and the injured falcon were left on Mount Purvenets.

And when the shadow of the Big Rock fell upon the Little Rock, the priest, Mircho, and the ten *haidouts* set out, and went to Momchil. And they saw from a distance that he had raised himself on his hands and his elbows, and was dragging himself around himself, and gazing about on all sides, as if he were seeking something. They could not see him well, for the sun was low and fell on his side, and melted him away. But they could see that he drew away from the earth with all his might and raised his head, but the earth drew him down to itself.

And they found him lying on his face, touching the earth with it. And when he heard their steps, he said to them :

'The earth smells of fine things.'

The *haidouts* sat him up, and rested his back on the stone.

And there they stood—the priest with Mircho and the ten *haidouts*, twelve in all, and Momchil in the middle—the thirteenth.

Momchil said :

'Tomorrow one of you will take my head and carry it down to Karaibrahim. And in the same bag you will put my knife.'

And they all stood there as if they had been turned to stone, and still they could not understand him.

And Momchil said further :

'That is the only way in which the knife can enter the accursed *Konak*. And when Karaibrahim rises to delight in my head, thrust my knife into his breast. And then not he, but I will remain the victor.'

And only now did the truth shine in their eyes and it blinded them. And they all raised their hands and hid their faces, as if, instead of Momchil, the sun had shone forth among them, and it seemed as if in Momchil's face there were thunder and the sun shone forth, so that it blinded them.

And Momchil said:

'Go into the forest, and when dawn breaks, cast lots for who is to take my head and kill Karaibrahim. I trust you all.'

And again they all set out, without speaking a word, and stumbled across the even meadow like blind men. And Momchil once more said to the priest:

'Father, stay.'

And taking the ring from his finger, and that was the same ring, which Manol had returned to Elitsa, and she had given it to Momchil, he stretched out his hand to the priest and said:

'Father, take this ring and return it to Elitsa. Tell her that she is as free as the little bird of the air.'

He spoke the same words that Manol had spoken. But he spoke them in his own voice. And for the first time it seemed to the priest that he had reached his father's stature. He added only:

'And let her look after my child.'

And the priest thought: 'May Manol forgive me, but never was he as handsome as Momchil is at this moment.'

His black hair was stirred by the breeze, his black eyes glowed, and the two straight veins on his swan-like neck beat, beat like two hearts. What was that beauty for, O God, if it was to go down into the earth?

And the priest said to him:

'Momchil, even if Karaibrahim dies, you will not be there to see it. And you will not be with us to see our joy.'

And he looked at the priest and said to him:

'How do you know that I shall not be there? And how do you know that I shall not be with you?'

And the priest heard weeping behind the rock, and realized that Mircho had hidden there and was weeping. And as he wanted to do something for Momchil, he begged him:

'Momchil, let me move you aside, that the sun may shine on you.'

And he smiled and said:

'The sun will turn, and the shadow will move away of itself. Before it sets, the sun will shine on me for the last time.'

And the priest suddenly understood, and believed. And he felt that time was flying. And the sun was turning, and time was flying and running out—like a herd, like a river, like a cloud. A new day would come and Momchil would no longer be there.

All night long Momchil played on his *kaval*. And all night long Mircho wept on my shoulder. But in the morning I dozed off, and when I opened my eyes from the cold—lo, day was breaking. And such a dense mist was falling that I could not see the tree opposite me.

And as on that memorable day, when I understood the great truth about the tree owned in common, I set out once more groping around in the mist. And it may be that truth is born of blindness and mist, and that is why on this day mist had to fall.

I found the *haidouts'* meadow.

The fire was out, and ashes covered the embers. And two steps away from the ashes, the grass was straightening slowly. And when I placed my hand on the ground, I felt that it was still warm from the body of the last *haidout*, who had endured the whole night long in the dark, but had not endured the break of day and in the first ray of light.

And I went back to Mircho, and the two of us found the tree under which Momchil was. And we found him with his eyes open, and the sleeping falcon in his arms. And I said to Momchil:

'They are men.'

And he shook his handsome head, and said:

'I am not angry with them.'

And in the mist he looked different, handsome, but terrible, too, and his face melted into the half-light. I saw that his big black eyes were piercing me.

And drawing back, I said to him:

'I cannot.'

Then Mircho stepped forward and said:

'Brother, I will take your head to Karaibrahim and I will kill him.'

And we looked at him, I and Momchil, and he stood straight in the half-light and the mist. He was but a lad—long-legged, like a stork, tall and slender. And when he saw that we were silent, Mircho said further:

'With this knife which you will give me, our father dug up the bones of my mother. And I have sworn an oath on it.'

Momchil said to him:

'Brother, may you be blessed.'

Then he said to me:

'Father, and you, Mircho, take me up to Purvenets. All night long this tree bent over me, with its broad leaves, and swayed, so that I could not see the stars. You ought to have put me under a spruce.

Yes, Father, bury me under the big spruce in ↘
every word is heard five times.'

And in a moment I lived through the long night, when the
foliage had hung over Momchil, and had whispered and
and stirred like a fallen black cloud, and he had not been able
drag himself aside and flee from it. And when I looked at the tree,
I saw that its foliage was not black, but red, as if it had been smeared
by a hot breath.

And we stood on the rock on Mount Purvenets. And it was all
one where we were, in the deepest valley, or on the highest summit,
For all around us was mist and nothing was to be seen.

And Momchil said :

'It is better that my leg is broken. Else I should have set out to
roam over the mountain. Could I have roamed all over it in one
day? But thus, I shall close my eyes, and wherever I turn my head
—to the east, to the west, to the north and to the south—wherever
I turn my head, my heart will set out there also. The heart, too,
has feet, so that it can roam over the mountains to the east, to the
west, to the north and to the south in the form of a cross—and I
shall go where I have been, and where I have wanted to be.'

Momchil said further :

'It is better that mist has fallen. Otherwise I should have looked
around, and what would I have seen? And thus I shall shut my
eyes and shall see the mountain in spring, and in summer, and in
autumn, and in winter, too, I shall see it by night and by day, in
storm and sun; in snow and verdure.'

And he was silent.

And we stood on the rock, alone amid the world, and around us
there was nothing but mist.

Was I a child, was I old or was I already dead? When was it—
a thousand years ago, today, or a thousand years hence?

The mist began to move, so that it flowed and was wafted past
the rock. And it seemed as if it was not that the mist flowed like
the waves of a river or a sea, but that the rock was sailing through
it like a ship, and cleaving it, and going ever farther and farther
away.

And I do not remember how much time passed, and the ship
sailed ever forward. And I stepped out and came down from the
ship, and the mist swallowed me like an abyss. And the ship passed
onward in the mist.

Now there were only two in it.

And the time would come when the second man would descend
from the ship, with a human head in his hands. And in the ship

ne man would be left, and it would sail on with him—on-
ds, onwards, through mists and time for ever and ever.

And my hands stretched out of themselves to seize the side of that
wonderful ship.

But it was already far away.

Here end the words of the Monk Grigorii, called Father Aligorko,
and later only Ali. I have written much, and far more have I left
out. And let those for whom I have not said a good word, forgive
me, for in those days the good numbered thousands. If one only
follows in their footsteps, my labours shall not have been in vain.

Tenth Excerpt

That morning a dense fog had fallen, but later the sun came out.
And once more a clear, brilliant light fell over the mountain, and
it seemed that autumn would never end. And once more the black,
moonlight shadows fell over the blue-black, yellow and red laps of
the forests.

I had deceived myself, thinking earlier that the women of the
Rhodopes gazed at the flowered meadows to embroider their green,
red and yellow aprons. And vainly had I looked for flowers with
orange-yellow and fiery-purple redness. The woman had gazed at
the forest in autumn.

I gazed and the mountains looked to me like Elitsa's face framed
with a dark kerchief, with shadows under the eyes, and all emaci-
ated by her stern and secret sorrow. Yet could sorrow darken her
chestnut hair and her eyes like a doe's? And the stern, sorrowful
Elitsa was still lovelier than the former happy girl, as the autumnal
forest, sunk in shadows, was lovelier than the green forest in summer.

So lovely was it, that I could not bear its beauty for long, and
I went back to the cool *Konak*. When I gazed at the mountain, it
seemed to me that I was gazing at Elitsa, that she was mine and
that I would always be able to gaze on her. And that thought was
unbearable. Who knows why, I went to Karaibrahim, and found
there the two Hodjas, Karaimam Hassan Hodja and the Sheikh
Shaban Shebil. And we heard shouts, as if the *Konak* were burning. The Turks were shouting :

'Momchil's head! Momchil's head!'

Karaibrahim's face grew terrible. And for the first time since
he had taken to his bed, he clutched the edge of his pallet with

his hands and stood up. And before the Hodjas could support him, he staggered across the room, then across the veranda, and fell against the wooden balustrade.

Out in the courtyard the Turks were crowding like wolves around fresh carrion, around something that we could not see. But Karaibrahim gave such an inhuman yell that they scattered.

In the middle of the yard, beneath the plane tree, stood Mircho— pale, thin, alone—clutching a bag made of goat's hair to his breast.

Karaibrahim coughed, sighed and asked:

'Is it the head?'

It seemed to me that there was horror in his voice.

Mircho merely nodded, and looked around, as if he expected the Turks to hurl themselves at him at any moment to seize his terrible burden. And they stretched their arms out to him, opening and shutting their hands.

Karaibrahim was transformed. He straightened up, grew taut and looked around like a madman who thinks that he is the master of the whole world.

With boundless arrogance and disdain he shouted to his men: 'Draw back, curs.'

And he nodded to Mircho to come up. And when the Hodjas wanted to take him by the armpits, he gestured furiously to them to leave him and returned to his room unsupported. His face was twisted with pain at every step—never before had I seen a face so distorted by devilish exultancy and pain, and may I never see such a sight again.

Karaibrahim sat down on his pallet. We heard the tramp of hundreds of feet mounting the stairs.

Karaibrahim coughed again, and said hoarsely:

'Sheikh, send the curs back. No one is to step on the veranda.'

He did not want to share his joy and his glory. He glanced at us, too, wondering whether to send us away, but probably he, nevertheless, wanted someone to witness that joy. Then suddenly he thought of something, and said to me:

'Go and fetch Elitsa.'

And I ran, though I wanted to go back, but I found strength to tell her, when she raised her eyes, like those of a doe, to mine, and asked me with a look why I had come to seek her:

'They have brought Momchil's head.'

And I did not tell her that Mircho had brought it.

She rose and staggered, but the moment I stretched out my hands to her, she made a commanding gesture that I was to draw back. And she set out alone with firm steps towards Karaibrahim's room. Hundreds of Turkish eyes watched from below, from the courtyard, as she hurried along the veranda. But no sound was heard.

In the room we found only the four—Mircho, Karaibrahim and the two Hodjas. All four were on their feet. Mircho was pressing the bag to his breast and looked like one that had lost his reason.

And Karaibrahim also looked to me as if he had gone mad. He was circling around Mircho—and the child was turning on his heels, too, so as to be always facing him—circling, bent double with pain, groaning through his teeth, now stretching out his hand, now drawing it back. And he kept shouting:

'His brother killed him! His brother!'

When he saw Elitsa in the doorway, he stopped. He wanted to show her the head himself, but who knows how, he restrained himself and said to her:

'Take it out.'

And he indicated the bag with a gesture.

But Mircho did not hand the bag even to Elitsa, he only allowed her to put her hands into it.

Elitsa drew out Momchil's head. And kneeling, then sitting down on the floor, she placed the head on her knees. And she bent her neck and her face, but she did not cover the head.

Momchil's head lay like a child in her lap, its face staring up. It was staring, for Momchil's eyes were open.

Karaibrahim knelt in front of the head, but did not stretch out his hand to it. The two Hodjas knelt on both sides of him, their backs towards me. I heard Karaibrahim gibbering like a madman:

'His brother . . . His brother . . .'

Then I saw that Mircho was standing erect behind the bent backs and that a knife was flashing in his hand. For several seconds he seemed to hesitate over the back of the one-eyed Hodja, then, with all his might, he thrust the knife into Karaibrahim's back.

And Karaibrahim fell forward, without even crying out, with outstretched arms, as if he wanted to seize the head.

With a scream Elitsa jumped to her feet, and pressed the head to her bosom. Her foot knocked over the lizard-green jar with Karaibrahim's wine. The cracked jar broke, the wine splashed and flowed over the floor. The dark stream reached the embers on the hearth and flowed over them. The fire hissed, and a white smoke rose.

Mircho hurled himself at the door leading on to the veranda, after him dashed the two Hodjas. When the one-eyed Sheikh passed by me, I gripped him firmly by the shoulder and turned his face towards me.

His sole eye opened like the muzzle of a pistol, and he put his hand to his waistband, looking for his dagger. I stood before him, defenceless. Someone touched me. Elitsa was handing me the rapier which hung on the wall, the same rapier, with which I had not dared to pierce Karaibrahim.

But I did pierce the one-eyed Hodja. And I stabbed him once more, when he fell on his back, I stabbed him with such fury, that the point of the rapier went into the boards and broke off.

I drew out the broken rapier.

Out on the veranda came the sound of countless footsteps; the entire *Konak* was shaking as if there were an earthquake. Dust fell from the ceiling.

And I heard Mircho shout :

'I have killed him ! I have killed him !'

I looked around. I seized Elitsa by the hand and dashed out on to the veranda. In my other hand I held the broken rapier, and with her other hand Elitsa pressed the head to her. The Turks were crowding one on top of the other over something I could not see. The crowd overflowed on the parapet, broke it, and the intertwined bodies fell out into the yard.

Elitsa pulled away to the throng and the yells, but I pulled her aside.

I remembered the secret passage.

I flew through Gyulfié's room, dragging Elitsa after me. I did not see if there was anyone there. With furious hands I opened the wooden door.

We fell down the stairs, and rolled on to the damp earth. I groped around, found Elitsa and dragged her after me.

Above our heads there was a trampling and an echo, as if devils were after us, and were thundering about, without being able to reach us.

It was dark, but I knew the way. I had lurked there to hear the revelation of the shepherds. On this soil I had possessed Gyulfié.

My hand sank into the side opening. That was the way to the forest.

I had not been through it. I stumbled and fell, and after me, a hundred times, Elitsa fell, for I was holding her with one hand, and with the other she was clutching the head.

The noise diminished and died away. I saw light.

We emerged into the cool shadow of the forest. I saw Elitsa's face, wet with tears, muddy, desperate.

I also saw the muddied, terrible head of Momchil in her hands.

His eyes were still open and were looking at me.

We buried Momchil under the Old Spruce in the Valley of

Petglassets. The men dug his grave with their knives, so as not to arouse the echo.

Elitsa placed Momchil's head by his body. Then all the refugees in Petglassets passed by him, and cast a handful of earth into his grave. It took a long time for them all to pass, for there were already a thousand refugees in Petglassets. The last to pass was Granny Srebra, and as she threw in a handful of earth, she was the first to speak since we had come to the grave. And she said:

'Let this village opposite be known from now on as Momchilovo.'

Then came the *Yurouk* Ismaïl Bey, and with him his seven sons. They bore Manol's silver *chans*. The clappers of the *chans* were bound. Ismaïl Bey stopped at the grave and said:

'I wanted to have the finest *chans* in all Rhodopa. But his head is a *chan* which, whenever it speaks, will be heard from sea to sea. May the *chans* of the father speak over the grave with the *chan* of the son.'

Momchil's *haidouts* climbed up on the spruce and hung the *chans* on its branches. The biggest, which was like a church bell, they placed at the top. Only then were the silver clappers unbound.

Not a voice was heard, not a ring. The sun was setting, shedding its peaceful radiance over the valley.

And the wind began to blow. The *chans* began to speak. First one, after it a second, then a third. Timidly at first, then clearly and loudly. The echo repeated their ringing.

The wind blew, and the fifty *chans* began to sing. Silver waterfalls splashed down and swept away. Amid the torrent of the chans I heard Granny Srebra's quavering voice. She was singing:

> Where was it ever heard,
> E'er heard or seen . . .

Thus the song of Momchil was born.

And to this day, whenever a storm sways the Old Spruce, the song of the *chans* is borne from summit to summit over Rhodopa Mountain.

[1] Tsar of Bulgaria (1187-1196).
[2] Tsar of Bulgaria (883-927).
[3] *Voivoda* (B)=head of a band of Haidouts or brigands.
[4] *Baté* (B) = a respectful form of address used in speaking to one's elder brother.
[5] River of the Dead.
[6] In folk songs and in the superstitions formerly current among Bulgarian peasants the Plague was personified as a swarthy and ugly woman.
[7] *Djanum* (T) = my soul.
[8] *Cherkovishteto* (B) = the church site.
[9] *Aman* (T) = have mercy!
[10] *Yamourlouk* (B) = shepherd's cape of homespun.

EPILOGUE

A Year Later

Elitsa died.

She was my wife, although I never once went into her at night.

After we buried Momchil, Elitsa was left alone. She went to Granny Srebra, who lived with one of her kin. And although he was not a bad man, it went against the grain with him to take the food from his children's mouths so as to feed the two women. And Granny Srebra was very old, and Elitsa was with child. And winter was coming.

Then I built myself a hut with the help of other men, and found Elitsa and Granny Srebra gathering wood in the forest. And I told Elitsa that I wanted her to be my wife.

Elitsa answered me :

'There were once three flocks, one spring and one pasture. The first flock, Venetian, that went in front of the others, drank clear water and grazed green grass. The second flock, Venetian, that went after it, drank muddy water and grazed muddy grass. The third flock, Venetian, that went last of all, for that flock there was nothing left. Neither water, Venetian, nor grass.'

I said to her :

'Come to my house.'

And, taking the load of wood from their shoulders, I placed it on my own. That evening the two women slept under my roof.

As long as the wind blew and it rained, it was cold in the hut. At night cold draughts came in through the cracks, and with them came the song of the *chans*. And however brave a man might be, he shivered, without wanting to, when he thought of the lonely tree, ringing amid the valley. For whom? It was like a clock ticking in a deserted house. It was deserted all around. And the echo answered the *chans*.

I would hear Elitsa weeping for whole nights on end.

Then snow fell, and buried my hut. The wind no longer blew in, it grew warm inside and the *chans* were no longer heard. The cold froze them. And Elitsa stopped weeping.

I had never looked after a house. But whatever I touched went

355

well with me. I shot well, I was brave, and feared neither blizzards nor wolves. Where other hunters left the tracks, I gave chase. It seemed to me that fate would not dare cut across my path, now that two women were waiting for me at home, and a little man was preparing to come into the world. Soon people drew aside into the deep snow when they saw me coming along the track. The meat from my hunt did not go to my house only, but also to the houses of my neighbours. Granny Srebra took it to them. I used to see that she never returned empty-handed, but always had something hidden under her apron. I was not angry with her, although I would have given the meat as a gift. Let Elitsa be well looked after.

I was poor, I lived hard, my lips cracked with the cold, and I sometimes slept burrowed into the snow like a bear. Yet I was happy. Looking back now, I see that those were the happiest days of my life. My heart sang. I was ready to endure anything, only to see Elitsa rise to her feet to welcome me, as soon as she heard me stamping the snow off my feet at the threshold. And she would look at me.

I felt that she came to me like a timid doe. And once, when I lay ill of a fever, she rose in the night and stroked my forehead. She thought that I was asleep.

Then came the spring. The rain-pipes began to sing, and after them, the *chans*. But Elitsa no longer wept.

I would often find her with her hands in her lap, staring somewhere ahead of her with her bright eyes. Her face was radiant and clear; she had become even more beautiful. She was waiting for something.

I would ask her :

'What are you waiting for?'

She would start and answer me with a shy smile :

'I am waiting for the child to quicken within me.'

Sometimes she would say :

'When we were fleeing, I pressed Momchil's head to my heart. Let us hope that the child will be like Momchil.'

I did not say so to her, but I thought that it would be like its grandfather—like Manol.

Then came the rains, and Elitsa's labour began. It lasted three days and three nights. I thought I would go mad. Many daughters have borne themselves with dignity, but she surpassed them all. She even found strength to smile at me with her bitten lips.

I wept like a child, and I was not ashamed of my tears.

Elitsa bore Manol and died. She heard the boy cry out and closed her eyes. Only her hair was left shining in the light of the pine torch.

I sat beside her dead body, thinking. What had her pain been for? Why had fate brought me here? Would it not have been better to have killed me in the *Konak*? Why had it given me such promises in the happy days of winter, yet had not fulfilled them now?

It was raining, the raindrops pattered on the stones of the roof. A strong wind was blowing and the *chans* were singing. Had she heard them before she died?

Someone touched my shoulder. I aroused myself. Granny Srebra handed me something wrapped in a brightly-coloured Rhodope apron, and said to me :

'This is your son.'

I took the child. It stirred in my arms. That was all that was left of Elitsa. And perhaps that was the sense of all that had so far happened.

Elitsa had had three husbands, but only one of them had once touched her. And she had borne this son. Fate had not wished to preserve the vessel in which this living fruit had ripened—Manol, son of Momchil, grandson of Manol. And it broke the mould so that no other like him should be born. And perhaps fate wanted a hundred mothers to nurse him, too, so that he would have a hundred brothers like the great man, his grandfather.

I did not think of that then. I knew one thing only—that Elitsa was not there.

I took wooden spoons, with which we had already eaten at home, worn wooden spoons, kissed thousands of times by human lips. There were seven spoons, and on each of them I wrote a name. The names of Manol, of Momchil, of Goran, of Sherko, of Old Galoushko, of Old Kralyo. I wrote my own name, too.

It was raining.

I went to the hole, into which the River Struïlitsa fell, so as to leave Petglassets. The river was flowing towards me, and thrusting its way amid the rocks, swollen by the rains. Then it disappeared in the Devil's Fall.

I lay on my stomach and bent over the terrible pool. One could not see its bottom. Darkness. And in the darkness water fell. Like frozen breath, mist rose in spirals, coming from somewhere very deep, from the darkness.

Damp rocks surrounded the cave. The drops on them shook from the thunder of the falling water. Rocks, and in the middle—nothing. The abyss and the darkness drew me downwards. I grew deaf and dazed.

Elitsa was not there.

The water fell, swift and strong, and vanished.

I needed only to relax my hand slightly.

Somewhere down below was the Dark Hole with the dogs and the bodies of Old Galoushko and Sherko. Down there somewhere was the Cheleveshtnitsa Cave, with those who had been walled up alive and smothered. I would not be alone in the Lower Earth.

My hand glided over the wet rock. The dark well gaped before me. Darkness. And in the darkness the thunder of falling water.

My breast rested on the cold stone. But I felt something warm pressing and stirring at my breast. Something living.

Elitsa had gone, but she had left me her child.

I straightened up with difficulty, being careful not to slip, and I turned my back on the Devil's Fall. And the rock beneath my feet shivered and my head was still dazed by the roar of the abyss.

I stood on the mossy rock, hanging over the swift-flowing stream, which shone in its narrow groove. And I saw floating towards me the wooden spoons. When the first came up to me, I seized it and drew it out of the water. And the other spoons, with the other names, vanished in a second in the black abyss from which nothing ever returned.

The name on the first spoon was :

Manol.

Granny Srebra warmed water in a big black cauldron and placed in it early basil and oil from the float light. Then she dipped the child three times in the cauldron, saying :

'Lord God, and Holy Virgin. This child was born a heathen, may he become a Christian. A bulb was he born, may he become a mountain. May the stone that he touches turn to silver. May he dance in his youth, and endure in his old age.'

And when she dipped the child into it the third time, she burst into tears, and cried through them :

'I baptize you Manol.'

She wiped him on a white woollen garment, made the sign of the cross on his forehead, his breast, his little hands and his little feet, and wrapped him in swaddling clothes. Then she handed him to me.

'A heathen you gave him to me, a Christian I return him to you !'

All around us stood the oldest folk in Momchilovo—the men with their fur caps in their hands, the women with tearful eyes. And they all said in one voice :

'Amen !'

And the child began to cry.

Granny Srebra stretched out her huge wrinkled hand and touched the babe's little forehead. And she added quietly, although these words were not to be found in the ritual of the baptizers:

'A Bulgarian you were born, a Bulgarian may you die.'

To Momchilovo came Manol's priest, the one who saved my life on the day of parting. Had he stepped to the left—this chronicle would never have been written.

A child called me out of the forest and told me that an unknown man was looking for me. And the man had not come into Petglassets, but stood at the cave. It was spring, it was growing warm, but my sweat froze when I passed through the cave and entered the terrible gorge of the Struïlitsa.

The priest was waiting for me there. And just as the sudden cold of the abyss had pierced and frozen me, so also the priest's face froze me. It was as if death were meeting me. If those same eyes were not shining in his face, I would not have known him. Were it not for those eyes, his face would have been like that of a skull.

'Are you ill?' I asked.

And I saw that at his feet lay a black cauldron and a gaily-coloured bag.

He made a vague gesture, and said in a toneless voice:

'You are the Venetian, are you not? Elitsa's husband?'

I only nodded, for his deathly face and Elitsa's name had saddened me. And I was shivering with cold in the abyss.

'You must help me,' the priest said in the same toneless voice.

He was no longer a priest, but was dressed in shepherd's garments, and wore a turban on his head.

'Come into Petglassets,' I said and bent down to help him carry his load.

He put a foot on the cauldron, then pulled it aside, frightened, and knelt before it.

'I shall not enter Petglassets,' he said quietly, with his hands on the black cauldron.

'Then why have you sent for me?' I asked.

'I set out on the journey alone, but my strength is not enough to carry my burden.'

And looking at me with his shining eyes, so that I felt still colder, he said to me:

'This cauldron holds the gold and silver vessels of the Monastery of St Elijah. And there are old chronicles in this bag.'

I looked at him and asked:

'Why have you come to me? Why have you chosen me?'

He answered:

'Elitsa chose you.'

But I saw that he had not said everything. And again I asked him :

'Why me?'

Then he said to me :

'Because, like me, you betrayed your God.'

I went to Petglassets, took a garment and bread, and returned to the priest. He was still kneeling in front of the cauldron and kept his hands on it.

And again I thought that this man would soon die. I gave him my garment and said to him :

'Father, are you not cold?'

He looked at me, and smiled so that he suddenly grew young, and said to me :

'I thank you for saying "Father" to me. It is colder in the grave.'

I shouldered the cauldron, and he the bag, and we set out. And the cauldron was so heavy that it nearly tore my shoulder off. I wondered how the priest had dragged it to Petglassets.

The road was easy to remember. We set out uphill along the valley of a river which flowed into the Struïlitsa. We went along it until we emerged onto pastures such as I have never come across in Rhodopa. They were so wide and lovely that it was impossible to walk all over them, and one wished one had wings. A blackish-green garland of wooded summits surrounded them. The forests did not begin at the meadows, but rose behind unseen deep precipices, in which rivers flowed. These precipices, which were not seen, but could be felt, this separation of the encircling mountains from the meadows made the latter still wider. There was a forest only on one side. And nowhere else in Rhodopa have I seen lakes so high up in the moutains. But here sparkled blue lakes, overgrown with reeds. They, too, made the meadows look still wider.

We set out across them, and walked and walked and they had no end. It was growing dark. At last we reached the forest at the end of the endless pasture. It grew cold. The sun reddened the last snowdrifts on the mountains around us. There were no flocks yet; it was deserted all around, wide and cold.

The priest said to me :

'Let us go into the forest.'

I looked at the forest and shook my head.

'The man who can pass through that forest has not yet been born.'

The priest said to me :

'A man can pass everywhere. More easily at some places, not so easily at others. But he passes.'

I don't know if there is a forest like this one anywhere else in the world. It is called Sheitanitsa, which means the Devil's Forest. The earth under this forest flowed like mud, or like dough, and lay in folds, but it could not shake the ancient pine-trees off its back. The trees bent this way and that, hurling themselves at each other, breaking their trunks and their branches. They fought each other for room, and interlocked. Where the earth had stopped moving, the leaning trees began to grow upwards, so that they writhed towards the sky like giant snakes, ready to attack. Other, slighter snakes wound around them: the long, wiry stems of unknown plants, which were neither grasses, nor trees, and resembled lianas, vines, couch-grass and ivy.

The priest was seeking something. He knelt and began to crawl beneath the entwined trees. I crawled after him, too, rolling the cauldron before me. What would I not have given to stop the rattling of the gold inside it—I was afraid of breaking the stillness and the peace of this extraordinary forest.

We crawled through black, stagnant marshes. I heard the earth around us licking its lips, as if it were a huge monster with soft lips. And although it was night, I felt that we were nevertheless keeping to some kind of a path. Who could have come this way before us? Men or beasts?

The priest stopped and said:

'We shall sleep here.'

He ought to have said—we shall stop here. Neither he, nor I slept. We did not light a fire, for there were no dry twigs, nor did we dare to do so. All night long we talked, and I was sorry that a man with such a mind and such a heart was soon to die.

That night, amid the Sheitanitsa Forest, Father Aligorko taught me to call the people I had loved and still love, every day, to pray to God for them, and to take counsel with them. The living, as well as the dead. Since then, I have never again been alone.

In the morning we rose and set out, walking, not crawling. We went through a vast forest, each tree having a trunk as big as a house, and a top rising high into the sky, and each tree standing far from the others, so that its strength and beauty could be seen. The weak trees had died, cast down, and had already rotted. There remained only the strong trees which blocked even the path of the earth with their roots. We walked amid them like lost children in an old tale.

Suddenly a lake appeared in the forest in front of us.

Father Aligorko whispered:

'The Samodiva's Eye.'

I looked up, and followed the huge trees until the back of my head touched my back. They had drawn aside, and formed a circle, and the lake lay in their midst, as at the bottom of a well.

This is a strange and terrible lake. All around it everything lives, dies and rots. The huge trunks of fallen trees, green with mould, moss and grass go down into its icy water and melt. Thick, juicy moss covers the rocks around it, so that no bare stone is seen and no step is heard. Damp, bearded lichens hang from the branches of the trees. Osiers and unknown green grasses grow in the midst of the still and icy waters.

I saw a black shadow glide slowly over the invisible bottom. I seized the priest by the arm.

He said :

'It is a trout.'

'If it is a trout,' I said, 'it must be the queen of all trout.'

'That is so,' said the priest, 'here everything is king or queen.'

A salamander emerged from under my feet—black, with yellow spots—and sank noiselessly into the water. A huge water snake with two yellow spots on its head came slowly out of the lake, and noiselessly glided away among the rocks.

The trees went down into the water, moss grew even on the stones at the bottom. Water dripped from the rocks on the shore, water seeped through the hanging moss. The trees, the grasses, the stones —all was steeped in moisture. The mountain and the water mingled and interpenetrated each other.

Suddenly I realized why everything around me made me hold my breath and my tongue, and tremble. The lake looked as if it had appeared out a fairy tale.

These were no trees, stones, fish and snakes around us, but bewitched living beings which had been turned into trees, stones and fish. They lived, breathed, and filled the air with their bated breath, but they could not speak. And perhaps at night the trout became a water nymph, the snake a forest dragon, the trees giants and the stones beasts?

'Father,' said I, 'let us go.'

'Cross yourself,' he said, 'and take the cauldron.'

I did not understand whether he was making me cross myself because of the lake, or because of the holy vessels in the cauldron.

Then he took me some hundred paces aside. There was another lake there—no, only a well amid the rocks. A green film covered the water, not green like grass or slime, but with a different, whitish, phosphorescent greenness. At night the entire lake shone. Here the trees stood so close to each other that the sun never reached the bottom of the well and eternal gloom, cold and damp, reigned here.

The priest bent down, took a broken branch and cast it into

the lake. The film opened, black water gurgled for a second, then swallowed the branch and closed over it. It did not float up, so water-logged was it.

'Carve a cross on these two spruces,' the priest said. 'There must be a sign.'

I carved them. And as I stood there, knife in hand, I turned. I saw the priest at my back, having come noiselessly up to the steep bank over the moss. He was gazing at the water and his eyes shone.

If he pushed me in, the green film would close over me. No one would ever find my body.

Shame welled up in me. And I realized that the priest wanted to jump into the lake himself. I seized him by the hand and he started.

'Father,' I said. 'Let us return. I could never find the way back alone.'

And once more he became the shepherd, whose duty it was to lead, even though it were but one soul.

Slowly we dropped the cauldron into the green lake. The phosphorescent film covered it. And the chronicles we hid in a cave, which is in the rocks above the lake, so high above the forest that sun shines in it.

The priest said :

'You go in. I do not enter caves.'

And when we emerged from the Devil's Forest, and set foot in the meadows, I turned and looked back at the bewitched kingdom.

Would anyone ever take the gold from the lake and the chronicles from the cave? And if he did, what would he find in the cauldron and the bag? There were no trees, rocks, trout and snakes there, but giants, beasts, nymphs and dragons.

The holy chalices and censers in the cauldron would become gold crowns, swords and shields.

And the chronicles in the cave would become a legend.

Rains fell, the like of which had never been known before. But the earth beneath the Old Spruce, where we had buried Elitsa, was still dry.

Granny Srebra gazed at the sky and said :

'A hundred years ago, when I was born in the spring, rains of this kind fell, too.'

That year she was a hundred years old.

The voice of the waters rose higher, until it was like the howling of a storm. The mountain drank water, the forests drank water, but they could not drink it up. And the rivers rose from their beds. In Petglassets, no one could enter, or leave the valley—the

Struïlitsa filled its narrow gorge and the path remained under water. The cave was still dry, but it was terrible for a man to pass it and show himself in the gorge. The water dashed against the perpendicular rocks that rose high up to the heavens, howling as one possessed, and rolling huge boulders along its bed.

The Elindenya folk could no longer possess their souls in patience, and sent three brave men through the forests to see what was happening in their valley.

On the fifth day the messengers returned, and the man who came from Podviss fell on his face before the multitude that had gathered and cried :

'The water has swept Podviss away !'

The holy forest was no longer there to stop the torrents. A muddy wave had dropped from the rocks above Chelevestnitsa, flowing swiftly over the burnt forest and dashing on to Podviss. Not one stone was left standing on another in that village.

Not a trace was left of Manol's home, into which he had thought to lead Elitsa and to rear his children.

The men of Podviss wept, even although previously only the bare walls of their houses had been left standing. They realized that until that moment they had hoped to return to Podviss one day. Now the torrent had torn up even their last roots.

When the water had subsided, I went to see what had happened to the Samodiva Lake and the cave in the rocks.

I passed through the Sheitanitsa Forest alone, I went to the lake alone. And I am prouder of that than of all my war deeds.

The lake was still there, as if it had not rained. I thrust a hand into the icy water of the green eye, and, shivering to the roots of my hair, I touched the cauldron. I did not take it out.

I found the cave with the chronicles, too. But here I could not restrain myself and thrust my hand into the gaily-coloured bag. I sat down in front of the cave and began to read. Wonderful and terrible, the history of Rhodopa unrolled before me. And at the end I read the Chronicle of Father Aligorko. I stopped when I could no longer distinguish the letters. It was evening. I could not pass through the Devil's Forest. I spent the night in the cave. I heard and saw much that night, and I thought still more.

I, too, would have to describe the destruction of Elindenya. The priest had seen it only from one side—from the side of the Bulgarians—I knew it from the other side, too—from the side of the Turks. Only thus would the story be complete. I did not feel like going back through the terrible days in the *Konak*, but I would have to do it.

I bore my decision within me for long years before I sat down to write. Now there is no longer time to put it off. That is how these notes that are now before you, saw the light of day, and they are the second half of Aligorko's nutshell. Let us hope, when you break the nut, that something will be left of its kernels, which Father Aligorko and I have tried to save from decay and from the worms.

Candia fell.

I felt it like a terrible blow. Later I realized that the entire west had trembled at the terrible news.

The great siege of a fortress, second in the history of mankind after the Siege of Troy had come to an end. And Candia, like Troy, stood on the shore of the sea. In the siege of Candia as in that of Troy, help had come from all the world for the besieged and the besiegers. Even the Moslem pirate states in North Africa sent ships and men to Küprüli; even the Christian pirates forgot that they had set out to rob, and died for sheer glory in defence of the Cross. The first difference between Troy and Candia was that there may never have been a siege of Troy, but there are still thousands of people living who have bullets in their bodies received at Candia. The second difference is that Troy had the good fortune to be lauded by Homer, and Candia has not been lauded by any-one. Yet I myself knew the men who defended Candia and who might well take their stand besides Achilles and Hector, and not look less in stature by a head.

So Candia fell. The big cross driven into the bloodstained earth-works, the cross, towards which the dying Christians turned their last gaze—while the Turks, when they saw it, went mad—that cross was torn down. Küprüli lost 108,000 dead and his bravest Pashas. Venice lost millions of ducats, its best ships and noblest soldiers. This was the last great victory won by the Turks, and the last defeat suffered by Venice, for, after this, the republic was unable to recover.

I think and say that Candia need not have fallen. Twenty-five years later the world saw at Vienna that Turkey was no longer the same. I curse the fools and traitors who unnecessarily sacrificed the 25,000 Christians who lost their lives there.

Our brave Frenchmen, who had come for glory and not for work, were among the first to flee. After the disappearance of the Duc de Beaufort, and the death of 600 knights and 1,000 sword-bearers, the Duc de Noailles led our men to the ships. Terrible laments and screams followed them to the very shores. What use was it that Louis XIVth punished the Duke?

Three hundred Frenchmen and three thousand Italians re-mained in Candia. Küprüli probably had 40,000 men.

Morosini gathered the commanders and told them : 'Candia is a pile of stones, and we are only defending an earthworks mixed with blood and bodies.' With tears in their eyes the commanders decided to defend Candia.

Immediately after the gathering, the Papal Captain Rospigliosi withdrew with his men.

Morosini had no alternative but to surrender Candia. During the time that the negotiations lasted, Küprüli sent Morosini fruit and cooling beverages every day. And to the messenger who handed over to him the eighty-three keys of the fortress, Küprüli gave a bag of gold.

Morosini passed through the camp of the Turks with the last defenders of the fortress, seen off with great honours and admiration. Küprüli entered Candia, welcomed by a Greek, a Jew and a Gypsy. There was not another living soul in the fortress.

Küprüli's mother, who had been with him during the entire siege, greeted her son in front of the entire army. When Küprüli returned to Turkey, Sultan Mohammed the Fourth gave him his own sword and said :

'I bless the bread and the salt which he and his father have eaten at the Padishah's expense. These two are an adornment to Islam, and pillars of the law.'

When the news of the fall of Candia reached the Turkish village, which the peasants still called Prossoina, the Turks became insufferable. Perhaps the news merely coincided with the moment when the Turks went wild, and they would in any case have set out to rob, but folk thought that the fall of Candia had driven them mad. The *bashi-bazouks*, brought by Karaiman Hassan Hodja, and those that came later, did not set about ploughing the Bulgarian fields and feeding the Bulgarian sheep, but took to robbing. And indeed, it is far easier to cut a man's throat and take his property, than to get your own property together, stake by stake and stone by stone. And it is much easier to throw another man's wife down on the earth and get her with child, than to feed and rear that child day by day, until it grows to manhood.

A clamour arose in the mountain around Elindenya against the Turkish village. The fields and pastures around it were deserted, but, on the other hand, new paths set out among the wildernesses and new graves appeared at the roadsides. Prossoina became the haunt of bandits.

What could the Bulgarians do? Bulgarian bands roamed the mountain, but they were not like the sun to pour their light on everything. And they could not set fire to the hornet's nest, for the cursed *Konak*-fortress rose in the middle of the village.

I stayed aside from the people's affairs, cut off by my grief, until one day I looked around and bethought me how to drive out the Turks.

And the Petglassets band raised a red flag on Mount Purvenets. For a whole week the *Voivodas* came one after the other with their bands, or sent messengers to ask about the flag. And when they heard why we were calling them together, they remained below Purvenets. Those who came were Mircho *Voivoda* and Doichin *Voivoda* of Raikovo, Doichin *Voivoda* of Ezerovo, Dimo *Voivoda* of Oustovo, Stoyan *Voivoda* of Ochinovo, Vulkan *Voivoda* of Peshtera, Velko *Voivoda* of Levochevo, Vitan *Voivoda* of Koutlovo, Chilo *Voivoda* of Petkovo and Delyo *Voivoda* of Belovidovo. Our men of Momchilovo were led by old Gordyo *Voivoda*. We got together over two hundred men, each one with a knife and a rifle in his hand.

It so happened that I was chosen to lead half the *haidouts*. This was not because I deserved it, but because I was the only one who knew the secret entrance to the *Konak*.

And one Friday, when the Turks had assembled for the big Friday prayer in the new mosque of Prossoina—it was right next to the ruins of the church—the bands went down in silence through the forests above Elindenya. And while I and my men entered the secret passage, and I prayed that the rains had not made it collapse, the other *haidouts*, headed by Gordyo *Voidova*, lay in ambush at the end of Prossoina.

We passed through the secret passage, and I pushed open the door of Gyulfié's room. There was no mercy in my heart—only wrath, for I remembered how I had fled with Elitsa and Momchil's head through the darkness and the thunder.

Gyulfié was in the room. I gagged her mouth. She bit me, and gazed at me with furious eyes full of hatred. I was on the left side, she—on the right. I do not know what she had thought of doing after Karaibrahim's death, but her eyes were shining. Perhaps she had wanted to entangle Karaiman Hassan Hodja.

When the room was overflowing with armed men, one of them went out on the veranda and fired a pistol. That was the signal for the men in ambush to surround the mosque.

And once more the *Konak* rang and shook to the tramping of feet and people's screams, and dust fell from the ceiling—as it had done on the day when Mircho had killed Karaibrahim and the Turks had torn him to pieces. I pushed Gyulfié aside and dashed out on to the veranda.

We caught all the Turks, those in the *Konak* and those in the

mosque. A hundred Turks were killed in the turmoil, but the rest
stood bound in the square beside the block that was black with
men's blood. The rains had not washed it clean.

We crowded the *bashi-bazouks'* womenfolk and children into
one of the inner courtyards of the *Konak*. Laments and wails rose
on all sides, but there was no mercy in my heart. It was the same
yard where earlier the Bulgarians had suffered and died.

I passed by the bound Turks and the first one I saw was
Karaimam Hassan Hodja. He gazed about him gloomily, but
there was not a trace of his fury. A few of Karaibrahim's Spahis
had also stayed behind. I had seen the other Turks, too—hangmen,
thieves, daylight robbers.

In front of the Turks, on the square, the *Voivodas* of the bands
took their places. And in the middle, on a white stone, sat Granny
Srebra, whom two young lads had brought to the top of the
mountain, to watch the attack on Prossoina. The *Voivodas* stood
there, with grim looks, ready for the slaughter, for one of the
Doichins, the one from Raikovo, had been killed in the clash.

The sun was shining, as it had shone on that day of parting,
when the Turks had beheaded Manol's hundred brothers on the
black block.

Two of the *haidouts* brought Sevda and Father Aligorko, now
Ali. The priest saw me, and smiled at me with his shining eyes.
He was still as mortally lean as ever, but his head was raised.

Sevda held a child in her arms, a little girl. She was still
beautiful, but her eyes were dark and lifeless, and her voice was
toneless. When I looked at her, I remembered that girl, the living
corpse, whom I had met on the stairs after the night of Manol's
wedding. I also remembered the girl who had hanged herself in
my room.

And I drew aside from the terrible judges, who were preparing
to try the first woman who had voluntarily given up her faith, and
the first man who had come down from the mountain and had
surrendered to Karaibrahim of his own free will.

I raised my eyes and saw beneath the Pass new stone houses in
the place of the crosses. It was the village of the Bulgarian
Mohammedans. The meadow was black with people, but not one
of the *haidouts* went up there, and not one of the new Moslems
came down to us. They brought only the former priest.

Granny Srebra said :

'Speak, *Voivodas*, and tell us what to do with this woman who
was the first to sell her faith? And went about with her slippers
clattering and her bracelets tinkling, while others wept?'

The *Voivodas* were silent. Then I spoke from the side :

'The child at her breast may be Goran's.'

I was thinking of little Manol.

Granny Srebra said:

'Speak, Sevda, whose is the child, Goran's or Karaibrahim's?'

Sevda said in a dull voice:

'I do not know.'

And she bent her lovely head over the child's little head.

Granny Srebra said:

'If that child is Goran's, we must look after it all the days of its life. If it is Karaibrahim's daughter, we must kill it—it and its mother.'

I said:

'Goran and Karaibrahim were brothers.'

The old woman gave me an angry look and said to Sevda:

'Say that the child is Goran's daughter, and you will have bread all the days of your life, and your daughter will marry the worthiest man in the mountain.'

Sevda repeated in the same toneless voice:

'I do not know.'

The *Voivodas* were silent.

Granny Srebra spoke slowly and quietly:

'Man is not a flower to be known by its leaves whether it has a poisonous root, or is a healing herb. Man is known by his deeds.'

Old Gordyo said:

'Let us wait until the child grows up.'

Granny Srebra said to Sevda:

'Draw aside, and wait!'

Then she said to the priest:

'Come hither, you, who welcomed me and blessed the land of Momchilovo. Why did you come down from the mountain bringing the people to Karaibrahim? Why did you betray your faith?'

The priest asked:

'What language do I speak, that you understand me?'

The old woman replied:

'Bulgarian.'

'Lo, that is why I did it. For I knew that with the cross or without it, we would always speak the same language. For I wanted folk to remain alive, even though they would be Moslems, rather than that they should be dead Christians.'

The old woman was silent.

I spoke up:

'Mother, you said that a man is known by his deeds. Do not then judge this man by his words. But by his deeds understand whether he has done well or ill. You founded one village, he founded another. Judge him by them. And a village is like a child.'

The old woman turned to me :

'Why do you stand aside, wise man? Either go to the Turks, or come to the Bulgarians.'

I thought that she wanted to silence me. I thought further : 'When you saw me for the first time, you cursed me for betraying my faith. Judge this man now, wise old woman.'

I gloated, but not for long. I saw that the *Voivodas* were silently drawing away from each other, to make room for me beside the old woman. I stepped forward with a beating heart and a tight throat, and felt my shoulders touching those of the glorious *Voivodas*, covered with the scars of wounds, saturated with the smell of blood and gunpowder.

Now I was looking at the priest face to face, not from the side. And again he smiled at me imperceptibly, only with his eyes. I heard the old woman say :

'Let this man, of whom we do not know whether he has done well or ill, become the father of this child of whom we do not know whether she is the child of good, or of evil. Let those who remain alive see by the child's deeds, whether it is good or bad. And let the mountain look at the new village and the deeds of those saved, or destroyed by this man, so that they may understand whether he has done well or ill. And if not today, then tomorrow, or a thousand years hence, it will be known whether it was better for men to die, or whether it was better that they remained alive.'

And she added :

'*Voivodas*, do you agree?'

And she looked around at them all, and to see me, she raised her head, for I was standing at her back. I saw in her eyes a childish pride that she had judged wisely. I also saw that she was not angry with me, but was deriding me.

The *Voivodas* replied :

'We agree.'

And the priest and Sevda withdrew to one side.

Now the crowd of bound Turks remained face to face with us— with the old woman and the *Voivodas*. And little by little they all bent their heads, until not even one pair of eyes was left opposite us, but only turbans and shaved heads.

And over the square, now absolutely still, rose Granny Srebra's voice :

'Evil has come to the earth, but woe to him through whom it comes.'

The Turks did not understand a single word. I went forward, and once more I became a man who translates words from one language into another, and puts nothing of his own into them. But there was not much to translate.

Granny Srebra said:

'They have slept amid walls which they did not build. They have reaped fields which they did not plough. They have ridden horses which they did not feed. They have killed and burned. What must be their fate?'

The *Voivodas* shouted:

'They must be killed.'

Granny Srebra said:

'And the women and children will go free, for they came here, led by their menfolk.'

I forgot that I was an interpreter, and decided to speak up, for among the Turks there were some who were innocent, swept away by the torrent. I said to Granny Srebra:

'Mother, among these men, there are also some who did not come of their own will, but were brought by Karaibrahim, Karaiman Hassan Hodja and the other chieftains. If you let the women and children go, why do you not let them go, too?'

The old woman cried angrily:

'Be silent! I seem to hear Old Galoushko the White One, God rest his soul. You would also absolve the sin of the son who killed his father. What I know, I know.'

And the *Voivodas* paid no heed to me, and Old Gordyo asked:

'How shall we kill them? Shall we behead them, hang them, or allot another death to them?'

Some said:

'Let us behead them, as they beheaded others.'

Others said:

'One hundred deaths for them, a different one for each, as they killed the martyred notables in different ways.'

But Mircho *Voivoda*, the other *Voivoda* from ' Raikovo, said:

'Let us hang them all on the other plane tree, from which so many Christian souls have hung.'

And he was listened to, for he had lost his foster-brother, Doichin *Voivoda*.

Then I had to speak again, and this time it was not to do good. But it had to be so.

'*Voivodas*,' said I, and pointed to Karaiman Hassan Hodja. 'That man must be impaled.'

And I told them of the curse uttered by the old woman with the eleven sons. And the priest spoke, saying:

'It was so.'

And the curse was fulfilled. He screamed and wept for water, and when he was given water to drink, it flowed down the stake.

The rest of the Turks we hanged on the plane tree. But so many nooses hung from its branches, and the hanged men shook it so hard with their writhing, that the ancient tree could not bear the weight, and its six branches broke at the same time with a crash. And its trunk was split into three, right down to the roots, and in its branches, half-alive Turks still stirred.

The fire, which turned the *Konak* to ashes, blazed up first in the split trunk, as if lightning from heaven had fallen upon it. And only four black walls were left of the *Konak*. The verandas, the doors and the cupboards, with carving that looked like fine embroidery on wood, the rafters of the ceilings and the cellars were burnt down. The roof fell into the flames, and the stone tiles crushed what the flames had spared.

Before this we had led the horses out of the stables. I took Karaibrahim's Arab stallion, for no one wanted such a horse for the mountain, but the huge horse, Syuleiman Aga's present to me, I returned to Gyulfié. She spat at me, but took the horse.

And I saw her, going up the path to the Pass, a fat woman on a fat horse. She did not weep, and I felt no pity for her. She seemed eternal to me; she was sure to find a place in which to strike roots. After Gyulfié went the rest of the women, with whole rows of children, barefoot and hungry, as they had come.

When the uproar and the weeping had died away behind the Pass, the *Voivodas* sent men to tell the Bulgarian Moslems of the new village that those who had been born in Prossoina, could come down and take what was theirs from their old houses. People came down, took this and that, and went up to their new village. The *haidouts* took out of the houses what could be of use to them.

Then one of the men from Petglassets, whose old house stood in Prossoina, cried :

'I want to set fire to my house with my own hands.'

And Prossoina blazed up. The third and last village of Elindenya, which had remained untouched, vanished in the flames.

Just at the top of the Pass, at the same place from which, a year ago, I had seen Elindenya for the first time, I turned my horse and looked at it once more.

Only a year had passed, and so many things had happened. Manol was no longer there, Momchil was no longer there. Elitsa was no longer there.

And the new Manol had been born.

There was no Elindenya.

Once more, the mountain and the forests lay before me in complete peace. Once more, no breath stirred the slim tops of the spruces, outlined against the evening sky.

Down in the valley, Prossoina still smoked. And the smoke did not rise, but slowly spread and enveloped the village. It seemed to have sunk in a dense fog; the walls of the houses looked like flies emmeshed in cobwebs, long dead and sucked dry. At the end, the burnt site of Podviss, swept away by the torrent, showed black. And above the dark sides of the valley hung clouds—grey-blue, ink mixed with milk, quite motionless, like real mountains. And that new mountain above the blackish-blue, wooded mountains, continued Rhodopa and raised it to the heavens, and made the ghostly, dead village at the end of the valley still smaller and still more dead.

Here ends the tale of the destruction of the Valley of Elindenya. Elindenya was no longer there.

No human foot would ever go down the cobbled road, weeds and nettles would cover it. The paths would go round it. Even hunters would not hunt the beasts that would hide in its ruins.

The Valley of Elindenya perished. But below the Pass, the chimneys of a new village smoked, and it had not even a name of its own yet. The road led to another village, to Momchilovo in the Valley of Petglassets. Elindenya gave birth to two villages, and although a muezzin sang in the one, and a bell rang in the other, they were the children of the same mother.

I turned away and I never saw Elindenya again.

Glossary

Aga (T) pl. *Agalar*=Master.
Agovitsa (T)=Aga's wife, mistress.
Akché (T)=Small Turkish silver coin.
Aman (T)=Have mercy.
Aspra (T)=Small Turkish copper coin.
Bairam (T)=Turkish festival.
Baksheesh (T)=Gratuity, tip.
Baté (T)=Diminutive of brat, brother. Usual form of address to men by their juniors, whether blood relations or not.
Bey (T)=Turkish title, also carrying certain administrative functions.
Beyler-Beg (T)=Governor of a province, Head-Bey.
Bilyuk-bashi (T)=Literally, commander over many, a sergeant in the army.
Cadi (T)=Civil judge, usually of a town.
Chan (T)=Long bells worn by the sheep, which had a smaller bell instead of a clapper. The shepherds chose their bells to make a chime.
Devitsa (B)=Maiden.
Dévsourmé (T)=The blood tax, by means of which the Sultan recruited his corps of Janissaries.
Grosh (T)=Silver Turkish coin worth about one fifth of a gold franc.
Haidé=Much-used expression all over the East, meaning 'Come on'.
Haidout (T)=Robber, bandit. The bands of Bulgarians, who took to the mountains and wreaked vengeance on the Turks for their oppression and misdeeds, were also called *haidouts*.
Haïrolsoun (T)=Good fortune go with you.
Horo (B)=Round or chain dance.
Janissary (T)=One of a body of Turkish infantry forming the Sultan's guard.
Kaimakam (T)=Governor of a county.
Kaval (B)=Shepherd's flute, usually made of wood in several sections.
Kehaya (T)=Shepherd, head shepherd, man possessing large flocks.
Konak (T)=House of a notable, castle, palace, government building.
Kyoshk (T)=Raised part of a covered veranda, projecting over a courtyard.
Maaneh (T)=Turkish folksong, sung slowly to a long-drawn tune with many flourishes and grace-notes.
Mashallah (T)=Praise be to you.
Odjak (T)=Tribe.
Oka (T)=Measure of weight of over 2 lbs.
Para (T)=Small Turkish coin.

Rayah (T)=Non-Moslem population of the Ottoman Empire.

Samodiva (B)=Wood nymph, fairy.

Sandjak (T)=Junior School for Janissaries.

Spahi (T)=Turkish cavalry men, to whom feifs were granted in exchange for their services when required.

Sultan (T)=A Turkish ruler, a higher title than Bey (T), also a ruler.

Teké (T)=Moslem shrine.

Temaneh (T)=Turkish salute. The ground, one's breast, lips and forehead are touched to do honour to someone.

Tougra (T)=Monogram of a Sultan with his father's name and the words 'Always Victorious' interlaced with it.

Tsar (B)=King.

Voivoda (B)=Head of a band of *haidouts*.

Yamourlouk=Hooded cape of homespun, worn by men.

Yataghan (T)=Curved sword used by Turkish soldiers.

Yurouks (T)=Moslem nomad tribe of stockbreeders.

Zashiv (B)=Sampler.

Zourla (T)=Primitive oboe.

Notes

Peasant Costumes—There was a bewildering variety of peasant costumes in the country, and one used to be able to tell where a man or woman came from by their dress. The women's costumes generally consisted of a smock with embroidered sleeves, and embroidery around its front opening. Sometimes the hem of the smock had a band of embroidery around it, or was trimmed with lace. A sleeveless woollen overdress, called *soukman*, was worn over the smock. It differed in colour in the various regions; it was also ornamented with embroidery, or braiding in gold and silver, or colours. The kerchiefs with which the women covered their heads, were tied in many different ways, often in such a way as to cover the lower part of the face to protect it from the sun. In the Rhodopes the kerchief covered the top of the head and left quite a lot of hair showing, apart from the braids which hung down the back. White kerchiefs were worn by girls and young women, black by old women and women in mourning.

By way of jewellery, the women wore chains of gold or silver coins, which were often their dowry, as well as a variety of ornaments in filigree work, or enamelled metals with inlaid stones or glass, and heavy silver, or silver-gilt buckles.

The men wore full-bottomed breeches, tied around their waists with a cord. Over this they wound a long piece of cloth, red (scarlet or crimson) or orange, sometimes vertically striped, and over the waistband they wore a leather belt, a cartridge belt, or a plain leather strap. Their shirts were also ornamented with embroidery. Braid was sewn round the pockets of their breeches and also on the edges and sleeves of their waistcoats and jackets. Their garments were made of homespun, which was left the natural colour if made from the wool of brown sheep, or was dyed brown with walnut leaves. Their leggings were made of thick white homespun, which they wrapped around the leg over their socks, from the ankle to the knee, and which were held in place by black cord, wound around in an ornamental pattern, 'cross-gartered.' They wore heavy, hooded capes of homespun, called *yamourlouks*, to protect them from rain and cold. On their heads they wore round or pointed fur caps.

Bulgarian Folksongs—Each of Father Aligorko's excerpts begins with a quotation from a folksong. For them, the author has drawn on the vast wealth of Bulgarian folksongs. During the period of the Turkish yoke, which lasted almost five centuries, these songs were virtually the only literary form that existed in Bulgaria, and they were handed down orally from generation to generation. In them, the folksingers poured out their people's joys and sorrows, their memories of historical events, their attitude to the earth that they tilled, to work, to social equality, to national and personal freedom, and last, but not least, to their dear ones. Rhymes are rarely found in them, alliteration is very frequent, and vocative forms abound, as the singer turns to his mother or his sweetheart, and anyone or anything else; the particle '*lé*', denoting tenderness, is often added to a name: Milka *lé*, Dimo *lé*, and so on.

I am indebted to Mr Kevin Ireland for the two verses of his very fine translation of the folksong about Tsar Ivan Shishman's last battle against the Turks, which the *Voivoda* Goran sings as he goes to his death.

Public Rooms—Some of the Rhodope villages were so remote and so poor that they had no tavern, and not even an inn. But as soon as they could afford it, they would build what were called '*achik odaya*'—'open' or public rooms, where travellers could spend the night and obtain food.

The Notables—The names of the notables present at the gathering on the meadow near Old Galoushko's water-mill are to be found in chronicles concerning the Rhodopes, in tax registers, deeds of property, court registers, and so on.

Nosegays Worn by Shepherds—On many occasions, when attending a wedding, or leaving for distant places, not only shepherds, but the menfolk in general, wore nosegays, stuck behind their ears or in their fur caps. These were made of flowers or crane's-bill (for health, as it is known as *zdravets*—the health plant).

Courtship—In the morning or evening, the girls went to the fountains to fetch water. The young men usually knew to which fountain the girls of their choice, or their sweethearts, went, and took this opportunity to have a word with them. Asking for a drink from a girl's water-jars expressed admiration, asking her for her nosegay was a further step, almost akin to plighting troth. If a girl gave her nosegay to a young man, it meant that she was willing to accept him as a suitor. So when Elitsa refuses to give Momchil a nosegay of crane's-bill, she tells him in so many words that her love has been bestowed elsewhere.

When Father Aligorko says that his sister-in-law had first given her nosegay to him, it means that she had shown a preference for him, although she had later married his brother.

Wedding Customs—Weddings were celebrated with great ceremony. There were many customs connected with them, which began the week preceding the actual wedding ceremony, and were always accompanied by singing and dancing. Finally, the bride was fetched, and those who went to fetch her were called '*momari*' from '*moma*', maiden. There was no time to send '*momari*' to fetch the bride for the hurried weddings which took place after the peasants had fled to the mountains.

The Curse on Momchil—In Turkish times, the peasants, who were quite helpless against their social and political oppressors, vented their indignation on men, whose actions were base or evil, by casting stones at a given spot and uttering a malison on them. The cairn thus formed was called a *Gramada*.

Personification—As few persons were educated and literate in the period of Turkish bondage, superstitions were rife, and the vivid imagination of the common people personified many phenomena of nature. *Samodivas* were nymphs, generally well disposed to humans, and were personifications of forests and rivers. *Yudas* were mischievous, wicked and revengeful fairies, whom it was dangerous to meet. *Halas* were evil spirits, personifications of whirlwinds. The plague was always represented as an ugly, swarthy old woman, with red-rimmed and bloodshot eyes, crooked and dirty nails, who marked the houses of her victims. Whoever she touched, died.